SUMMER *of* FIRE

KITTY PILGRIM

SUMMER *of* FIRE

RIVER GROVE
BOOKS

Published by River Grove Books
Austin, TX
www.rivergrovebooks.com

Distributed by River Grove Books

For ordering information or special discounts for bulk purchases, please contact River Grove Books at PO Box 91869, Austin, TX 78709, 512.891.6100.

Design and composition by Greenleaf Book Group
Cover design by Greenleaf Book Group
Cover image: ©Shutterstock/Natalia Barsukova

Publisher's Cataloging Publication Data is available.

ISBN: 978-1-63299-025-9

First Edition

Other Edition(s):
eBook ISBN: 978-1-63299-026-6

To the elements it came from
Everything will return
Our bodies to earth,
Our blood to water,
Heat to fire,
Breath to air.

—Mathew Arnold, 1852,
Empedocles on Etna

Iceland has produced some of the most destructive volcanoes in history. In 1783, the Laki eruption released a haze of ash, basaltic lava, and sulfur dioxide into the atmosphere, immediately killing tens of thousands of people. Ashfall destroyed crops and livestock as far away as England and Northern France.

PIAZZA UMBERTO I, CAPRI, ITALY

The golden afternoon was coming to an end. Dusk was falling, creating shadows in the main square of Capri. Storeowners were pulling down their aluminum gates with a rattle and a bang.

Cordelia Stapleton walked up to a flower stall where a proprietor was preparing to close up for the day.

"*Un momento,*" she said in halting Italian.

The man stopped pouring water out of the plastic buckets and waited for her to choose. She looked over the selection. In the heat of the afternoon, the air was filled with the scent of flowers. The sweet scent of the petals mingled with deeper notes of damp green vegetation. It was amazing how many varieties were in season on the island of Capri.

Living in London, she was used to the pale pastels of northern blooms. But here in the Mediterranean, vivid hues prevailed: reds and pinks, oranges and yellows—all different. It was almost impossible to decide. John would know which ones would be best for tonight.

She turned to look for him. John Sinclair was a block away, talking on his cell phone.

"Over here!" she called, waving to him with a sweeping gesture, as if signaling at sea.

He disconnected and covered the distance rapidly, with a long-limbed stride.

"We need to get a bouquet for the dinner party," she said.

He nodded. "Yes, sorry. I had to take that call. A volcano is erupting in Iceland. They say it will be enormous."

"Oh, which one is it?"

"Ela . . . ka . . . " he said, stumbling over the Icelandic syllables.

"You mean, Eyjafjallajökull?" she said.

He cocked his head, amused. "Now, *that's* impressive."

"Why?" she asked.

"There aren't ten people who would know how to pronounce that correctly."

She laughed, pleased at the flattery.

"I was a geology major in college," she explained.

"So, what do you know about Efyal . . . Iceland?" he asked, his eyes worried.

She tried to remember. It had been a while since she studied the region, but the geology was simple enough.

"There are four volcanic zones in Iceland, and Eyjafjallajökull is in the Eastern area—one of the biggest. Eruptions there can be enormous."

"What about this one?"

She shrugged. "I have no way to tell. It depends on how long the eruption goes. But what's your worry? We're in Italy."

"I have an archaeological dig going on in the Mosfell Valley, an ancient Viking site in Iceland. I was wondering if I should tell my team to evacuate."

"It might be prudent," she said.

The buzz of a cell phone vibrated in her purse. "WHOI" flashed across the screen. Though she now lived in London, she still served on the board of the US-based Woods Hole Oceanographic Institute.

"It's Woods Hole," she told him. "They're probably calling me about the same thing. Give me a second."

The head of the ocean research department spoke over the line. "Delia?"

"Hi, Joel. What's going on?"

"Sorry to bother you. NBC News wants to talk to you about that volcanic eruption in Iceland. The impact on the ocean."

She looked around at the town square. There was nowhere private to talk.

"I think you should handle it, Joel. I'm in Italy."

"But I always get tongue-tied on TV."

"Just take a deep breath before you start," she said. "You'll be fine."

"Come on Delia. You could do it over the phone."

She looked over, and Sinclair was glancing at his watch, waiting for her to finish up. They were overdue for the dinner party.

"Joel, you'll be fine."

She said goodbye and turned back to Sinclair.

"NBC News wants the institute's opinion on the impact the volcano could have on the ocean. Joel's going to handle it."

Sinclair smiled. "Then let's pick out some flowers and get a move on. We're late. Charles is expecting us at seven."

Their friend Charles Bonnard had a little villa up on the cliffs, in the hamlet of Anacapri. They were going to stay with him for a week.

Cordelia turned back, and the proprietor of the flower stall was still standing there, patiently waiting.

"I couldn't decide," she said, looking at the array. "Do you know if he has a favorite?"

"I'm not really sure, but these should work," Sinclair said.

He reached for three bunches of brilliant red poppies, lifted them from their pail of water, then handed them, dripping, to the vendor. As the man wrapped them up, Cordelia examined his choice. The flowers had long green stalks, silk-soft petals, and a subtle fragrance. They reminded her of a Monet painting.

"What are they?"

"Tuscan poppies. They're very special," he said, pulling a twenty-euro note from his wallet.

"How so?"

"The ancient Romans used to remove the pistil and then boil the center to brew tea."

"Tea?

"Yes. Supposedly it would soothe the aches of love," Sinclair said.

"Hmm . . ." Cordelia said, impressed

As an archaeologist, Sinclair's grasp of classical Greek and Roman culture was encyclopedic; it was almost as if he had lived in ancient times.

"Ever brew any?" she asked.

"No, but from what I hear, Charles is going to need it," Sinclair said, taking the paper-wrapped bouquet and handing over the euros to the vendor. "He's really in love this time."

"Who is she?"

"I have no idea. Apparently, she's famous."

Cordelia raised an eyebrow. "You didn't ask?"

"I didn't want to pry."

"*Pry* . . . he's your best friend!"

"Delia, it's called a private life for a reason."

"Charles is not allowed to have secrets from us."

"Men can have secrets," he joked. "Women do."

"Really? Tell me your worst," she teased, and stretched up to kiss him on the cheek. "I want to know everything."

"Another time," he said, and smiled.

As they walked across the piazza, she slid a hand around his waist. She could feel his warm skin underneath the cotton shirt. He hugged her in return, looping an arm over her shoulder and pulling her tight. Body against body, they fit perfectly.

It was her first time to Capri. What a wonderful place! Yachts were anchored in the harbor, and designer shops lined the narrow cobblestoned lanes. Yet somehow this island was more interesting than the other glitzy vacation spots on the Mediterranean. There was a magical timelessness to Capri. A special atmosphere, and a sense of history. This island had once been an ancient Roman settlement.

The enclave at the top of the island was called Anacapri. It would be a half-hour drive up the cliffs. Sinclair flagged down a cab and held the door open for her.

"I can't believe Charles finally has a new girlfriend. I'm just dying to know who she is," Cordelia said as she climbed in.

He smiled. "You won't have to wait long. She'll be at the villa when we get there."

VILLA SAN ANGELO,
ANACAPRI, ITALY

Charles Bonnard wiped his forehead with a towel and glanced over at the woman lying next to him. Personally, he would have preferred sitting under the awning, but Victoria insisted they sunbathe on the terrace by the pool.

"V?"

No response. She was asleep, face down. Her yellow bikini top was untied, her body bare except for a triangle of fabric that covered the twin mounds of her magnificent derrière.

Charles leaned over, speaking softly.

"Victoria, be careful you don't burn."

No answer. He noticed that her arms were turning bright pink, so he reached for a towel and draped it across her shoulders, then turned to admire the panoramic view.

His house was oriented high above the Bay of Naples where the ocean breezes blew. The sky was clear, and he could see the cone of Mount Vesuvius on the Italian mainland. Out on the water there were lots of white sailboats and motor yachts—everyone was out enjoying themselves.

Unfortunately, he and Victoria were housebound. All day long he had a distinct feeling of being watched. It was textbook paranoia. At a thousand feet, nobody had a direct line of sight to where they were sunning. But still, he worried.

Suddenly Victoria woke up and glanced over, her eyes blinking against the glare.

"What are you thinking?" she asked.

"Nothing in particular."

What a liar he was turning into. He had been agonizing about their predicament all day.

The situation began when Victoria arrived two days ago. He planned to be alone. But then she turned up, assuming he would be interested in a romantic tryst.

A fair assumption. But, if they were photographed together, the scandal would be international. The girl on his terrace was Victoria, Crown Princess of Norway.

Victoria appeared so often in the headlines, the press shortened her name to V to conserve space.

The articles were always flattering. V was often praised as being someone who behaved with royal dignity. Her reputation was above reproach. She had no serious romantic interests. In fact, the whole world was waiting to find out whom she would choose for a husband. Her parents had vetted all the young eligible men in Europe.

And therein lay the problem.

Charles wasn't included. He wasn't even royal. So forget the short list. The Norwegian Royal Palace didn't even have him on the long list of appropriate aristocrats.

Not that he didn't have a noble pedigree. His mother's family descended from a French duke who ruled Languedoc in the 1600s. But there was a vast age difference between Charles and Victoria. He was a mature man, at least a decade older than any of her other suitors—a lothario, by all appearances.

If anyone saw her lounging on his terrace in her current state of undress, it would be a complete scandal. The princess had never been photographed while wearing anything more revealing than an evening gown.

If he were an honorable man, he'd put a stop to this. But he couldn't. His emotions were too strong.

Reaching over, Charles trailed his fingers down her spine to make certain she was not a mirage. Her back was slim and strong. He kneaded the muscles just above her bathing suit bottom.

"Your skin is hot. Are you all right?"

"I have sun cream on."

"Shall I put on some more?"

"Hmmm. Would you?"

Charles squeezed a dollop onto her back and rubbed it in, still marveling that she allowed him to touch her like this. Her body was magnificent. Victoria was a biathlon champion and an expert fencer. Every inch of her was firm and beautifully proportioned.

"Don't stop," she murmured.

Her eyelids dipped twice and closed. Asleep again. Charles scrutinized her face, beautiful in its tranquility. But it was more than her looks. V had that indefinable power some women had over men. When he met Victoria, he lost all reason.

In fact, they were both acting crazy. Victoria slipped away from her security escort two days ago, and her guards were searching for her throughout the streets of Capri. Sooner or later, she'd be photographed.

Charles took a sip of his tea. The cubes had melted, diluting its strength.

"V? You awake?"

She stirred. The wind was whipping tendrils of her hair, the blond locks slowly coming lose from the ponytail.

"What's wrong?" she asked.

"Nothing. It's just that it's getting late."

Victoria turned over, pulled the towel off her shoulders, and sat up, delicately blotting her face and neck. Her small, firm breasts were exposed for a moment as she fastened her top. Charles politely averted his eyes.

"I can't believe I fell asleep again."

"It's hot," he said. "You're not used to the Med. I'll get you a glass of ice water."

Charles stood up and started toward the house.

"Oh, don't bother," she called. "I still have some here."

Charles hesitated halfway to the door.

"Is it cold enough? I could get you some ice cubes from the freezer," he offered.

She laughed, squinting at him, shielding her eyes. " I don't drink *ice* water. What do you think I am, an American?"

"Do Americans drink ice water?"

Charles returned and stretched out again. He was half American on his father's side, but that was not something he talked about.

Victoria picked up the glass near her chair and drank deeply. When it was empty, she ran a thumb across the condensation.

"Water is one of the four basic elements."

"Mmmhmm."

"So tell me . . . which of the four elements am I?"

Charles hesitated.

"There are four natural elements: earth, water, fire, and air," she listed, ticking them off on her manicured fingers. "You have to decide which one is your basic nature."

"I see," he said, not comprehending at all.

"So, which one am *I*?" she asked.

"Earth?" he said.

Her smile fell in disappointment.

"Why?"

"Your country. Norway."

"No, I'm talking about *me*."

"So am I . . ."

"But *earth*? How could you say that?" Victoria sighed as she swung her long legs off the chaise. "Is that all I am to you? A *country*?"

"V . . . you know I didn't mean it that way."

She pulled the elastic out of her ponytail. Long blond hair cascaded over her shoulders. Her mouth turned down, eyes focused on the terrace.

"I adore you. You know that, don't you?" he blurted.

Victoria smiled. "I know."

"So if I'm not earth which *other* element would I be?" she asked.

He looked up sharply.

"What element am I?"

Charles met her gaze squarely, trying not to reveal his chagrin. "What do you want me to say?"

"Tell me what element you think I am."

He shrugged, while mentally reviewing his choices.

"I guess you're fire," he ventured.

"Why?"

"I see fire in your eyes."

"But they're blue—more like ice."

"You are *not* ice," he vowed.

A flicker of satisfaction crossed her face.

"If I'm fire, what are you, Charles?"

"I am . . . air."

"*How* are you air?"

He had no idea. Now he had to come up with something clever.

"I am air with great V-locity," he improvised. "I am wind."

"That's good. We're compatible. Wind fans a fire."

Oops. Fire. That reminded him. Charles checked his watch and stood up, draping a towel over his neck.

"Listen, I hate to leave you, but I'd better get going on grilling that fish."

Victoria looked up at him. Her hair cascaded over her eyes.

"Is it late?"

"It's six thirty. You can stay on the terrace if you like."

"Oh, no. I'll come in with you."

She stood up, reaching to retrieve her beach wrap from under the lounge chair. As she bent over, the tiny yellow bikini rode up. That bathing suit was *not* palace-approved.

"Should we get dressed?" she asked, tying the pareo around her waist.

"No need to fuss," he said. "My friends won't care."

"When are they due to arrive?"

"Any minute. They probably came over on the six o'clock ferry."

Charles reached down to collect the empty drinking glasses and towels.

"How did you first meet Sinclair?" she asked.

"We met about ten years ago in Monaco. He asked me to run his charity."

"Is he very wealthy?"

"Yes. He made a bundle in the tech world. But he gave up his career in the States to become an archaeologist."

Victoria half-turned. "And Cordelia?"

"She's an oceanographer—a rather famous one. I've known her for two years. In fact, I introduced her to Sinclair."

Victoria smiled. "Oh, that's nice."

"I think they're compatible," Charles agreed, smiling to himself.

"So what elements are they?"

He hesitated. "I've never thought about it. Why?"

"I want to get some idea of what they're like before I meet them."

"Well, I suppose John Sinclair is earth. He spends a lot of his time at archaeological digs."

"And Cordelia?"

"Water of course. She's an oceanographer."

Victoria smiled. "Water and earth go together. She soothes him and provides the way for him to flourish and grow. And he, in return, provides stability and solidity in her life."

Charles laughed. "That sounds about right. Without Cordelia, Sinclair is a bit of a dusty old bachelor."

Victoria turned to him. "Charles, do you realize that *all* the essential elements will be present tonight? Earth, water, air, and fire."

"Is that significant?"

"It's fantastic! The four of us will be in perfect balance! . . . I do hope they like me."

They started toward the house

"They will *love* you, V."

HOTEL CAESAR AUGUSTUS, ANACAPRI

Two blocks away from Charles Bonnard's villa, a police car pulled into the village square. The revolving red light flashed onto the façade of the Hotel Caesar Augustus. Detective Jaccorsi of the Naples Police Force climbed out of the driver's seat.

The night was starting to get oppressive. The heat turned muggy as the sea mist pervaded the island. Detective Jaccorsi cut across the darkened plaza, wiping the perspiration off his forehead with a handkerchief.

Curious onlookers milled around the street, speculating about what was happening. Rumor had it that there had been a theft and a murder in the hotel.

As he entered the lobby, the desk attendants were huddled together, whispering.

"*Scusi*, detective?" the manager called over.

Jaccorsi didn't even break stride as he crossed to the elevator. The hotel staff could be interviewed later. The crime scene was more important.

This was the first time he'd been inside the hotel, although he'd heard many tales of the splendors. The Caesar Augustus was an old mansion, used by Italian nobility in the 1920s that was now converted into a five-star resort. Rooms here went for astronomical sums, with suites costing two thousand dollars a night.

The finest of these was the Vesuvius Suite, famous for its view of the historic volcano. Here guests would drink Bellini cocktails on the balcony while observing the jagged peak of Mount Vesuvius on the mainland.

The entrance hall was spectacular. The white marble floor was well polished, and a crystal chandelier chimed slightly in the breeze.

He followed a corridor past several large bedrooms and entered the large salon. The spectacular double-height ceiling had skylights, giving the room a soft glow. A shaft of late afternoon sun was coming in, cutting through like a ray from heaven.

A body was on the floor in a pool of crimson.

"I'm here," he announced.

The medical team stepped aside, so he could approach the corpse. A clipboard was thrust at him, and he drew a pen across it in a hasty scrawl, giving them permission to transport the body.

He looked down. It was an assassination-style hit. The point of entry was clean and small, 9 mm. There was a small dark hole in the middle of the forehead—the signature of a notorious Camorra gangster.

Only one person killed like this—Salvatore Mondragone—a mobster nicknamed "Cyclops" after the Greek mythological creature with one eye in the middle of its forehead.

Jaccorsi checked the wall. As expected, small particles of brain matter spattered the paint. This was either Mondragone's handiwork, or that of one of his henchmen.

The corpse was sprawled awkwardly, staring at the ceiling, mouth slightly open. Jaccorsi bent down to take a closer look.

The face was gray-white. A fly buzzed around the pale lips, crawling in and out of the oral cavity. Rigor mortis had already set in. Soon the skin would begin to swell and discolor. In this heat, putrefaction would be rapid.

"Alejandro Castillo, from Spain," the policeman read, handing over the passport.

The passport was in the hotel safe. That ruled out robbery as a motive. Any average thief would have taken the passport. Government-issued documents went for a lot of money on the black market in Naples.

Jaccorsi stood up and started to type his notes on an electronic tablet.

"If anyone asks, it was a heart attack. Chief's orders."

The medical examiner gave a glum nod, uncomfortable with the lie.

Four medics lifted the corpse. Its dead weight thudded onto the gurney. On impact, air escaped from the lungs, and the mouth emitted a faint *ahhh* as if the man were trying to get in a final word.

Jaccorsi resisted the impulse to make the sign of the cross.

VILLA SAN ANGELO,
ANACAPRI, ITALY

Cheerful music filled the kitchen as the fish sizzled on the grill. Charles leveraged the sea bream off the brazier, its silvery skin bubbled to perfection.

He and Victoria had eaten almost nothing all day. In fact, they'd never even considered going into the kitchen.

He rolled a lemon on the countertop to release the juice inside. Victoria had just picked it from his garden. The citrus smell was intense.

As he cut wedges, a 1960s Italian pop song started up on the music system—"It Had Better Be Tonight."

> *If you're ever gonna kiss me*
> *It had better be tonight*
> *While the mandolins are playing*
> *And stars are bright.*

The kitchen was a refurbished farmhouse, with the cooking and dining areas combined. All the appliances were of professional quality: thermostat-controlled refrigerators for food and wine, a gourmet stove—a *La Cornue*, with eight gas-flame burners.

Charles took a stainless steel spatula and moved the fish onto a platter. A saucepan boiled over and began to spit on the stove, so he quickly redirected his energy to saving the mushroom risotto. Fragrant steam billowed out as he lifted the lid. The small kernels were golden and perfect.

Suddenly, he felt a pair of slender arms slide around his waist. Hips pressed into him from behind.

"You are the sexiest chef I've ever seen."

Charles dropped the pot lid.

"V, you're a real distraction."

She tightened her embrace, nibbling his ear. His concentration wavered and a piece of lemon slipped to the floor.

"You'd better stop. I can't multitask."

"Seems to me you were multitasking pretty well this morning."

"Cooking's different."

"If it wasn't so late, I'd drag you back to bed," she breathed.

He laughed and wiped his hands on a dishtowel, then turned around. Her pink Indian tunic was transparent enough for him to see the outline of her breasts.

"They'll be here any second," he cautioned.

"Then kiss me quickly."

His lips found hers. Soft and compliant. He pulled her body tight, leaning back against the kitchen counter. Just then, the sound of a doorknocker shattered his concentration. Victoria flinched and giggled with nerves.

"Right on time," he said.

"What should I do?"

"Why don't you set the table?"

He sprinted out into the corridor, the heels of his loafers clicking a rapid staccato. After the heat of the kitchen, the hallway was cool and pleasant.

Cracking the door open cautiously, he found John Sinclair on the threshold, holding a bottle of wine. Next to him was his *inamorata*, Cordelia Stapleton.

"Sorry we're late," Sinclair apologized. "We ran into some traffic—"

Cordelia cut him off. "There was an ambulance outside that big hotel."

"At the Caesar Augustus?"

"I think so. The one at the end of your street."

"I hope it's not serious."

"There must have been five or six policemen."

Charles thought about it, wondering about the proximity of law enforcement to his house. Clearly they were not looking for Victoria. Not if an ambulance was there.

"If someone's hurt, they might have to evacuate them by helicopter," he said. "The last ferry leaves at nine. Anyway, come in, come in."

Cordelia strode inside, giving him a quick hug. A crisp, white linen dress draped off her body with simple elegance. Flat Greek sandals laced up her shapely legs. Fetching indeed.

"We brought you some flowers," she said, holding them out.

In the dark hallway, the bouquet looked spectacular. The white cone of paper offset the brilliant red poppies.

"Wow, Delia. Those are gorgeous."

He took the bundle from her and examined them.

"What are they?"

"Tuscan poppies," she said.

She shot Sinclair a look, and they exchanged a smile.

Charles observed the two of them with renewed interest. They were so well matched. She was a pale, willowy beauty, with dark hair and green eyes. Sinclair was tall and broad shouldered, with the deep tan that came from year-round exposure to the sun at his archaeological digs.

Charles turned to Cordelia. "I'm so glad you finally decided to come. Sinclair said you might be tied up at work."

She smiled and plucked his sleeve. "I escaped at the last minute. Joel is taking over my duties for the week. Besides, I wouldn't miss seeing you for the world."

"Well it's the perfect season to come here. Capri is incredible this time of year," Charles agreed.

"I hear you have a new girlfriend," Cordelia probed.

He hesitated. "Well, not a *girlfriend* exactly."

"Then what would you call her?" she asked.

Charles stopped, uncertain how to continue.

Sinclair cut in, handing Charles a small plastic case.

"We thought you'd enjoy this."

Charles breathed a sigh of relief, grateful for the diversion.

"Music. How nice," he said

Sinclair tapped the CD with his index finger. "'Les collines d'Anacapri.' It's by Debussy."

"*The Hills of Anacapri.* What's the story behind it?"

"Claude Debussy composed it in the summer of 1909. He used to vacation here on the island."

Cordelia stared at Sinclair as if she couldn't believe he was interfering with her cross-examination. She turned and stalked off down the hall.

"Delia, wait," Charles objected. "What's wrong?"

"I won't be put off *that* easily," she said, and kept walking.

"I think she's lost interest in our musical discussion," Sinclair joked.

"Delia, where are you going?" Charles asked.

"I'm going to the kitchen. These flowers need water. And I want to meet your mystery woman."

Charles's house, the Villa San Angelo, had been built partly into the cliff. It had the simple stucco style of a monastery, and there was a long corridor leading back to the kitchen. Pieces of marble fragments were mounted on the wall for display. Sinclair had said that they were shards of carved Roman marble. Charles found them when he dug up the vegetable garden.

Cordelia barely gave the artifacts a glance as she walked along the corridor. Ancient history was not her chief interest tonight. She was more concerned about the woman Charles was dating.

He rarely had a steady girlfriend. Not that he wasn't attractive. Charles Bonnard was the quintessential fair-haired charmer. He enjoyed life to its fullest, and everything about him was carefree and fun.

Sinclair always dismissed the rumors that Charles was a playboy. He said that an Italian expression summed him up better: *sprezzatura.*

It described a quality that was rarely found in most individuals. People with sprezzatura were highly accomplished, yet made everything seem effortless. It was a characteristic that was prized at the royal court in the 1400s. A courtier had to be equally skilled in diplomacy, sword fighting, music, poetry, and dancing—all gracefully executed without any self-aggrandizing fuss.

That was Charles.

When Cordelia entered the kitchen, Charles's latest girlfriend was setting the table. She was a real glamour doll: tall, blond, and slender. And when she glanced up, her blue eyes were fringed with dark lashes.

Cordelia blinked in astonishment.

It was Princess Victoria of Norway!

There was no mistaking the slim body and the loose chignon of pale blond hair. Victoria was one of the most recognizable European royals of her generation.

The princess spoke first.

"Hello. You must be Cordelia."

The Nordic accent was barely discernable. She stood there looking utterly regal, head held high. Cordelia stared, speechless.

Just then, Sinclair and Charles came into the kitchen and stepped forward, smoothly dispelling the awkwardness.

"Your Royal Highness, an honor. I'm John Sinclair. May I present Cordelia Stapleton."

The princess smiled. "Delighted to meet you. Please call me Victoria. Everyone does."

Cordelia felt Sinclair's hand on the small of her back. It was a nudge, or a reassuring pat. Clearly, she needed to say something.

"Nice to meet you . . . "

"And you as well, Cordelia," Victoria said.

"Actually . . . my friends call me Delia," she added.

"Then I shall also, in the hope that we will become good friends."

The formality of the exchange left Cordelia searching for a response. Sinclair jumped in to keep the conversation flowing.

"Are you enjoying Capri?"

Cordelia barely heard the answer. The conversation rose and fell as she struggled with the facts.

Charles and *Princess Victoria*? It was incredible she was here in this little farmhouse. She looked exactly like the pictures in the magazines.

Victoria was only about twenty years old. Too young for Charles. Yet when you really thought about it, Charles was of correct rank. He was an aristocrat in the true meaning of the word. The Bonnard family was one of the oldest in France.

Cordelia glanced over at Sinclair and saw that his eyes were troubled. He clearly didn't approve of the situation. So much for a relaxed dinner.

Cordelia finally found her voice. "So Charles, what are you cooking tonight?"

He looked at her with relief.

"Gazpacho, sea bream, and mushroom risotto. I expect you are starving."

"I'm famished."

"Well, it's ready. Can you give me a hand?"

"Absolutely," she answered, grateful for something to do.

Anything was better than standing around staring at Princess Victoria. Sinclair could handle the diplomatic chitchat.

Charles went over to the oven and pulled on some mitts. "I have the vegetables warming on the stove."

"Why don't I put these flowers in a vase," Cordelia suggested.

"Oh, right. I think there's one under the counter."

She found a tall glass container and filled it with lukewarm water.

"I'll open the wine," Sinclair said.

Charles turned to Victoria. "*Chéri*, would you bring the bread?"

Cordelia's head snapped up, surprised. Charles had just called Princess Victoria *chéri*—the French equivalent of *darling*.

Cordelia shot a quick glance over at Sinclair. He hadn't noticed and kept his attention on the red metal seal of the wine bottle. Sinclair inserted the corkscrew and gave it a solid pull.

He looked up and smiled. "I'm really looking forward to hearing the story about how you and Victoria met."

HOTEL CAESAR AUGUSTUS, ANACAPRI

Detective Jaccorsi pulled his car out of the shadowy plaza. The moon gave off enough light for him to see. It was a winding road, and only a low wall delineated the edge. Beyond, there was a thousand-foot drop, straight down to the sea.

Even though it was late, lights blazed from a few private residences. August was high season, and people stayed up until well after midnight. The windows of Villa San Angelo were illuminated. The Bonnard house was right next to the plaza. He made a mental note to come back tomorrow. Maybe Charles had noticed something unusual.

"*Madonna*," he said aloud.

He usually didn't curse, but no one could hear him inside his empty car. The implications of tonight's events were just becoming clear to him.

The Camorra, an organized crime organization, controlled the Italian mainland, which was twenty-six miles away. But up until now, Capri had been relatively free of mob influence. If Salvatore Mondragone had sent an assassin here to the island, it set a dangerous new precedent.

Mondragone was one of the most powerful bosses in Naples. No public official would ever stand up to him. This murder would never be reported to the press, or even to authorities in the capital city, Rome. Naples police always turned a blind eye when it came to the Camorra.

But moral duty was clear. Jaccorsi wasn't going to allow Mondragone to get a foothold on Capri. The Jaccorsi family had lived on the island for countless generations.

It had been his childhood home. He personally knew every inch of the place. His youth had been spent diving off a small skiff out on the bay and climbing all over the rocky hillsides. And at night, under the grape arbor, his grandpa would tell him stories about the old days.

Eventually he had moved to Naples to become a policeman. But his mother still lived here. And every week he came over on the ferry to visit her.

He parked at the local precinct and got out of the car. The station was only manned during the day. Whenever duty called him to the island, he used the precinct as his base of operations.

He opened the office door and flipped on the light. The air smelled stale. It was warm, so he opened the window and let the place air out.

The phone sat prominently on the empty desk. He stared at it, trying to decide. There might be another way to report the murder. Rome was a separate jurisdiction, and his cousin was an inspector.

He dialed a home phone. A sleepy voice answered.

Jaccorsi spoke. "Hello, Leonardo? It's me."

His cousin's voice was immediately cautious.

"What's going on?"

"You know our local Camorra boss, Mondragone?"

"Are you talking about Cyclops?"

"Yes. He just killed a guy in Capri. They're telling us to say it was a heart attack."

"Capri? That's strange."

"It was a 9mm to the forehead."

"Of course it was. I'll pass it along to my chief."

"Just don't say my name."

"Of course."

Detective Jaccorsi put down the receiver. Nobody had heard the conversation, but it still gave him chills. He stood up and paced around the little office, working his neck to get the kinks out.

It was too late to go back to the mainland; the last ferry had left. So, he'd get a good night's sleep and start his investigation early.

He pulled off his tie and unlaced his shoes. The pants and shirt went carefully over the chair to be worn again tomorrow. A shame the suit would be wrinkled, but maybe his mother would offer to press it. Finally, clad only in his boxers and undershirt, he padded over to the jail cell and stretched out on the cot.

The air was cool now, and he pulled up the blanket for warmth. The scratchy wool smelled slightly of dust. But no matter; just lying down was bliss. He closed his eyes and tried to sleep, but the vision of the ugly little hole in the man's forehead just wouldn't go away.

VILLA DEL MARE,
TORRE DEL GRECO, ITALY

The most powerful crime boss in Naples was getting ready for his midnight meetings at the dockyards. Salvatore Mondragone always worked at night while others were asleep; it was safer that way.

He had just taken a shower and finger-combed his wet hair in the bathroom mirror, surveying his own naked flesh. His body was strong and muscular, his abdomen flat. In thirty years, the scale hadn't budged, but his skin still bore traces of violence from decades ago.

All across his pectorals, fourteen ridges of raised tissue looked like little worms, the mark of a serrated knife. He ran his thumb over a welt near his sternum. They had missed his aorta by a quarter of an inch.

Enemies had tried to kill him. Miraculously, he had survived and spent the next six months hunting his assailants down, putting his trademark bullet between their eyes.

That vendetta had established his criminal identity as "Cyclops." People never said his name out loud. They simply touched the space between their eyebrows.

His army of foot soldiers roamed the streets, pistols tucked inside expensive black leather jackets. Fleet-of-foot in Adidas sneakers, or zipping around on motor scooters—they were a cloud of flies, alighting on unsuspecting victims. It was his own private army, and tonight, a dozen of them would accompany him to the dockyards.

He walked into his wood-paneled dressing room and selected one of the 200-thread count, double-twisted Egyptian cotton shirts. Next, came the right-handed, custom-fit chamois holster and the Glock.

A slim gold watch went on his wrist. The timepiece had been stolen from the King of Spain. Pilfered articles delighted him, especially if they came from royalty.

It reinforced his sense of entitlement to be using objects that had been handled by kings and queens.

For that reason, he always employed a personal thief. Renato Balboni was sent out to fetch whatever Mondragone desired. Just this evening, he had ordered his henchman to steal two valuable objects from Capri:

One, a Roman betrothal ring owned by a guest at the Hotel Caesar Augustus.

The other, a beautiful sapphire necklace belonging to Princess Victoria.

NAPLES, ITALY

The nine o'clock Capri passenger ferry plowed through the oily water. The sun was sinking as the boat approached the main dock in Naples. An aluminum gangplank slammed into place, and the crowd surged forward. Most were clutching plastic souvenir bags.

Renato Balboni walked in the middle of the pack.

He was disguised as a tourist, a killer among innocents, and wore a dark T-shirt, camp shorts, and running shoes. His pistol was in the plastic souvenir bag, along with a guidebook of Capri. Renato was responsible for the corpse on the floor of the Hotel Caesar Augustus.

He thought back to the events of the afternoon.

"Is someone expecting you?" the manager of the hotel had asked in a haughty tone.

"No," Renato had said, giving an icy glare.

The clerk's eyes widened, but he bravely tried to uphold the standards of the hotel.

"All visitors must be announced, sir. Who shall I say is calling?"

Renato reached over and jabbed the man's forehead, clearly enunciating the name that most people would never say out loud—"Cyclops."

It had the desired effect. The manager took a blank key card and punched in the door code for the Vesuvius Suite.

What followed had just been business.

On the ride up to the fifth floor, Renato pulled on a pair of thin, black leather gloves. He'd been instructed to shoot the man in the forehead. That would serve as a warning to the authorities not to investigate too carefully.

His victim was standing, admiring the view. The man must have noticed some movement, because he turned in surprise. Renato fired, and there was a dull thud as a bullet pierced the man's skull.

The gold signet ring was in the safe.

Stealing it was easy enough. But there was another item he was supposed to get while he was in Capri—a sapphire necklace belonging to Princess Victoria of Norway.

It should have been a simple break-in at the Contessa Brindisi's villa. The princess had gone off somewhere, and her guards were out looking for her. So nobody was at the house.

But when he reached the street, about fifty paparazzi were standing around waiting to take pictures, so he couldn't even approach the gate.

Now back in Naples, Renato dashed across the Via Nuova Marina and headed into the labyrinth of streets, cutting through an alleyway behind the commercial district. Laundry lines were strung above; forgotten bed sheets wafted in the dark. At the back door of the Trattoria il Molino, voices were raised in a kitchen dispute.

These were *his* streets—he had been recruited as a child to be a Camorra drug runner. Since the age of six, he had ferried narcotics in his school backpack. The vials were color-coded: green for heroin, red for cocaine, white for crack.

His lost youth didn't matter. There was always plenty of money, and he basked in the reflected glory of Mondragone. It was like being an aide-de-camp to a famous general.

Renato had earned the sobriquet "Thief of Princes" on a recent trip to London. He had managed to amass a haul of jeweled tiepins, gold buttons, watches, and cuff links from St. James's Palace, all belonging to Prince Charles. Mondragone loved wearing them.

Renato dialed a number, and a rough voice answered.

"Tell him I got it," Renato said.

"The necklace?"

"No, just the ring."

"Wait. You were supposed to steal the necklace, too!"

"I couldn't get near the place."

"He's not going to like that."

"Do you want the ring? Or not?"

"Yeah. Meet me. And be sure you're on time."

VILLA SAN ANGELO,
ANACAPRI, ITALY

It was nearly midnight. Cordelia stirred a spoonful of sugar into her espresso. The dinner was delicious. Charles prepared a light meal, perfect for a sultry evening. Now they were all seated around the table, helping themselves from a ceramic serving bowl of tiramisu.

Suddenly, Sinclair's cell phone rang. He checked the number.

"Sorry, I have to take this. It's my team in Iceland."

He stood up and stepped away from the table.

"What's going on in Iceland?" Charles asked.

Cordelia answered. "A huge volcano is erupting. It just started this afternoon, but they think it might impact air travel over the next few days."

"Is it serious?" Victoria asked.

"They think so. It's Eyjafjallajökull. Do you remember the eruption back in 2010? I'm sure Norway was affected."

"Vaguely," the princess said. "I cant quite . . . "

"Volcanic ash went up into the jet stream. International air space was shut down for a week. Every airport in Europe was closed, and people were stranded all across the continent."

"Oh, yes. I remember," Charles said. "I was stuck in Paris. So do you think that will happen now?"

"Well, John and I have been monitoring the situation all afternoon. They're saying the debris may hit Northern Europe."

Victoria frowned. "I better check with my staff in Norway. I might have to fly back home."

Charles's face fell. "This all seems very sudden."

"Volcanoes can be unpredictable, even when they are monitored," Cordelia said. "Most people don't realize that volcanoes erupt constantly. There are fifty or sixty volcanic eruptions a year. More than once a week, on average."

"One a *week*?" Charles said. "Why don't we hear about them?"

"The majority occur in remote areas. Very few people are affected."

Sinclair came back to the table.

"Sorry about that. I moved my team back to Reykjavik. That's about eighty miles away from the eruption zone, so they're safe for now. I'll fly them back to London if it looks like the airport is about to close."

Cordelia nodded.

Charles passed the bowl of tiramisu for everyone to have seconds.

"All this talk about volcanoes reminds me of what Victoria and I were discussing this afternoon."

"What was that?" Sinclair asked, helping himself to the dessert.

Charles turned toward Victoria.

"V, why don't you tell everyone about your new philosophy."

"Oh, yes. It's called the Theory of the Four Elements."

Victoria leaned forward, wisps of blond hair escaping from her chignon.

Cordelia marveled, once again, at her beauty. No wonder Charles was so enthralled with her.

"The four elements are the basis of all life," Victoria intoned, her voice taking on a mysterious cadence. "Everything in the world is made up of these elements."

"I'm not sure I understand," Cordelia said.

"Each person is either earth, air, water, or fire. I'm fire, for example."

"Fire?"

"Yes. This afternoon Charles identified my element right away."

Cordelia glanced over at Victoria. What an unscientific theory. Why would anyone give it any credence? But Charles was mesmerized. His gaze stayed riveted on Victoria's face.

The princess continued breathlessly. "It's fascinating. Everyone in Oslo is talking about it."

"Is it like a zodiac?" Cordelia asked, pretending to play along.

"Horoscopes are just superstition. What I am talking about is an ancient *philosophy.*"

"Absolutely," Sinclair interjected.

Cordelia flashed him a look. Was he buying into this also?

The princess zeroed in, sensing her skepticism.

"I like to keep an open mind about these kinds of things," she said to Cordelia.

Cordelia swallowed her pique and replied civilly.

"I do . . . within reason."

"Personally, I try to study all kinds of philosophies: Tibetan Buddhism, Japanese Shinto, Hindu transcendental meditation. I think it's important to open your life to all kinds of new things."

Cordelia nodded and retreated into silence. Victoria was blathering. There was no way to have a rational discussion with her.

Cordelia reached over and helped herself to another spoonful of dessert. A huge lump of tiramisu quivered on her plate, and she spooned it down, oblivious to the calories. The mascarpone dissolved on her tongue in a cloud of sweetness. Tiramisu translates as "pick me up," because the cake at the bottom is soaked in coffee and cocoa. It was certainly giving her new energy. Suddenly she felt absolutely alert. And that made things worse. Her mind was whirling as the conversation droned on.

Sinclair was leaning forward on his elbows, listening to Victoria intently. His white shirt glowed in the candlelight, the sleeves rolled up to reveal muscled arms. He was always tan and fit from shoveling dirt at his archaeological digs. Tonight, he looked more handsome than ever.

This week was supposed to be a special time for them both, filled with sightseeing, shopping, swimming, and long walks along the cliffs. Sinclair loved Capri and had promised to show her the ancient Roman ruins. It was going to be a private, romantic getaway. How many of those precious days would they have now, with Victoria and Charles around all the time?

Cordelia spooned down the last of her dessert. The two men were still focused on the discussion. Rather than be rude, Cordelia picked up her coffee cup and started listening. The monologue had progressed to the heights of religious rapture.

"So you see, the four elements are necessary for the universe to be balanced."

Cordelia took a sip of her coffee.

"Why don't you give us an example," Charles suggested.

Victoria beamed, only too happy to proceed.

"So let's say the four of us are perfectly compatible: earth, water, fire, and air. Now, if too many people were fire, for example, something terrible would happen . . . the earth would . . . "

"The earth would *what?*" Cordelia said. "Spontaneously *combust?*"

Victoria stared. There was complete silence at the table. It was meant to be a funny remark. But Cordelia's derision had inadvertently come through.

Charles looked at her with hurt eyes. Sinclair didn't glance up. He sat for a moment with a slight frown and then turned toward Victoria. The way he angled his body away from Cordelia seemed to be a rebuke.

"I find it astonishing to hear you describe the cosmogenic theory of the Four Classical Elements," Sinclair said gently. "You realize that Empedocles proposed the same theory."

The princess managed a weak smile and grabbed the lifeline Sinclair had thrown her.

"I'm sorry . . . is that a philosopher?"

"Yes. You are basically framing the same theory as Empedocles."

"So what did he say, exactly?" Charles asked.

"Precisely the same thing. Empedocles believed that four elements— earth, air, fire, and water—constitute the physical world."

Cordelia sat in silence, her face flaming with embarrassment. Sinclair was trying to make amends for her gaucherie. Making a mockery of the princess was unforgivable.

Charles cut in again. "Victoria says I'm wind."

Cordelia pressed her lips together, determined not to say a word. Not a peep. But her mind still rebelled against the skewed logic of the conversation. Sarcastic quips tumbled around in her head.

Charles was wind, and Victoria was fire. So, combined, were they hot air?

"I've never heard of Empedocles," Victoria admitted. "I had no idea that this theory came from a particular school of thought."

Sinclair smiled. "It's Greek. Pre-Socratic. About 430 BC. Empedocles was a major figure of his age."

"Sinclair knows everything about ancient cultures," Charles declared.

"Did Empedocles become emperor?" Victoria asked.

Sinclair shook his head. "No. Philosophers were outside the power structure in those times. They functioned as oracles."

"So what happened to him?" Victoria asked.

"One version of history says he threw himself into the volcano at Mount Etna to prove to his disciples that he was immortal," Sinclair said.

"That must have been painful," Charles laughed.

Victoria smiled. "Well, now that I know the origins of Empedocles' theory, I am definitely going to read more about him."

Sinclair regarded the princess with a gracious smile. "I'd be happy to suggest a few books, if you like."

"I would love that."

Cordelia stretched. Wasn't it time to move on? Her chair scraped back, signaling her desire to end the discussion.

Sinclair took the hint and drained his coffee and stood up. He extended a hand to help her from her chair. As they came face to face, he brought her fingers to his lips. Their eyes connected. She tried to convey her regret for being so rude to Victoria.

He planted a kiss on the back of her hand. All was forgiven.

Then he turned to the others. "Now I ask you—why are we talking about ancient history on a beautiful night like this? We should live in the moment."

"Exactly," Charles agreed, jumping to his feet. "What shall we do now?"

Victoria replied. "Let's have a bottle of wine out on the terrace."

Cordelia stood outside watching the moonlight glimmer on the Bay of Naples—a brightly lit, romantic seascape.

But Sinclair was still inside, chatting with the others. Their comments were barely audible. Someone made a joke and she heard Charles laugh. Then there was the low rumble of Sinclair's voice, deep and sexy, and everyone laughed again.

Sinclair knew how to keep things light. He was sophisticated and intellectual, with just the right touch of humor. They had been together for two years. He was the only man she had ever felt entirely comfortable with.

They lived in London—a Mayfair townhouse that had been in her family for many generations. Right from the beginning, he fit in perfectly. They would spend entire days together. He would putter around, humming opera, pulling down texts, and researching his ancient sites. She would plan her expeditions.

She had two bases of operations, one in the States for marine research, and another in London where she worked with the Royal Geographical Society on deep ocean exploration.

Sinclair often served as a consultant to the British Museum. But primarily he funded archaeological digs all over the world through his Herodotus Foundation.

They were both world-renowned explorers, perfectly matched. Their maps and nautical charts were always mingled in a messy pile on the library table. Sometimes, he'd call her over to look at archaeological projects, or she'd show him some new discovery in the ocean. They could go for months without a ripple of discontent.

It was only when they were apart that the relationship frayed. Neither of them was any good at communication, and small things would become stumbling blocks. Misunderstandings would mushroom into arguments.

She could always tell when Sinclair was going off on expedition again. He would become non-communicative. Insomnia would follow. And she'd wake up to find his side of the bed empty, the light burning on the floor below.

Finally, after weeks of restlessness, he would pack his battered Gladstone bag and declare a need to "get his hands dirty." His main dig was in Ephesus, Turkey, although he worked in many other sites in Greece and the Middle East, even as far away as Ethiopia.

So off he would go, with a kiss and a promise. Weeks would pass before he'd reappear, sunburned and exuberant.

She always tried to be sympathetic about his need to go away. Sinclair had a full excavation schedule. And there was no reason for him to give that up now they were together. There was no use complaining. She knew from the start they would have to spend long periods apart.

Of course her oceanographic work was equally important. So being alone should not have been so difficult.

But the fear of abandonment was an old emotional scar. Her parents had been killed when she was twelve. Ever since that tragedy, any departures of loved ones evoked irrational anxiety. It took decades of therapy to even come this far.

His footsteps approached. She wouldn't mention any of her worries to him now. Nothing should interfere with their time together in Capri. All distractions would be ignored—especially those created by royal houseguests.

Sinclair stood next to Cordelia, collecting his thoughts. The stone parapet was cool to his hands as he looked out over the Bay of Naples. It was a beautiful night. Several sailboats were anchored, and the white lights on the masts were pinpricks against the indigo sky.

Dinner had been difficult. Clearly the two women didn't get along. Cordelia's razor-sharp intellect outstripped the fuzzy-thinking princess. And Cordelia didn't suffer fools. She always wanted to voice her opinion.

But that didn't work with Victoria. The princess was used to approval. Most of the time her comments, no matter how outlandish, were met with sycophantic agreement.

For the rest of the week, he and Charles would have to keep the two women apart. Leaving Cordelia and Victoria alone together would be about as dangerous as combining two incompatible elements.

Besides, he had bigger plans. He brought Cordelia to Villa San Angelo to ask her to marry him. He'd been thinking about proposing for months. It was obvious that Capri would be the place to do it. Nowhere on earth was more romantic.

If he asked her tonight, that would solve everything. They'd have the perfect excuse to go off on their own, without Charles and Victoria. Who would dream of interfering with a newly engaged couple?

And there was another reason to propose sooner rather than later. It seemed that the volcanic ash from Iceland was starting to disrupt air flights. In another day or so they might have to leave and cut the trip short.

He took a deep breath and assessed the situation. The setting was perfect. A beam of moonlight led straight across the water to where they were standing. The actual proposal speech had been on the tip of his tongue all day, and the engagement ring was in his pocket, ready to go. He reached in and ran his finger ran over the sharp angles of the five-carat, emerald-cut diamond.

"Aren't you glad we came?" he asked.

She stood looking at the sky, the corner of her mouth tilted up in a smile. "Yes, it really is wonderful."

"I've always wanted to share Capri with you."

She turned to him. Her eyes were pools of darkness, unreadable.

"I love you, Delia," he said.

There was a quick intake of breath. She clearly wasn't expecting such a declaration.

"Oh, John. I love you, too," she replied.

He reached out to take her in his arms, and she tilted her lips up for a kiss. Her perfect mouth was delineated by the glow of the moon. He took his time, memorizing the curve of her face.

"I want to ask you something . . ." he said, his mouth inches from hers.

"Later," she instructed. "Kiss me."

He smiled and pressed his lips to hers. She melted into him, winding her arms tighter around his neck. As they embraced, his brain formed the simplest way to say it. *Marry me.* But when their mouths parted, she spoke first.

"Come to bed," she said.

"Yes, but first— "

There was a noise from the kitchen.

"Oh damn, they're coming out . . ." she said, breaking out of his embrace.

Charles's voice was louder, and a tinkle of laughter escaped from Princess Victoria. The two lovebirds had gone off to fetch another bottle of wine and were now tipsily trying to open it.

Cordelia cast the princess a critical glance.

"Charles must be crazy in love. I don't know what he sees in her."

Sinclair put his hand in his pocket and fingered the ring. Maybe now wasn't the right time after all.

"She is very naive," he agreed. "But you were a bit rough on her at dinner, don't you think?"

Cordelia nodded. "I know. I'm sorry. The whole thing was so ludicrous. I just couldn't take it anymore."

"She can't help it. She's young," he explained.

"*Too* young," Cordelia amended.

Charles and Victoria were standing in the doorway, kissing passionately. It was torrid. Charles was holding a wine bottle in one hand and stroking Victoria's neck with the other.

"Does he always carry on like that?" Cordelia asked.

"Not at all. Charles may look like a playboy, but he is basically a simple family guy."

"Family? He wants children?" she asked.

"No. I mean that he takes care of his mother and his sister. He's very devoted to them."

"Well, Victoria can't exactly move to Paris."

"You're right about that. She's supposed to ascend the throne in Norway next year."

"So soon?"

"Victoria is turning twenty-one. Old enough for the succession."

"But what about her parents?"

"Her father has to step down for health reasons."

"Well, I don't care if she becomes queen. They're not a good match at all. Charles is still much older than she is," Cordelia pointed out.

"Don't worry. There's probably some Norwegian prince lined up for her. I'm sure she'll be married within the year."

"So you think her affair with Charles is a fling?"

Sinclair nodded.

"Still, it's dangerous," Cordelia fretted. "If the media get wind of it . . . "

"I agree," Sinclair sighed.

"You should say something to him," she whispered.

"Yes, but how? He's never alone."

"Invite him for a midnight swim," Cordelia suggested.

"What about you?" he asked.

"I'll go to bed."

"Without *me?*" he objected, half-joking.

Cordelia smiled.

"You can come later."

His spirits sank. The proposal would have to wait until another time; the moment was gone.

Charles and Victoria stood silhouetted in the light from the house, arms around each other. Sinclair reached down and laced his fingers through Cordelia's in solidarity.

"Hey, you two," he called over. "Come on out and join us."

VILLA SAN ANGELO, ANACAPRI

It was well after midnight on the terrace of the Villa San Angelo when Charles and Sinclair opened the last bottle of wine. Both men were wrapped in large beach towels, their hair wet. At this time of night, the underwater lights of the pool shimmered, but there were deep shadows everywhere on the patio.

Sinclair poured a glass of 2004 Chateau Lynch-Bages and passed the bottle over. Charles helped himself, drank deeply, and put the glass down on the flagstones.

"I've been miserable all day," he said.

Sinclair laughed. *"Miserable?* There's a beautiful woman in your bed, waiting for you."

"I know," Charles said. "But what if we get caught? There will be hell to pay."

Sinclair looked out at the view. "That's something you should have thought of before this."

"I've been thinking about it all day. I can't stop."

"So why did you invite her?"

Charles ran a hand through his wet hair, combing it back from his forehead.

"That's just it. I didn't."

"She just came here on her own?" Sinclair scoffed.

"Basically, yes. Victoria and her brother Prince Karl were visiting in Capri. She just showed up at the house two days ago."

Sinclair leaned forward, suddenly realizing what Charles was saying. That meant that someone else knew that Victoria was here.

"Who helped her get into your house?" he asked.

Charles shot him a tentative glance.

"Brindy."

Sinclair groaned. The Contessa Georgiana Brindisi—or "Brindy"—was his ex-girlfriend. She summered on the island every year. Her roof was visible from the terrace.

"Why would you give Brindy a key?" he asked.

Charles shrugged. "In case of an emergency."

"Are you insane?"

"Come on. She's not *totally* evil."

"You're aware that Machiavelli was her *direct* ancestor," Sinclair pointed out.

Charles sniggered. "Now you're just being dramatic."

"I assure you, it's true," Sinclair said, walking over to pick up the wine bottle.

Sinclair had been in love with Brindy, until she revealed an almost pathological talent for lying.

Charles stood up and stretched. "So what do I do about Victoria?"

"Are you asking me?" Sinclair ascertained.

"Yes."

"Tell her to go home to Oslo," Sinclair said. "And don't see her again."

"You make it sound so easy. But tell me, how does one break up with a princess?"

"Pretend she's any other girl," Sinclair suggested.

Charles pinched the skin between his eyebrows and sighed. "But that's just it. She isn't."

Sinclair raised his eyebrows. "Is *that* the reason you like her?"

Charles nodded. "At first, yes. I was flattered she approached me. I think I was trying to prove something."

"Because of the circumstances of your birth, you mean?"

"Yes."

Now they had waded into Freudian muck. Charles was more or less illegitimate. His mother discovered an unwanted pregnancy and had quickly married a French aristocrat. Charles had never met his real father.

Sinclair took a sip of wine and spoke. "Listen, why complicate things? There are plenty of other women."

"Not like Victoria. I honestly think I might be in love with her."

"She's so young."

"Not really. In some ways she has a lot more responsibility than most women her age. And she's old enough to make up her own mind about who she wants to be with."

"Well, if that's the case, you should stop sneaking around and ask her father's permission to get engaged."

"Engaged? Don't you think we should date first?"

"No," Sinclair shook his head. "Princesses don't date. They marry."

Charles looked morose. "That's the problem. Even if I asked her, she couldn't accept. Just imagine the complications with my family history."

"I realize that," Sinclair agreed.

Charles finished his wine and put the glass down on the terrace.

"I'm going to bed," he said.

"Listen, my friend. You're going to make a mess of Victoria's life and yours. You have to either cut it off or go to Oslo and talk to her father."

"I know, I know . . . "

"So *do* something. Before it's too late."

Charles turned, his shoulders slumping. "Her family would never accept me. I have to cut it off."

"Then the decision is made," Sinclair advised briskly. "Now *do* it."

"You're right. All this has to stop."

"When will you tell her?"

Charles shrugged. "Soon. She has to leave tomorrow."

"I thought she was staying the whole week?"

"No. It's the volcano," Charles said. "They're saying the debris is going to shift toward Norway, and the Oslo airport might shut down. She can't afford to get stuck in Capri. She has a few public appearances next week."

Sinclair stood up and started toward the house. "I'd better tell Cordelia, if she's still awake. We might have to head home early as well."

He stopped halfway to the door.

"By the way, how is Victoria getting back to the Villa Brindisi tomorrow?"

Charles caught up to him, carrying his towel.

"Funny you should bring that up. I was going to ask for your help."

EYJAFJALLAJÖKULL VOLCANO, ICELAND

Jude Blackwell unzipped his parka as he entered the Café Grai Kotturinn on Hverfisgata. He'd been in Reykjavik for two weeks now, waiting for the volcano to erupt. This little restaurant had become his nightly haunt, a cozy place where people came to talk, have a meal, and play chess. Plus, there was a cute little waitress who always gave him a nod when he came in the door.

Jude found a place in his usual spot. The girl came over and served him a Skjalfti with a flirty smile. She was a sweet minx, with dark, cropped hair and three silver studs in her left ear.

"Hello again," she said, elongating the vowels.

They always spoke English. He had no comprehension of Icelandic. It was a series of throat-clearing glottal stops. And the written language looked like a smashup of vowels with accent marks that flew around like shards of broken glass.

"What's the special tonight?" he asked. "Anything interesting?"

His intonation made the question sound like a flirtatious overture. She blushed, her ears glowing pink against the jumble of silver.

"Lamb stew."

"I'll have to settle for that, then, won't I?"

She went off to fetch it for him. He took a pull of Skjalfti, enjoying the light, bitter taste. Beer was one of his chief pleasures, and he could identify a hundred different kinds, even blindfolded.

Within minutes, the waitress returned with his meal.

"Sorry I can't talk this time," she said. "So many people tonight."

"What time are you off from work?"

"Eleven."

"Eleven's not too late for a drink is it?"

She blushed.

"No, eleven is not too late."

"Good, I'll see you later."

She went off, and he got down to business with the lamb, using a piece of bread to mop up the gravy. Just as he was swallowing his last bite, his cell phone started bleating . . . alert . . . alert . . . alert.

He took out a dented four-generation-old Blackberry. It was patched with duct tape to keep the battery in, and the plastic had been singed from various volcanic encounters over the years. He'd resisted upgrading it, because the buttons were better for his bulky fingers. He couldn't see himself poking at a touch screen—ping, ping, ping—like a teenage girl.

The alert messages were alarming.

Volcano warning . . . Reykjanes Zone eruption . . . Seek shelter immediately.

He grubbed some krona out of his jeans, then forced his way through the bodies to go outside to the rental car.

On the twenty-minute ride to the airport, Jude calculated a plan of action. He needed to get video of the eruption as it happened. The volcano had been off-gassing for days. Seismic readings had been predicting a huge eruption. The moment had arrived.

Suddenly, he spotted the green sign for Keflavik airport and the bright, cold lights of the terminal. Five minutes later, he pulled up to the tarmac. The rotors of the chartered helicopter were already whirling, stirring up a cloud of dust. Struggling under the weight of his camera equipment, he yanked the helicopter door open and scrambled up the metal steps.

"*Let's go!*" he shouted, buckling in.

The rotors speeded up, and the pilot manipulated the controls. They were airborne—the Bell 206L4 LongRanger swaying as if it were a children's swing. They reached altitude and powered over the pockmarked landscape. Two pairs of eyes searched the glacier with its jagged rocks, ice, and snow.

Thirty active volcanoes had formed the entire landmass of Iceland. The country lay smack in the center of the mid-Atlantic ridge. The area around Eyjafjallajökull had been sending out earthquake-swarm tremors for a week, and tonight the seismic readings were off the charts.

Iceland was the location of some of the largest and most disruptive volcanoes in history. From all the indicators, it seemed that tonight, this eruption might make the record books.

Jude looked down at the digital camera and set the ISO, f-stop, and shutter speed. It was 10:00 p.m., but the "white night" of summer would last until well after midnight. In these conditions, the volcanic ash would shimmer like diamond dust. Suddenly, there was a glimpse of a vertical shadow—a slender plume undulating out of the earth like smoke from the end of a cigarette.

He tapped the pilot's arm and gestured toward the ground. At a mile away, this would be a safe place to record the action. The helicopter skids kissed the snow and settled. Jude stumbled out the door and onto the glacier.

Frigid air smacked him in the face, and his eyes watered as he ran forward. At fifty yards, he dropped to one knee. Grit was flying around in the helicopter rotor wash, stinging his skin. Adjusting for the light levels, his hands shook with impatience. As he set the dial, a dark funnel cloud shot up several hundred feet into the air.

The vibration sounded like the far-off rumble of a train. Then it hit him. The initial shock wave passed over his face, nearly knocking him flat. He turned away to protect his camera lens from the blast and noticed the pilot gesturing. The man's mouth was contorted, eyes frantic. *Get back! Now!* Luckily the engines were still running.

Jude dragged his gear, spitting grit out into the wind. He flung himself into the aircraft. It shuddered and lifted off in a steep vertical ascent.

"Are we going to make it out?" he asked.

The grim-faced pilot did not offer any promises.

Volcanic vapor was changing from dark gray to pure white. The cloud soared a quarter of a mile into the sky. All around, scalding steam and ash were roiling the air.

Sweat streamed down Jude's face. With the buzzing of the rotors, he felt like he was sitting in a microwave.

He had once heard a wives' tale that during the famous eruption of Mount Vesuvius, people's brains boiled and exploded out of their skulls. True or not, it felt like his brain was about to do that right now.

Suddenly, the helicopter blades became labored, and the gears started to grind. Debris was infiltrating the motor. Jude looked over and saw the pilot's jaw clench, his hands in a white-knuckled grip on the controls.

The atmosphere was now barely breathable as the mephitic gases reached poisonous concentrations. The stench was awful, and the lamb dinner started to climb in his esophagus.

They careened sideways and dropped a couple of feet. Jude smacked his head against the doorjamb. His vision broke into kaleidoscopic shards. When he reached up, his palm came away, red with blood.

The sight of it startled him. They might die. A jab of fear chased his mind toward the dark side of panic. So he raised the camera and fired off a couple of shots—not for the pictures, but to steel himself against the loss of control.

The volcano was now actively erupting. Brilliant orange sparks were licking up out of the earth, and the cone was glowing red, throwing up huge splatters. Crimson streaks of molten magma were coursing down the side of the mountain, glowing in the dark.

This was going to be a disaster of epic proportions.

ANACAPRI, ITALY

On Sunday morning, Charles Bonnard tiptoed out of the bedroom carrying his shoes. He silently closed the door with one last look. Princess Victoria was asleep under the covers. The only visible part of her was a tousled head.

He slipped out of the house through the long corridor and went outside. There, just outside the door, he stopped, balancing on one foot and then the other, to brush off the soles of his feet and put on rope-soled espadrilles.

The morning air was cool. It felt good to be outside again after being confined for two days. The main piazza of Anacapri was deserted. Sinclair and Cordelia mentioned that a police car had parked here, but now it was nowhere to be seen.

Birds were screaming in the trees. Were they always so loud? Or was it just last night's wine?

Passing by the Hotel Caesar Augustus, he traversed the side streets, until he reached the footpaths that led outside the village. Within a few minutes, he was walking along the cliffs.

The local hiking route led high above the sea. It was a simple track of trampled dirt and loose stones. The Bay of Naples was below, a vast stretch of cobalt blue, glimmering in the sun. There was a nice breeze, and he could smell the earth as it warmed up.

The confinement of being housebound with Princess Victoria was mentally exhausting. It had been a wearing couple of days. His own fault really, although it was she who had initiated the affair.

He had only told Sinclair half the story.

About two months ago in Paris, he and Victoria had indulged in an impulsive and torrid one-night stand. Not that he planned it that way. The princess had invited him to join her after midnight in her hotel room. He'd arrived, assuming they'd have a cozy little drink and maybe a stolen kiss. And, at first, it was perfectly innocent. They sat together on the settee, flirting, making small talk.

He didn't suggest anything more. After all, she wasn't like any other girl. But then suddenly, she stood up, reached behind her neck, and undid the halter top of her dress. The silky folds slipped to the floor.

She was naked underneath.

He should have stopped it right then and there. She was too young for him. But he couldn't resist. A real princess wanted him. And not just any princess—it was Victoria, the darling of Europe. And he was flattered.

Then came the shock of his life. The day after they slept together, Victoria was finished with him. She never got in touch and never returned his calls. The reality dawned on him slowly. He had only been a diversion for her, a fling and nothing more.

The sting of rejection had been acute. For three weeks, whenever he saw her picture in the newspaper, he would turn away. This kind of thing had never happened to him. Though he certainly had many girlfriends, all of his past relationships had been tender and respectful. He had always found casual relationships to be repellant.

His self-esteem suffered a blow. He became restless and irritable and didn't want to remain in Paris. When August came, he decided to go to his house in Capri to nurse his wounded ego.

Thinking about it now, Charles walked faster and faster. He climbed along the path, until he suddenly became breathless with exertion and stopped.

Looking up into the azure sky, he inhaled deeply and tried to quell the anxiety. It was a beautiful day. The morning haze had burned off, and the sun was rising in the sky. Capri had always been his place of solace. He came here to relax and take stock of his life.

He should be doing that now.

Except Victoria had invaded his island, shattering his peace of mind. He read about her arrival in the local papers and was determined not to let it rattle him. He planned to simply avoid places where she might go.

Little did he expect to find her sitting in the dark hallway of his house one night when he came home. As he opened the door, she was a pale face among the ancient artifacts.

Before he could react, she threw her arms around his neck, saying she missed him and thought about him all the time. All the bitterness melted away in an instant. He had misread the situation. She cared for him after all.

Still, the pain of the past few weeks made him cautious.

"V, I don't think you should be here," he said, removing her arms from around his neck.

"It's fine. Nobody saw me."

"But they'll be out looking for you," he objected.

"No, Brindy will cover for me. We can be together for the *whole* week."

"A *week*!"

"Yes. Please. Let me stay with you, Charles."

"No, I think it's too dangerous."

"Well, I can't leave now," she said stubbornly. "Too many people are around. I'll have to wait until it's dark before I can go back."

Of course that was pure manipulation on her part. She could leave any time she wanted to. But he didn't argue.

"Maybe just for dinner . . ." he demurred.

About halfway through the evening, he realized she had no intention of leaving. That night he called Sinclair and dropped a hint that "someone special" was spending the week.

Initially, Sinclair seemed enthusiastic on the phone. But, upon seeing the princess, his disapproval was a harsh dose of reality. Even Cordelia was politely doubtful about his royal liaison.

And they were right.

It was only a question of time before the media found out that Victoria was secretly seeing an older man. The girl's reputation would be destroyed, and their lives would be turned into a circus.

Last night, after speaking with Sinclair out by the pool, Charles joined Victoria in the bedroom. Determined to cut it off, he told her with brutal honesty that they should stop seeing each other. She needed to stop sneaking around and marry an eligible prince.

It was an obligation. For the good of her country.

But she simply laughed and said that her parents had selected horrible partners for her. All the men bored her. They were dolts. She'd rather die than marry one of them.

Then she enumerated all his sterling qualities: his looks, his charm, his worldly sophistication, punctuating each remark with a kiss. After that, his resolve had faded.

Charles reached the end of the walking trail. The dirt track turned into pavement, so he started down the narrow street toward the town.

This couldn't continue. He'd go to the café to think about the right words to say. This morning he was going to tell Victoria goodbye.

VILLA SAN ANGELO, ANACAPRI

Out on the terrace, John Sinclair checked the BBC News app for information about the volcano. The video was impressive. Eyjafjallajökull was now in full eruption, and ash was coming out of the cone like black paint from a giant spray can.

Air travel was turning into a nightmare. The wind and jet stream were disseminating particles into the atmosphere some 20,000 to 40,000 feet above the Earth. The debris cloud was sweeping eastward toward England and Northern Europe. In another few hours, Norway would be unreachable by air.

So far, fifteen European countries had put restrictions on flights. The UK Civil Aviation Authority was warning that in the next twenty-four hours, all but non-emergency traffic in British airspace would be shut down.

This quashed Sinclair's plans for remaining in Capri. They had to leave the island before they were stranded.

He took the ring out of his pocket and looked at the brilliant sparkle in the sunlight. His proposal would have to wait. He wanted to show Cordelia the island. Capri had always been a special spot for him, and he had spent many summers exploring the ruins.

The archaeology here was fascinating. The historian Tacitus had written about Capri, particularly the period when the emperor Tiberius had moved his court. The emperor had feared assassination in Rome and had fled here to construct his palace, the Villa Jovis, overlooking the Bay of Naples. After that, Capri became known as the "Imperial Island."

One of Sinclair's favorite pastimes was to wander through the ruins of the ancient palace and sit on the warm marble fragments, conjuring up what it must have been like to live in those days.

Charles built his own house on a nearby precipice, calling it Villa San Angelo, after a local legend. Some old women in the nearby village claimed that Archangel Michael often frequented the exact cliff where Charles now lived. They had seen a winged creature staring out to sea. Sinclair didn't really believe the wives' tale, but the proximity to the ancient ruins made Charles's villa one of Sinclair's favorite places on earth.

Cordelia stepped out onto the terrace, interrupting his thoughts. She had a light blue robe over her nightdress. Her hair was tousled, her feet bare. Padding over, she sat on an adjacent lounge chair, nursing a cup of coffee.

"Anybody up yet?"

"I guess it's just us," Sinclair replied.

He palmed the ring and put it in his pocket.

"What were you checking?" she asked, assuming he was putting away his phone.

"BBC News. The volcano. It looks like we can't stay."

"Is it that bad?"

"Yes. We should get back to London while we can. They may close down airspace for quite some time."

"Why don't we stay until it clears up? Charles won't mind," she said, relaxing back with a sigh.

He looked over at her; she was radiant, even without makeup.

"I can't get stuck here indefinitely. I have some important meetings in London next week. And we have that big gala for the Herodotus Foundation. I need to get organized for that."

"Oh, right. I forgot," she said, leaning back and closing her eyes, as if determined to absorb every last ray of sun.

"The weather won't stay as nice as this," he cautioned. "It might get cloudy."

"You're right. I suppose the air quality will deteriorate here as well," she said.

He looked over with regret. "I'm sorry, Delia. We'll just have to come back to Capri some other time."

VILLA BRINDISI, CAPRI

The Contessa Brindisi stood on the balcony of her house watching the Bay of Naples. It was a rare moment of leisure, away from her famous Brindisi Luggage Company in Milan.

Ever since childhood, she had come to this house to spend a month in the summer. The villa was one of the most beautiful on the island, a large white structure of graceful architecture with terraces and balconies and a view out over the water.

August was always a time of enjoyment, but this year everything seemed different. The threat of ashfall from the volcano was worrying everyone. And her household was in turmoil because of her royal houseguests. Princess Victoria and her younger brother Prince Karl brought their security teams with them. Big Norwegian men crowded her kitchen, annoying her housekeeper.

Worst of all, the arrival of the princess generated a flock of paparazzi at her gate. Hordes of tourists lingered in the street, hoping to catch a glimpse of the girl. Of course their efforts were futile. Victoria was still up at the villa with Charles Bonnard.

The Norwegian guards were confident they could locate her without a fuss. They were quietly searching the town, convinced she would turn up. It wasn't the first time Victoria slipped away. Of course, the Royal Palace had not been notified. At least not yet.

Brindy helped Victoria plan the caper. The princess only packed a small bag to visit Charles, per Brindy's suggestion. Travel light, she said. And Victoria agreed.

The rest of Victoria's luggage stayed at Villa Brinidisi. One of the large suitcases held her evening gowns and jewelry, including a valuable sapphire necklace. This was the bag the princess used when she attended a gala in Rome. It was foolhardy to leave it lying around. The contents were priceless.

Brindy walked into the guest room and opened Victoria's valise on the luggage rack. Everything was neatly folded. She felt along the sides of the suitcase, looking for the necklace box, pressing her hand down on the silky folds of the dresses. Her fingers came into contact with something hard—a black leather case. She opened it.

The sapphires were still inside!

They were supposed to be stolen by now. Salvatore Mondragone's thief was instructed to take the necklace while everyone was out of the house.

Brindy walked quickly to the living room and dialed the phone. The normal rough voice answered. It was Tito, disgruntled as usual.

"The necklace is still here. Why didn't your man take it?" she asked.

"He couldn't get through the paparazzi. There were too many people outside the gate. We'll have to try another time."

The contessa's voice grew aggressively louder. "If you want that necklace, you have to hurry. The princess is coming back to the villa today."

"I thought she would be away all week?" Tito asked.

"No. She has to go back to Norway. The volcanic ash is causing a problem with the flights."

"OK, we'll send Renato back."

"Just so you know, I held up my end of the deal," she said firmly. "Any mess-ups were on your side."

There was a dry, mirthless laugh.

"I wouldn't take that attitude, Contessa. People don't tell Cyclops that he screwed up."

"Hey, he's your boss, not mine," Brindy replied.

"Salvatore Mondragone is *everyone's* boss. And if you make a deal with him, you deliver."

Detective Jaccorsi walked through the narrow streets of Capri. The village was empty, except for the stray cats sniffing at trash bins. The retail shops would be shuttered until noon, but the café was open, and a few grizzled men sat nursing their morning espressos in silence.

Every Sunday, Jaccorsi came to the island to visit his mother. For the past fifteen years, she had been the cook and housekeeper for the young Contessa Brindisi. This morning, Jaccorsi would make the trip over to the house for breakfast. But it was still a little too early to show up.

He had been on the island since last night to investigate the murder at the Hotel Caesar Augustus. After sleeping in the cramped little precinct, he was wearing the same clothes from the day before. It wasn't comfortable, but at least he could count on a good meal.

He walked through the silent streets, enjoying being back on the island of his youth. Glancing over at the town café, he saw Mr. Charles Bonnard at one of the little tables, drinking a double espresso. They knew each other as passing acquaintances.

Jaccorsi approached to question him about last night.

"Ciao, Mr. Bonnard," he said, walking up.

"Good morning, detective. You're up early."

"I'm on my way to Villa Brindisi."

Charles frowned, confused.

"Are you part of the princess's security detail?"

"No, nothing to do with that. I'm going to see my mother," Jaccorsi explained. "She's the housekeeper."

"Oh, of course. How could I have forgotten? Do give her my best."

Jaccorsi gestured to the opposite chair. "May I sit down?"

Charles nodded. "Please. Would you like some coffee?"

Jaccorsi shook his head. "No, thank you. I just wanted to ask . . . did you notice anything unusual up near your house last night?"

Charles sat up straighter.

"Not really. I was with some friends. We didn't go outside, except on the terrace."

"I see."

"An investigation?" Charles asked.

"Nothing important," Jaccorsi said, standing up again. "One of the guests at the Hotel Caesar Augustus had a heart attack. Just a routine matter."

"Oh," Charles said.

They both knew that was a fabrication. Medical emergencies didn't require follow-up questions. Murders did.

There was an awkward pause.

"Well, it looks like the summer season is ending early," Charles remarked. "I hear a lot of people are leaving today because of the volcano in Iceland."

Jaccorsi looked up at the china-blue sky. There was not a single cloud.

"Yes. A pity," he said without much feeling.

"Are you sure I can't get you an espresso?" Charles asked again.

"No, I'd better be getting along now," Jaccorsi said. "Thanks for the help."

"Take care," Charles said.

Detective Jaccorsi rang the kitchen bell and listened for the shuffling footsteps. For the next two hours, he and his mother would sit at the wooden table in the kitchen. There'd be coffee and fresh *panettone* and lots of local gossip.

It was a big week at the Villa Brindisi. His mother would probably tell him all about it; the entire island was talking about the royal visitors.

Footsteps approached the door and the lock clicked open. Jaccorsi was always surprised to see how old his mother was. In his mind she was still young and beautiful. She stood there now, her face shining with joy at seeing her only son.

Somehow the sight of her caused him to think about the grisly murder he had witnessed last night. The Hotel Caesar Augustus was not even a half mile away.

He pulled his mother into his arms and squeezed her with affection.

"Mama, come stai?"

TORRE DEL GRECO, NEAR NAPLES, ITALY

Naples crime boss Salvatore Mondragone sat under the shade of a grape arbor. Out on the lawn, his fishpond glimmered in the sun. He lived in the charming suburb of Torre del Greco on the lower slopes of Mount Vesuvius. It was pleasant to sit in the garden where the sea breezes gently stirred the oleanders and umbrella pines.

He did not grow up in such idyllic surroundings, but rather spent his blighted youth in the slums of Naples. The family apartment was on a street nicknamed "the Tunnel of the Dead"—where mobsters had their gun battles, taking advantage of the narrow alleyway to corner their enemies.

Mondragone turned at a noise behind him on the terrace. It was Tito. His second in command was a strange looking man, with a shock of Warholesque white hair and a perpetually hostile expression. Tito's lower body was deformed, and he scraped his feet along with a painful gait, as if his hips had been knocked out of alignment.

"*Buongiorno*," Mondragone said. "Did you bring anything from Renato?"

"Here's the ring."

Tito wormed something out of his pocket and handed it to his boss. Mondragone held it up to the light.

At first glance, it wasn't impressive. The gold wasn't very heavy, and there were no jewels or fancy ornamentation. The design was common enough—two clasped hands—a standard wedding ring that was traditionally worn by the wealthy women of ancient Rome. Similar artifacts could be found in the British Museum or the Pergamon Museum in Berlin.

What made this ring special, according to Sotheby's, was the inscription on the inside—"*Te amo parum.*" The Latin phrase was etched into the ancient gold.

The translation of *te amo* was straightforward enough—"I love you." The inclusion of the word *parum*, however, was enigmatic—it meant "very little" or "not a lot."

"I love you very little" was an unusual thing to declare to one's betrothed. But experts came up with a less literal meaning, interpreting the phrase as "I don't love you as much as you deserve."

Mondragone found that to be a perfect sentiment when it came to his wife. Fabiola was a legendary beauty and an opera diva of international fame. Being with her proved that he was cultured and not just a common thug. But he didn't really love her. He was incapable of the emotion.

Her fortieth birthday was coming up, and he needed several expensive presents for the occasion. It would be a big party in London, and he had to appear generous. Not for her sake. Her approval didn't matter. The rest of the world should see that he was successful.

"Did he give you anything else?"

"No, boss. He didn't."

"I guess the 'Thief of Princes' has lost his touch. *Cazzo,*" Mondragone swore. "I told him to go to the Villa Brindisi."

"He says it was too heavily guarded."

"Brindy made sure everyone was out of the house," Mondragone growled. "What more does he need, an engraved invitation?"

Tito shrugged and made a big production out of opening a pack of cigarettes, banging it on the heel of his hand. He pulled one out and put it between his lips.

"What do you want me to do, boss?"

The unlit cigarette bounced like an orchestra baton beating out the syllables, as he searched his pockets for the lighter.

"Tell him to go back to Capri and get it."

"*Va bene,*" Tito nodded, lighting the cigarette.

"Make sure Renato knows he's a dead man if he doesn't."

"Want me to hurt him?" Tito asked, flicking ash onto the terrace as he awaited instructions.

Mondragone thought about it, looking off at the garden. He answered with utter dispassion.

"Sure. Just a little."

VILLA BRINDISI, CAPRI

Sinclair stopped the car in front of the gates of the Villa Brindisi and honked. He was on a fool's mission, secretly returning Victoria to the house where she was supposed to be staying.

The car belonged to Charles, and ludicrously, Victoria was now concealed under a blanket in the backseat. Her body was so slight, she barely made a bump.

At first, Sinclair refused to chauffeur the girl back. But Charles begged, saying he was perfect for the job. Sinclair and Brindy were former lovers and had been seen together on the island for years. No one would think it strange if he turned up at her house today.

As Sinclair pulled up to the gates, there were a few cameramen, but it was too early in the day for the majority of the paparazzi to be here. After all, it was Sunday.

As Sinclair eased the car forward, no one reacted. Clearly, they did not spot Victoria in the back seat.

The portals of the Villa Brindisi swung open. It was Brindy's son, Luca. The teenager flashed a grin as Sinclair drove through and then shut the doors.

The interior of the stone courtyard was sunlit and deserted. As expected, Detective Jaccorsi's police car was parked next to the kitchen door for his weekly visit with his mother.

Sinclair got out of his vehicle without saying a word to the princess. He'd let her sweat it out for a while.

Luca Brindisi ambled over, a typical teenager, shy with awkwardness.

"Luca, ciao. I've got a delivery for you."

"Yeah. Brindy just told me."

Luca's eyes were enormous, uncertain about how things would be between them. Sinclair and Brindy had broken up when Luca was still a boy.

"Come here and give me a hug," Sinclair said, dispelling the tension.

He affectionately gripped Luca and pounded him on the back.

"I can't believe how big you are. How old are you now?"

"I just turned fifteen."

Sinclair took his measure. Luca was wan and pale. He had just come through a bout of cancer and his pallor was waxy. But Sinclair didn't comment on that.

"Well look at you! You're almost as tall as I am!"

Luca shuffled, pleased with the remark.

"Will you come in and say hello to my mom?" the boy asked.

Sinclair realized that Luca probably wished for some kind of reconciliation. That was not going to happen. Still, there was no need to be rude.

"Oh, sure," Sinclair relented. "I'll pop in, just for a minute."

He turned toward the house just as two Norwegian security men came lumbering out into the courtyard, scowling.

"Where is the princess?" one of them asked.

"In the car," Sinclair said.

He purposely didn't open the rear door. He was not going to play footman as well as chauffeur. At the sound of their voices, Princess Victoria pulled off the blanket and climbed out. She ignored the guards and turned to Sinclair.

"Thanks for helping me."

Sinclair stiffened and signaled a warning. Jaccorsi was coming out of the kitchen entrance. The detective's eyes were taking in the scene with professional attention. His gaze went immediately from Sinclair to the princess, widening in surprise.

"Hello, detective," Sinclair hailed him casually. "Been seeing your mother?"

"*Buongiorno*, Sinclair. Yes, as usual."

They clasped hands warmly like old friends. Sinclair met Jaccorsi when he was dating Brindy. The detective would come by once a week, and sometimes they would talk about the history of the island. A few times they even explored the hillsides of Capri together. Jaccorsi knew all the secret passages in the ruins of Villa Jovis.

Sinclair turned to Victoria with studied nonchalance.

"Your Royal Highness, may I present Detective Jaccorsi?"

"Pleased to meet you," she said.

Sinclair continued. "Your Highness, I think you may have met Detective Jaccorsi's mother, Carmela. She's a member of the household."

Victoria understood immediately.

"Oh yes, detective. You mother is absolutely marvelous."

Jaccorsi attempted a small bow of thanks, which he aborted in mid-execution. He looked both smitten and embarrassed.

"Very nice to meet you, your Highness," he said, then turned back to Sinclair. "So how have you been? Spending much time in Capri this summer?"

"I've only just arrived with Cordelia. But now it looks like we have to leave."

"Because of the volcano?"

"It would seem so."

"That's a shame. I'm also here for a short time," he said. "An investigation."

"Have you been up to the ruins lately?" Sinclair asked.

Jaccorsi knew all the hidden parts of the island, from childhood.

"Not in years. We really should plan to go again," Jaccorsi replied. "That last time was fascinating. And I hear they have excavated a lot more of Villa Jovis."

"Absolutely, let's do that. I'll let you know the next time I come to Capri."

"Excellent," Jaccorsi nodded.

"And if you ever get to London, be sure and look me up," Sinclair added. "I'd love to show you around."

"London? I guess it's possible," Jaccorsi said, to be agreeable.

Sinclair smiled. "Well, it's nice to see you again."

Jaccorsi shook hands, giving him a strong grip, but his gaze shifted once again to the princess. He made another abbreviated bow. Then he walked to his vehicle, got in, and started the engine. Luca opened the gates to let him out.

"That was close," Victoria exhaled.

"He was too starstruck to suspect anything."

"Thanks ever so much. I *really* appreciate it . . ."

Sinclair nodded and turned to go inside. From now on, Victoria was on her own.

But that didn't mean he was rid of troublesome women. His ex-girl-friend, the Contessa Georgiana Brindisi, was waiting for him inside. As he entered the living room, she stepped in from the balcony, her long dark hair blowing in the breeze. Strong, sensual, exotic, her dark eyes flashed in welcome.

It had been seven years since they last dated. Brindy hadn't changed at all. There was the usual flamboyant attire: jeweled sandals, an arm-load of gold bracelets. Her orange silk caftan clung to her body, defin-ing ample breasts. Even on a Sunday morning, she was not reluctant to flaunt her sexuality.

"Hello, Brindy," Sinclair said quietly.

"John, *darling!* How *kind* of you to drop in."

She stretched up to kiss him on each cheek. He was assailed by her perfume, "Aphrodite." Years ago, Brindy had invented the scent, recon-stituting an ancient perfume oil found in one of the Greek amphorae Sinclair discovered on a dig. It was now sold in every duty-free shop in the world. Sometimes he'd catch a whiff of it on a passing woman, and it always brought back memories.

"I thought I'd stop by to say hello," he said, hesitating in the middle of the room, fighting the urge to flee.

"Come in, come in."

Brindy gestured to the upholstered settee.

"I can only stay a moment," he said, sitting down.

Brindy settled in next to him.

"How good to see you," she said, patting his arm.

She was often touchy-feely in conversation. Intimate, confidential. But she could turn that off and on. Sometimes, she could be as aloof as an empress. Her manner changed depending on whom she was manipulating.

Deceit was in her genes. In terms of social rank, her Brindisi ances-tors included princes and popes. The family had rivaled the doges of Venice in terms of power. They had amassed their wealth by their wits and cunning. And so had Brindy. She was a true Brindisi.

Her appearance revealed the family bloodlines, and her features matched those of her ancestors in the portraits. Her profile had the purity of a classical marble statue—hooded eyes, a full mouth, dominant nose. Sinclair often thought that she would have fit in as the wife of a high-ranking senator during Nero's reign.

"John, it's been *ages.*"

She reached for a small silver bell to ring the housekeeper.

"Coffee?"

"No, thank you. I really have to get back."

Her hand hesitated, then she put the bell down. Disappointment registered in her eyes.

"Well, stay a moment anyway and tell me—how have you been?"

Her manicured fingers made a quick brush of his knee and then moved away.

"I'm fine. Living in London now," he said.

She really had no right to all his personal details. He chose another direction.

"How's your family?" he asked. "Is everyone well?"

Her smile faded a bit. That question was a blunder, Luca was still recovering from cancer. So he pressed on, trying to cover his gaffe.

"I was actually wondering about your grandmother. Is she still in that beautiful old house in Rome?"

The old Contessa Brindisi was ninety-five and still a prominent social figure in Italy.

Brindy smiled. "Yes, I don't see her often. But she's going as strong as ever."

She looked up, and their eyes connected.

"Of course you heard about Luca," she said.

Sinclair nodded quickly. "Yes. I was so sorry . . . I wrote to him a couple of times. I wish I could have come to see him, but I was away on expedition. How's his prognosis?"

Brindy sighed. "They say he's in total remission. There's a six-month checkup in another week or so, but the doctors are optimistic."

"Please, keep me informed, will you?"

"Of course. He thinks the world of you, John."

"Well . . . I've missed . . . it's so nice to hear he is doing better."

There was a moment of silence as Brindy looked around furtively. She leaned closer, speaking softly. "I wanted to ask you. Have you heard about the murder last night?"

"*Murder?*"

"Yes, apparently a guest was killed up at the Hotel Caesar Augustus. My housekeeper, Mrs. Jaccorsi, just told me."

Sinclair felt the hair rise on the back of his neck.

"There was an ambulance in the square last night. But I didn't realize it was a murder. What happened?"

"A man was shot through the forehead."

"That sounds like a Camorra hit."

"Yes. Apparently the victim was a banking executive."

"What does Detective Jaccorsi say? This case must be generating a lot of interest."

"To the contrary. They're hushing up the whole thing."

Sinclair frowned. "Why?"

"Nobody wants to answer questions about the *Camorristi*."

"That's terrible."

"I'm really worried, John. You know we have security issues, especially with the princess."

He fixed her with a cold stare. "If you're so worried about Victoria, what was she doing up at Charles Bonnard's house?"

Brindy's eyes were all innocence. "How could I stop her? She's in love."

He gritted his teeth in exasperation.

"Brindy, you shouldn't encourage the girl. This kind of liaison will *never* work."

"Why not?"

"She's first in line to the throne."

"That's no problem. Charles is from a noble family."

"Well, yes and no," he corrected her.

"His father is Alphonse *Bonnard*," she countered.

"You know Charles's family history as well as I do. He is not Bonnard's son."

"But none of that information is public."

Sinclair shook his head. "If the press starts digging, he's going to be humiliated."

"We shouldn't interfere in affairs of the heart, John."

Sinclair felt his patience evaporate.

"What about Charles's mother and sister? They'll be dragged into it as well."

"I'm sure it will all work out," she purred, putting her hand on his thigh. She gave his leg a squeeze. Her dark eyes were cunning.

He stared back, wondering what she was scheming.

Luca Brindisi and his boarding school friend, fifteen-year-old Prince Karl of Norway, were lounging on the terrace of the Villa Brindisi, looking for new ways to get into trouble.

"So your sister is going back home?" Luca asked.

Prince Karl nodded. "Yeah, they're afraid she'll get stuck here. There is some kind of public appearance in Oslo next week."

"What about you? Do you have to go, too?" Luca asked.

"No, I can stay until school starts."

"Cool," Luca said. "You know, we should do something incredible, so we can brag to the other guys when we get back."

Karl sat down opposite him.

"Why don't we sneak away and go off somewhere."

Luca grinned. "The Blue Grotto?"

"No, that's for tourists. How about climbing Mount Vesuvius?"

"You want to climb *that*?" Luca asked, pointing to the volcano on the mainland.

"Yup."

"Are you sure it's safe? I mean, that other volcano is erupting in Iceland. The same thing might happen here."

"Don't be ridiculous. Volcanoes are not connected underground. It's not as if one magma chamber is linked to the others. Iceland is on the other side of the planet."

"Wow," Luca exhaled. "How do you know that stuff?"

"I've been studying volcanoes since I was eight."

"Well, I guess we could always just go to Mount Vesuvius for a few hours."

"I was thinking more like a day or so. And there are some awesome volcanoes right nearby—Stromboli and Mount Etna."

"We could take the ferry," Luca suggested.

"Do you have any money?"

"My mom gives me a little. Or we can pay with a credit card."

"They can trace a card. Cash would be better. And we'd have to sneak away."

"I don't have much money," Luca confided.

Karl looked off in the distance, eyes narrowed. "Don't worry, I'll find a way."

"When do you want to go?" Luca asked.

The young prince looked at him with an impish grin.

"Now."

Karl pulled open dresser drawers in his sister's room, looking for cash. He ransacked the bureau and night table and turned up nothing. Then, he went through Victoria's suitcase on the luggage rack with its evening gowns and shoes. Not even a euro.

Just to be sure, he stuck his hands into the silky garments and felt along the sides of the suitcase. His fingers came into contact with something hard and square, and he lifted it out. It was a jewel case—a black leather box with a Norwegian royal seal. Inside was a blue necklace.

He hesitated, an idea suddenly dawning on him.

Why not sell the necklace?

This didn't belong to her personally. These jewels belonged to the royal palace. Of course he really shouldn't, but Victoria had so many she'd never miss this one. It would be their only chance for a source of cash.

He heard Luca in the hallway.

"Karl, where'd you go?"

Karl made a fast decision. He snatched some tissues off the bureau, wadded up the necklace, and stuffed it into his backpack.

He stepped out into the hall. Luca was waiting, sunglasses in hand, backpack slung over his shoulder.

"Are you ready?"

"Yeah."

Luca nodded. "We'd better get out of here before anyone notices."

NAPLES, ITALY

The "Thief of Princes" was eating dinner on a tray in front of the television. A napkin was tucked into his collar, and the two corners were spread across his chest to prevent splattering. His eighty-five-year-old mother sat beside him, watching the news. Since she broke her ankle, Renato had to cook the noonday meal.

The broadcast ended and a commercial started. Over the sound of a musical jingle, Renato heard a knock. His mother didn't turn but continued to stare.

"Somebody is at the door, Renato."

"I got it, Mama."

He shoveled in another forkful and stood up. Walking into the tiny hallway, he checked for his pistol and then turned the knob. Tito was standing on the doorstep.

His appearance was always startling. Tito was puny, with misshapen legs and a mane of white hair that stood up as if electrified. He stood scowling, clearly in a foul temper.

"What do you want?" Renato asked.

"I got a message from Cyclops. He wants to know why you didn't get that necklace from Capri?"

Renato puffed his cheeks and blew out dramatically. "I told you. There were too many guards. Paparazzi and the police were patrolling the villa."

"Well he wants you to try again. His wife's birthday is in three weeks."

"OK. But half the population of Capri is standing outside trying to get pictures of the princess. It's pretty hard to sneak in."

"Well, you'd better try."

Renato began to shut the door, thinking the conversation was over, but Tito stuck his foot in.

"What now?" Renato asked.

Without warning, he saw a flash of blue and the unmistakable pulse. It was Tito's notorious Taser C2.

The electric current shot through his body, dropping him to the floor. For a full thirty seconds he writhed in excruciating pain, his body in the grip of neuromuscular spasms. Totally incapacitated, every cell burned, and it felt like his heart would burst through his chest. His nerves were on fire—legs and arms jerked in spastic contortions. There was a faint metallic taste in his mouth.

"Agghhh . . ." Renato gasped.

The Taser treatment was legendary. Tito was weak because of his physical deformity. He needed to drop his victims to the floor before he could beat them up. The Taser had been set on stun mode to incapacitate Renato. Now came the assault. A foot smashed into his groin. Phosphorescent dots danced before his eyes.

"Stop, please . . ." Renato begged.

"Get the necklace."

"O-K."

Tito left Renato on the doorstep. Renato dragged himself back inside and kicked the door shut. He felt like he had been flayed alive. Even his eyeballs hurt. He lay on his back. Vomit rose up in his throat. It was tinged with the taste of tomato sauce from lunch.

"Renato?"

"Just a second, Mama."

Miraculously, his voice sounded almost normal. It took him a few minutes to be able to move, but then he groped his way over to a table to stand up. The hall mirror reflected a pale face. He did a quick pat down of his hair and smoothed his clothes.

Tito's beating left no visible trace. That was intentional; fights among Mondragone's men would never be advertised.

Renato walked back into the living room and sat down, wincing as his privates pressed against the cushion of the chair. Luckily, his mother barely glanced over at him. He looked down and stared at his tray of spaghetti, nauseated. The TV program ended, and a commercial jingle started up again.

"Who was at the door, Renato?"

"Nobody important, Mama."

CAPRI–NAPLES FERRY

Detective Jaccorsi was out on the deck of the ferry as it pulled into the Naples dockyard. The pier was stacked with shipping containers, boxy metal freight modules in various colors, filled with every kind of consumer good imaginable: sneakers from Taiwan, cocoa from Africa, electronics from Korea, fresh produce from Latin America.

Naples was one of the busiest ports in Europe; ships unloaded 30,000 tons of cargo a year, and revenue was in the billions. Salvatore Mondragone was in charge here and took his cut on everything that passed through.

Each kingpin in Naples controlled a separate industry: clothing factories, garbage collection, fishing, smuggled counterfeit goods, cigarettes, liquor . . . The Camorra was like a hydra; killing it was impossible. Eradicating so many heads was too much for the police, and consequently, the organization was integral to the functioning of the economy.

Mondragone was universally feared, and the police let him operate with impunity. But his position in the hierarchy of Camorra ranks had to be defended. To stay in power, he had to kill. And because of Mondragone, Naples had one of the highest murder rates in Europe.

Jaccorsi knew the real reason behind Mondragone's madness. In recent years neuroscientists had been able to scan the brains of men who had been classified as psychopaths. The amygdala region was markedly less active than that of normal people. In the orbital frontal cortex, the receptors for empathy, remorse, or fear were impaired.

Mondragone was a textbook example of a psychopath, even down to the charming manner in which he manipulated people.

Jaccorsi stepped off the Capri ferry and walked along the dock, making a silent vow to get rid of the monster. When Mondragone targeted Capri, he went too far.

TORRE DEL GRECO, ITALY

The Camorra boss was sitting in his living room reading the *Financial Times* newspaper, sipping an afternoon Campari and soda. The article was about the famous Brindisi family—an aristocratic dynasty whose wealth and power had dominated Italy for generations.

There were two powerful women in the family—the young contessa, whom everyone called Brindy, and her grandmother, the "old contessa," who was ninety-five and lived in Rome.

Mondragone knew Brindy well. She paid him protection money. In exchange for regular cash payments, the mobster made sure that nobody interfered with her factories. Brindisi Enterprises was off-limits to the Camorra gangs.

It cost her plenty. Mondragone upped the prices lately, and she was complaining. So instead of arguing, he cut her a new deal. In lieu of payola, she now gave him information.

Brindy was in the perfect position to know where all the rich people were and what they were doing. She was connected to everyone who mattered in Italy.

The article Mondragone was reading in the *Financial Times* was a profile of the *old* Contessa Brindisi, an enormously wealthy woman who had been a big player in national politics. She had long retired from public life. This was one of the first articles written about her in years.

Mondragone examined the grainy image. The ancient contessa was looking at the camera with rheumy eyes, her white hair pulled into a scanty topknot.

The article mentioned her private collection of *objets d'art*. The two-page write-up read like a Sotheby's catalogue, describing the valuable gold collectibles that were displayed all over the house. This kind of bounty was too tempting to resist.

Salvatore Mondragone started formulating a plan. He'd tell Renato to break into the old contessa's house and clean the place out. Brindy owed him for that sapphire necklace. Now her grandmother was going to pay.

ROME, ITALY

Renato Balboni sat in an outdoor café on the Via Condotti in Rome. It was a beautiful Sunday night and couples strolled by, arm in arm.

The thief had a chameleon-like ability to blend in. Tonight, drinking his Cinzano Blanco with a splash of soda and lemon, he looked like any other classic boulevard dandy. He chose a black suit with an open-front shirt and smoked an MS *filtro*. From time to time, he would check his watch, as if he were impatient for a girlfriend to arrive.

Just in front of him, beyond the magnificent sweep of the famous Spanish Steps, was the fifteenth-century Brindisi Palace. Brindy's grandmother had lived here all her life and so had the rest of the Brindisi clan going back to the 1600s.

He'd been watching the house, calculating his timing for the break-in. Monday through Saturday, the staff came and went; the schedule was like clockwork.

Sundays seemed ideal. At a quarter to ten in the morning, the old lady, clad in a severe black suit and a lace mantilla, would totter off to Mass. In the afternoon, she'd have a four-course lunch with the local Roman Catholic monsignor, and they'd spend a few hours in conversation. But Sunday night the contessa was alone—without staff.

That was the only real window of opportunity for Renato to steal her precious *objets d'art*.

At exactly 9:00 p.m. Renato drained his glass. As if on cue, across the square, the light in the upstairs bedroom went out. The old lady was down for the night. No one would be back until 6:00 a.m. when the housekeeper arrived to prepare breakfast.

Renato dropped a few euros on the zinc tabletop and casually sauntered across the street. There was a small alley that led to the back of the house and the kitchen door. There, in the shadows, he pulled on a pair of thin leather gloves. Inserting a small metal pick into the old keyhole, within ten seconds he heard the distinctive click of the tumblers.

Inside, it was dark and silent. He crossed through the kitchen and found a back stairway leading up to the main hall—a stately foyer with a Carrera marble floor and a fifteenth-century iron chandelier. In the dim light he could see a long, curved staircase leading up to the second floor.

He felt his way along the marble railing. The house was airless, stuffy, and smelled heavily of old upholstery. The main salon was pitch dark. Thick damask drapes were drawn across the windows, blocking the streetlights.

He felt his way to the nearest piece of furniture and extracted a small LED light. As he stepped forward, a floorboard creaked.

Merda!

He froze and then eased his weight off the parquet. It would be better to take an alternate route through the room. In the bright pinpoint of the beam, he saw a Fabergé cigarette box and three solid gold snuffboxes.

All around the grand salon were *objets de vertu*—eighteenth-century gold snuffboxes from the French kings Louis XV and Louis XVI—small, portable, and priceless.

Renato walked around casually, as if this were an antique shop. No reason to rush. He wanted to select the most valuable pieces to put into his knapsack. Some were gold, others brilliant *emaille en plein* enamel. Renato noticed a Johann Christian Neuber box made of jasper and carnelian.

Suddenly, the room was ablaze. The overhead crystal chandeliers nearly blinded him, and a reedy voice came out of nowhere.

"Che fai?"

Renato followed the sound and saw a little old woman standing in the doorway. The contessa wasn't any bigger than a twelve-year-old girl and looked very frail in her little pink bathrobe. She clutched a pistol in both hands, but the muzzle was doing loop-d-loops.

"Sei un ladro!"

Renato sprang, his movements a blur. In a single bound, he knocked her to the floor. As they landed, he could feel her bones crunch under his weight. Her pistol skittered across the parquet and disappeared under a curio cabinet.

Renato sat astride the woman, pinning her with an elbow to her sternum. She was writhing and clawing like a little cat, calling out rude names.

Time to shut the old witch up. He stood up and placed a foot on her ribcage to keep her down. The silencer was already in place.

As she opened her mouth to curse him, he shot her directly through the forehead. Her little head popped up off the floor as the bullet made contact, then dark red blood began to flow through her white hair. Her eyes were open. Renato noticed they were strangely blue and coated with cataracts.

Blood was beginning to seep into the carpet fringe. He tiptoed around the growing puddle, trying not to make tracks, then unzipped his backpack. As he prepared to load up, he saw the famous green chrysoprase and diamond snuffbox that once belonged to Frederick the Great of Prussia.

Madonna, what a haul this was going to be!

NAPLES, ITALY

Renato walked through the back streets of Naples carrying the stolen loot in his backpack. Mondragone was going to have a hard time finding a market for all this stuff.

Europe was nearly broke. Italy, Greece, Spain, and Portugal were racked with unemployment, budget problems, and banks going bust. Most wealthy Europeans were too concerned about their finances to splurge.

Cyclops would probably keep it all for himself. He had that kind of insatiable greed.

Renato walked through the old neighborhood until he came to a flight of stone steps. The city of Naples was built on soft volcanic rock, and subterranean tunnels lay beneath the streets. This labyrinth, a remnant from ancient times, was largely unexplored, except during World War II when the caverns were used as bomb shelters.

Renato knew all the various hiding places; as a child, he often slept here when avoiding the police.

As he descended, he noticed the sharp, strong smell of urine in the passageway where people had ducked down to relieve themselves.

A man was standing at the bottom of a flight of stone stairs. It was Tito—white hair, dead eyes, working away at his teeth with a toothpick.

Renato greeted him with deference. There was no use in making him angry again.

"Ciao, Tito. I hope I didn't keep you waiting."

"Just got here," Tito asked, tonguing the toothpick to the other side of his mouth. "How'd it go?"

"Good. I got it all. The old contessa caught me, so I had to shoot her."

Tito froze.

"Through the *forehead*?" he asked, touching the space between his eyebrows.

"Of course; that's how we always do it."

Tito took the toothpick out of his mouth and flung it on the ground. His face turned crimson.

"Idiot! Cyclops didn't want to be associated with this."

"He didn't?"

"Of course not. The contessa lives in Rome!"

"So?"

"They aren't part of *il Systema*."

Renato felt his mouth go dry. This was a colossal blunder. *Il Systema* was the tight net of Camorra influence over the entire Naples region. Local law enforcement would turn a blind eye, but the police in Rome would have no qualms about prosecuting.

"Don't tell him, please," Renato pleaded.

Tito shrugged. "It's out of my hands. The papers will get the story."

Renato's eyes widened.

"You know he's gonna kill you."

Renato felt faint. He stared down the black void of the tunnel that now looked like a grave.

"Did you bring the stuff?" Tito asked.

"Yes," Renato said, hastily handing over the backpack.

"The sapphire necklace, too?"

"No, I went back the next day. It was gone."

VILLA SAN ANGELO, ANACAPRI

Charles Bonnard stepped out onto the terrace of the Villa San Angelo and noticed the wind had shifted again. A hot breeze blew, and there was a dramatic absence of birdcall. Could the strange weather be a result of the eruption in Iceland? The jet stream had picked up the emissions of ash, and a cloud of debris was headed toward Europe.

In the distance, he could just make out the silhouette of Mount Vesuvius. Millions of people lived in the dangerous "red zone" and would be killed if there were an eruption. Computer models proved that the roads around Naples were inadequate if evacuation were necessary.

Not that anyone seemed to care. The residents of the city were totally blasé. During minor alerts housewives would go out shopping, holding umbrellas up to protect themselves from volcanic ash.

Charles turned to go back into his house and noticed a newspaper ruffling in the wind. It was caught under the leg of a chair. Cordelia or Sinclair must have left it. He walked over to collect the pages, so they wouldn't blow away. On the front page was a picture of the volcano in Iceland. The photo credit was Jude Blackwell, the famous volcano photographer.

The eruption looked positively awful. He'd better get the ferry to the mainland soon and return to Paris. Everyone else had gone. Sinclair and Cordelia had flown back to London, and Victoria was on her way to Norway in the royal jet.

Charles scanned around for anything else that had been left behind. He noticed a bright object under the lounge chair. It was a white hair elastic from Victoria's ponytail. He picked it up and slipped it over his wrist as he walked back into the house to pack.

HOTEL FRON,
REYKJAVIK, ICELAND

Photographer Jude Blackwell sat on his bed staring into space. He was still shell-shocked from his near-death experience in the helicopter. It had been a very close call. Up until now, risking his life had always seemed like a game. But not this time. He could still taste the sulfur from the volcano in the back of this throat.

Of course, he had sent his pictures of Eyjafjallajökull out to the major news organizations. And they wanted even more.

He picked up his laptop and began to scroll through the photos again. The plume of the volcano extended more than four miles above the earth. That put it at a level five out of eight on the Volcanic Explosivity Index. That kind of VEI reading was considered cataclysmic, making it one of the most dangerous eruptions since primordial times.

In the video, the roiling ash cloud filled the screen. The column of dark and light volcanic debris looked like marbleized granite. He knew the science. The dark streaks indicated that magma pressure had developed deep underground. The white ash was characteristic of a steam-driven eruption.

The photo shimmered with electric charges. Lightning storms sometimes flared up during a volcanic explosion, generated by friction of the ash particles. In this case, the large thunderbolts had turned into balls of lightning, an extremely uncommon phenomenon.

There was no question about it. He would have to leave Iceland before all the planes were grounded.

OSLO, NORWAY

Princess Victoria stepped out of the limousine, dismissed her bodyguard, and walked up the steps to her apartment. Her little flat in downtown Oslo was her private refuge, a haven away from palace life.

Not that she was alone here. Official staff included a housekeeper, laundress, driver, and chef. But there was only one security guard. Her parents were willing to give her a little freedom while she was still young.

The door opened, and Mrs. Erickson, the housekeeper, came forward to greet her. The woman skimmed a quick curtsy and held out her hands for the suitcase and raincoat.

"Welcome back, your Royal Highness."

"Good evening. I trust you are well?" Victoria inquired.

"Yes, thank you."

The older woman hung up the coat, fussing with the exact placement of the hanger.

"I sent the other suitcase up to the palace to be unpacked," Victoria told her. "It contains some jewels—the ones I wore at the gala in Rome."

The housekeeper turned to reply, her expression studiously neutral.

"Very good. Would you care for anything else?"

"No, thank you. I already had something to eat on the plane."

Mrs. Erickson's gaze shifted to the floor. She seemed nervous. Victoria stared at her, puzzled.

"Is there something you want to tell me?" Victoria asked.

Mrs. Erickson looked up. "No, just that I've left some mail and a newspaper on your desk . . ."

"I'll have a look."

In her private sitting room, Victoria sank into an oversized armchair and put her feet on the ottoman. She took out her smartphone. It was still powered down from the flight. Should she turn it on?

Charles was unlikely to call. They agreed to speak later in the week. There was no one else she wanted to talk to.

Now that she was back in Oslo, there would be all kinds of messages about her schedule and obligations. Tomorrow would be soon enough to deal with it all. She dropped the silent phone into her purse and leaned back in the chair to think.

Her fingers reached up and toyed with the new necklace. It was an 18-karat gold volcano charm. Charles gave it to her as a memento of her trip to Capri.

"It's Mount Vesuvius," he said. "Sorry I couldn't find something nicer, but the souvenir stand was the only place that was open on Sunday morning."

"Its adorable," she said. "Put it on for me."

"It's your element. Fire."

With clumsy fingers, he fastened it around her neck, fumbling with the clasp.

"Goodbye, V," he said.

His voice was so somber. So final. Was he saying goodbye forever?

Victoria sighed as she came out of her reverie. What would happen to her and Charles? Everything was so complicated.

She realized it was growing late. Tomorrow's schedule would be demanding. Not only would she resume training for the Norwegian Olympic biathlon team, but the royal protocol office would also have set up a schedule of appearances.

She moved her feet off the ottoman and picked up her jacket. Weary, she walked along the small corridor that led to her bedroom. The lights were dimmed, and the bed was turned down.

Victoria caught a glimpse of herself in the dressing table mirror—a mature young woman with a serious expression. How melancholy she looked tonight.

As she glanced at the dressing table, she noticed that a newspaper had been placed next to her perfume bottles. Her name was in the headline. Not "V" as usual. This time they used her full title, "Princess Victoria."

Victoria picked up the paper and gasped aloud in shock.

GROSVENOR STREET, LONDON, ENGLAND

John Sinclair stepped out of the cab in front of the London townhouse and reached back for Cordelia's hand. She emerged from the car, her eyes sparkling, happy to be home.

"Let's just have a quiet evening, shall we?" she suggested.

"I'm all for it." he said, happy to have a relaxing, romantic dinner.

The door of the townhouse opened, and his assistant, Malik, came out to help carry the luggage. The young man had an uncanny ability to appear whenever needed.

"Good evening, sir."

Malik had originally been a helper on Sinclair's archaeological dig in Turkey. Now he served as the official majordomo of the London household. The young man was indispensible, taking care of everything from booking flights to ordering groceries.

As Malik came down the steps, he was pushed off balance by a blur of silver and black fur. It was Kyrie. The dog began a wild dance on the front sidewalk, running up and down, barking in paroxysms of joy. Kyrie was looking for some roughhousing from her master.

"Down, girl," Sinclair said, grabbing for her collar.

Sinclair first encountered the Norwegian elkhound as a half-starved stray in Ephesus. Their friendship began over a shared sandwich. Every day thereafter, the dog returned to sit in the dust and watch him work.

Sinclair got used to her. He even started talking to the pup about archaeological finds, informing her whenever he found something important. Kyrie always listened with quiet intelligence. When Sinclair moved to London, there was no question that the dog would come with him.

Kyrie barked while wagging her tail. Cordelia laughed. "She's insane, John. You'd better take her for a walk."

He looked down. Cordelia was on her knees, her arms wrapped around Kyrie's neck, trying to avoid being licked in the face. There was something so maternal in the tableau; his heart contracted. It was foolish to wait any longer. Tonight he would ask Delia the big question.

Sinclair crossed the beautiful rectangular lawn of Grosvenor Square as Kyrie nosed around, sniffing under the trees. He unclipped the leash and let the dog wander, grateful for a moment to collect his thoughts.

Grosvenor Square was a quiet oasis in the middle of London—a small park rimmed with townhouses. The area had long been associated with American expatriates. John Adams had established the first US mission to the Court of St. James here in 1785. Now, the modern American embassy stood at the far end, the largest diplomatic post in Europe.

Sinclair usually walked to the perimeter of the embassy and passed by the Marine guard posts. This was where Kyrie usually did her business, and then they would return home. He gathered the leash and prepared to go back to the townhouse.

What exactly should he say to Cordelia? Would she accept his proposal right away? He had everything he needed—the engagement ring was still in his luggage, a bottle of champagne was cooling in the refrigerator. But it might be nice to pick up some flowers.

What about Tuscan poppies? Delia loved the story about the Romans boiling the center of the blossom to "soothe the aches of love." But that particular variety was indigenous to the Mediterranean. Poppies would be difficult to find in central London. A dozen roses would have to do.

A rumble of thunder sounded overhead, interrupting his thoughts. He'd better get a move on, or he'd be soaked. And tonight especially, he didn't want to deal with a wet dog.

The nearest flower shop was at Claridge's, on Brook Street, a block away. As he started toward the hotel, the liveried doorman waved, and Kyrie started to pull on the leash.

"Good evening, Mr. Sinclair. Hello there, Kyrie," the doorman called out.

Sinclair stopped for a moment and allowed the doorman to pet the animal.

Pulling a dog biscuit out of his pocket, he broke off a piece, and Kyrie sat politely to accept her treat. It was their normal ritual. Kyrie gobbled down the first portion and kept her eyes on his hands for the rest.

"It's nice to see you, George."

"You haven't been around lately, Mr. Sinclair. Where've you been? America?"

"No, I just got back from Capri. We had to come home early. That volcano in Iceland is acting up."

"Oh, I know. It's a mess. All the flights are cancelled, and the hotel guests are stuck."

"Sorry to hear," Sinclair sympathized. "Look, I've got to run. It feels like rain, and I need to grab some flowers for Cordelia."

"Keep the missus happy, that's what I always say," George said as he winked.

Sinclair smiled to himself. Cordelia wasn't a missus yet, but after tonight that ring was going to be on her finger.

The hotel flower kiosk was open. There were beautiful mauve roses, the petals soft and layered in perfect bloom. Cordelia would love them.

Sinclair bought a dozen and turned to leave. His eye caught the headlines in the newsstand. The *Sun.* Something about Princess Victoria.

Intrigued, Sinclair pulled out the newspaper and read.

"Princess Victoria Smuggled into Capri Love Nest"

What?

He shifted the flowers and thumbed through the pages. This was worse than he could have imagined. The reporters had caught him driving into the Villa Brindisi.

He was seated at the wheel of the car and had been identified as the paramour of the princess. There was an arrow indicating where Victoria had been hidden in the back seat.

This was awful. The article described him as "international playboy, John Sinclair." According to the *Sun,* he was an absolute cad. There were dozens of pictures of his former girlfriends. In fact, they had listed the name of every woman he had ever dated. Even some he hadn't.

For the briefest second, he considered hiding the paper from Cordelia. But it was pointless. It would be better to get it all out in the open and be done with it.

George gave him another wave as he passed by again.

"Say hi to the missus for me."

Sinclair nodded and kept going. This wasn't going to be quite the evening he had planned.

It was starting to sprinkle, so he picked up his pace. Their townhouse was only a few blocks away. As he walked along, he couldn't get over the absurdity of the situation.

Did someone tip off the reporters? Who would have done that?

As he turned the corner into Grosvenor Street, a gaggle of photographers were setting up their tripods. The spindly black sticks and long-distance lenses looked like a battery of artillery, trained on the front door. Sinclair gathered Kyrie's leash and started to walk at a brisker pace.

"Here he is!" someone shouted.

The cameras sounded in a continuous staccato until he and the dog retreated inside. Sinclair shut the door firmly. The entrance hall was empty.

Cordelia called out from the parlor. "In here, John."

"Kyrie, go," he said, opening the door to the basement kitchen.

Kyrie headed down. The housekeeper, Margaret, would deal with the wet paws.

Sinclair composed himself and walked into the living room, dreading the impending conversation.

Cordelia was sitting with her feet tucked up on the Regency sofa, a Wedgwood cup of Earl Grey tea halfway to her lips. The low table held a Georgian silver teapot and a plate of English ginger biscuits.

She beamed at him. "You brought me flowers?"

He looked down and suddenly remembered.

"Yes, I'll go put them in water."

"Don't be silly, I'll ring for Margaret."

Bellpulls were a holdover from Victorian times. She gave the tassel a firm tug. Sinclair put the roses on the chair and hesitated, uncertain how to begin.

"Would you like some tea?" she asked. "It's turned a bit chilly, don't you think?"

"It's starting to rain," he said, walking to the windows to check the photographers.

They were all still there with lenses poking out from underneath rain-slicked ponchos, like some kind of strange primitive beasts. By now it was pelting, and cars were splashing through the puddles. A gust of wind lifted the lace curtains, so he shut the sash. When he turned toward Cordelia, she was staring at him, nibbling on a ginger snap.

"Why did you get the *Sun*? You don't usually read that paper, do you?"

"There's a headline you might want to take a look at."

"What's wrong?" she asked, popping the rest of the cookie in her mouth, wiping her fingers on a napkin.

She read a few lines, chewing slowly. Then she swallowed and looked up, her eyes troubled.

"John, they think *you* seduced Victoria!" she said, putting a hand through her hair.

This was the gesture she made when completely unnerved. Clearly, the article about all his former girlfriends was what concerned her most. Cordelia had no idea that he had such a lively past when it came to women.

"I'm going to kill Charles for getting me involved," he swore.

"And what about all these women?"

"I barely know half those girls."

She stared at him, her eyes hurt. "Half would still be too many."

"But most of them are just friends."

"Well, you certainly have a lot of attractive friends."

"Including you," he countered. "Not a friend . . . I meant . . . you are also very—"

She cut him off. "You realize this is rather embarrassing for me."

He decided he should take a stronger position. "This isn't about you, Delia."

"I beg to differ," she shot back. "According to this article, I'm the 'jilted girlfriend.'"

"Well, you know these tabloids just invent whatever they want."

Her face was stricken. "How many were there?"

"Delia. I would think that question were *beneath* you," he stonewalled.

But she didn't back down. "Under the circumstances, I have every right to know."

"So a full confession would satisfy you? " he asked, irritated.

She stared in silence.

"You should try to fix the mess you got yourself into," she said.

"It's not my mess. It's Charles's."

"It's *you* being labeled the biggest cad in Europe, not Charles."

"A boldfaced lie."

"Do you have any other girlfriends now?"

He stared at her, appalled.

"Delia, I've been with you for *two years*. Of course not."

"How do I know you've been faithful?"

He sputtered. This was preposterous! She was becoming completely unreasonable. Furious, he walked toward the window. The photographers were still there.

"You'll just have to trust me," he said tersely. "And as for the past, I don't see the point in dwelling on it."

"I'm not *dwelling* on it," she huffed.

"There's something else you should know," he said.

"What else could there possibly be?"

"There are about ten paparazzi right across the street."

"I told you not to get involved," she muttered.

He whirled, fuming. Now that was too much.

"Wait just a second, Delia. You were the one who asked me to help."

"I did not. I told you to get rid of her!"

"I did get rid of her. I drove her back to Brindy's house," he said a little too loudly.

He realized he was dangerously close to losing his temper.

"I'm sorry, Delia," he said in a conciliatory tone. "I don't think fighting about this is constructive."

"So what do you want to do?" she said coldly.

"I probably should go talk to Charles."

"Where is he?"

"In Paris, with his mother. Why don't we both go there?"

"You mean run away?" she asked.

He came over and sat down next to her on the sofa.

"Why not? Or we could go to Ephesus," he suggested.

"We can't. The planes are grounded."

"We can take a boat or a train."

"You're using this as an excuse to leave again," she accused.

"That's not true."

He reached out to take her hand. "Come with me."

She recoiled. "Please don't touch me."

"You can't mean that."

"I do."

He stared at her, horrified.

"Delia, don't let this destroy us."

She moved farther away.

"You're the one who's destroying everything," she accused. "Go ahead. Leave if you want to."

Their eyes met. He swallowed, trying to comprehend why she was forcing him to abandon her. The ticking clock measured a full minute. Margaret ambled into the salon.

"You rang, miss?" she asked, but her cheery expression faded as her eyes traveled from one to the other.

"John brought me some flowers. Could you please take them away?"

"Shall I put them in your room?"

"No."

Cordelia's tone was pure ice. Margaret looked around for an explanation, but he remained silent.

Sinclair silently cursed himself. Those roses now implied guilt. Cordelia probably thought he had bought them as a peace offering. If only she knew his real intentions.

"I'll put them on the table in the entrance hall," Margaret declared. She picked up the roses and trudged out.

Cordelia watched her go, her face impassive, then turned to him.

"Before you leave, I want to get something clear between us. I want to know how you feel about me. "

He took her hand in both of his.

"Delia, you *know* how I feel."

"Actually, I don't."

He realized that this whole thing could be solved with the words "marry me." Those two little words would do it. But under the circumstances, he settled for three.

"I love you."

Her face remained warily expectant.

"*Do* you?"

"Yes, Cordelia. I do."

"Have you *ever* considered the future?" she asked.

His heart sank.

"Of course I think of the future, Delia. All the time."

"So why are you so reluctant to talk about it now?"

"It doesn't seem appropriate, with all this going on."

She looked up at him, eyes shimmering with tears.

"Who is John Sinclair? I feel like I don't know him anymore."

She looked small and frail, sitting on the far side of the couch. He leaned forward, speaking urgently.

"Delia, I'm the same man I have always been. A newspaper doesn't change that."

"So why don't you answer me?"

"I did. And I really don't know why you are suddenly questioning my intentions."

"I don't question your intentions. I just want to hear how you feel."

He closed his eyes and shook his head, refusing to budge.

"We can talk about it after this is over."

His tone was firm, but part of him was racked with doubt. If he asked her to marry him now, she'd never know if he really loved her or if he'd been pressured by circumstances. Their life together shouldn't start with a scandal.

Sinclair stood and paced toward the window.

"I'm going to go," he said and looked out at the rain.

RUE DE VAUGIRARD, PARIS

When Charles Bonnard entered the breakfast room, his mother was at the table looking at a tabloid newspaper. A neighbor subscribed to the publication. Madame Bonnard would never buy it herself, but she wasn't above accepting it secondhand after her friend had finished reading it.

Charles sat down, poured some café au lait, and added two lumps of sugar with a pair of silver tongs. At this hour of the morning, his mother was already fully dressed in a beautiful Yves St. Laurent wool suit and a lovely filigree gold bangle on her right wrist. On her left hand was the emerald wedding ring that Alphonse Bonnard had given her all those years ago.

The reality of her life was very different from the impression she presented. Since her husband's death, the family fortunes had dwindled alarmingly. The Bonnard family still had the house, which could fetch millions if need be, but Madame Bonnard was clinging to it with something akin to panic. She was unwilling to give up her aristocratic lifestyle.

For Charles, this created enormous pressure. After a gilded and carefree youth, it was now up to him to support the household.

So far, they were scraping by.

His sister was a fashion designer and chipped in. Her business was good, but seasonal. Charles was the only steady income earner in the family. His job at Sinclair's Herodotus Foundation paid well. But keeping up to his mother's standards took all his resources.

Madame Bonnard dabbed her lips daintily with a linen napkin and dropped the newspaper onto the tablecloth.

"Good morning, Charles."

"Good morning. Anything interesting in the gossip columns?"

"There's an article about your friend, John Sinclair."

That was no surprise. As a wealthy philanthropist, Sinclair was frequently in the news.

"What are they saying about him?"

"He has another woman."

"No he *doesn't*. They're making things up again."

Madame Bonnard's smile of satisfaction was barely hidden.

"Her picture is right here. The usual kind of girl, young and pretty. Except this one happens to be famous."

"Ridiculous. I just saw him in Capri."

"Alone?"

"Of course not. He's still with Cordelia."

"Then he's cheating on her," Madame Bonnard proclaimed.

"Sinclair doesn't cheat."

"Well apparently he's moved on to someone else."

Madame Bonnard picked up her orange juice and redirected her argument. "I think Cordelia Stapleton should marry *you*, Charles."

His mother had been pushing Cordelia on him for a long time, and he was used to fending off that suggestion.

"I'm afraid Delia has other ideas about whom she wants to marry," Charles said tersely.

"Well she might be changing her mind about Mr. Sinclair."

Charles held his hand out for the newspaper.

"Let me see."

He was one of the directors of the Herodotus Foundation and should be aware of any negative press. Charles unfolded the tabloid and glanced down

"Princess Victoria's Lover—Playboy John Sinclair."

He swallowed hard, reading the words twice.

"*This isn't true!*"

Madame Bonnard spooned strawberry confiture onto her croissant.

"It's a disgrace. Princess Victoria is only twenty years old."

"*Twenty! No she isn't!*"

He felt the blood drain out of his face.

"It says right here, she's twenty," his mother declared.

"I thought she was twenty-five," he said feebly.

He tried to recall the exact conversation he had with Victoria about age. She had made a joke of it, brushing off his inquiry.

He pushed back his chair. "I have to make a call."

"Charles, please. Finish your coffee. I don't want you getting involved."

"Sinclair's in trouble. I have to warn him."

His mother shook her head firmly.

"You will do nothing of the kind. This is not about the Herodotus Foundation."

"But he's also my friend."

"That may be so, but John Sinclair can take care of his own sordid affairs."

GROSVENOR STREET, LONDON

Malik stood in the doorway of the bedroom, as Sinclair pulled shirts from the top shelf of the armoire and flung them into his calf-skin satchel. He was using the Gladstone bag—the luggage that usually went on expedition. His exact travel plans were a mystery, but by the look of things he was headed to a warm climate.

"I assume Mr. Bonnard will handle all calls about the Herodotus Foundation while you are away?"

Sinclair stuffed a shirt into the bag.

"Yes. I just spoke to him."

"I thought I heard you on the phone with him just now."

Sinclair looked up, sharply. "I expect the whole house heard me, Malik. What are you getting at?"

"Is everything all right, sir?"

"We had some difficult things to discuss."

Malik had witnessed Sinclair and Charles quarrel many times before. But it was usually amiable, like brothers. Now apparently there was a more serious issue.

Malik spoke in Turkish, using a common expression from his native country: "Only friends can speak bitterly to each other."

"Then Charles and I must be very good friends," Sinclair said in Turkish.

Charles and Sinclair had met a decade ago, and Sinclair had suggested they work together on the Herodotus Foundation. It was a successful partnership.

At that time, he was an American billionaire from Boston, newly arrived in Europe. Charles, with his aristocratic lineage, was connected to everyone of importance on the continent. Under Charles Bonnard's tutelage, the Herodotus Foundation became internationally recognized.

"Sir, the planes in the UK have been grounded," Malik volunteered gently. "With that volcano in Iceland, *nothing* is taking off from Heathrow."

"That's why I'm traveling by train. I'm booked on the Eurostar out of St. Pancras Station."

"How will I get a hold of you, sir?"

"I'll forward you a landline number when I get there."

Again, Sinclair did not reveal his destination.

Malik tried another approach. "When will you return?"

"When I'm ready to deal with civilization again."

"Will that be long?"

Sinclair snapped his bag shut and buckled it firmly.

"Yes, it will be quite some time."

ST. PANCRAS STATION, LONDON

St. Pancras Station was filled with people who had been stranded by the airline shutdown. Sinclair had never seen such bedlam. The counter clerk thumbed the dog-eared passport, fanning through twenty extra pages of stamps and visas.

"I see you travel frequently," she said.

"Yes, I'm an archaeologist."

"Destination, please."

"Paris, then Sicily."

She surveyed his paperwork, taking an extra moment to examine his photo, then handed everything back with a smile.

"If you're going to Sicily, you'd better take care. I hear Mount Etna is starting to rumble."

Sinclair tucked his passport into his inside pocket.

"My dig is in Morgantina, about sixty miles away."

She glanced at the clock on the wall.

"You'll have to hurry. The train is about to leave."

He rushed through the luggage scan and ran down the escalators. On the platform, several trains were about to depart. Sinclair dodged the crowds and stepped into the premiere carriage of the ultramodern Eurostar just as the train doors slid shut.

It would take two hours and fifteen minutes to make the trip from London to Paris. From there he'd take an overnight sleeper straight to the tip of Italy. His dig in Sicily was free of ashfall; the prevailing winds had blown the debris away. So he could work there for a while. A couple of weeks of hard labor would help him sort out his feelings. There was nothing like shoveling in the dirt to set a man right.

GROSVENOR STREET, LONDON

And there was nothing like a long soak in a hot bath to set a woman right. Cordelia came into her room toweling her hair. The ivory silk bathrobe was soft against her skin as she tied the belt.

For the hundredth time, she wondered about Sinclair. Speculation about his whereabouts had become almost a constant thrum in her mind.

The evening stretched ahead of her, empty and alone.

Why had he left without telling her where he was going? Grim-faced, he said he would get in touch in a few weeks. Sinclair could be stubborn when he was angry, and so could she. This wasn't the first time that they'd had a falling out and he had stormed off. He'd probably relent in a day or so and call her.

"Take care, John," she had replied, displaying frosty indifference.

And foolishly, she let him to go.

Now the house was too quiet. Malik was finished for the day, and Margaret was sitting with the dog watching the telly in the kitchen. Cordelia opened her laptop, hoping to find out the latest about the ashfall that was shutting down Europe.

According to the BBC, the Eyjafjallajökull volcano was causing the biggest disruption of air travel since World War II. The videos of the event in Iceland were heart-stopping. Jude Blackwell's pictures on You-Tube already had 1.2 million hits.

Jude Blackwell was a legend. He lived on the edge—literally. In a spectacular feat, he had donned a thermal-resistant "hot suit" and zip lined across the lava lake of Ethiopia's Erta Ale volcano—a solitary figure flying across a sea of fiery orange, lava splatters missing him by inches.

He was quite the daredevil. She knew him by reputation long before they met. Their paths crossed a few years ago. It was in the South Pacific, where he was photographing volcanoes and she was on a geological expedition to study the seabed. They struck up a casual conversation over a drink in a crummy little bar in Tuvalu.

She noticed immediately how attractive he was. Rugged male energy radiated off of him like heat. When he suggested a walk on the beach, her heart had skipped. This was the kind of man who would waste no time in putting the moves on her. She said yes anyway.

As they walked along the deserted beach, she listened to his voice, half distracted by her own thoughts. Relationships were hard for her. Ever since the death of her father, becoming attached to a man was risky stuff. Her heart was usually locked up. And Jude Blackwell looked like trouble. If she fell for him, what would happen? In most likelihood, she'd just be one more conquest for him to brag about.

Without wasting any time, Jude had taken her hand and pulled her toward him. The kiss was demanding and sexy. But she pulled away.

"Something wrong?" he asked.

"Timing."

"Got another fella?"

"Something like that."

His grin was wicked.

"Well, don't tell him," he said and kissed her again, lifting her off her feet.

Nothing more happened that night except a half-dozen torrid kisses on the deserted beach. But they did become good friends, albeit at a distance. He emailed from time to time, always very flirty.

She scrolled down to the comments section for the video of the volcano.

Her fingers paused over the keyboard.

"Spectacular photos, Jude!" she typed. "But a little too close for comfort—take care."

KEFLAVIK AIRPORT, ICELAND

Jude saw the comment from Cordelia Stapleton as he was checking in at Iceland's international airport. He smiled as he read it.

Delia was one brilliant woman. And to be perfectly honest, she appeared in his fantasies quite often.

But then, ladylike types always intrigued him.

Delia was more than an illusion. She was very down to earth—intellectual and sexy—the kind of woman who would never be boring. He had half a mind to look her up next time he was in London to see if she was free. Even if she weren't, she'd be worth the effort.

But, first things first. He had to get out of Iceland.

The flight status window on the departure board was spinning like a slot machine.

CANCELLED, CANCELLED, CANCELLED.

"Rome," he said. "Please, not Rome."

There it was: KEFLAVIK to ROME—BOARDING. The ashfall had shut down most of Europe. But Southern Italy had been relatively spared. Apparently the drift had not yet reached Sicily.

Mount Etna was still a possibility.

He walked over to the counter.

"Are you calling flight 75W?"

The counter clerk pressed her lips together in annoyance.

"Yes, sir. One moment please."

Jude hoisted his backpack and stood by the gate, anxious to go. He'd fly through Rome and take a train to Sicily.

Every news network in the world was clamoring for volcano video—from Hawaii's Kilauea to Mexico's Popocatepetl. Some pundit on television had proposed the theory that this was a "Summer of Fire," as if all the volcanoes were going to light up simultaneously like some kind of a pinball machine.

Of course, that was complete rot.

Seismic activity in one part of the world did not automatically generate eruptions in other hemispheres.

But it didn't stop the news networks. They were convinced there would be hundreds of eruptions this year. And they wanted pictures. So that meant he was going to make a lot of money.

The only problem was that Iceland wasn't photogenic anymore. Magma splatters had died down, and a haze obscured everything. The best shots were over. It was time to move on.

The Discovery Channel had commissioned him to get footage of any volcano in the world. His choice.

He chose Mount Etna.

In terms of beauty, it was the ultimate caldera. There were constant puffs of white gas from the southeast crater, which contrasted nicely with the blue Mediterranean sky.

The airline attendant began the boarding process and scanned his ticket.

"Have a safe flight."

The words gave him a chill. Flight conditions were deteriorating. Westerly winds were carrying the ash into the upper stratosphere.

The sulfuric acid corroded the metal skin of the plane. Grit was abrading the cockpit windows. Each speck of ash was as fine as baby powder. During flight, that debris was sucked inside the engine. The superheated chamber was 1,400 degrees, and the grains of silica would melt and fuse onto the turbine blades.

This wasn't just a paranoid fantasy. In the past three decades, more than one hundred civil aviation accidents had been from volcanic ash. An organization known by the acronym VAAC monitored air quality conditions from twelve sites around the world.

There had been a few near misses with commercial liners. Once, ash from Mount Galunggung in Indonesia caused a jumbo jet to stall. All four engines shut down. Luckily, the pilot switched to glide mode and was able to restart. In Alaska, a 747 flying over Mount Redoubt plowed through volcanic ash and plunged for two miles in a near free fall.

The thought of something like that made his knees weak.

When he entered the plane, the economy section was entirely empty. Who would be crazy enough to fly today? He said a quick prayer as the seatbelt sign pinged on. It was too late now. They were closing the cabin door.

GARE DE LYON, PARIS

The trip from London to Paris on the Eurostar was quick and easy. Sinclair sat in the back of a cab that smelled of stale cigarettes. Traffic was awful. The driver was cursing his way through the City of Light.

Sinclair had planned to stop off and see Charles at his house in the sixth arrondissement. But the only train out of Paris this afternoon was almost fully booked. He had no choice but to grab a seat while he could.

Besides, Charles had his own decisions to make. They'd fought bitterly on the phone. Another confrontation seemed pointless.

Instead, Sinclair got out of the cab at Gare de Lyon. The station was crowded, and people milled about. Inside the terminal he summoned his command of French and collected his tickets on the Thello sleeper train for the fifteen-hour trip from Paris to Rome.

It would be a scenic ride through France and Italy. He carried his Gladstone bag up the steps of the train and gestured for the attendant to unlock the door of compartment twenty-seven. The private compartment was simple and functional, with a bed, a table, and a reading light with an electrical outlet for his phone. There was plenty of space for his luggage in the overhead rack, so he put his bag up top. He'd need a change of clothes once he arrived.

Malik had given him a food basket. Inside was a bottle of *St. Estèphe*, apricots, brie, a baguette, and dark chocolate—provisions for later.

He took off his jacket, hung it on the hook, then stretched out on the bed just as the train was pulling out of the station.

Sinclair awoke to the sound of a knock on the door. A pretty blond girl in a uniform had come to collect his passport. They would keep it overnight as standard procedure for customs inspection between France and Italy.

As he gave her the travel document, the girl gave him a flirty smile.

"Is there anything else I can get you, sir?"

"No, thank you," he said and shut the door.

Women! The last thing he needed was another girl to add to his romantic résumé. He walked wearily over to the window and sat down.

It was dusk, and he realized he hadn't eaten today. Famished, he ransacked the basket. He ate as he watched the countryside go by.

Tonight the sunset was blood red. The haze from Iceland was already affecting the atmosphere in Europe.

Cordelia had explained that after a volcanic eruption, the refracted light from the ash and debris sometimes caused vivid red sunsets. The crimson color over France this evening had a personal significance. It was the same bold red as those Tuscan poppies in Capri.

He sipped his wine and thought about the aches of love.

OSLO, NORWAY

At 8:00 a.m., Princess Victoria drew back the curtains of her Oslo apartment and saw a gray Mercedes idling at the curb. Two security men were in the front seat; one was dangling his cigarette out the window. Her father had sent them. They were bringing her back to the palace. Permanently.

Victoria fingered her cell phone. Mobile transmissions could be hacked. She would have to get a new phone with a different number. Until then, it would be impossible to communicate with Charles.

There was a rap on the door. Mrs. Erickson was gently reminding her that it was time to leave.

Victoria checked her hair once more in the mirror and forced a smile. As she stepped out of the apartment building, a security officer got out of the car.

"Good morning, your royal highness," the officer said as he opened the car door for her.

She looked down the street and noticed there were camera lenses glinting a block away. Paparazzi. She buckled her seatbelt and watched as the van approached the security cordon. Police officers drew aside the wooden sawhorses. A few bold videographers stepped up, filming through the windshield.

It was bedlam. Everyone shouting. Camera lights pinned her to the seat. She sat, looking neither right nor left, remembering to smile slightly. Within moments, the driver drove clear of the barriers. As the van sped up, she looked down. Her hands were clenched together, knuckles white.

VILLA BRINDISI, CAPRI

Contessa Georgiana Brindisi stood looking out the sliding glass doors of her living room. It was dawn. With all the ash in the atmosphere, the sky looked blood red.

The boys did not come in last night. When she checked their room this morning, the beds had not been slept in. Hopefully, they would reappear soon. But she wasn't too worried. Camping was always popular with Capri teenagers during the hot summer months. Sometimes, they slept in the ruins.

Brindy walked over and picked up the newspaper. She scanned the front-page article about the princess and John Sinclair. In the photo Sinclair was devastatingly handsome and very believable in his role as the seducer of the fairest princess in Europe.

All his lovers had been listed. The editors had chosen a particularly nice photo of her swimming in the Blue Grotto. She remembered the day well. Sinclair and Luca had spent the morning diving off the boat, and then they all went into town for lunch. Those were wonderful years.

She missed him terribly. But ever since their breakup, Sinclair had kept his distance. There was no hope of ever attracting him again.

Not long ago, a scheme had occurred to her. It was on Luca's fifteenth birthday. Her son was being treated with chemotherapy, and she had arrived at the hospital with presents and a cake. When she walked in, Luca was sitting in bed reading a letter.

The envelope immediately gave away whom it was from. A light residue of sand fell out. Sinclair always included a pinch of earth from wherever he was digging. The handwriting was distinctive. His script was blocky and strong with flourishes borrowed from the ancient languages: Greek, Sanskrit, and even hieroglyphics.

Luca was brimming with happiness. "I'm so glad he remembered my birthday."

"Of course he would, *caro.* He loves you very much," she said, forcing a smile.

That's when she realized that if Sinclair came back, it would be so much better for Luca. So much better for them all. Right then and there, all the elements of deceit fell into place.

First, she suggested that Victoria should go up to visit Charles at the Villa San Angelo. And then she had made sure that the paparazzi were waiting when Sinclair returned with the princess in the car.

The concept was simple: Sinclair's reputation would be tarnished, and his girlfriend, Cordelia, would leave him, freeing up Sinclair to marry.

She rubbed her neck and stretched. It was 7:00 a.m. Where were the boys?

Suddenly, the phone rang—unusual at this time of morning. The housekeeper Carmela was not up yet, so she sat down at the desk to answer the call.

"Hello," she said.

An unfamiliar male voice came on the line.

"May I speak to the Contessa Georgiana Brindisi, please."

"This is Contessa Brindisi."

"Inspector Soldini in Rome. I'm afraid I have some terrible news, Contessa."

Her heart stopped. *Luca!* She couldn't speak.

"Your grandmother has been found dead in her home," the inspector continued. "The housekeeper came across her body this morning when she arrived. I'm terribly sorry."

Brindy nodded, not really surprised. Her grandmother was ninety-five years old and in poor health. A call like this had been expected for years.

"I understand, inspector," she said smoothly. "Thank you very much for telling me. I will come to Rome as soon as possible to make the funeral arrangements."

"There is a complication, Contessa," he said. "I haven't explained properly."

"Complication? What do you mean?"

"Your grandmother was murdered. Shot through the forehead."

Brindy bolted to her feet, knocking over her chair.

"*Cyclops!*" she gasped. "*Why?*"

"We don't know. Except maybe because of the valuables in her home. Pretty much everything was taken."

Brindy felt her knees start to shake. She had paid Mondragone millions in protection money every year. And now he had murdered her *grandmother*! Why had he turned on her?

A horrifying thought came to mind. *Was it because she hadn't delivered the sapphire necklace?*

"I'll be in Rome in an hour."

NAPLES, ITALY

A million people were crammed into the densely packed city of Naples. For Luca and Karl it was the perfect place to hide. No one paid any attention to two fifteen-year-old backpackers, shabbily dressed, wandering around like tourists.

The greasy smell of cooking oil and gasoline hung over the Via Carmignano. They found a grubby café with a half-dozen plastic chairs and a menu that offered a slice of pizza for four euros. A man in a stained apron called for them to come in, gesturing with both hands. He apparently served as both hawker and cook. Behind the counter, the radio was blaring, and the announcer's voice sounded like automatic weapons fire.

"This isn't a good pizza place," Luca cautioned, taking on the role of local expert.

Hungry and irritable, Karl ignored him. "I'm starving. It doesn't matter."

Luca flung his backpack on the floor and ordered two slices of pizza margherita and two cans of Limonata, then carefully doled out the money. The food came immediately—slices oozing with hot grease onto the paper plates.

Karl took a swig of his drink and put the can down.

"I'm going to go find a bank. Wait for me here."

Luca looked out at the street with concern. "Karl, no. You can't wander around here on your own."

"I'm not going that far. There has to be a bank right nearby."

"Let me come with you."

"Everybody knows you," Karl argued. "You're a Brindisi. I'm not even Italian. I look like a tourist."

Luca sighed. "OK, but hurry back."

Karl picked up his rucksack and walked briskly down the crowded street. Within a moment, he found a small jewelry store. It wasn't an expensive place; the window was filled with gold chains and trinkets.

He went inside, and a bell clanged. The owner stood up, an older man in a threadbare shirt.

"*Buongiorno*," Karl said.

The man nodded a greeting.

"I have something to sell," Karl said.

Uncomprehending, the storeowner fanned his hand over the counter.

"Just a minute," Karl said.

He put his backpack on the counter, pulled out the wad of facial tissue, and unwrapped a magnificent sapphire necklace.

"How much will you give me for it?" Karl asked.

The man stared in disbelief. Without taking his eyes off the treasure, his right hand felt around for a jeweler's loupe. He fitted the magnifier into his eye socket and examined each gem, taking his time. There were fifteen blue-violet stones set with small diamonds in between. Karl felt his nerves twitch with anxiety as he waited.

The man's neck looked frail, and his shirt collar was a couple sizes too big as he bent over the sapphires. White hair sparsely covered a pink scalp. The proprietor of the shop took the loupe away from his eye with an expression of astonishment.

"Will you buy it?" Karl asked.

Slowly, reluctantly, the man shook his head, no.

Karl reached for a notepad and pen on the counter. He wrote down 10,000 euros.

The man's eyes widened in shock. It was a pittance compared to what the necklace was worth. His expression wavered. Karl crossed out the figure and wrote 5,000 euros.

The man's gaze shifted to the door and then back to the necklace. The watery old eyes were canny. That's when Karl knew he had a sale.

The man indicated that Karl should wait, and shuffled to the rear of the shop. The green velvet curtain swayed as he went through. Then all was quiet.

Karl could hear his own breath, ragged and nervous. After a few minutes, the old man came back carrying one-inch stacks of euros, secured with rubber bands.

Just then Karl's cell phone rang. It was Luca, sounding stressed.

"Where are you?" he asked.

"I'm getting some money. I told you. Are you still at the pizza shop on the corner?"

"Yes," Luca replied.

"Don't worry. I'll meet you at the restaurant in five minutes."

"Hurry up. My mom is calling me nonstop."

Karl hung up the phone and resumed the transaction. The old man slid the stacks of bills across to the counter a few at a time. A 500-euro note topped each packet.

Karl reached for the bundles of euros and stuffed them into his rucksack.

The necklace still lay on the glass countertop, gleaming with an indigo shimmer. A small ping of guilt crossed his mind. He shouldn't have sold it. But V had so much jewelry; hopefully she wouldn't miss the necklace.

The old man in the jewelry store waited a moment before he reached for the phone.

A few minutes later, Renato walked into the shop with a swagger.

"Ciao, Bartolomeo. What have you got for me?"

"You won't believe it," the old man said and pulled out the necklace, putting it on a faded black velvet display pad.

"Where did you get *that?*" Renato exclaimed.

"From some kid."

"It looks like a million-euro necklace? Am I right?"

Bartolomeo nodded. "I've never seen anything like it in my life. These are not the kind of stones that are sold commercially, and the setting is handmade. This wasn't designed in a cheap factory in Hong Kong."

Renato grabbed the man by the arm.

"Where did he go?"

"He was meeting his friend at the pizza shop on the corner. I heard him say it on the phone."

"What'd he look like?"

"Blond, red T-shirt, jeans, and thick glasses. A little stocky."

"I'm going after him," Renato said, yanking the door open, the bell clanging wildly.

"What should I do?" the old man asked.

"Hold on to it, and don't tell anyone."

Prince Karl sauntered up to the table and pulled out a chair. The burnt smell of pizza crust and tomatoes now seemed appealing. Luca had finished. There was only a rind of crust on the paper plate, but Karl's slice was still there, the cheese congealed. Emotionally exhausted, he picked up his can of Limonata and took a long swig.

"You took so long. I thought you had been robbed," Luca complained.

"Sorry."

"My mom called me twelve times. I let it go to voice mail," Luca said, holding up his phone for Karl to see.

"Don't worry, she'll be fine."

"She'll be mad at me."

"Nah, we'll just be gone for a couple of days," Karl said, belching slightly at the carbonation. "We're all set. I just got a couple thousand euros from the bank."

"Why'd it take so long?"

"They had to verify the account."

"So where do you want to go?"

"We need to find a hotel."

Karl bit into the pizza and pulled out a long string of mozzarella like a piece of spaghetti.

"You want to stay overnight in Naples?" Luca asked.

"Yes, and tomorrow we can go to Herculaneum."

"How are we going to get there?"

Karl leaned forward to keep the grease from dripping on his shirt. He swallowed before answering.

"Trust me. I have it all worked out."

Renato sat down at the table next to the two boys and ordered a slice of pizza. The kids had absolutely no clue that they were being watched.

After years of knocking around, Renato could tell if someone came from money.

This blond boy had wealth written all over him. He was really somebody—the straight spine, the imperious tilt of the head. The dark-haired boy also looked rich. He was wearing a two-hundred-dollar sports watch, a Lacoste polo shirt, and a leather backpack.

They were planning some kind of trip. Probably they were on some kind of joy ride and couldn't use their parents' credit cards. They must have sold the necklace to pay for their expenses.

The sapphires were a big mystery. Obviously they weren't from a store. Not even Bulgari had a necklace like that. So the boy must have taken it from home. Clearly it had been lying around the house and he had nicked it.

Now, what kind of house had this kind of jewelry lying around? A thought struck him and he almost gasped out loud. He had been sent to steal a necklace from Princess Victoria not twenty-four hours ago, but it had been gone. Now an heirloom necklace of the same description had turned up in Naples.

This kid must be Prince Karl of Norway!

Renato scrolled through the Internet connection on his phone and checked. Yes, this was Prince Karl—the same face and blond hair. A brilliant idea came into his mind. Why not make some money for himself? A little side action. A kidnapping wouldn't be difficult to pull off. The crime-infested Secondigliano neighborhood was his backyard, and there were plenty of places to hide the boy while he waited for a ransom. Something told him the payoff was going to be huge, if he just bided his time.

The boys stood up and started to gather their things. Prince Karl walked over to the counter and paid for a bottle of water, then the boys started off down the street, consulting a map. Renato followed ten paces behind, keeping the red T-shirt in sight as he dialed the number for the jewelry shop owner.

"Hey, it's me . . . You know that necklace? Put it in a fancy box. I mean a *real* fancy box with velvet. It's for Mondragone. I'll come and get it. Do not let anyone know that you have it."

Detective Jaccorsi tied his cream silk necktie and adjusted the knot. It was going to be a hot one, and at only 8:00 a.m., the weariness of the day was already upon him. The apartment phone rang—it was his cousin from the police precinct in Rome.

"They need you," his cousin said.

"Who needs me?"

"My boss. They're going after Mondragone. The prime minister is outraged. He's given orders that Mondragone should be stopped, no matter what. Agents from the US and Britain are coming to help."

"An *international* effort?" Jaccorsi asked.

"They're going to shut down the money laundering and get him on financial fraud."

"How?"

"They'll bankrupt him first. But they need your help."

"*My* help? I don't know anything about finance. I told you not to get me involved. Someone will see me if I come to Rome. I don't want Cyclops to go after my mother."

"Don't worry," his cousin assured him. "They don't need you in Rome. You are going to meet the Brits."

"Where?"

"London. The order comes from the GDF."

Jaccorsi blinked in surprise. The Guardia di Finanza was the Italian government's special agency that dealt with financial crime and drug enforcement.

"So Mondragone is connected with the UK? I thought he was just here in Naples."

"No, he runs most of his international operations out of his house in London. That's where he does all his global business . . . you know, money laundering . . . with New York, Switzerland, Cyprus, you name it."

"But I don't know anything about international finance. Why me?"

"Your department cleans up his messes every day. Nobody knows how he operates better than you."

"Well, I guess that's true."

"You should expect a call today from the GDF. I just wanted to give you a warning."

"Right. Thanks."

Jaccorsi hung up the phone and stared at his pale face in the mirror. He was now going to make an enemy of one of the most powerful criminals in Italy.

ROYAL PALACE, OSLO

Princess Victoria slipped the ice blue chiffon gown over her head and turned to her assistant to fasten the buttons down the back of the dress. Tonight was a formal occasion—an official state dinner with the Prime Minister of Japan.

The princess looked at her reflection in the mirror and was surprised at how serene she appeared—a young woman just back from vacation. There was still a pink sunburn across her nose from spending the after-noon lounging on the terrace in Capri.

"All done, your Highness."

"Thank you."

She walked over to put on the thick, red grosgrain ribbon. The cer-emonial sash would be worn crosswise over the bodice of her gown, along with the Cross of the Order of St. Olaf.

"Will you have the aquamarines, your Highness?" her assistant asked.

"The sapphires, please."

"If you wish."

Hostility was apparent in the woman's tone of voice. Victoria and her "personal dresser" had never gotten along. And now, with the scandal in the papers, her assistant's displays of contempt had gotten worse.

The assistant disappeared into an enormous wall safe the size of a walk-in closet. She soon emerged with a flat necklace box and a smaller one on top for matching earrings. All of Victoria's tiaras and necklaces were in velvet-lined cases. There were additional jewels downstairs in the Palace Treasury for elaborate ceremonies, coronations, and weddings.

"Here they are," she said, placing them on the dressing table.

Victoria absently reached for the larger box. The last time she wore this necklace was at the gala in Rome, just before she met Charles in Capri. That seemed ages ago.

Victoria opened the case, then shut the lid and handed it back.

"Did you change your mind your Highness?"

"No. You gave me the wrong box. This one is empty."

The assistant opened it, her jowly face trembling in astonishment.

"*The necklace is gone!*"

"Well, it can't be. I just wore it last week."

"Yes, I know," she nodded. "I unpacked your jewel case when you came back."

"And the necklace was there?"

"I assume so. I just put the box back in the safe."

"You should have looked."

"Did you have the necklace with you in Capri?"

"Yes."

"Could it have been left at the Contessa's villa?"

"No, of course not."

"Was it . . . stolen?"

"How?"

"While you were off visiting your American friend, Mr. Sinclair."

Victoria seethed at the impudence.

"No. Security was tight. And I never even opened that suitcase. It only had my formal wear."

"Well *somebody* took it."

Victoria felt her heart sink. It was enormously valuable, a gift from the Queen of England to the Princess of Norway in 1830. The gems themselves were irreplaceable, an unusual color—deep indigo mixed with royal purple.

"Should we ask the Contessa Brindisi?"

"How can I do that? It would be like accusing her."

"Well, it's either that, or we will have to notify your mother."

Victoria frowned and shook her head.

"Please bring me the aquamarines. I don't want to be late for dinner."

ROYAL PALACE, OSLO

The Queen of Norway looked up and saw Princess Victoria's personal assistant standing in the doorway.

"Yes, what is it?"

"I'm terribly sorry to disturb you, but I think you should be informed."

"Of what?"

"It's the sapphire necklace, your Highness. The one that was given to Queen Astrid?"

"Yes? Does it need repair?"

"No, I'm afraid it's missing. It was stolen in Capri."

"*Stolen!*" the Queen exclaimed. "By *whom?*"

"I suspect it may have something to do with Mr. Sinclair."

The queen stiffened at the comment. Discussing her daughter's romantic fling was not something she would normally do with one of the palace staff.

"What makes you think that Mr. Sinclair was involved?" she asked in her most austere tone.

"Princess Victoria seemed very reluctant to report the loss."

The queen stood up and walked her to the door. "You were right to come to me with this. I'll look into it."

"I thought you should know, your majesty," the woman said smugly.

"I will count on your discretion. Please say nothing to Princess Victoria. I don't want to give her a reason to contact Mr. Sinclair again."

LONDON, ENGLAND

Two Metropolitan Police detectives walked up to John Sinclair's townhouse and banged the heavy brass knocker. There was no response. For the next few minutes they surveyed the morning traffic. Then, one of the detectives checked his watch.

"He's probably at work. We should come back. Perhaps later this evening?"

"Let's give it one more minute," the other replied, looking out over the neighborhood.

Just then, a slight young man in a white tunic opened the town-house door.

"May I help you?" he asked.

"Is a Mr. Sinclair available? We're from Scotland Yard."

"I'm afraid he's traveling at the moment."

"Where is he, exactly?"

"He didn't give me a destination. I am happy to convey a message when I hear from him."

"When would that be?"

"I really couldn't say."

"You are telling me that Mr. Sinclair has left with no word of when he will return?"

"That is correct, sir."

"And he is your employer?"

"Yes, he is."

"And who might you be?"

"I am Malik Akçam, Mr. Sinclair's personal assistant."

"Well, Mr. Akçam, perhaps you had better come with us. We're going to need to take a statement from you."

The man turned pale. "Is that really necessary?"

"Yes. It is. Now, is there anyone else who lives here besides Mr. Sinclair?"

"Yes, this is Miss Stapleton's house."

"And her connection to Mr. Sinclair?"

Malik paused, thought about it, and then answered with perfect accuracy.

"Mr. Sinclair and Miss Stapleton are usually together. But now she is alone."

Cordelia Stapleton walked down the steps of Scotland Yard apprehensive about the questions she just answered. They wanted to know about her relationship with John Sinclair and clearly assumed she was covering up for him. The senior officer had regarded her with frank disbelief.

"You have been living together for how long?"

"Two years."

"And Mr. Sinclair leaves without giving you a phone number?"

"His cell sometimes doesn't work. Sometimes the digs are too remote."

"And you don't find that suspicious?"

"Why should I? He's an archaeologist."

"And he doesn't leave a hotel number?"

"He usually stays in a tent."

"In a *tent*?" the policeman had asked.

Cordelia shrugged. It did sound absurd when you said it out loud.

"He usually tells me where he's going."

"I see. Any reason why he didn't this time?"

"We had a disagreement."

"About what?"

"About Princess Victoria."

"So he *is* acquainted with the princess."

"He only just met her last week."

"And now he's disappeared with her necklace," the policeman concluded, lifting an eyebrow.

The two policemen had exchanged looks. The older, heavier policeman leaned forward and spoke gently.

"We will need your permission to search the house."

"Of course," she agreed. "But you won't find anything."

At 2:00 p.m., the front doorbell rang, and Cordelia walked across the marble foyer to answer. The policemen from earlier that day were on the doorstep, their avuncular manner gone.

"May we come in?"

"Yes, of course."

They wiped their feet on the mat before stepping inside.

"We'll start in his bedroom."

She led them up the stairs, feeling foolish. This whole thing was so preposterous.

Sitting on the bed, she watched them go through the drawers of Sinclair's dresser. She viewed the procedure with emotional calm, totally confident they'd find nothing. They lifted shirts and socks out in neat little piles, running their hands along the wood, looking for hidden compartments. They must do this often. There was a real system to it.

It was funny, but you could tell a lot about a person from the contents of their dresser drawers. Sinclair's things were arranged with military precision, stacked in neat piles—light blue and white Swiss-made boxers, Pantherella merino wool socks in black, brown, and navy. His pajamas were all white 160-thread count cotton, custom-made by Luigi Borrelli, with mother-of-pearl buttons and a thin band of sky blue piping on the cuff and around the collar.

The contents of a black cuff link box were examined and put back. There was a small leather case that held Sinclair's father's watch. His cell phone, left behind, drew an eyebrow raise. One of the policemen removed her love letters to Sinclair, written on pale-blue Smythson stationery, tied with a bit of string.

"Those are mine," she said, and they gently tucked them back in the drawer.

She waited, wondering how soon they would be done. There was work to do. With the volcano erupting, the media had been calling her for comments about climate change. Thankfully, all the tabloids were leaving her alone. Apparently, they had moved on to other stories.

"What's this?" one policeman asked, holding out a small red-leather jewelry box.

"I've never seen it before," she replied.

"It was here in the shirt drawer," he said.

"Well, I have no idea."

He opened it slowly, and then turned the box around, so she could view the contents. There, nestled on a satin pillow, was a square-cut diamond engagement ring. It sparkled in the light from the window.

Cordelia got up to look at it more closely.

"May I?" she asked, reaching for it.

The policeman nodded. She took it out and slid it onto her finger. The band fit perfectly.

He planned to propose.

A thousand emotions coursed through her—surprise and delight. And mostly regret. Cordelia looked up at the inspector, her eyes swimming with tears.

"I've never seen it before."

A flicker of sympathy passed over his face.

"We'll be taking this along as evidence. If it's not stolen property, then we'll be returning it to Mr. Sinclair, of course."

She nodded mutely, slid it off her finger, and handed it back to him. Then she walked out of the room toward the circular staircase. On the second-floor landing she leaned on the banister, determined not to cry.

HERCULANEUM, ITALY

Prince Karl and Luca stood in the hot afternoon sun, looking down at the ruins of the ancient Roman town of Herculaneum. The city had been destroyed during the eruption of Mount Vesuvius in AD 79, along with another more famous town, Pompeii.

"Should we hire a guide to give us a tour of the site?" Luca asked.

"No, let's keep a low profile. I'll buy a book at the kiosk."

Luca and Karl walked down the steel suspension ramp, their footsteps clanging on the metal. As they descended, the excavation pit of the archaeological dig stretched out before them like a gigantic 3-D map.

Once on the lower level, all signs of the modern world dropped away. Suddenly, they were walking down a two-thousand-year-old street paved with marble. There were houses, shops, and a market square with a fountain, all still intact.

Luca looked around, agog.

"Its almost feels like a movie set," Luca said.

"Yeah, except it's *real*."

Karl consulted his guidebook and then went over to examine some words carved onto a wall.

"Look, this is Latin graffiti. It's about a local politician."

Luca grinned. "I guess they didn't have spray paint back then."

"I can't believe this is still legible," Karl said, squatting down.

"You know, I always heard that Herculaneum was much better

preserved than Pompeii. But both cities were destroyed when Vesuvius erupted, right?"

"That's right," Karl affirmed

"So why is Herculaneum in better condition?"

"Pompeii was downwind from the volcano and everything burned."

"But not here?"

"No. Herculaneum was hit by a mudslide. That preserved everything."

"Incredible," Luca said, poking his head into the doorway of an abandoned structure.

Inside was airless, with a pungent scent of herbs. The floor was packed earth, and there were intact clay amphorae still on the shelves. Luca came back outside and looked around in awe.

"That must have been a shop. It feels like everyone just stopped what they were doing and left. Like a ghost town."

"I know. Creepy isn't it?" Karl agreed.

They stood for a moment, deciding what to do next. Wavy lines of heat radiated off the white marble surfaces of the buildings and pavement.

Karl pulled out his water bottle, took a long swig, and handed it over. Luca didn't drink but poured it over his head until rivulets ran down his cheek and dripped off his jaw.

"You look like you're melting," Karl laughed.

"It must be 110 degrees," Luca said, using the bottom of his T-shirt to blot his face. "Let's find some shade."

"I think there's a house along here," Karl told him, consulting the guidebook.

At the end of the main street was a large classical villa with columns. As they entered, the temperature felt several degrees cooler. Karl and Luca walked around a large square atrium with twenty-foot ceilings and a small pool, or *impluvium*. The pool, now dry, would normally be filled by rainwater falling through a hole in the roof.

They made their way through the villa, sticking their heads into the various rooms on the way. The *triclinium*, or dining hall, was painted with scenes of abundance—gods and goddesses, fish and animals. The walls were the deep oxblood color known as "Pompeii red." The colonnade encircled a lovely interior garden. It was a beautiful private oasis, in full bloom.

"Let's just rest here for a while," Luca said, shrugging off his backpack.

He lay down on the mosaic floor, using his backpack as a pillow. Karl looked down at him and laughed.

"Make yourself at home, why don't you."

"Ahh . . . this is perfect. You should try it."

They stretched out side by side.

Karl read from the guidebook. "It says they replanted the same flowers that were originally here by analyzing the roots in the soil."

"Looks like pomegranate trees and some kind of roses."

"Yeah, I guess."

"I like archaeology," Luca mused. "John Sinclair used to take me to his digs like this when I was young."

"Was that fun?"

"Yeah, except his digs were just chunks of rock. This feels like we're visiting someone's house."

"Wouldn't it be great if we could stay overnight?" Karl fantasized.

"Yeah. We could sleep right here. But it's a little sad, knowing that the people died."

"That's not true. Most of the residents of Herculaneum escaped."

"They did?"

"This was a really wealthy town, so people sailed back to Naples."

"So what happened in Pompeii? Everybody got killed, right?"

"Yes. Pompeii was a real working city, and the people stayed to protect their businesses. That wasn't a good decision."

"It sure wasn't," Luca agreed. "Karl, why aren't you studying to be a scientist? You love all this geological stuff so much."

"My parents won't let me. I have to go into banking to help Norway with its financial situation when my sister takes over the throne."

"That stinks," Luca said with feeling.

"It sure does."

They stared up at the portico ceiling for a while in silence.

Karl yawned. "You know, if I don't get up now, I'm going to fall asleep. We should go."

As they walked back down the hallway, Luca noticed that another visitor had come into the villa. The man held his camera close to his face, snapping pictures. Once or twice he stepped back to take a wide shot.

"Let's get out of here," Karl whispered. "I don't want to turn up in anyone's vacation album."

"Yeah, that would be hard to explain," Luca laughed.

Renato scrolled through his viewfinder to look at the photos of the two boys. Herculaneum was the perfect stalking ground—so many places to hide. He stared at the features of the blond kid in playback. These photos matched the Internet images of Prince Karl exactly. He'd use these pictures later for ransom. Kidnapping the boy would be tricky, but hiding him in the underground caverns of Naples for a couple of days wouldn't be a problem. Then, once he got the money, he'd move on to Rome, or even America. Somewhere beyond the reach of Salvatore Mondragone.

NAPLES–PALERMO FERRY

On the six o'clock Naples–Palermo ferry, Luca Brindisi and Prince Karl dangled their arms over the railings. The craft was now out in open water, and the wind was brisk. Renato observed them from the snack bar, and both boys were clearly visible through the window. Karl was talking nonstop, and the pale dark-haired boy looked a little queasy as the ferry bounced around.

They were traveling down the Mediterranean coastline to Sicily, an island located just off the tip of the mainland of Italy. For now, the ferry was hugging the shore until it passed the island of Stromboli, and then it would skirt by the Strait of Messina, and finally dock at Palermo.

The wind was in their faces as they stood on deck. The day had been scorching, but out on the water, it was surprisingly cool.

"I just love living like this! I feel so free," Karl shouted in high spirits.

"I can't believe we got away without anyone stopping us," Luca observed.

"See how easy it was?" Karl bragged.

Karl angled his body to feel the salt spray. When he turned back, he noticed Luca was shivering.

"We better get some heavier clothes if we're going to climb Mount Etna," he remarked.

"I'm not so sure . . ." Luca said, worrying about the volcano.

"Do you feel nauseous?" Karl asked, thinking he was seasick.

"No. I'm a pretty good sailor," Luca lied.

"Well, in a few minutes, we're going to pass by one of the most interesting volcanoes in the world. Stromboli."

"I've never seen it," Luca admitted.

"I've only read about it. The island of Stromboli is the top of a volcano, and most of it is underwater."

"Cool," Luca smiled. "Won't it be too dark to see it?"

"No, it erupts all the time. They call it 'The Lighthouse of the Mediterranean.' Jules Verne put it in his book *Journey to the Center of the Earth*."

"You really love this stuff, don't you?" Luca said.

"I first read it when I was thirteen. After that, all I wanted to do was become a volcanologist."

Karl broke off, suddenly pointing at something on the horizon.

"There it is!"

Luca turned around and shouted in excitement. "Wow!"

As the ferry moved closer to the island, they were able to get a better view. Velvety green slopes rose up to form a perfect little volcanic cone. At the top, a continuous spray of orange sparks lit up the sky. Every few minutes, a little puff of smoke billowed out.

"It's so small, it looks like a toy," Luca observed.

"I just love it," Karl said. "See the little village at the bottom?"

In the fading light, Luca could just make out a tiny beach and a cluster of small white houses. The ferry passed close by, and he could see a few cows in the pasture.

"How can they *live* there!" Luca said, astonished. "I'd be terrified."

"I know. Stromboli's been continuously active for the past 1,400 years," Karl told him.

They watched as the orange sparks sprayed up like a welder's torch. Every once in a while, the fire fountains of basaltic lava shot up in large incandescent sheaves of flame. The colors were spectacular—deep garnet, blazing orange, golden yellow. The flames off-gassed continually with a whooshing sound.

"It's like the soundtrack for a war movie," Luca shouted.

"I read that eruptions are louder on Stromboli than other volcanoes because of the high gas content."

"I wish I had a camera."

"You don't want a camera. This is living, man!" Karl yelled.

They stood watching as the ferry passed by. The other side of the island looked completely different. Instead of meadows, there was a dark streak of black ash and lava.

"The locals call it *Sciara del Fuoco*, the Stream of Fire," Karl said.

"Cool," Luca said.

The stood and watched until the volcano passed out of sight.

"Let's go inside," Karl suggested. "I'm starving."

They walked into the café, ordered prosciutto sandwiches, and sat gazing out at the water. Both boys were oblivious to the man right behind them. Renato sat nursing a coffee and listening to Karl outline plans for their arrival in Sicily. The Camorra gangster heard every word.

ROYAL SPORT TRAINING CENTER, OSLO

Princess Victoria lay on her stomach squeezing the stock of a .22 caliber rifle against her shoulder, aiming at a metal knock-down target. After five rounds, she put the gun down and ran a lap around an oval track, then came back to fire from a standing position.

This was standard biathlon training. The Olympic event emphasized cross-country skiing and shooting. It had been originally devised by Norwegians to hone their hunting skills during their long, frozen winters.

Victoria knew she was preforming badly this morning. Her pulse was highly elevated and her aim way off. She missed her target three times.

Managing adrenaline was key. During the skiing portion of the contest, participants would drive their heart rates up to 180 beats a minute. Yet, to accurately fire a rifle, her pulse needed to be half that. Forcing the heart rate lower took a lot of mental and physical skill.

"I'm terribly sorry," Victoria apologized to her coach.

She took a towel from the bench.

"We all have our good days and bad," he said diplomatically.

"Tomorrow will be better," Victoria promised, wiping her face.

"We will try running laps. It may help with your breath control."

"All right. I'll see you in the morning," Victoria said, putting on her training jacket.

She pushed through the double-glass doors of the sports center and climbed into her chauffeur-driven Mercedes.

The streets of Oslo were shadowy and dark. An overcast day turned into light rain. When they reached the palace portico, Victoria jumped out and strode inside.

A long, narrow passage led to private royal apartments. She walked softly on the crimson carpet. Her mother and father had a suite of rooms on the first floor, and she and Karl had smaller accommodations upstairs.

As she walked by the security office, she heard people shouting in anger. She recognized their voices. Incredibly, her father was in a blazing row with the security guards.

"What's going on?" Victoria asked as she entered the room.

Queen Ingrid turned to her, distraught.

"Your brother is missing!"

"He left Capri?"

"Yes, he's gone somewhere with the Brindisi boy." Her mother turned to her with worried eyes. "Go up to your brother's room and see if you can find anything. And don't tell *anyone* about this."

"What am I looking for?" Victoria asked, confused.

"Maybe he left something lying around that would give us a clue."

Victoria nodded and left the room. She immediately took the lift upstairs to her brother's private apartment on the third floor. Entering cautiously, she found the suite deserted. The living room had the disheveled look of a scholar's lair. A cognac-colored calfskin couch was piled high with books, and an original Biedermeier writing desk was laden with paraphernalia—the detritus of a scientific mind.

Even at his young age, Karl was a dedicated naturalist. The desk held a microscope and a box of glass slides. There was an anemic-looking plant labeled with a Latin botanical name, clearly unsuited to the climate of Norway. A stuffed otter lolled on its back, its row of little pointed teeth horribly bared in a permanent grimace.

Victoria picked up a book titled *Arachnid Advice—Keeping a Tarantula as a Pet.* Suddenly, a rapid flittering movement caught her attention, and she jumped. But it was only Karl's iguana in its octagonal glass terrarium surrounded by fiddlehead ferns.

She let out a nervous chuckle and continued to look around. A page of a notebook was filled with doodles that resembled volcanoes. She sighed. Who could fathom the mind of a fifteen-year-old boy?

Just as Victoria was about to leave, she caught sight of his map and a couple of posters on the wall. There was a publicity glossy of a handsome man autographed in thick black pen: "Life's a Blast, regards, Jude Blackwell."

A topographical chart was marked with colored pins indicating all the major volcanoes he wanted to climb: Kilauea, Hawaii; Popocatepetl, Mexico; Erta Ale, Ethiopia; Chimborazo, Ecuador.

The largest was of Mount Etna, under which Karl had written "taken by the Advanced Land Imager, NASA's Earth Observing-1 satellite."

She focused on the photo. Mount Etna was on the island of Sicily, surrounded by the dazzling blue Mediterranean. In the high-def image, the slopes of the volcano were blackish-green, similar to the skin of an overripe avocado. A white plume of smoke flared up from the summit. A chart of "Seismic Signatures" resembled an electrocardiogram in which the patient was having a heart attack—the lines oscillating wildly. It was dated July of this year.

Victoria immediately realized the implications of what she was seeing. The volcano was only a short boat ride away from Capri, and Karl would certainly want to see it.

MOUNT ETNA, SICILY

Jude Blackwell stood in the center of the scientific monitoring center weighing the odds of whether Mount Etna would erupt. There were increasing signs it would happen.

This was one of the most explosive volcanoes in the world. Mount Etna was a so-called composite volcano, which meant that it had formed along the edges of a tectonic plate. As one plate moved against the other, the lower one would melt, creating magma with heavy concentrations of silica. That molten liquid would be thick, and the volcano chamber would plug up easily. Enormous pressure would build up until the final eruption.

The problem was, it was almost impossible to tell exactly when that would happen. The only way was to monitor the distortion of the ground; a slight bulge could be discerned as the magma rose to the surface.

Jude had plenty of experience with composite volcanoes, and he knew they often gave very little warning. So right now, timing was everything. If he ascended while the volcano was simply off-gassing, the pictures would be magnificent. But if he miscalculated, he wouldn't be around to talk about it.

It would take a couple of days to map out his route and prepare his gear. But Jude made up his mind—he was going for it.

PARIS, FRANCE

The leaves on the trees hung limply, and the streets were empty. August in Paris was always like this—the summer doldrums. Businesses were closed. Everyone was away on vacation. The Cote d'Azur and the beaches of Saint-Malo and Deauville were crowded, but, unfortunately, Charles Bonnard and his family were stuck in the city.

Charles offered his mother and sister the use of his little villa in Capri, but the ash from the volcano curtailed all travel. Besides, the end of the summer was always a busy time for his sister, Clothilde. Her fall collection was only a week away, and she was busy making the final arrangements for the runway show. Madame Bonnard kept herself busy as well. She went out to play cards with her friends and have lunch every day. Charles was left alone with his dog, Watson.

A week ago, he would have tried to sneak off to see Princess Victoria. But ever since the scandal broke, they had not spoken.

Bored and restless, he decided to take a walk. He and Watson left the house, crossing the street to go into the Luxembourg Gardens. It was the former grounds of the historic Medici chateau, with acres of shaded paths. He started a semi-jog, passing by the marionette theater. There was a slight breeze, and the water jets in the large central fountain dispersed into white plumes in the air.

The dog kept pace effortlessly. Watson was a wolfhound, one of the largest breeds in the world. As they trotted, the enormous beast looked up at him intermittently, his eyes filled with adoration.

"Come on Watson, let's run," Charles said as he picked up the pace.

They rounded the ornamental fishpond and took off down an allée of chestnut trees. His cell phone rang. He saw it was Brindy calling and turned it off. The last thing he wanted to do was discuss his private affairs over the phone.

Charles was suddenly aware that his dog was no longer with him. He turned, and Watson had stopped, his tongue lolling.

"OK, boy. Let's go back."

They retraced their steps home, passing through the interior courtyard. The Bonnard house was a typical Paris *hôtel particulier*—a white limestone mansion in the Haussmann style with a slate mansard roof. As was usual, there was an interior cobblestoned courtyard where the family parked their vehicles. Madame Bonnard's little green Peugeot was gone. That was a relief. He'd finally get some peace.

Inside, Charles walked up the broad marble steps to the second floor and unclipped the leash. He gave Watson a pat. The wolfhound looked up, shaggy fur partially obscuring liquid brown eyes.

"Good dog. Now stay off the furniture."

Watson dropped down on four paws and headed toward his favorite couch in the grand salon. Charles walked down a silent corridor and knocked lightly on his sister's door.

"*Entrez,*" a female voice said from within.

He stepped inside. No matter how often he came here, there was always a moment of wonder. His sister, Clothilde, was one of the most celebrated fashion designers in Paris, and her studio was breathtaking. It was creative chaos. Every wall surface was pasted with cuttings from magazines: fashion shoots, glossy magazine covers, tear sheets from catalogues and art books. A large worktable had been pushed against the window, and she was bent over, sketching.

Many years ago, Clothilde had been the toast of Paris because of her beauty and vivacity. She was tall and angular, with hauntingly ethereal features and a cloud of blond hair. As slim as a model, she was the most successful fashion designer of her generation.

Her life changed when a horrible accident left her partially paralyzed. She was still an acclaimed designer, but her life diminished considerably. She now lived at home with Maman and didn't go out socially anymore. Charles constantly pleaded with her to look up old friends and get out to parties, concerts, and theater. But her work was everything to her now. She claimed she didn't need all the rest.

Now, as she sat at her drafting board, her infirmity was not imme-diately apparent. A visitor would need a second glance to notice the state-of-the-art wheelchair.

"*Salut, chéri,*" he said as he strode in. He kissed her on the cheek then went to claim his usual spot. There was an old upholstered chair by her worktable. He always had to examine it first to make sure there were no straight pins in the cushions.

This room had always been a refuge for him. His mother was a martinet about the rest of the house, but this was a *sanctum sancto-rum* where he and Clothilde could talk freely. No one entered without Clothilde's permission.

"I was hoping you'd drop in," Clothilde said. "A woman named Victoria called."

Charles sat bolt upright.

"Where is she?"

Clothilde wheeled around to give him a slip of paper.

"I have no idea. It's a new cell number, she says."

Charles stared at it, frozen with indecision.

"Who's Victoria?" Clothilde asked.

"I'll explain later."

Charles dialed the number, and Victoria picked up on the second ring. Her voice was very quiet.

"Call me later," she whispered. "I'm at a reception and can't talk."

"When?"

"Around seven tonight. I'll be alone."

"Is anything wrong?" he asked. "Tell me quickly."

"Yes. Luca and Karl are missing. Charles, it's awful! And Brindy's grandmother was murdered in Rome."

"Oh my . . . that's *horrible!*"

"Brindy thinks it might be a Camorra revenge killing. The boys might be in danger. I'll explain more later."

Charles hung up and stared at the floor.

"What is it?" Clothilde asked.

He looked over at her, his mind spinning.

"Can you keep a secret?"

"Don't be ridiculous. Of course I can."

"Remember the magazine article about John Sinclair being Princess Victoria's lover?"

"Yes. I was very surprised . . ."

She stopped and gasped, her eyes enormous.

"Was that the same Victoria who called here?"

"Yes."

"*Princess Victoria* called you?" she repeated, incredulous. "Why?"

"She's not involved with John Sinclair. It's me. "

Clothilde's mouth dropped open.

"Oh, Charles. I can't *believe* that. She's so young!"

"I swear I didn't know her age," Charles protested.

"How could you not *know?*" Clothilde gasped. "She's all over the papers, all the time."

Charles ran his hand over his forehead wearily, as if to massage away a headache.

"I don't read that stuff. I guess I'm an idiot. Don't gape at me like that."

She gulped. "I'm sorry . . . what are you going to do?"

Charles stood up briskly.

"I promised I would call her later tonight. Right now I need to think."

Charles Bonnard always went to the top of the house to work out complicated problems. The entire top floor was a large photo studio, reachable by the ornately gilded elevator. Clothilde often used the space to photograph her designs, but Charles also kept his darkroom up here.

He strode through a forest of light stands and walked directly into the small closet, flipping on the safelight. There, in the lurid red glow, he started to develop the film from Capri.

His passion was black and white photography. Today he needed to do something to calm down. Photography was methodical and precise, conducive to deep thought. He started working, knowing that about halfway through he'd settle down and be able to focus on thinking through the problem about Victoria and Karl.

First, he checked over his wet and dry stations. Then he poured out the chemicals to make silver gelatin prints. He had shot some photos at Villa San Angelo, most of them of Victoria.

It took several minutes of preparation. After immersing the contact paper in the solution, he lifted the dripping photo out with tongs and transferred it to the stop bath. The image of Princess Victoria floated in the clear liquid, moving as if it had a life of its own. He had captured her in a moment of carefree joy, head thrown back in a spontaneous laugh.

Charles tilted the tray back and forth to soak the paper, and then, with a fresh set of tongs, shifted the contact sheet to the sodium thio-sulfate fixative. That step would take at least ten minutes before he could do a final wash. Time to think.

ROYAL PALACE, OSLO

Victoria sat at the makeup table. Her eyes kept returning to her own image in the mirror. She was dressed in a green silk sheath, stockings, and high heels. The perfectly made-up face gave no indication of the turmoil she was feeling inside.

Karl must have taken the sapphire necklace. How else would he be funding his little excursion? Neither he nor Luca had any real spending money—only enough to pay for a gelato or a snack. Security teams were looking for the boys in Capri and Naples. The strategy was to start at the Villa Brindisi and then fan out, possibly going as far as Mount Vesuvius or even Mount Etna.

She pressed them to try Sicily. Her parents weren't convinced that Karl would travel that far. Somehow, they assumed because of his age, he'd stick closer to what was familiar. But Karl loved Mount Etna and knew every inch of it as if it were his own backyard.

Not a word had been spoken to the press. The media still thought Prince Karl was visiting a friend in Italy. But that story would not hold for much longer.

The cell phone vibrated on the table, and she answered.

"Hi, V," Charles said, sounding breathless.

"Oh, Charles. Thank God you called. I missed you so much."

"Same here, V. But first, have they located Luca and Karl?"

"No, and I'm just sick about it."

"Well if it's any help, I've known Luca Brindisi since he was a kid, and he's very sensible. They should be fine together."

"Brindy is worried they might have been murdered. The Camorra killed her grandmother, and she doesn't know if it's some kind of vendetta."

"Does she have any idea where they might have gone?"

"No. But Karl has lots of pictures of Mount Etna in his room."

"That's in Sicily. I'll see if I can get hold of Sinclair. He knows the area very well."

"Charles, I'm coming to Paris to be with you."

There was a slight pause on the phone. His voice was cautious.

"All the flights have been canceled."

"I can go by overnight ferry from Oslo to Le Havre."

"What would you tell your parents?"

"That I'm going to fall fashion collections."

"I don't know, V. Maybe we should keep apart for the moment."

"But I need to see you. I feel like . . . I just can't take it anymore . . . Like I am going to explode. Maybe I should just tell my parents about us, and be done with it."

She sounded desperate. Charles sighed.

"All right, V. But be careful. I'm going to have my sister call you when you get here. It's safer that way.

Charles walked back into Clothilde's studio, feeling drained.

His sister wheeled her chair over, reaching for his hand. He sat down in a daze.

"What is it, Charles?"

"I need you to tell Princess Victoria about my father. I haven't mentioned it to her yet."

Clothilde pressed her lips into a firm line.

"Of course. But don't worry, I am sure she will understand."

"Well, I trust you to put the best spin on it."

"And what about you? How do you feel about *her*?"

He looked into her pale gray eyes and smiled. Clothilde was the one person he trusted most in the world. She knew all his secrets and fears.

"I love her," he said.

"Then I will make sure she understands."

OSLO-LE HAVRE FERRY

Victoria pulled her collar up and looked out over the water. She was alone for the moment. A male attendant waited inside, where it was warm, and the Norwegian Embassy driver would pick her up at the dock in Le Havre. From time to time, she was allowed to travel incognito. When she dressed down and didn't wear makeup, she had the ability to look absolutely ordinary. As she boarded the ferry, no one had noticed the young blond woman wearing a knit cap and a navy blue pea coat.

Her parents were insisting that she stay at the official Norwegian residence in Paris, under the sharp eye of the ambassador and his wife. Frankly she was astonished that her parents allowed her to go. Especially after what happened in Capri. But she needed new clothes from the fall collections. Normally her mother would accompany her, but the queen was too caught up in the search for Karl.

Now that she thought about it, Karl was probably fine. Her brother was one of the smartest, most resourceful kids she knew. He'd surface in a few days, and everything would be back to normal. Brindy's fear about the Camorra was probably overblown. Victoria pushed down the flicker of fear and tried to relax.

The sun was setting, and the sky was turning brilliant red over the water. The sunset was so intensely crimson, it almost hurt her eyes.

Karl had told her about the beautiful red sunsets that accompanied volcanic eruptions. He said that Norway was often particularly affected because the debris was carried along the jet stream.

He mentioned a famous painting, *The Scream* by the Norwegian artist Edvard Munch. The painting showed a person howling in horror against a swirling red background, which was meant to depict a volcanic eruption. Most people didn't realize that the iconic masterpiece was originally titled *Der Schrei der Natur*—*The Scream of Nature*.

Edvard Munch had witnessed a volcanic red sky after the eruption of Krakatoa in 1883. Munch wrote in his diary that he stood trembling, because the color of the sunset was so powerful—he actually claimed to have heard a shriek that came from nature.

Victoria felt tears well in her eyes. She felt the same way. It seemed that everything in her life was erupting right now. She had never felt so nervous and unsure. It was as if the whole universe were undergoing some violent change.

NORWEGIAN EMBASSY RESIDENCE, 28 RUE DE BAYARD, PARIS

Clothilde put her teacup down gently in anticipation of the difficult conversation to come. She and Victoria remained discreetly silent as the waiters cleared the lunch table. She and the princess were meeting at the Norwegian Embassy Residence in the chic eighth arrondisement in Paris. This small, intimate dining room was used for entertaining heads of state and other dignitaries, but today they were by themselves.

Clothilde took the opportunity to look around the room. If it had been a purely social lunch, she would have enjoyed it very much. The elegance was delightful. The china on the table was hand-painted *Flora Danica*—a set of botanical-themed plates that had been originally designed for Catherine II of Russia in 1790. There was heirloom silver and delicately etched crystal goblets.

Victoria presided over the table wearing a blue linen dress, accessorized with a gold filigree bangle bracelet and pearl earrings. Her hair was caught back in a loose chignon, and she looked absolutely regal.

But Clothilde noticed the princess was nervous. Victoria had barely touched her food even though the Norwegian repast had been delicious: puree soup, lute fish with potatoes, and yellow cake with whipped cream and lingonberries. After the waiters left, Victoria turned to her guest.

"I am so happy to finally meet you," she said, signaling that the serious conversation could begin. "It was good of Charles to suggest it."

"Yes, but he thinks there is something you should be aware of before you continue any further."

"What is that?"

Clothilde paused and took a breath.

"Alphonse Bonnard was not Charles's father."

Victoria looked up, surprised. "So Alphonse Bonnard is . . . ?"

" . . . my father. But I'm afraid my brother's biological father never married my mother."

"I don't . . . understand," Victoria said slowly.

"My mother never married Charles's father."

"Charles is illegitimate!" Victoria gasped.

Clothilde recoiled from the harsh word.

"Not technically. My parents were married when Charles was born. But his real father never acknowledged him."

Victoria was staring at her, horrified.

"You realize his parentage determines if I can marry him or not," Victoria said through pale lips.

"I know. That is why I am here."

"I don't know what to say," Victoria said, shaken.

She picked up a water glass and took a sip.

Clothilde kept her voice calm and factual.

"My mother fell in love with an American student in Paris. They had a brief affair."

"So Charles is half American?"

"Yes. His father was recalled to the States by his parents. They didn't approve of him marrying a French girl."

Victoria frowned. "Why?"

"They were a major political family. A foreign wife would have been a detriment to a political career. The boy later became an important US senator."

"I see."

"My mother was devastated when he left. The Americans tried to make amends. They offered a trust fund to pay for Charles's education, if she would keep his paternity a secret."

"Surely your mother didn't need the money."

"Of course not. She simply hoped to keep the connection alive. She hoped that Charles would get to know his real father someday."

"But that never happened?"

"It was wishful thinking. In fact, years later, when the man became a politician, she was again forced to sign another legal document saying she would never reveal the baby's paternal origins."

"So who was Alphonse Bonnard?"

"He was a family friend who stepped in to marry my mother, to shield her from scandal."

"That was very honorable of him."

"Actually, it was rather romantic, because my father had been in love with my mother since she was very young. He was much older, you see. So for him it was a lucky turn of events, because he never thought my mother would ever look at him."

"But she did," Victoria said, toying with her spoon.

"Yes. Alphonse Bonnard saved her good name, and I think she always loved him for it."

"When did Charles find all this out?"

"When he was a teenager. It was devastating to him."

"Oh, how awful."

"My father made it work. He embraced Charles even more and took him everywhere with him. They became inseparable."

"He sounds like a lovely person."

"Yes. I think that is why Charles is so honorable. He understands that doing the right thing under difficult circumstances is very important."

Victoria sat back in her chair, thinking. "Thank you for telling me."

"Charles thought you should know. But he finds it hard to talk about."

"Well, it does matter, I'm afraid. I'll have to tell my parents."

"I should add one thing," Clothilde said.

Victoria turned, her eyes questioning.

"You are the first woman Charles has ever loved. He told me."

Tears welled in Victoria's eyes, and she took a moment to compose herself, blinking hard and looking out over the lawn. But then, with supreme effort, she spoke.

"So just to be clear, none of this has ever been made public?"

"That is correct," Clothilde assured her.

"So technically, on paper, it would still be a perfect match."

"Yes, but the press will certainly investigate Charles."

"Well, let them. I like that he is half American. And I suspect my parents will approve."

"They will?"

"Your mother's aristocratic heritage is sufficient."

"But there's still a problem," Clothilde pointed out.

"What?"

"My mother risks her reputation by opening up the past."

"I'll meet with her," Victoria said, lifting her coffee cup to her lips.

"I don't think you know what you are saying. She can be extremely difficult."

Victoria laughed. "Mine is much worse. Now, how do we arrange this?"

"Are you free tomorrow? I can set up a meeting."

"Yes, of course. And thank you, Clothilde."

"Don't thank me quite yet. You haven't met my mother."

The small bedroom at the top of the Norwegian residence was cozy and pleasant. The ambassador and his wife were off to a dinner party, and no one was here except for her security guard downstairs.

Victoria walked to the window and looked across the dark rooftops of Paris to the beautifully illuminated Eiffel Tower. Just beyond in the sixth arrondissement, Charles Bonnard and his family were all at home, having dinner. Clothilde had called with a daring plan. Everything was set.

Victoria walked over to the closet to select an outfit to wear tomorrow. It was important to look her best when she met Charles's mother.

CARROUSEL DU LOUVRE, PARIS

At eleven o'clock in the morning, six hundred people sat in an auditorium waiting for a fashion show to begin. It was the famous glass pyramid of the Louvre—La Pyramid Inversée.

Madame Bonnard walked hesitatingly down the aisle, looking for her seat in the first row. She settled in next to a lovely young girl with her blond hair pulled up into a graceful chignon.

The lights dimmed. Right on time, the boom of rock music throbbed, and pink lasers sliced the air. Then a curtain opened, and a young model walked out, her skinny legs scissoring in time with the beat. The skirt—a drift of gray chiffon—swirled around her knees.

The girl next to her made a comment.

"I like the color of that dress, don't you?"

Charles's mother turned, surprised.

The girl introduced herself in a cursory fashion. "We haven't met. I'm a friend of one of your children."

Madame Bonnard brightened up, delighted.

"You must know Clothilde? Are you one of her models?"

"No, I'm Princess Victoria of Norway."

Madame Bonnard nearly gasped, but then responded smoothly.

"Oh, I thought I recognized you, your Highness. So how do you know Clothilde?"

"Actually, I know both Clothilde and Charles."

Madame Bonnard looked astonished.

"*Charles?* He never mentioned . . ."

"Yes . . . both your children are lovely. They speak so highly of you. Would you have time to join me after the show for lunch?"

HOTEL GEORGE V, PARIS

Le Cinq restaurant in the Hotel George V was the perfect spot for a private tête-à-tête. As Victoria walked in, the maître d' did a double take, then smiled and bowed.

"Two for lunch, please."

The man frantically searched his seating chart.

"Somewhere discreet," she told him. "Perhaps over there, away from the window, if you don't mind."

"Of course, your Highness."

He led the way, carrying the menus. Victoria kept her eyes focused on the center of the room as they walked. The restaurant was crowded, and conversation flowed at a high pitch. Suddenly people started to notice, and they passed through a wake of whispers, as they settled into their small table in the corner.

Victoria and Madame Bonnard remained quiet as the waiters set silverware, poured water, and offered bread. The head waiter took out a pencil and wrote down the order as carefully as if he were drafting the Magna Carta: lobster bisque and grilled lamb for the Princess, green salad and halibut for Madame. The man bowed and set off to supervise.

Victoria surveyed Charles's mother. Madame Bonnard sat as erect as a ballet mistress. Her lavender couture suit was the picture of respectability. Nothing about her appearance now would suggest her history of youthful passion.

If Madame Bonnard was curious about the invitation, she didn't let on. Her lips were set in a pleasant smile; her bright little eyes watched as waiters placed an amuse-bouche on the table. She bent over to survey the thimble-sized puff pastries: one filled with beet mousseline, the other a single braised scallop topped with a drop of Japanese tamari sauce.

"Bon appétit," Victoria said and saluted with her Perrier.

Madame Bonnard responded with her glass of champagne.

She started the conversation with an observation of the Parisian weather. The summer had been so hot, and airless. They moved on to fashion and art, and the conversation flowed effortlessly. But by the time the desserts were served, small talk was getting smaller and the conversational pauses were longer.

"It's remarkable that you were able to make the trip to Paris from Norway," Madame Bonnard said as she finished her crème brûlée.

"Because of the volcanic ash, you mean?" Victoria asked.

The waiter poured the demitasse and left the silver coffeepot on the table for them to help themselves.

"Yes, I understand that European airspace is closed right now."

"I came on the ferry from Oslo."

"There was no mention in the press."

Victoria smiled. A plate of macaroons was within her reach, and she selected a light pink raspberry-filled confection and bit into it, taking her time to answer.

"There are ways of keeping things out of the press."

Madame Bonnard raised an eyebrow.

"Apparently it doesn't always work."

Victoria laughed. "Oh, poor Mr. Sinclair. They were wrong about that."

Madame Bonnard took another spoonful of crème brûlée, smiling coyly.

"I see you are skeptical," Victoria said.

"Your personal affairs are really not my concern, my dear."

"I'm afraid they are. You see, I was with Charles."

Madame Bonnard's spoon stopped halfway to her mouth.

"That is *impossible*! He would have said something to me."

Victoria let the facts settle in. Madame Bonnard put the spoon down, her gesture abrupt.

Victoria soothed her over with superb diplomatic tact. "*Of course* Charles would respect my privacy. You have raised a perfect gentleman."

"What is it you propose to do about this liaison?"

Victoria took her time before she answered, calming her pulse, as she knew so well how to do.

"I would like to continue to see Charles. With your permission, of course. And I must tell you that I am aware of his American heritage."

"What does Charles say about this?"

"He is naturally cautious, and wants to protect my reputation, as well as yours. But I'd like to do this formally and introduce him to my parents. I see no need for continued secrecy."

"You realize that it will not be easy." Madame Bonnard said and took a sip of coffee. "The media will uncover his past."

"I understand that is a risk. But if my parents give their approval, the story will die away quickly enough. There will be no scandal. And the press might never investigate Charles further.

"One could only hope," Madame Bonnard said speculatively.

"Will you give me permission to make our liaison public?" Victoria asked, her heart pounding.

Madame Bonnard paused, dabbing her lips with her napkin. She focused on the young princess with a serene smile.

"Charles's real father passed away last year, so I have no further obligation to uphold the secret."

"And you would be willing to endure the bad publicity?"

Madam Bonnard gave a Gallic shrug. Her look of noble resignation rivaled that of Marie Antoinette facing the guillotine.

"If you are willing to risk the furor, then so am I."

"I was hoping you would say that."

"The happiness of my son is all that concerns me."

"I want Charles to be happy also. And I think he is, with me."

"How should we proceed?" Madame Bonnard asked.

"When I return to Norway, my parents will be informed. There will be a formal announcement from the palace."

"Are you sure they will agree so quickly?" Madame Bonnard asked.

"They *must* approve of Charles."

"Must?"

"Yes, you see, there is no choice in the matter. I have just discovered I am carrying his child."

PARIS, FRANCE

Clothilde Bonnard was following her usual custom of sipping a Lillet before dinner. The sun had just dipped behind the trees, casting a golden glow across the Luxembourg Gardens. Madame Bonnard entered the large salon, smiling smugly.

"Is your brother still here?"

"He's going out."

"I must speak to him first," Madame Bonnard said and rang the bell for the housekeeper.

Annette entered, carrying a silver tray. She was well aware of Madame Bonnard's cocktail of choice and had already mixed a Kir Royal. At that exact moment, Charles strode into the room freshly showered and dressed for an evening out. Clothilde noted his new navy linen, unstructured suit, cut in the latest fashionable Italian style.

He pointedly ignored her scrutinizing his clothes and requested his usual aperitif, Punt e Mes—a bittersweet Italian vermouth—with a splash of soda and an orange twist. As Annette set off to fetch it, Madame Bonnard confronted her son.

"Whom are you seeing tonight, Charles?"

"Mother, you know very well. You had lunch with her today at the Hotel George."

Clothilde gave a little snort into her glass and pretended it was a cough.

"What are you planning on doing about her?" Madame Bonnard asked in an impatient tone.

"I am trying to decide."

"Trying to *decide?*" Madame Bonnard demanded, drawing the words out with drama.

"Charles, that is not acceptable. Surely you understand the seriousness of the situation."

"I understand, mother."

Charles accepted his drink from Annette, and they all stayed silent until she left the room. Clothilde kept her eyes on her mother's face.

Madame Bonnard took a long sip of the champagne cocktail, her narrowed stare burning into her son.

"You must marry her, Charles. There is no other way."

Charles flagged a taxi and gave the address—135 rue Saint-Dominique. Settling into the backseat, he thought about what had just transpired. His mother was enthusiastic about Victoria. And she was right about marriage. It was exactly as Sinclair said. Princesses don't date. He'd have to propose soon.

Victoria gave every indication that she would agree. But the public acceptance wouldn't be quite as smooth. The tabloids would uncover his past and the King and Queen of Norway would *not* be thrilled about their daughter marrying an illegitimate son of an American senator. Of that he was certain.

The cab pulled up to the curb, and he paid the driver. Victoria was meeting him here. The restaurant Le Violon D'Ingres was young and lively—completely different from the stodgy formal dinners she usually attended.

As he got out, he noticed a young, blond bohemian girl in a leather jacket, long skirt, and sandals standing outside the restaurant. It took him a second to realize it was Victoria.

Victoria and Charles walked into the restaurant in total anonymity. The flowing skirt was unlike anything she ever wore, but she also wore her long hair hanging down her back in a braid. Clothilde also suggested a touch of bright red lipstick and hoop earrings. Those style changes transformed her from a demure princess to a contemporary young woman of the Left Bank.

They took their places and looked around at the other patrons. Everyone was too busy to notice. Victoria immediately lost all self-consciousness.

"What would you like to drink?" he asked.

"Oh, I think I'll stick to mineral water tonight, if you don't mind."

"Come on V, let's have a nice glass of red wine."

"I can't Charles . . . I'm in training for the biathlon team."

"Oh, right. Of course."

He returned the wine card to the sommelier, ordered two Perriers with lemon, then sat back, utterly relaxed.

This was how things should be between them, informal and stress-free. Charles looked around the restaurant with satisfaction. Everyone was laughing and talking loudly.

"I thought you'd like it here," he said.

Victoria was leaning back against the banquette, her skin glowing. She was lovelier than ever. If he and V could date like this, it would be fun, instead of all that sordid sneaking around.

The waiter came over with the drinks. Just then, his cell phone vibrated.

"It's Cordelia. I called her to contact Sinclair, so he can help find Karl."

"Go ahead, Charles. Take it."

Charles pushed back his chair and answered the call.

"Hello? Delia? What's up?"

He walked through the restaurant with the phone pressed to his ear. "Just a second. I can't hear you."

Victoria took a sip of mineral water. Tonight was going to be a big moment. After dinner, she'd tell him she was pregnant. Not a soul knew about it, except for Brindy and Madame Bonnard.

The funny thing was, Victoria hadn't planned on divulging the secret to Charles's mother, but if she was willing to put her reputation at risk for the sake of her son's happiness, then she deserved to know about her first grandchild.

Incredibly, the baby must have been conceived the first night she and Charles were together. It had been a colossal miscalculation on her part. She knew about prevention, but buying birth control products was too awkward. She couldn't just walk into a pharmacy like anyone else. So she'd decided to take her chances with timing. A very stupid move, as it turned out.

Of course, Charles wasn't to blame. He never imagined the evening would be so passionate. When it had become obvious that things were progressing rapidly, he stammered an apology about not having brought the necessary precautions. She had assured him it was fine, leading him to believe that she was taking something. But she wasn't.

About five weeks later she began to feel unwell in the mornings. Then she gained a few pounds. Soon after, panic set in.

She couldn't confide her secret to anyone at the palace. So Brindy had been her confidant. The contessa had come up with a plan to invite her and her brother to Capri.

It had been thrilling to see Charles again at the villa. He seemed even more charming and special, and she was awed by the ease and sophistication with which he handled everything. There was no doubt in her mind that she loved him.

That weekend she tried to bring up the subject of the baby, but she was afraid it would be too much of a shock for him. What would he think of her?

Victoria came out of her reverie to see Charles enter the restaurant, walking rapidly. As he slid back into his chair, his expression was worried.

"You never mentioned that your sapphire necklace was missing."

"I know. I seem to have lost the silly thing."

"V, that's a big problem."

"Why?"

"Your parents have called Scotland Yard. They think John Sinclair stole it."

Victoria gasped.

"Do you know where you put it?"

Victoria sighed. "That's just it. I had it in my suitcase at the Villa Brindisi, but when I got home, the box was empty."

Charles frowned.

"The household staff at Villa Brindisi would never touch it."

"I know," Victoria said, her eyes serious. "The problem is, I think Karl may have taken it and sold it for cash."

Charles looked shocked. "Are you *sure*?"

"The necklace is missing, and Karl has been gone for almost a week. He couldn't afford to travel on the spending money he had."

"Then we need to find him and the necklace. Scotland Yard is searching for Sinclair."

"Does he know?"

"No. He left the country a few days ago."

"Can't you just call him?"

"No cell phone. What I can do is to go to London to talk to Cordelia and Malik. I want to meet with Sinclair's lawyer. We'll figure it out together."

Victoria felt her sprits sink.

"You mean you have to go away to London for a few days?"

"Or more. I might have to go find Sinclair. Some of his archaeological sites are very remote."

Victoria slumped back against the cushions of the banquette.

"Charles, you can't leave me here!"

"V, don't be silly. I'll only be gone for a day or so."

"But we don't have that kind of time . . ."

Charles looked at her in confusion.

"I don't understand. What do you mean?"

Panic was rising; she needed to tell him about the baby. But this was not the place to say such things. As their voices rose, the couple at the next table glanced over.

"V, what's the matter?" he said, regarding her with alarm.

Somehow, she couldn't tell him. She sat silently, looking at him, taking in the details of his appearance.

The moment was crystal clear. His hair was slightly mussed, and he wore a deep midnight blue suit with a white chambray shirt, fashionably wrinkled. A white hair-elastic was on his wrist, almost hidden by his watch.

"Is that mine?" she asked, touching it.

"Yes, I found it on the terrace."

Her eyes filled with tears.

"What is it darling?" he asked, reaching for her hand.

If she told him about the baby, nothing would ever be the same. Charles Bonnard would be irrevocably altered. The carefree charmer would be gone, and he would have to take on the burden of fatherhood. She didn't want to rob him of his last moment of freedom. The weight of duty and obligation had crushed her for years. How could she do it to someone else?

The room was crowded and loud. The people next to her were entirely too close. She felt her eyes fill with tears.

"Can we go?"

Charles paid quickly and ushered her out of the restaurant. Once they were in the dark street, he put his arms around her.

"Tell me what's wrong. I don't understand."

Just then, a group of people walked by giving them a curious glance. He took her wrist and pulled her along.

"C'mon V, we can't stay here. Let's go somewhere we can talk."

RUE DE VAUGIRARD, PARIS

Madame Bonnard was sitting in her boudoir with her feet up re-reading *Chéri* by Colette. Her concentration was poor. She unwrapped the silver foil from a Fauchon caramel and popped it into her mouth, rolling the buttery flavor across her tongue.

All this business about Charles marrying Princess Victoria was too exciting. Her son had attracted the love of a royal princess and would finally take his proper place in the world. And the prospect of a royal baby was almost too much to consider. Imagine the christening, and a long lace dress, the King and Queen . . . It would be in all the magazines.

Downstairs, she heard the door open, and there was the sound of voices. Charles must be home. *Did he bring the princess back with him?* Madame Bonnard put down the book and tiptoed out to the landing for a peek.

The Bonnard house had four floors and a spiral marble staircase connecting them. In the middle of the landing, there was an ornate and gilded elevator, the kind installed in many European houses at the turn of the century. The shaft was Madame Bonnard's secret listening post. The narrow space served as a sound amplifier, and voices on the ground floor were clearly audible outside her bedroom.

"Don't worry, my mother is asleep," Charles said in a low voice.

Madame Bonnard smiled smugly to herself. Little did he know . . .

" . . . or maybe she's up there eating caramels and reading romantic novels, like she always does."

Madame Bonnard's eyes widened in surprise.

"Where can we talk?" a woman's voice asked, a Norwegian accent clearly discernible.

"Let's go into the salon. No one will disturb us there."

Victoria followed Charles into the living room and put her jacket and purse on the chair. Her lobes ached, as she removed the earrings and shook her long hair out of the braid. She deftly twisted it up into a chignon. Now she felt like herself again.

Charles was watching her silently. He'd become somewhat withdrawn and pensive in the cab on the way home, and he now walked over to the window. The treetops in the park had turned silver in the light of the full moon.

"Tell me what's wrong, *chéri?*" he asked, turning to her. "Aren't you comfortable with the way things are between us?"

She took a deep, shaky breath, uncertain where to begin. "Yes, actually. In fact, I think we should tell my parents about us. You could come back with me."

Charles looked shocked.

"Victoria, I can't just run off to Oslo. There are other things I have to take care of first."

"You mean finding Sinclair?"

"He's facing *criminal* charges. I have to find him. In the meantime, you need to figure out what Karl might have done with that necklace."

"But that is not . . ."

"V, it's really important that we solve this as soon as possible."

Victoria's heart sank. A fatalistic mood came over her. Maybe now was not the right time to tell him about the baby.

"I'm sorry V, but if that necklace doesn't turn up, Sinclair could be facing jail time."

Victoria nodded, almost relieved that the conversation about the pregnancy could be avoided, once again.

"All right, Charles. But don't tell anyone about Karl stealing it. We can't disgrace the family."

"Understood. Now, will you go back to Oslo? All this might take a while."

"She will stay in Paris," a voice said from the doorway.

Madame Bonnard walked into the room with a determined look on her face. Her purple velour robe and high-heeled mules were elegant, and the carriage of her head was imperious.

"Princess Victoria can stay with us while you are away," she said.

"I don't think . . ." Charles started.

She ignored him, turning to Victoria. "Your Royal Highness, you can say that you are consulting with Clothilde on a new wardrobe. I believe you will need some new clothes fairly soon."

Madame Bonnard gave Victoria a raised eyebrow.

"That's perfect," Victoria agreed hastily.

"I'm sure your mother would approve of you being with an established family, instead of on your own."

"I am sure she would prefer it."

Charles looked from one to the other, not understanding what was transpiring.

"I'll go to London tomorrow to talk to Cordelia," he declared.

"Perfect," Madame Bonnard smiled.

Charles picked up his jacket.

"Now, I'd better get Victoria back home to the Norwegian embassy before we have any more trouble. She promised to be back before midnight."

The ride back was not convivial. Charles slumped morosely in the backseat of the cab.

"What's wrong, Charles?"

"I'm not sure it's a good idea to stay in Paris. My mother can be a bit overbearing."

Victoria turned, her expression unreadable.

"Nonsense, I'm delighted to spend some time with her."

"Listen V, she won't be able to resist flaunting you to her friends."

"So you want me to go back to Oslo?"

"Not at all. I know some people who have a big estate close to London. Why don't you stay there? We could see each other privately."

She brightened at the prospect.

"I could invite your sister to come with me. We can discuss a new wardrobe."

"Excellent idea. My sister would love a little vacation after her fashion show. I'll call my friends the Skye-Russells. Cordelia introduced me to them a few years ago. They're a very nice older couple. Their estate, Cliffmere, is an organic farm."

"Oh Charles, that's perfect."

"Now, how do we get permission for you to go?" he asked.

"Its simple really. I just have to ask the protocol office to clear my schedule. They'll send a couple of security men with me, but they don't have to stay on the estate. They can lodge at a nearby inn."

"I'll set it up right away," Charles said patting her hand. "There's a good chance I can come and see you in a day or so. "

RUE DE VAUGIRARD, PARIS

Clothilde took a pencil and sketched out the graceful silhouette of the Norwegian princess. With Victoria as a muse, the new collection would be the sensation of Paris.

There was a light knock at the door.

"Anybody home?" Victoria asked as she stepped into the workroom.

"Come on in. I was just thinking about some new designs."

Victoria bent over the drawing board.

"Mmmm, navy. I never wear that color much."

"It would be stunning with your hair. More sophisticated than pastels."

Victoria sat down on the overstuffed chair and crossed her legs. Clothilde had a quick memory of her brother in that same spot; he and Victoria were a perfect match.

"I need to ask a favor," Victoria said.

"Of course."

"I'll need some new clothes . . . maybe in another month or so."

"I don't follow . . ."

Suddenly she realized what Victoria was hinting at. Without thinking, her eyes fell to her waistline.

Victoria nodded. "I'll start to show soon."

Clothilde sat, staring blankly. The sunlight poured in the studio windows, and the sound of traffic rumbled by on the Rue de Vaugirard. In that instant, she realized that everything had changed.

Charles was going to have a baby, and they would lose him. Neither she nor her mother had ever thought that Charles would marry. He just didn't seem the type. Now he would be off in another country, with his own family. And Norway was so far away!

Clothilde laid her pencil down.

"Are you sure you are . . . ?"

"I'm sure."

"What did Charles say?"

"He doesn't know yet. I only told your mother."

"What! You told Maman, and you didn't tell Charles?"

"Telling your mother seemed the right thing to do, considering the impact on her life."

"But you also need to tell Charles, right away!"

It was only then that Clothilde noticed the red-rimmed eyes and the dark circles. The princess clearly had not been sleeping.

"I'm sorry, I didn't mean to . . ."

Victoria sighed. "After he finds Sinclair. In the meantime, he thinks I should go away to England to stay with friends of his. I would love it if you would come with me. We could work on a wardrobe together."

Clothilde looked up in surprise.

"Oh, that would be wonderful. I've been stuck in Paris all summer."

Victoria smiled. "So you'll come?"

Clothilde grinned. "Getting out of Paris will do us both a world of good. And there's nothing like a quilted English Barbour coat to hide a baby bump for a week or two."

25 THE NORTH COLONNADE, CANARY WHARF, LONDON

At 1:00 p.m. Detective Jaccorsi stepped out of his hotel in London, wearing a silk Armani suit and dark sunglasses. He had splurged on new clothes, figuring it would be better to look sharp in London. He was meeting with the big boys. British Special Intelligence Service, also known as MI6, and the British Financial Conduct Authority, or FCA. MI6 was pushing hard for any possible shred of evidence against Mondragone. Prosecution would be primarily on financial malfeasance. There would be charges of money laundering and racketeering.

Three different national governments were cooperating: the British, the Italians, and the Americans. Up until now, Britain's National Crime Agency had left Mondragone alone. But now, everyone had decided that enough was enough, and Mondragone was in the crosshairs.

Jaccorsi checked the sky, uncertain whether he'd need an umbrella. The street was still wet from the morning rain, but the precipitation had stopped. London had strange weather—island weather. He climbed into the spacious backseat of a taxi and gave an address. As traffic lumbered, he watched pedestrians rushing to work, jumping over puddles on Oxford Street.

Jaccorsi's destination was the East End, Canary Wharf, where the world's most prestigious banking firms were located. Ironically, they were cheek by jowl with the FCA—a government watchdog agency that was in charge of banking regulations.

At the ground-floor security desk at 25 The North Colonnade,

Jaccorsi went through the prerequisite sign in, searching through his wallet for his identification. His contact was waiting on the twelfth floor to greet him.

MacDonnell was a Scotsman, and at 260 pounds, he was a walking indictment of his nation's diet of meat pies and pints. After a painful hand crush, he made the usual pleasant inquires about hotels and traffic. With the strong Glaswegian burr, Jaccorsi only understood a fraction of what he said. Finally, after what seemed like miles of corridors, they entered a glass-paneled office with a minimalist steel desk.

The view of the Thames was a conversation stopper. Jaccorsi removed his sunglasses and paid silent homage to London in all its glory. In the morning light, the serpentine river shone gunmetal gray. The Union Jack snapped briskly from the roofs of the surrounding buildings. MacDonnell heaved his bulk into an ergonomic chair and sighed. Jaccorsi carefully pulled up the knees of his trousers before he sat down.

The intercom buzzed.

"What is it Mary?" MacDonnell barked.

"Your trip to the States is cancelled, sir. The airport is closed."

"All right. Thank you."

"Is that a problem?" Jaccorsi inquired.

MacDonnell shrugged, indifferent.

"The guys at FinCEN will have to wait."

"FinCEN?"

"Financial Crimes Enforcement Unit. It's a division of the US Treasury."

"So the Americans are prosecuting also?" Jaccorsi asked.

"Yes. But with the planes grounded, I can't go anywhere. It might set the case back a day or two, but the noose is closing in on Mondragone. We're about to shut down his banking accounts."

"I'm glad."

MacDonnell smiled. "So detective, tell me, what do *you* know about Cyclops?"

KENSINGTON PALACE GARDENS, "BILLIONAIRE'S ROW," LONDON

Detective Jaccorsi had been warned to stay away from Salvatore Mondragone's house in Kensington. It was good advice in theory, but the temptation proved too much. So after his meeting at FCA, he took a taxi and stood diagonally across the street, casing the place.

The residence was a beautiful Edwardian house on "billionaire's row"—a line of embassies and private residences in London's most expensive neighborhood.

The utter size of the mansion was a shock. Somehow in the squalor of Naples, Mondragone's vast wealth could be overlooked. The little villa in the Naples suburb of Torre del Greco was not particularly lavish. But here in London, Cyclops lived like a prince financed by dirty money.

Jaccorsi shook his head in disgust. Thank God the Brits were going to prosecute. This was disgusting. But there was not much he could do about it himself. Procedures were moving slowly. But, by all estimates, Mondragone would be apprehended by the end of the month. Until then, Jaccorsi knew he would have to remain in London.

The detective glanced at his watch. It was too early for dinner, but there was plenty of time for a nice walk. He turned and headed to the lovely green oasis of Hyde Park.

His friend John Sinclair lived on Grosvenor Street. Maybe he'd cut straight through the park to Mayfair. They'd have a drink together. Sinclair was the only person he knew socially in London, and right now he needed a friend.

The British lifestyle was wearing on him: difficult accents, briskly impersonal pleasantries, and tasteless food. There was no decent pasta, and he simply couldn't eat another potato. A visit with Sinclair would boost his spirits.

Twenty minutes later, Jaccorsi lifted the knocker on John Sinclair's door and let it fall with a heavy bang. He wasn't expected, but Sinclair didn't usually stand on ceremony.

The knob turned, and a young man in a crisp linen tunic opened the door.

"Yes. May I help you, sir?"

"Does Mr. Sinclair live here?'

"Yes, sir. But he is not home at the moment."

Jaccorsi felt his spirits sink.

"Tell him the Detective Jaccorsi of the Naples police was here to see him."

The young man frowned.

"We have already talked to Scotland Yard, sir."

Jaccorsi stammered in confusion.

"No . . . no, I'm a friend. This has nothing to do with law enforcement."

"Oh. I see. Well, he's not in the country, sir."

Jaccorsi scribbled a phone number on the back of his business card.

"Would you please give him this when he returns?"

The young man examined the card carefully.

"I'll tell him you called."

"Thank you so much," Jaccorsi replied and walked down the steps to the street.

Salvatore Mondragone's men watched Jaccorsi approach the elegant townhouse and converse with the young butler.

They followed him across the park. Jaccorsi was ridiculously obvious about casing Mondragone's house. Did he really think he blended in wearing a black silk suit and Armani sunglasses? Even in the grainy video from the surveillance camera on the roof, his clothing screamed southern Italy.

"Doesn't that guy look familiar?" one of the Camorra guards asked, staring at the security monitor.

They zoomed in to get more detail of Jaccorsi's face.

"Yes, it's that detective from Naples. I know him well. He put my cousin in prison."

They watched him walking along the sidewalk and trailed him all through Hyde Park to Mayfair. Now, at the townhouse on Grosvenor Street, the conversational exchange between the detective and the butler seemed brief. Something passed between them, a slip of paper or a note.

"Let's find out who lives there," Mondragone's security man said. "Whoever it is, they're working with the police."

LIBRARY, GROSVENOR STREET

Cordelia glanced over at Charles Bonnard, lounging in a leather chair in her library. The word "disheveled" pretty much summed up his appearance. He had pulled his tie loose, and his suit was rumpled beyond redemption. They had been at it for hours, trying to figure out how to locate Sinclair.

Now it was early evening. Sinclair's dog, Kyrie, was at her feet. The small circle of light from the table lamp cast shadows, creating a cozy feeling of intimacy. She sighed heavily and looked up at the wall of bookcases, deep in thought.

The room had twenty-foot ceilings and ornate second-floor iron balconies that gave access to the upper reaches of the stacks. Tonight the shelves were cloaked in darkness, except for the occasional shimmer of gilt on the spine of an old book.

Everything here had once belonged to Cordelia's great-great-grandfather, Elliott Stapleton. He had been a renowned Victorian explorer and had used this library for planning his expeditions.

"Do you suppose that Malik is telling the truth?" Charles suddenly asked.

"About what?"

"About not knowing where Sinclair is?"

"Oh, he would be too terrified to lie to Scotland Yard."

"What did he tell them, exactly?"

"That Sinclair took the Eurostar to Paris."

"And they believed that?"

"They're checking. If John crossed any borders they can find out."

"Could he have gone to Ephesus?"

"No. If he went to Turkey he would have brought Malik."

Kyrie's ears twitched at a word she knew. Cordelia trailed a hand down to give the dog a gentle stroke.

"I can't understand why John is so out of touch. He was supposed to call Malik once he got to where he was going."

Charles sighed and shook his head.

"When he's upset he usually goes off on a dig and disappears. Let me tell you, it's hard to run the foundation when he's like that."

"It's ridiculous," she fumed. "How *dare* he just fall off the map."

Just as the word left her lips, her gaze rested on an enormous table piled high with a dozen atlases and loose charts.

"*Map!*"

"What of it?"

"I just thought of something," Cordelia exclaimed.

She strode over and began leafing through the charts. Sinclair's messiness had a benefit; he always left a paper trail. Somewhere on this table was a topographical map of the place where he had gone. The only problem would be figuring out which one of the archaeological sites he had chosen.

Cordelia tossed aside a nautical chart of the Mediterranean and focused on the land drawings, scanning the maps of Greece, Turkey, and Italy. Charles hung over her shoulder.

"Where do you think?"

"I just don't know . . ." Cordelia trailed off. "Hit the switch on the wall bracket over there. I want to see something."

A large brass lamp was hung above the library table. Cordelia blinked in the sudden glare.

"Sinclair always works with the lights on, so he can see all the details," she explained, looking through a magnifying glass and lowering her nose inches from the paper.

"What are you looking for?"

"A pencil mark."

She laid the magnifying glass down and raised the chart up to the light, scanning the Tyrrhenian Sea. Still nothing. Then she tried the reverse, flipping the paper over to the blank side. In the harsh illumination she could see a pimple where a pencil had pressed down on the paper.

"I think I have it!"

Moving the magnifying glass over the paper, she confirmed that there was a raised bump, barely visible, made by a pencil point.

Cordelia turned the map over to look for the corresponding location on the printed side.

"Sicily," she announced.

"He went *back* to Italy?"

"This is a dig in Morgantina."

Charles looked at her in astonishment.

"I can't believe you found him!"

"I've seen him do this a hundred times. He says, 'That's it!' and dots the place on the map."

"Thank you, Delia. I'll take a train and find him. I'll be back in a week or so."

"A *week*?"

Charles counted off on his fingers.

"Three days to get there by train, a day or so to find him, and another three days to come back. Commercial planes aren't flying yet."

"What other options do we have?"

"We could send someone. Brindy's in Italy."

"Would she get him?"

"I don't see why not. I'll give her a call."

"What will you do in the meantime? Go back to Paris?"

Charles rubbed his face and then looked over at her, trying to decide.

"No, I'd better stay here in London. That way I can meet with Scotland Yard."

"Can't you do that by phone?"

"Well, Victoria is visiting nearby in Oxfordshire, so I can go see her."

"Whom is she staying with?"

"Tom and Marion Skye-Russell."

Cordelia started in surprise. "The *Skye-Russells*? Whatever for?"

"I suggested it. V needs to get out of Paris. And don't worry, she's under supervision. Clothilde is with her. That should keep everything on an even keel."

"She's certainly gotten hold of your family, hasn't she?"

"Yes, my mother already adores her."

There was an awkward silence as Cordelia tried not to comment.

Charles stood up and stretched. "Well I'd better be going. I haven't booked a hotel yet."

"Don't be silly. Stay here."

He smiled, embarrassed. "I've brought you so much trouble already."

"You *have* to stay. I will be very offended if you don't," she insisted.

"Are you sure you don't mind?"

"Actually I hate to admit it, but I'd feel safer with you upstairs."

"What about Kyrie? She seems like a good watchdog."

"Totally useless," Cordelia laughed. "She'd make friends with Jack the Ripper if he had a biscuit."

Charles laughed.

"Well I'm happy to play bodyguard, for you, if that's what you want. Is it this way?"

"Right upstairs. Top floor. I'll show you."

"Oh, don't bother," Charles said, collecting his jacket. "I can find everything I need."

"Well, holler if you don't."

"Absolutely. Goodnight, Delia. See you in the morning."

CATANIA, SICILY

The second biggest city on the island of Sicily stood in the shadow of Mount Etna. The residents of Catania had seen many eruptions, some cataclysmic. The worst had been in 1669 when lava had flowed through the streets, killing more than 20,000 people.

The volcano brought blessings as well as death. Ash contributed to the fertile soil, giving the local wine a wonderful flavor. Tourists flocked to see the steaming caldera, which boosted the local economy.

Over the years, Jude Blackwell climbed Mount Etna many times. Now, the seismic readings were showing that a catastrophic eruption might be imminent.

There had been fluctuating vibration levels with an increase in gas and ground deformation. Magma was moving below the surface. Each volcano had a seismic signature, or a pattern of vibrations that were considered normal. Volcanologists usually noticed when something was different, but not always. Sometimes other things could interfere with the reading: a herd of elk, a hovering helicopter, snowfall, avalanches, or earthquakes could look the same on a printout.

Often, the tremors would diminish. Then, at other times, an eruption could occur with very little warning at all. In the end, no one could predict the exact timing of when a volcano would erupt.

And that posed a problem, because the local people made a nice living guiding tourists to the summit and selling food and souvenirs to anyone who rode the cable car up the mountain. Curtailing visitor activity had an immediate impact on the economy.

This morning readings were intensifying. Soon they would increase the alert level to "orange," which would mean that the volcano would be exhibiting "heightened levels" and "increased potential of eruption." During an orange alert, tourists would be stopped from ascending by funicular.

As he stood in the main monitoring station, Jude stared at the screens. Real-time cameras recorded the action. The Institute of Geophysics and Volcanology was buzzing. Several Italian volcanologists huddled, discussing the possibility of the Civil Defense Authority shutting down the cable car.

If he was going to photograph the summit, the time to do it was now. Jude left the volcano center and walked briskly back to where he was staying.

It was a low-budget hotel. The lobby was forlorn, with a plastic plant, a crudely painted mural of Mount Etna, and a weary desk clerk.

Jude gave the man a nod and took the elevator to his room. All his equipment had been laid out in advance. Much of it was beaten up, frayed, and scorched.

There were silver, heat-resistant aluminized coveralls and a helmet, along with a glass-paneled facemask with a bias-cut shoulder-gusset that served as a neck protector. Gauntlet-style gloves covered his hands to the elbow with shiny silver fabric that could reflect high heat. Every article of clothing was stitched with special Kevlar thread.

He staked his life on his footwear. Ordinary running shoes would melt. So he always wore Hathorn Explorer boots, the kind forest firefighters wore. They had specially formulated vibram soles, and were constructed without the normal metal instep, which would heat up.

The last necessary piece of equipment was a self-contained breathing apparatus. That was absolutely critical for protection from noxious gasses.

Most scientists would never approve of him going up Mount Etna during an orange alert. But this was a final farewell to the profession.

The near miss in Iceland gave him the jitters. The past few nights were rough, and the nightmares were increasing. After he sold these pictures, he was planning on retiring from volcanology and switching to fashion photography. From now on, the hottest thing he wanted to photograph would be a Brazilian model in a thong.

MOUNT ETNA, ITALY

Renato Balboni knelt on the floor of the men's room and felt around in his backpack until his fingers came into contact with the cold steel of the Beretta. He shifted the gun to his outside jacket pocket and zipped it.

The boys were climbing Mount Etna today. It was the ideal place to kidnap the prince. Up until now there was no opportunity. There were too many witnesses in the city streets. But up on the mountain, no one would see.

He stood to check his appearance in the mirror. Hard, flat eyes stared back at him, wool cap pulled low across his brow. In this outfit, he looked like a classic thug.

Renato curved his mouth into a disarming smile, brightened his eyes, and set his cap at an awkward angle. The transformation was miraculous. Here was a novice mountain climber, ready to climb Mount Etna. He picked up his backpack. It was time to make friends with Karl and Luca.

Prince Karl and Luca Brindisi stood at 6,200 feet on Mount Etna in an area known as Rifugio Sapienza. It was a typical staging area for mountain climbers. The facilities included souvenir kiosks, restrooms, a snack bar, and a coffee shop. Karl checked the zippered pockets of his backpack: energy bars, water, and extra fleece jackets. They were both wearing jeans. The thick denim would protect them from cuts and scrapes, and if there were any kind of eruption, the cotton fabric would not melt in extreme heat.

A few dozen tourists in shorts and T-shirts hung around waiting for the cable car. Most would stay for a few minutes at the midpoint and then descend. But Karl and Luca wanted to climb higher and that meant a trained guide should accompany them to the top.

Karl scanned around for a likely candidate and noticed a young man in an official tour company parka. He waved, and the man came jogging over.

"Do you need an escort?" the guide asked in heavily accented English.

"Yes, could you take us up?" Karl asked.

"Of course."

Luca conducted the rest of the interview in Italian. Matteo, as he was called, produced solid credentials. He was a former Italian military officer and belonged to several alpine associations in Europe. His current position was with the local guiding service ITAL-TREK, which maintained several vehicles on the upper slope of Mount Etna.

"I have summited this mountain three hundred times," Matteo said.

Karl gave him a quick nod, and they immediately came to terms on a timetable and a price. Satisfied, Matteo looked at his watch and suggested they leave immediately. The funicular would close in a few hours, but there was enough time for a quick ascent.

Karl turned to Luca. "Are you sure you want to summit?"

"Absolutely," Luca assured him.

They both walked with Matteo to the cable car. Just as they reached the funicular, another man came rushing up to them, slightly out of breath.

"May I join your group?"

Matteo shook his head, no. "I'm already engaged by these two gentlemen. But I'm sure you can find some else."

The man seemed very distressed. "No one is available. Please. I'll pay you double."

Karl saw Matteo's eyes light up at the prospect of earning more money.

"Would that be a problem?" the guide asked the boys.

"No, it's fine," Karl agreed.

"*Grazia mille.*" The man beamed. "I've traveled all this way, and I didn't want to miss it."

They shook hands all around, the stranger smiling happily.

"My name is Renato."

Karl pointed to his chest "I'm Karl, and this is Luca."

With that, they stepped over to the cable car.

There was no waiting in line; only a dozen people were willing to ascend. Matteo explained there was going to be a "code orange" later that afternoon, and they'd have to move quickly.

The cable car arrived in the station. Karl and Luca got on first, crossing to the far side to claim the uphill view. Matteo and Renato stepped in with the other tourists. The doors swung shut with a pneumatic wheeze, and the cabin lurched forward to begin the ascent.

Suddenly, they were suspended twenty feet over the barren slope. It was a smooth, silent glide as everyone took in the scenery. Karl looked down at the great expanse of black cinders. Some patches of ground were as smooth as glass, while others were rough with gravel and sand. As the little car gained altitude, the earth became darker and more charred in appearance.

The connecting axle of the cable car bumped over a thirty-foot support tower, and there was a nervous titter of laughter. Karl turned to see Luca white-faced and grim. He was silently looking up, his hands still gripping the handrail. Karl followed his line of sight. Above them, the smoking cone of the volcano loomed like a malevolent beast.

"I'm not too good with heights," Luca confessed.

"We'll be on the ground in a minute. Do you feel strong enough to climb?"

Luca nodded.

"You don't mind this other guy coming with us, do you?"

"No, I'm glad. It's always safer to have a few people together."

Renato looked at the two boys on the far side of the cable car surveying the scenery. He was calculating his odds of kidnapping the prince.

It would not be a problem to overpower the boys. The Italian kid looked weak, and Karl was just a teenager. Neither of them would have enough nerve to resist a gun.

As the cable car approached its highest point, the wheels glided to a stop. The doors whooshed open, and everyone headed to the exit.

This was the terminus for tourists. There were restrooms and places for taking photos. The drink counter was doing a brisk business in hot chocolate, and there were multiple advertisements for a red liquor, a local 70-proof concoction, called Fuoco dell'Etna—Fire of Etna.

This staging area was not a good place to tarry on a day like today. Most of the visitors shivered through their snapshots and hurried inside the shed to wait for the ride down. The cable car operators were issuing warnings. The mountain might have to be evacuated by this afternoon.

An involuntary shiver shook Renato's body. It was freezing. At the higher elevations, it would be even colder. At the guide's insistence they had all donned warmer clothing—puffy down jackets and fleece—supplied by the tour company.

Renato looked up at the mountain. The volcano was smoking heavily against a perfect china-blue sky, and the noise was ominous: a deep rumble, alternating with high shrieks of off-gassing. He felt his nerves jump. It sounded like incoming rocket fire.

"We have to make this quick," Matteo said. "They're closing the mountain in a few hours."

"How will we go up?" Renato asked.

"We'll drive to 9,000 feet and walk up from there."

Matteo led the way over to a row of 4x4 jeeps with the logo of the guide company printed on the door. He unlocked the vehicle and climbed in the driver's seat. The boys took the backseat, leaving the front passenger side for Renato.

They set off, the vehicle straining up the incline. Matteo explained that the road was built directly over the cooled lava field, a remnant from the last eruption. The rutted track was a winding single lane with steep drop-offs on either side.

"This is the Torre del Filosofo, or Tower of the Philosopher, named after the famous Greek sage Empedocles who died on the summit."

Matteo began a tourist monologue, and Renato listened intently—anything to distract himself from the horrible sounds of explosions in the distance.

Matteo droned on. Mount Etna was one of the most active volcanoes in the world, and its eruptions could be observed from the International Space Station.

Suddenly, the guide stopped mid-sentence, cranking the steering wheel around a hairpin turn. The falloff was sheer cliff. Renato snuck a glance back at the two boys. The Italian kid looked pale with worry, but the prince was staring down the chasm with a grin on his face.

The guide resumed his recitation. Etna was designated as a so-called Decade Volcano—there were only sixteen in the world, so labeled by the International Association of Volcanology and Chemistry of the Earth's Interior. That moniker meant that it was one of the most dangerous volcanoes in the world, based on the proximity of the local population and the potential loss of life.

The volcano sent up a deafening explosion. Everyone flinched except Matteo, who hand-over-handed the steering wheel onto a narrow overlook. He parked and set the emergency brake.

"*Andiamo,*" he said briskly.

They all climbed out. This parking spot was a mere ledge with a flimsy wooden guardrail. From here a steep track meandered through the barren landscape. All around were large shards of broken rock. Matteo handed out pairs of leather gloves.

"OK *regazzi,*" he said, "There may be some volcanic activity, so we have to make it quick. The climb takes an hour, and we'll have about ten minutes at the summit."

They all looked at him, speechless.

"If any of you think it's too much, there's a hut right here where you can wait out of the wind. But once we start climbing, nobody leaves the group. Understand?"

Matteo turned to Luca. "Are you going to be all right?"

"Yes, I'm good to go," Luca insisted.

"OK then. Keep your wits about you. If there is any activity, stay close to me," the guide warned.

"Do you expect a sudden eruption?" Karl asked.

"Possibly," Matteo affirmed, "Sometimes we'll see a burst of lava fountaining and have to wait until it subsides. It doesn't happen often."

"Do you think we'll get an eruption today?" Luca asked.

"Maybe later. We had a small plume of ash yesterday, and there was a small trickle of lava not far from here, but nothing more. We'll be OK for the moment."

Karl looked over at the others. Renato was quiet, studying the slope with a focused look. Luca's lips were chattering. It was hard to tell whether it was from fear or the wind.

"Cold?" Karl asked.

"No, I'm OK."

"Re-tie your bootlaces," Matteo instructed. "I don't want any stumbles."

They knelt down and made sure their laces were tight and the knots secure.

"Karl first," Matteo decided. "Then Luca, then me. And Renato, you take up the rear."

They all set off at a steady pace, the wind tearing at their clothes and whipping their hair. Karl felt the lift of pure adrenaline as he looked out over the ash fields. It was a raw and desolate place, smelling of sulfur, a rare glimpse of where the earth's molten underworld revealed itself on the surface.

Karl forged ahead of the others. The fragments of lava crackled underfoot like shards of broken glass. At times, there were streaks of black cinders they had to wade across. It was extremely slippery underfoot. In some sections, the slope was so steep they had to place their hands on the ground and scramble up on all fours using ragged pieces of rock to pull themselves along. Without gloves, it would have been impossible.

Karl felt his leg muscles heat up, his calves knotted with painful cramps. After a mile or so of tough going, Matteo called a halt.

The wind was fierce now. The guide pulled out a few pairs of goggles and handed them out.

"These will protect you from the flying particles of light basaltic rock."

They all put them on. Matteo checked his watch, gave them a brisk nod, and set off at a steady pace.

As they climbed, the air seemed to get thinner, and soon Karl was panting. After about twenty minutes, Matteo called another stop at a natural plateau. He leaned over and picked up a solid black chunk of hardened lava.

"*Questa e una bomba,*" he remarked, holding it out for them to see. "This is a bomb."

Everyone leaned in, so they could hear. He explained that the rock had been tossed skyward during an explosive eruption. Volcanic bombs were not lava, but igneous rocks. They could range in diameter, up to the size of a basketball.

"How do you know when these rock-bombs are going to start flying?" Luca asked.

"It's usually during 'code red.' They can land up to fifteen miles away. But don't worry—nobody is allowed up here during code red."

The guide gestured to the ground beneath their feet. During flowing eruptions, he explained, the melted lava would run down the hillside like burning liquid syrup. In the case of stratovolcanoes, this liquid lava would harden and build up. It was sometimes possible to walk over lava when it cooled. The configurations looked like twisted ropes on the ground. He cautioned them never to step in molten lava, or they would suffer serious burns.

Matteo pointed to the sky. "Quick! Look up there,"

Karl saw a perfectly formed smoke ring floating above the summit.

"Is the volcano doing *that*?" Luca asked, agog.

"Yes. Etna is one of the few volcanoes in the world that can blow steam circles," Matteo explained. "The crater on top is shaped like a mouth."

"That's enormous!" Luca exclaimed.

"Each ring is about 600 feet across," Matteo recited, "and can rise up to 3,500 feet in the air."

"Unbelievable!" Luca said in awe.

Karl grinned. "Aren't you glad you came?"

Before Luca could answer, he fell to the ground, gasping for air.

"What's wrong?" Karl asked.

"I feel dizzy."

"Rest a minute," Matteo encouraged. "Drink some water. Maybe this is as far as we can go."

Karl glanced up the hill to gauge the distance to the summit.

"Do you think you can make it?" he asked.

"No," Luca gasped. "I'm sorry."

"But it's only about 300 feet more," Karl encouraged.

Luca didn't respond. He tore off his goggles, doubled over, and retched on the ground.

"Maybe a touch of altitude sickness," Matteo declared. "Not bad. He'll be OK. He needs to rest. We might have to go down now."

"Can't we leave him for a moment?" Karl asked. "I could just run up there and take a peek at the caldera."

"No," Matteo, said firmly. "I'd have to accompany you. We're not allowed to leave a client alone, not even for a minute."

Renato stepped forward. "I could stay with him."

"No, wait. I can make it," Luca said, wiping his mouth on his sleeve. He wobbled and attempted to stand up.

Matteo shook his head, grimly. "No, I don't think you should go up."

"Yes! I can do it," Luca rallied. "Let me try."

He straightened up with determination. Karl helped him on with his pack, and Luca stood before the guide, wobbly but determined. Matteo scanned the group, skeptically.

"OK, but we need to stay together."

"Fine," Luca said and started up the path.

Karl followed, watching closely.

Halfway around the first switchback, Renato assessed the condition of the boy. Luca was staggering along with his head down, concentrating on getting to the top. Karl was distracted by his friend's weakness.

Now was the time to make his move. Renato unzipped the outside pocket of his jacket and fingered the pistol. The guide would be the first to die, then the Italian boy. He'd force Karl back down the slope and then they'd take the jeep and drive down the mountain and grab the ferry to Naples. A plan was formed. Renato caught up to the boys.

Karl stood at the lip of the South-East Voragine Crater with Matteo next to him. They were both panting heavily. Climbing to 11,000 feet was tough. Karl bent over, resting his hands on his knees.

All around them, a fog-like mist crept across the landscape. The volcanic miasma seeped up out of the crater and flowed over the lip, bringing with it the sickening stench of sulfur.

"Luca!" Karl shouted over to him. "Just one second. I'll take a quick look and then we'll go down right away."

Luca waved and gave him the OK sign. He sat on the ground, gray faced and breathing heavily.

"Go ahead. Take a look," Luca called over.

Karl moved closer to the edge of the caldera, trying to see if there was a lava lake. But the lip of the crater was too deep, with no view of the bottom. The magma would be 1,000 feet down. Still, he could see a faint glow from the interior of the pit. Molten particles were spewing up regularly as if the volcano were juggling hot rocks.

Karl watched for a minute, entranced. The projectiles looked like glowing orange tennis balls that rose and fell. A timpani chorus of booms and explosions were coming from inside the mountain.

Matteo put a hand on Karl's arm with a cautionary gesture. All around were signs that pointed to the potential hazard:

Attenzione/Attention

Pericolo/Danger

"Is this the main crater?" Karl yelled, gesturing to the open pit.

"Yes, but there are more. Voragine is the largest. This is normal Strombolian activity. Etna is always active."

Karl unzipped his parka. "Is it getting warm, or am I just feeling that way from the climb?"

"It's a lot hotter standing on the edge," Matteo affirmed. "We're safe here, but we wouldn't want to get any closer. Sometimes the rim collapses. We lost a hiker at this exact spot about ten years ago."

Just then they heard a loud rumbling lower down in the pit. Karl flinched. Matteo scanned the other peaks a half mile away, and a dark gray cauliflower-shaped cloud of ash was billowing out of the earth.

"The eruption is over there," Matteo indicated with a gloved finger. "That crater is called Bocca Nuova. It's sending up ash. I think it's time to leave."

Just as he said it, the far crater started off-gassing. The noise was a low fizz that immediately climbed to a jet-engine whine. The decibel level was deafening.

Matteo turned and shouted over the racket.

"Let's go! It's too dangerous to stay!"

Karl looked over and saw Luca gesturing emphatically at Renato, shouting something.

That's when Karl saw the danger.

At the National Institute of Geophysics and Volcanology monitoring station in Catania, the chief scientist picked up the phone. Mount

Etna was starting to erupt. As with all stratovolcanoes, it was almost impossible to predict the exact timing of an eruption. They had been expecting some activity, but nothing of this magnitude. He had to alert the Civil Defense authorities. Sawhorses were set up on the roads surrounding the volcano, in the event they needed to block traffic. The mountain was completely evacuated, but the ITAL-TREK tour company reported that a few tourists were still unaccounted for.

There was no time to lose. Lava fountaining had begun, and dense fallout of ash was being recorded three miles away. The reservoir of magma about twenty miles beneath the summit was becoming super-heated from the friction of tectonic plates. Within the hour, huge sheets of flame would shoot up into the sky and everything on the slope would be destroyed.

Karl shouted "No!"

Matteo saw the glint of a gun muzzle. Then there was a burn in his chest. Another pain bloomed in his shoulder. All of it happened silently. The sound of the pistol was drowned out by the volcano. Time stopped, and there was only searing agony.

His legs collapsed, and he fell to the ground. His cheek was pressed into the basaltic gravel, as if weights were holding him down. Blood was pooling on the ground, soaking into the volcanic rock particles.

Painfully, he turned his head. The lip of the volcano was only two feet away. Foul gasses were pouring out in heavier concentrations. Molten lava would soon follow. He closed his eyes in despair. He was dying. His body would be buried in the eruption. No one would ever know what happened.

Karl looked in horror as the guide lay gasping, eyes glazed over. He had no idea how to save Matteo. *Renato had shot him!* The gunman's eyes were hard, and his mouth turned down in a sneer. This was not the jovial fellow who joined them on the lower slope.

Slowly, the pistol swiveled toward Luca. The boy sat on the ground, cowering in fright, with no ability to resist or flee. Something had to be done, or Luca would die.

Karl felt a hot flush of panic. He could not give in to fear. He had to do something quickly. The only thing in his possession was a small backpack. But, weighing about thirty pounds, it might be of some help. He held it by the strap and sprinted across the distance, swinging it in a wide arc.

Karl let out a huge bellow, to draw Renato's attention away from Luca. The gunman turned at the noise, and his eyes widened. It was too late to duck. The bulk of the pack slammed solidly into Renato's chest, driving him toward the edge of the volcano. As he stumbled backward, his foot hit a rough patch of scoriae.

The next moments played out in agonizing detail. Renato's mouth opened into a perfect O as one foot left the ground. He balanced on one leg, flailing wildly. His body, top heavy with the weight of his backpack, cantilevered toward the yawning chasm. Arms windmilled in an attempt to fight the pull of gravity, but the desperate struggle was too late.

Slowly, as if in a dream, Renato toppled into the volcano.

Karl stood motionless as the gunman did a backward somersault, his form splayed against the glowing sparks. And then Renato was gone.

Karl gasped in horror.

It was unbelievable. He just killed a man. The look on Renato's face as he tumbled would haunt him forever.

Karl turned back to Luca and saw his friend slumped on the ground panting like a sick dog. Luca was almost in complete collapse.

Karl started toward his friend. A deep trembling under his feet told him there was no time to lose. Mount Etna was erupting!

Luca realized that several of the vents near him were shooting up hot gasses. Suddenly, molten lava oozed out of the earth and started down-hill. It was glowing orange. Longer and longer it came, never ending.

"We have to leave, now!"

"What's happening?" Luca asked confused.

Karl spoke urgently. "Forget it. We have to go!"

Karl started down the trail, and all around him the ghostly vapors of volcanic emissions floated up out of the ground. He tried to place his boots carefully, so as not to step on the molten lava streams. Walking downhill, it was difficult to stay upright. Tremors shook the ground, nearly knocking him down.

Visibility was awful. The particles of black ash were as dense as a blizzard. The volcano behind them was belching sparks and ash. Off-gassing sounded like bottle rockets. The intensity of the eruption convulsed the earth under their feet.

Karl had no idea if they had wandered away from the main trail. This seemed to be the way, but the risks of going astray were considerable. There was the danger of getting stuck in a ravine, or ending up wandering aimlessly across the landscape. That would be catastrophic, as new fissures were opening up every minute.

Then, suddenly, through the vapor Karl had a glimpse of something square and solid. There was a building! The outlines of it were barely visible in the smoke. As they approached, he could see it was the climbing hut. They had barely glanced at the structure on the way up, but now Karl realized it was the perfect place to seek shelter. The building was fashioned into the earth like a root cellar with a stout wooden door and a tile roof.

Karl let go of Luca's arm and walked over to read the sign on the door. An orange neon sign was nailed to the wood planks with the word VULCANO. Karl pushed the door open and bent down to enter.

As he stepped inside the climbing hut, it was suffocating, like drawing breath inside an oven. He took off his parka and jettisoned it. Luca stumbled in and fell onto the floor, gasping.

"Thank God," he mumbled.

"Drink some water," Karl advised, handing him his backpack.

Luca began looking for his water as Karl began to rummage around. The interior of the hut was very dark, and there was not much to see: a wooden bench; a built-in cot with a flame-retardant mattress; a large, red metal box containing medical supplies. Several aluminum cylinders with breathing masks were mounted on the walls. Karl examined them and realized the air canisters were bolted and secured by a thin band of metal.

He seized a mask and placed it over his face. It was not like a scuba regulator. This was a full respirator that covered the entire nose and mouth. Karl turned the valve and breathed in, filling his lungs with air. Then he set one up for Luca.

After two or three inhalations, Karl's head stopped spinning. His mind cleared. He was finally able to think. He now understood why they had been attacked.

Renato had followed them up the mountain. Why would someone come after two kids like that? Karl felt a flush of shame. *All this must have something to do with the stolen necklace.*

Jude Blackwell photographed Mount Etna and filled two 64 GB San-Disc memory cards with digital images. The caldera was deserted. He had climbed using the little-used western route. By the time he finished taking his photos, activity was visibly picking up. Pea-sized pebbles of glowing rock were pelting the earth; the Strombolian activity was reaching the height of the crater rim.

Conditions were deteriorating, and the downward trek would be treacherous. As he started down, he could feel the heat through his thermal boots. His "hot suit" was keeping him from being burned, and the stiff fabric chafed his elbows and knees.

He rapidly retreated back down the slope, keeping his eyes on the ground. There were only the faintest of marks made by previous climbers; the indentations of boot treads, barely discernable. He trudged down blearily, eyes watering from the sting of chemicals. Mercifully, his air supply partially eliminated the stench of sulfuric off-gasses.

Rather than dwell on the danger, he focused on the mission. The trip was a success. He made it to the top and got some incredible shots just as the activity picked up.

He reached a ridge and looked out over the barren landscape. As far as he could see, fissures had opened up, and hot gasses were shooting out like steam from a boiling kettle. Visibility diminished as the ash blocked out the sun. In the dim twilight, molten lava streaks were glowing like orange ribbons trailing down the slope.

The noise from the mountain was exactly like the sound of combat. The rhythm varied: the volley of pistol shot, the stutter of a machine gun, or a sound like a supersonic jet. Sparks cascaded like a fireworks display. There was no question in his mind—this "code orange" was rapidly deteriorating to "code red."

He flinched as a rock whizzed by, missing him by inches. Volcanic bombs were starting, and one of them would kill him outright if he didn't take shelter soon. It was time for a strategic decision. He'd go into a nearby climbing shed, then pick a lull in the activity to continue his descent.

The ground shook with a deep cough. There was a convulsive rumble, and a blaze lit up the mountain. For a beautiful, awful moment the peak was silhouetted in a perfect ring of fire.

Jude shouted in surprise and glanced quickly at the distance to the door of the hut—only a short sprint away. As the debris rained down, he hurtled himself through the opening.

It was like diving into an inferno. He stumbled over something on the floor at the doorsill. Overbalancing in the awkward suit, he fell forward, losing his footing entirely, and landed on something soft in the dark.

There was the squish of a body and the feel of bones. Trying to get a better view of what had tripped him up, he ripped off his hood and goggles. A pair of eyes was staring at him in the dim interior.

The figure spoke to him.

"Have you come to save us?"

It was a teenage boy: thin, dark-haired, and bug-eyed with terror. The kid launched forward and clung to his arm.

"Hey, steady there," Jude said.

He gave the kid a manly hug and thumped him reassuringly on the back. There was an awful smell of sulfur in his hair. Jude pulled away to get a clear look in the dim light.

"What's your name?"

"Luca Brindisi."

"Well Luca, you and I are going to have to get off this mountain pretty fast. There's an eruption going on."

Another voice emerged from the blackness.

"Are you from the Geological Institute?"

There was another boy. He had a slight accent, which Jude placed as Norwegian.

"Don't be ridiculous, the institute would never let anyone up in the middle of this."

"Then who are you?"

Jude was tempted to ignore the question, but under the circumstances they should all know each other's names. They'd have to descend together.

"I'm a photographer," he explained. "Jude Blackwell."

"*You're* Jude Blackwell?"

"Correct. And you are . . ."

"My name is Karl. I know who you are. I have your autograph on my wall at home."

Even in the dim hut, Jude could see the glassy-eyed stare of hero worship.

"That's great," Jude said. "Tell me about it later. For now, I suggest we all get out of here."

Inside the climbing hut, Jude was organizing the descent. Technically it was just a walk-down, nothing difficult. No fancy climbing gear would be necessary. But an auxiliary air supply couldn't hurt.

He went over to the wall and examined the air canisters. With a quick pop, he sprung the cylinders from their mounts and lined them up on the cot.

"I didn't know they came off," Karl said. "I thought they were bolted in place."

"There's a release button," Jude explained. And these straps go over your shoulders. You wear it like a backpack. Now, everybody grab one."

Jude helped Luca on with his canister, and they all got ready to leave.

"Here's how it works. I'm going to start a count. I'll say 'one,' Karl you're 'two,' Luca 'three.' We count out loud and keep it up until we hit the bottom. You're going to have to yell. If I don't hear your number, we stop, and I go back. Got it?"

Karl looked at him with rapt admiration. "Everything I read about you is true."

Jude laughed deprecatingly. "Hopefully not everything. Now let's get going."

"One," Jude shouted as he stepped out the door.

"Two," Karl answered.

"Three," Luca shouted, giving it every ounce of his strength.

Luca realized immediately that he was not able to walk. So Jude helped pull him along. As they stumbled downhill, Luca observed his companion.

The famous volcanologist looked like a spaceman. His body was encased in shiny fabric—hood, face protector, and gloves—and there was an air tank strapped to his back and a bulky mask covered his face. Descending the slope, his steps were careful and slow like a moonwalker.

Luca tried to emulate the surefooted tread, but he was too weak. His lungs ached and burned. Each breath was torture as he pulled from the air canister.

This was absolutely terrifying, but somehow the photographer instilled a new confidence in him as he led the way down. It was almost as if Jude Blackwell, in his magic silver suit, was invincible.

"I got altitude sickness," Luca confessed to him. "But I feel better now."

"You're going to make it. Keep walking."

Jude looped his arm around Luca's waist, but the boy kept stumbling on the loose debris. He'd had seen plenty of cases of mountain sickness before, but this kid wasn't suffering from high altitude. Something else was wrong with him.

The other kid, Karl, was a great help. He was strong as an ox and was able to support Luca from the other side.

"I can't believe I'm climbing on Mount Etna with Jude Blackwell," Karl gushed.

Just then, another explosion went off. Jude couldn't help but marvel at Karl's youthful stupidity. There was a fair chance they wouldn't make it out, but he'd keep that to himself.

Mount Etna was in between paroxysms. The debris had been raining down heavily, and it was like being peppered with grapeshot. But they were farther down the slope, so the particles of magma had time to cool.

He told the boys to strip off their parkas, and they tied them over their heads like babushkas. As they did so, Jude remembered the citizens of Pompeii. They had tied pillows to their heads to protect themselves from falling rocks. It didn't help them much in the end. They all died in the pyroclastic flow.

Many victims of volcanoes perished because of this phenomenon. The volcanic debris and ash would typically shoot up about a mile into the sky. Initially, the eruption would carry all the debris upward. But sometimes, depending on the atmospheric conditions, that column of debris could eventually collapse. Then superheated gases, steam, water, ash, and pieces of rock would flow down the slope of the mountain.

If that pyroclastic flow happened, there was no chance of survival. The surge could travel at speeds of hundreds of miles an hour. People would suffocate, and their bodies would be buried. Jude had read about such an event. During the eruption of Krakatoa in 1883, the kinetic surge passed over the ocean. According to eyewitnesses, the superheated gases actually boiled the sea.

Jude looked at the two kids. They were going to have to move quickly. Right now the momentum of the blast was still skyward, but there was no way to tell how long that would last.

Suddenly, he became aware of the crackle of burning vegetation. Sparks ignited a large brushfire, and all the grass and small trees on the slope were going up like torches.

That was a good sign. More vegetation meant that they were reaching lower elevations where rescue would be possible. Jude stepped over a foot-wide stream of lava and turned to the boys.

"C'mon. We're almost there."

Then he forced himself to believe it.

FERRY TO SICILY

Brindy stood alone at the railing watching the wind whip the Tyrrhenian Sea into three-foot peaks. No one else was out on deck, as she watched the coastline of Sicily come into view. The landscape was low and flat, except for the impressive cone of Mount Etna. Right now the smoking peak looked like a throwback to prehistoric times.

She watched a black cloud streaked with orange at the summit. There was a distant rumble, like thunder. Large flashes of lightning were visible—a bad omen, surely. It felt like her whole world was spiraling out of control.

If Luca and Karl were in danger, it was her fault. She should have paid more attention to them while they were at the house, instead of being involved in her own schemes. Norway's security forces were looking for the boys throughout Naples, but she had no faith in that. The Norwegians were completely out of their element in Italy. She needed Sinclair to handle the situation; he'd know how to make inquiries.

A surge of warmth washed over her heart. John Sinclair was the most capable man she knew. He was solid and dependable. When Charles called, she jumped at the chance to go to Sicily to find him.

Sinclair would know how to go about finding Luca and what to do about Mondragone targeting her family. Now she needed him more than ever.

MORGANTINA, SICILY

Sinclair looked up from his dig and suddenly noticed the ash cloud over the mountain. The gust of black smoke thickened and was turning into a large funnel. He watched for a moment, enjoying nature at its most terrible.

It suddenly reminded him of the conversation with Princess Victoria about Empedocles and the four elements. It was hard to imagine that was only a week ago. At that time, he'd never guess he'd be standing here watching the exact volcano that claimed the Greek philosopher's life.

He turned at the sound of footsteps. A young graduate student came over with a bottle of cold water. The kid looked at the volcano, fascinated.

"They say it's going to be the biggest eruption in the history of the mountain," he said, his voice high with excitement.

"They always say that."

"I hear all the tourists were evacuated and road blocks are being set up."

"Have they declared 'code red' yet?" Sinclair asked, taking a long swig of water.

"It's 'orange,' but they are moving it to 'red' in another hour."

"I saw Mount Etna erupt three years ago," Sinclair said, finishing the water and wiping his mouth. "You'd think the world was ending."

"In a way, I'm sort of looking forward to it," the student said. "So long as nobody gets hurt."

Just then, a flame shot up out of the summit and flashed against the sky. They were too far away to hear anything, but the visual effect was impressive.

"I guess the fireworks are starting."

Just as the words left his lips, Sinclair heard his name being called. He turned. To his utter astonishment, Brindy was picking her way across the archaeological ruins toward him.

"John! Thank God I found you!"

Her sports car was parked out on the dusty track—some kind of vintage roadster, brilliant red—totally incongruous against the ancient marble fragments.

His mind leapt to unspeakable tragedies. Cordelia? Charles? Luca? Why would Brindy come all this way?

He dropped his spade and started toward her, launching over the chunks of marble scattered on the ground.

"What's going on?" he asked.

She looked up at him with terror.

"I . . . we need your help."

Her dark eyes were swimming with tears.

"Who's in trouble?"

"I am. And Luca."

In the excavation tent, Sinclair offered Brindy a seat on the neatly made cot. He sat perched on the edge of an old wooden trunk that served as his table. It was a Spartan accommodation—a tent with a packed dirt floor. Both flaps were open and a hot breeze blew through. Sinclair's assistant had brought them cold water, and the plastic bottles were beaded with condensation.

Brindy looked around and marveled at Sinclair's capacity for monastic simplicity. He had been here in the dust for about a week with nothing but the clothes on his back.

She took in his appearance: the tanned forearms, white shirt unbuttoned at the neck, the dusty Clark's desert boots. When she met his eyes, he gave her a smile of encouragement.

She leaned forward, keeping her voice low.

"My grandmother was shot by the Camorra."

His eyes widened, then he reached for her hand and held it.

"I'm so *sorry*, Brindy. How horrible!"

His grasp was warm and reassuring. The poignancy of the moment brought fresh tears to her eyes. She nodded, choking back her distress.

"Its awful. But there's more. Luca and Prince Karl have run off. They're missing."

He frowned.

"How long have they been gone?"

"About four days. The Security Service of Norway did a bank audit and credit card trace and came up with nothing."

"That's strange."

"Very. The problem is that Luca doesn't have any cash and neither does Karl. Victoria thinks her brother stole her sapphire necklace to pay for the trip, which is why I am here to see you."

Sinclair frowned.

"You shouldn't care about the necklace. What counts is finding the boys."

Brindy regarded Sinclair with a look of operatic tragedy.

"Actually the necklace is important, John."

"Why?"

"Because they think *you* stole it. The Norwegian royal family is having Scotland Yard investigate you."

Sinclair let go of her hand and stared at her with absolute astonishment.

"You must be joking! They think *I* stole the necklace! What on earth gave them that idea?"

"I know it's ridiculous. That's why Charles sent me to find you. They're going to arrest you when you come back."

"This is preposterous!" he said. "And Victoria? Why hasn't she defended me?"

"She can't say anything, or it will implicate her brother, so she is playing dumb."

Sinclair shook his head. "I can't believe Charles is involved with this kind of girl. What's gotten into him?"

"Love," Brindy said seriously.

Sinclair clenched his jaw in irritation.

"Well, that's just great. So what am I supposed to do now?"

"We could find the boys and ask Karl where he sold the necklace," she suggested. "It has to be somewhere in Naples."

"I'm not sure we should go poking around in the criminal under-world of Napoli. Especially if Mondragone is after your family."

"I know," she agreed. "But I figured you would know what to do."

Sinclair nodded, thinking. "Any idea where the boys might have gone?"

"Victoria says Karl had a real passion for volcanoes."

"Well, hopefully he's not climbing Mount Etna."

"But that's just it. Victoria thinks Karl and Luca might be there."

"Are you *serious*?"

"Yes. Victoria says Karl had a map marked with all the active volca-noes—sort of a wish list of the mountains he wanted to visit. Etna was number one."

"Brindy, it's erupting right now!"

He glanced over at the mountain. The peak was a good thirty miles away, but they could see it visibly steaming.

Sinclair spoke with controlled calm. "I was told they evacuated the mountain earlier this afternoon. Let's go to Catania. If they're in Sicily, they're probably somewhere in the city."

An hour later, Brindy and Sinclair were speeding toward the volcano in a bright red Lancia Aurelia convertible. On any other day it would have been a glorious ride. The vintage roadster yowled through the gears, and they had the entire road to themselves.

Sinclair leaned back, contented to let Brindy drive. She could han-dle a car like no other woman he knew. Her dark hair was flowing, her strong face set in a determined expression.

"Look out ahead, there's a roadblock," he cautioned.

Brindy slowed down and stopped to speak to the Civil Defense offi-cer. Her Italian was rapid and urgent.

"I am a volcano expert," she explained, flashing the ID in her wallet quickly. "We need to get to Catania to check the seismic readouts. It's very important."

The young man nodded and waved them through. Brindy put the car in gear and accelerated past the roadblock.

"That was clever," Sinclair remarked. "What card did you show him?"

"My membership in the World Heritage Fund."

He chortled. "That's not exactly relevant, is it?"

"It worked. And besides, I *am* a volcano expert."

"Brindy don't be ridiculous. You're *hardly* a volcanologist."

"I can see Vesuvius from my living room window; I spend hours studying it."

"I see your mendacious abilities are still intact," he said, half in jest.

She took the dig cheerfully. "Yes, I must admit, I have a devious nature."

"You should turn over a new leaf. All that fibbing will get you into trouble someday."

"I'll reform when you do, John," she shot back. "You give up your women, and I'll start telling the truth."

He was about to reply when a loud boom came from the direction of Mount Etna, and the sky lit up orange.

"Oh my God," she cried out, flinching involuntarily. "What should we do?"

"It's OK. Keep driving. We're almost there," Sinclair assured her. "Take a left at the next fork in the road."

"I don't know where to even begin to look for the boys," she said.

"We should go to the hospital, just in case."

"I blame myself if anything happens to Luca. I should have watched him more carefully."

Her hands were tight on the wheel, tears shimmering in her eyes.

"Don't beat yourself up over it, Brindy. Teenage boys are almost impossible to keep track of."

Another loud boom came from the volcano as he spoke. Sinclair averted his gaze to the landscape ahead. Mount Etna was raining ash, blanketing the ground with thick gray sediment.

He reached over and turned on the windshield wipers.

"Pull over, Brindy. We'd better put the top up."

Jude Blackwell noticed a checkpoint on the road ahead. Two military policemen were armed with walkie-talkies, standing next to an all-terrain vehicle with huge pneumatic tires. They had reached the mid-summit parking lot where all the tour guides left their vehicles. This meant they could get a ride down the rest of the way. They were saved!

"Hey!" he shouted, waving at the men.

Two of the guards did a double take at the sight of the three stragglers and started toward them at a jog.

Jude turned to the boys for last-minute instructions before the officers came over.

"We'll have to get Luca to a hospital. Somebody should check him out. He doesn't look good."

"I can't go to the hospital. I need to stay out of sight," Karl said urgently.

"Why?" Jude asked, intrigued.

"I'm not supposed to be here."

Jude laughed. "None of us are supposed to be here, kid."

Karl shuffled. "Yes, but especially not me. I'm Prince Karl of Norway."

Jude started to laugh at the joke and then stopped.

"What did you say?" he said, uncertain.

"I'm serious," the boy insisted. "I'm Prince Karl."

"So what's that got to do with anything?" Jude asked, baffled.

"I ran away. Everybody is looking for me. I have to call my sister right away."

"And your sister is . . ."

"Princess Victoria," Karl replied, exasperated.

Jude fought to keep his composure. Everyone knew Princess Victoria. Photos of her sold for tens of thousands of dollars. And now her kid brother was right in front of him.

Jude improvised quickly. "Here's what we'll do. When we get to the hospital, I'll sign the paperwork to get Luca admitted. And then you can leave with me."

"What if they ask our names?"

Jude scanned the area. Two guards were rapidly approaching, carrying water and blankets, but they were still out of earshot.

"How will we explain it?" Karl whispered.

"We'll say that we came across Luca on the trail. I'm a scientist and I work with INGV, and you're my assistant."

"Thanks," Karl gushed. "I really appreciate it."

"Hey, no problem."

Jude couldn't help but stare at Karl, as they went through the motions of checking Luca into the hospital in Catania. Could the kid really be who he said he was?

Afterward, when they went back to his room at the Caldera Hotel, Jude did a quick scroll through the Internet while Karl used the bathroom. Identity confirmed.

"It was tough to get that grit off my face," Karl said, wiping his face with a towel." Can I take a shower?"

"Be my guest," Jude said, waving his hand graciously. He held back the impulse to add "your highness."

HOSPITAL GARIBALDI NESIMA, CATANIA, ITALY

Sinclair stood next to Brindy at the hospital. Luca was asleep, his face a pale contrast to his raven-black hair. The starched white sheet was drawn up across his chest. At least the boy was safe, even though there was no word yet of Karl.

Sinclair looked down and had a quick recollection of how, as a young boy, Luca would fall asleep after a long day's excursion at the beach. He and Brindy would tuck him in with whispered exchanges. That was a lifetime ago.

Restless with anxiety, Sinclair walked over to look out the window. The sky was darkening with ash, blotting out the sun. Catania was in chaos—traffic snarled, people frantic. The hospital emergency room was jammed with people suffering from asthma. That was probably what was holding up the doctor, who was supposed to be here by now.

Sinclair looked over at Brindy. She was gray-faced with worry as she waited. The minutes dragged by. Finally a white-coated physician put his head into the room.

"Any relatives here?"

"I am," Sinclair said without thinking.

Brindy cast him an affectionate glance.

"We *both* are," she amended.

"What's his condition?" Sinclair asked.

The doctor perused the chart, his eyes scanning the checklists of drugs and treatments.

"He's exhausted and dehydrated. A touch of altitude sickness. He came in very agitated, so we gave him a sleeping pill. That's why he's so unresponsive right now."

"No other issues?"

"Not really."

"Did he tell you he has just been treated for cancer?" Brindy asked.

"We contacted his physician in Rome who had a good prognosis."

"When will you discharge him?" Sinclair asked.

"I'd like to keep him under observation for another day. Who will sign for his release?"

Sinclair hesitated.

"His mother should do it."

"And the nature of your relationship with the patient, sir?" the doctor asked, his pen poised over the chart.

Sinclair tried to think of a description that would sum up the way he felt about Luca.

"I'm his godfather, in a sort of unofficial way."

Luca's brown eyes opened, and he looked at the nurse and doctor. Then he noticed his mother. But when he connected with Sinclair, a glorious smile lit his face.

"Hey, thanks for coming," Luca croaked, his throat still raw from the burning fumes.

Sinclair was nearly delirious with relief.

"How are you feeling?"

Luca paused to take inventory, shifting his legs and drawing his hands out from under the covers.

"Fine," he said and struggled to sit up.

"Where's Karl?" Brindy asked urgently.

"I . . . I don't know for sure," Luca replied, confused.

"He was with you on the mountain, wasn't he?"

"Yes, he came down with me," Luca said "But our guide . . . Matteo. He fell in."

"Fell in where?" Sinclair asked.

"He fell in the volcano," Luca said, his eyes enormous, as if realizing the magnitude of the tragedy for the first time.

"Your guide *died*?" Brindy gasped.

"Yes, and Karl and I had to go down on our own. It was pretty scary."

"That's incredible! They told us the Civil Defense came across you. How did you manage to find your way to the checkpoint?" Sinclair asked.

"Jude Blackwell helped us."

"Where do I know that name?" Sinclair said, frowning.

"He's a world-famous photographer," Luca supplied.

Sinclair nodded. "Oh, yes. He's a friend of Cordelia's. A real daredevil. So was it Blackwell who suggested you climb the volcano in the first place?"

"Not at all. Karl wanted to go up. Jude found us later and got us out of there. I guess Karl must be with him."

"I can't believe that Karl would go off and leave you at the hospital alone," Brindy said, irritably.

"I think he was afraid to be recognized. He wanted to keep away from the press."

"Any idea where they might have gone?" Sinclair asked.

"Back to a hotel, I think," Luca said, looking confused. "I can't remember."

"I'll check it out," Sinclair said, starting to the door.

"Take your time," Brindy assured him. "Luca has a lot of explaining to do."

CALDERA HOTEL,
CATANIA, ITALY

The clerk at the reception desk of the Caldera Hotel rang Jude Blackwell's room, talked for a moment, and then turned back.

"He says he doesn't know you."

"Please mention that I've come to see about our mutual friend, Karl."

The next exchange produced the desired effect.

"Mr. Blackwell has requested you meet him upstairs. Number 413. The elevators are on the left, sir."

"Thank you."

Sinclair took the small lift to the fourth floor and peered down the corridor. The hallway was dimly lit with a frayed gray carpet and florescent lights. It was clearly a budget accommodation and rather shabby for the likes of a Norwegian prince.

Sinclair rapped sharply on door 413, then heard the thud of heavy footsteps approaching. The door opened a crack, and the man who peered out at him was in his late thirties, very muscular, and dressed in a simple white T-shirt and jeans. His hair was still wet from a shower, and a towel was around his neck.

"Are you Jude Blackwell?" Sinclair asked.

"Yeah. Come on in. Karl is here."

Karl was standing near the window, shifting from foot to foot, as if ready to flee. He looked healthy and fine. Apparently, there were no ill effects from climbing Mount Etna.

"Karl, you are in a heap of trouble."

"How did you find me?"

"That doesn't matter. You need to come with me right away. Your parents are frantic."

"I don't have to do what you tell me. This is not your concern."

Sinclair bit back his anger. He had every impulse to grab Karl by the scruff of his neck and thrash him.

"What *is* my concern is the sapphire necklace," Sinclair said with controlled patience. "I believe you have taken it, and now I'm being accused of stealing it."

Jude Blackwell had been moving around the room sorting out gear. He glanced up when he heard the animosity in the exchange. Sinclair raised an eyebrow, as if to tell him not to intervene. Jude understood immediately.

"I'm going to go get a coffee," Jude said, grabbing his leather jacket.

Sinclair nodded. "Thanks for the help with the boys. It was very kind of you."

"No problem," Jude said. "I wasn't going to leave two kids on the mountain, now was I?"

When the door clunked shut, Karl opened his mouth to begin a long explanation, but Sinclair cut him off.

"Save the sob story for your parents, Karl. I'm not interested. Just tell me where the necklace is."

GROSVENOR STREET, LONDON

Charles Bonnard bounded up the steps of Cordelia's townhouse and rang the bell. Malik answered the door with his usual polite reserve.

"Good evening, Mr. Bonnard."

"Is Delia home?" Charles asked with a smile.

"She just came in. You can find her in the library."

Charles entered the stately black-and-white marble foyer and tossed his jacket on a chair. By now, the townhouse was becoming like a second home.

It was a good thing he decided to stay in London. Scotland Yard had been here to question Cordelia about Sinclair's whereabouts almost every day. The police simply didn't believe she didn't know his location. It was heartrending to see Delia under suspicion, and now virtually a prisoner.

The police were insisting that she remain in London until Sinclair returned. She kept on with her work, spending her days at the Royal Geographical Society, writing a research report on the Mariana Trench. But In the evenings, Charles was made aware of her discontent as she railed about the bizarre twist of circumstances that left Sinclair free to travel while she had to remain under the thumb of Scotland Yard.

In fact, until Sinclair was cleared, they *all* had to stay in the UK. But being kept in the UK was not a hardship for Charles. Victoria was at a nearby country estate, along with his sister. He could visit whenever he liked.

Malik took Charles's jacket.

"Cordelia's upstairs, Mr. Bonnard."

"Hallo," Charles shouted up the stairwell. "Anyone home?"

Delia poked her head over the banister.

"Hi, Charles. I'm here in the library. Come on up, we're just starting tea."

Charles sprinted up to the second floor.

"Who's we?" he asked as he entered the large book-lined room.

Afternoon sun was pouring in, illuminating the lovely old leather-bound tomes and the rich colors of the Tabriz carpet. He looked around and saw that nobody else was in the room. Cordelia was standing, holding out a piece of muffin to Kyrie. The dog was sitting upright, offering a paw as if to shake hands.

"What do you mean, who's we?" she asked as she dropped cake into the dog's open mouth.

"Well I don't know about Kyrie, but you shouldn't eat too much cake," Charles admonished.

"Oh really," she said, laughing. "And who put you in charge of my figure?"

Charles blushed.

"Your figure is fine. I just wanted to take you out to dinner."

"No you don't; I'm taking you," Cordelia said biting into a muffin. "What's the latest on Sinclair."

Charles smiled with delight.

"Brindy found him, and they managed to locate Luca and Prince Karl."

"Oh, what a relief!"

Mondragone's right-hand man, Tito, stood outside Cordelia's town-house. His collar was turned up, but that did nothing to hide the strangeness of his pale eyes, the shock of white hair, and the pronounced limp. Because of his bizarre appearance, Tito was not the best person to send on a surveillance mission. But he was a master at breaking and entering.

Mondragone wanted the place checked out. The boss heard that someone in London was feeding information to the police. Detective Jaccorsi of the Naples police had come here a few days ago. The question was: Who lived here? And what did they want with Mondragone?

According to the real estate listing, Cordelia Stapleton owned the house. He had seen her coming and going. There were also various members of the household who took the dog for a walk at least a couple of times a day.

Daily patterns were as predictable as clockwork. The servants were not much of a problem. The housekeeper lived in, but she left every Wednesday for a day off. And the young butler went home every evening at 7:00 p.m. The only thing Tito needed was a little patience, and the rest would be easy.

Cordelia came down the staircase wearing her nicest Clothilde Bonnard original. It was a white silk sheath with an appliqué of embroidered pink flowers at the hem. She had paired it with simple white high-heeled sandals and a natural-colored straw purse. As she came to the landing, she glanced down and saw Charles looking up at her.

"Delia, what a vision you are," he joked. "Or am I not allowed to say that?"

"Your sister designed this dress," she replied. "So I'll accept the compliment on her behalf."

"Oh, I must say, you wear it very well. Now where are you taking me?"

"Just a few blocks away."

They left via the front steps. Cordelia locked the door and turned toward the street.

"Oh, Malik must have left this," she said, noticing the garden hose draped over the banister. "He was watering the window boxes earlier."

She regarded the long length of hose coiled messily on the steps.

"Want me to get it?" Charles offered, starting to reach for it. "I could put it in the garage."

"No, our reservation is at eight o'clock. I'll get it when we come back. Let's just go."

GROSVENOR STREET, LONDON

Checking his watch, Tito walked quickly to the service entrance of the Grosvenor Street townhouse and entered the garage with an electronic skeleton key. The lights were off, but in the dim illumination he could see many expensive vehicles—a Triumph Speed Triple motorcycle, a black Aston Martin DBS, and a silver Range Rover.

Just as he traversed the garage, a dog barked. He paused. The low growl that followed seemed only half-hearted. The dog poked her head out of the doorway, eyes curious.

Tito moved slowly, reaching into his canvas satchel. The animal seemed interested. Tito extracted a ziplock with several chunks of steak. He opened the plastic bag and placed the meat on the floor. Then he took out a 12-ounce bottle of commercial antifreeze. It contained the chemical xylitol, which was toxic for dogs. He opened the screw cap and poured the mauve liquid all over the meat. It glugged out with a thick viscosity and pooled around the chunks of meat.

The dog walked over to the antifreeze and gave it a tentative lick. It was sweet, and dogs were known to enjoy it very much. First, she lapped up the liquid, and then she wolfed down the chunks of meat. Tito was sitting on the floor of the garage, eyes shut, listening to music when the dog came over and nosed him a few times. He didn't make eye contact with the animal, so the dog wandered off.

After a few minutes, Tito checked his watch. In another half hour, the dog would exhibit signs of intoxication, then shortly thereafter, vomiting and respiratory distress. After six hours, there would be seizures, rapid heartbeat, and ultimately, kidney failure.

Tito finally stood up and walked through the kitchen. The animal was already lolling on its bed, panting for breath, eyes rolled up in terror.

Cordelia couldn't help noticing that Charles Bonnard was employing his full powers of *sprezzatura* tonight. His conversation was delightful, as they walked to a neighborhood restaurant a few blocks away.

Corrigan's was one of her favorite places. It was fancy enough for a good dinner but not fussy. The décor was informal and witty. Pop-art photos of famous jazz artists like Dizzy Gillespie and Duke Ellington were on the walls, and a live pianist played all evening.

Cordelia watched Charles perusing the menu, wishing with all her heart that she and Sinclair could get back to this kind of normalcy. Dinner out. Why did the simple things always elude them?

Charles never took his food lightly. He ordered an appealing combination: asparagus with grated Parmesan and balsamic vinegar, followed by a lamb cutlet with peas, and rhubarb crumble for desert. Cordelia chose the spicy corn soup, the lamb, and rum raisin ice cream.

She immediately commandeered the wine list, treating him to a fabulous vintage—Chateau La Mondotte Saint-Emilion 1996.

"Cordelia," he admonished. "How extravagant."

"I'm celebrating tonight."

"What are we celebrating?" Charles asked.

"Finding the boys. That means John will come back soon."

"Are you two going to be OK?" Charles asked, looking at her with concern. "He seems to be in a bit of a funk."

She was about to reply when the waiter came over and interrupted. He poured a bit of wine for her to taste, and she nodded her approval.

When the man left, she continued. "Sinclair and I had a terrible fight the day before he went away. I think I misjudged him terribly, and it was unfair."

"It will work out. He loves you. But I'm sure you know that already."

Cordelia nodded and smiled.

"To love," she toasted, and they clinked the rims and drank.

"So tell me what is going on with Luca and Karl," Cordelia asked.

Charles leaned forward to speak quietly. "Apparently, Prince Karl sold the necklace in Naples. The Norwegian royal family can't afford another scandal. So Sinclair has to try to quietly find the person who purchased it."

"Isn't that dangerous?"

"Sinclair has contacts in Naples. He used to help recover stolen artifacts for the Italian government. Brindy is staying around to help."

Cordelia felt her heart sink. That woman again. All she could see was the tabloid picture of the Contessa Brindisi in a bikini, diving off a boat in Capri with her lover, Sinclair.

"What's wrong?" Charles asked, sensing her mood shift.

"I don't like John spending so much time with Brindy," she confessed. Charles shook his head.

"You have no idea how much he detests her. He's more likely to strangle her than to get involved in any romantic entanglements."

"He hates her?" Cordelia asked, astonished.

"You can't imagine how much. It's all I've been hearing for years. So don't worry." Charles took another sip of wine. "This is fantastic, by the way."

Cordelia ignored the wine. "But Charles, if he hates Brindy, why does he have anything to do with her?"

Charles gave her a knowing look.

"It's Luca. He absolutely adores the kid."

Cordelia opened the door to her townhouse and flicked the light switch. The house was strangely quiet.

"Kyrie?" she called, tentatively.

"Where do you suppose she is?" Charles asked, tossing his jacket onto the hall chair.

"Its odd, she usually runs to greet me . . ."

Charles walked up the main stairs, looking around, his face serious.

"Delia, I don't like this, at all."

She got a sudden chill.

"Let's check the kitchen," she said.

"Do you think she's down there?"

"She sometimes sits with my housekeeper."

"I thought Margaret wasn't here tonight," Charles said.

"You're right, she isn't."

Charles opened the door to the basement and listened.

"Stay here," he whispered and started down in the dark.

He crept through the hallway to the kitchen, passing the pantry shelves filled with bottles and jars. His senses were hyperaware.

There was no light on in the kitchen, but the iridescent clock on the stove painted the room with an eerie green glow. Passing by the counter, Charles slid a cooking knife out of the rack. He was faster with a fencing blade than almost anyone else in the world, and the ring of a steel knife against marble made a faint sound that boosted his confidence. Arm extended, he readied himself for any surprises. But all was silent.

There was nothing in the kitchen but the hum of the refrigerator. A slight breeze fell on his cheek as he went over to the cooking island and looked around.

Nothing.

The fresh air was coming from the hallway that led to the garage. The door must be open. As he started over, he saw the dog sound asleep in her bed. But something was wrong. Kyrie never stretched out like this. Marked by her years as a stray, the dog always slept upright, always vigilant.

"Kyrie, wake up."

Again the feeling of danger passed over him.

Kyrie was lying on her side, breathing heavily, her tongue lolling on the pillow. Charles bent down and smelled a sickly sweet scent, overlaid by the acrid stench of chemicals.

He spun around and flew up the basement stairs to the foyer where Cordelia waited.

"Go outside now!"

Her gaze fell on the kitchen knife in his hand.

"What's wrong?"

"Go outside, Delia. Someone is here," he told her. "I'm going to look through the house. Call the police and a vet."

"A vet?" she asked.

"Yes. Someone has poisoned Kyrie."

Cordelia walked down the front steps, her knees shaking. The vet's number was in her contact list. Just as she dialed, the side door to the garage opened a fraction. A head popped out, with a shock of white hair. Then a middle-aged man emerged and looked cautiously around.

Cordelia disconnected the call and flattened herself against the front door. From this angle, the man couldn't see her standing on the steps. She kept quiet. He was only a few feet away, near the service entrance to the townhouse.

Her mind went into battle mode. Somebody had to stop him. If she made a call to the police, he would certainly hear. But accosting him seemed risky. He might have a gun.

The man was moving slowly out of the service drive, scanning the street to make sure that he wasn't observed. As he moved, she noticed a terrible limp, his legs were half bent, and he walked with a shuffling gate. He was not strong. Perhaps she could stop him. But what should she do?

Looking around, her eyes fell on the garden hose. Quickly she twisted the spigot on the wall to allow water to flow and raised the nozzle like a gun.

"Stop right there!" she shouted, pointing the hose at the man.

He turned and stared in astonishment.

"I warn you. Stop! I know you broke into the house, and I have just called the police."

He took a step toward her, as if to grab the nozzle, but she backed up. The three steps of the front entrance gave her a slight height advantage over the man. He'd have trouble climbing up with his limp.

"Don't tempt me, lady," the man said, reaching for his canvas satchel.

She squeezed the nozzle as hard as she could, the rubber hose jerked with the force of the water, and a high-pressure stream caught him in the chest.

He sputtered in astonishment and then started toward her.

She pointed the nozzle directly at his face, shooting him in the eyes and forcing water up his nose. He staggered back with the impact of the blast and then slipped on the wet pavement and nearly fell.

With a murderous look, he turned and hurried off toward Grosvenor Square. Constrained by his heavy limp, it took him a while before he disappeared into the trees. She got a good look at him. His clothing was soaked, and the shock of white hair hung like seaweed on his head.

Just then the front door opened.

"*Delia!*" Charles gasped. "*What are you doing?*"

"I shot him," she said, too shaken to move.

Charles grabbed the hose away from her as if it were a dangerous toy.

"Delia, what if he had a gun? This hose wouldn't have protected you."

She looked up at him.

"It doesn't matter. How's Kyrie?"

It was five o'clock in the morning, and Cordelia was slumped in the waiting room chairs at Streatham and Wallace Veterinary Surgery in Mayfair. The young veterinarian, a woman named Harriet, had been quietly reassuring. It was good that they detected the poison early. Kyrie had a better chance of pulling through.

The vet administered an emetic—apomorphine—to make the dog vomit. But the antifreeze had already entered her system. They tried other antidotes—activated charcoal to absorb any remaining xylitol in her gastrointestinal tract, an IV of fluids, including ethanol—but so far there was no real indication of whether Kyrie would make it.

Charles came in and tossed his raincoat on the chair.

"I just finished up with the police," he said. "The house is secure."

"We need to get John back here right away," she said.

He came over and sat down.

"The police want to talk to you tomorrow. But from your description, they think they know who it was. Not too many people look like that."

"Who was it?" Cordelia asked. "Why do you think he broke in?"

Charles sat up straighter, pulling his jacket down.

"It wasn't a robbery. The police went all through the house and found nothing disturbed. You'll have to inventory all the valuables, of course. But nothing appears to be missing."

Cordelia sank back in her chair, bewildered.

"What was he looking for?"

Just then, Harriet emerged from the waiting-room door. "Kyrie's vitals are returning to normal," she said. "She's going to recover."

"Oh, thank . . ." Cordelia broke off, overcome with emotion.

"I am very glad to hear that," Charles said, standing and picking up his jacket.

"Can I see her?" Cordelia asked.

"Not right away. She'll have to stay for a few days while we monitor her kidneys."

"Please. Just for a minute," Cordelia begged.

"I'm afraid not—" the vet began.

Charles interjected. "Delia, why don't I take you back home, so you can get some rest. I have a few more things to tell you."

"Of course," she conceded. "I'll be back tomorrow."

They thanked the vet, gathered up their things, and went outside to Cordelia's Range Rover. She climbed into the driver's seat, buckled her seatbelt, and turned to Charles.

"OK. Who was it?"

Charles looked grave.

"A Camorra boss named Tito. He works for Salvatore Mondragone in Naples."

"I know that name, Mondragone. John told me they crossed paths once, when he recovered some stolen antiquities. Apparently there were a few threats exchanged, and Mondragone told John to stay out of his turf."

Charles pressed his mouth into a tight line.

"We should tell Sinclair right away. This might be some kind of warning for him to back off and stay away."

"You think so? I can't imagine how they would know Sinclair is in Naples."

"I have no idea," Charles said, rubbing his face with exhaustion. "But I do know that Mondragone is one of the most dangerous men in the world."

NAPLES, ITALY

Sinclair hung up the phone and tried to quell the urge to fly straight back to London. It was stupid of him to have left Cordelia to fend for herself. Having a dog in the house was not enough protection. And Charles was no match for the Camorra.

He ran a hand through his hair, wishing he could leave right now. But that was not possible. If he didn't get the necklace, his name might never be cleared. And the minute he stepped back into the UK, Scotland Yard would detain him. This little hunting expedition would have to pay off, and quickly.

He and Luca now sat in the little pizzeria where the boys had eaten before. Karl had only a vague recollection of where he had sold the necklace and couldn't give them any specifics. The prince said he was so frightened at the time, he couldn't remember the name of the store or even the exact street where he had gone.

Karl's parents whisked him away to Norway, so Luca was now trying to remember where they had been. He and Sinclair went to the same pizzeria and stopped for a bite to orient themselves

"Who was that on the phone?" Luca asked, tucking into his pizza. "Is everything OK?"

"Yes," Sinclair said distractedly. "My dog is sick, but she'll be fine. Now look around and tell me. Where did Karl go to sell the necklace?"

"It was up there, by the corner," Luca said. "Now I remember."

"So Karl went that way?"

Luca nodded. "Yes. He was only gone about ten minutes."

"Then we need to find the nearest jewelry store from that point," Sinclair said. "I don't think he would have shopped around."

Sinclair assessed the risk. Apparently, the Camorra was on to him, and now Luca was here—a dangerous situation. This was a rough neighborhood near the Piazza Garibaldi—Camorra territory. Sinclair swiveled around to examine the establishment where they sat. The man serving the counter wore a stained apron and an indifferent expression, but his eyes were watchful.

At a glance, it was easy to see that the street held the normal menace—a dozen or so thieves invisible to all but the trained eye. A ragged man shuffled. He had the haggard look of a long-time addict. Two thugs were riding a Vespa, spooned together on the single motorcycle—clearly on a purse-snatching mission. The boy riding in the back would be carrying a short, curved knife for cutting the shoulder straps.

Sinclair was familiar with this type of milieu. The governments of Greece, Italy, Turkey, and Egypt often commissioned him to find artifacts that had been pillaged from ancient sites. The last time he was here, it was to recover a priceless Etruscan vase. At that time, Mondragone warned him to stay away from his territory.

But this time, the hunt for missing valuables was personal. The chief problem was that the sapphire necklace could have already been broken up. The stones may have been removed from the settings and sold individually. Still, he had to try.

"Finished?" he asked Luca, indicating the pizza.

"Yup."

Sinclair pushed back his chair. "What do you remember about Karl on that day? Was he upset?"

"No," Luca said. "Not at all. He told me he went to a bank."

They started walking, and Sinclair noticed a small bakery on the corner.

"Let's ask in here about a jewelry store."

He pulled open the door and smiled at the woman behind the counter.

They had planned in advance to let Luca do the talking. Sinclair's attempts at Italian tended to drift into classical Latin, and his archaic vocabulary often caused confusion.

Luca inquired about a jewelry store. The old woman lumbered to the front window, pointed down the street, and waved her hand twice, speaking in Neapolitan dialect.

"She says there is one just two blocks away," Luca said.

Sinclair frowned.

"I'm having second thoughts about you coming with me. Why don't you go back to the pizza shop and wait."

Luca turned to him, his expression drooping with disappointment.

"I'm probably safer with you. You don't want me sitting out on the street by myself, do you?"

Sinclair acquiesced. If Mondragone's men were around, it would be better to keep Luca close by.

"All right. But do exactly what I tell you."

"I promise."

"I'm going to pretend to be an American tourist. I've hired you to translate for me. Got it?"

"Let's go," Luca said and flashed a brilliant smile.

The jewelry store windows were filled with gold chains, small charms, and trinkets—keepsakes for tourists.

"Ready?" Sinclair asked.

"Yes," Luca said with a grin.

The boy seemed to be enjoying the lark. Sinclair felt a twinge of affection. He missed Luca tagging along with him. But now was not the time for sentiment; this required his full focus. He pushed his feelings down and continued to examine the window of the shop, planning his approach.

Undoubtedly everyone on this street paid for protection and traded information for favors from the Camorra. He and Luca were probably putting themselves in danger, but there was no other way to get the necklace back.

Sinclair took a deep breath and turned the doorknob. A bell clanged, and the proprietor stood up—an older man in a threadbare but neatly-pressed shirt. The shop smelled slightly of dust and silver polish. The man smiled tentatively and Sinclair began the charade, speaking slowly as Luca translated.

"I am looking for a necklace for my wife."

The man waved in the direction of the cases.

"Please take a look."

"I would like something with sapphires."

There was the tiniest shift in the eyes—a wariness. The man explained that he didn't usually carry stones. He pulled out a few dusty trays of jewelry, gnarled old hands picking up cheap 14K gold trinkets. Finally, the shopkeeper held up a gold heart with a small diamond suspended from a chain.

"This is very beautiful," the old man told Luca, hoping to make a sale.

Sinclair shook his head.

"I was thinking of something more like this." Sinclair reached into his inside jacket pocket and pulled out the tear sheet from a magazine. Victoria had been photographed wearing the necklace at a gala in Rome.

The old man stood staring down at the paper for a full thirty seconds, then looked up at Sinclair with a closed face. It was a good attempt at composure, but his eyes could not hide the shock of having been discovered.

"Maybe you know where I could get something like this?" Sinclair probed.

"I could ask around," the man said slowly. "What is your price range?"

"Fifty thousand. Cash."

The eyes wavered. "No, I don't think so."

"Sixty," Sinclair bartered. "If you could find it in the next hour."

The man looked around and ran his palms down the sides of his slacks.

"I can inquire."

"I'll wait."

"It will take more time," the old man said.

"No, an hour. Not more."

"You would pay cash? Euros? Dollars?" the man ascertained.

Sinclair nodded. "Either."

He had 50,000 in euros and 50,000 in US currency in a canvas expedition satchel over his arm.

"Come back in an hour."

VIA NAPOLI, ITALY

When the tall American and the young Italian boy left, the proprietor walked to the door and flipped the sign to "Closed," then went behind the green curtain to open the safe.

He took out the box and opened it. The necklace looked more rare and precious than he first remembered. Why had Renato never returned to collect his loot? Clearly, the sapphires were intended for Salvatore Mondragone.

If he sold the necklace, Renato would be furious. The thief had told him to put it away until he collected it. But now Renato had disappeared. What should he do? This was too much for him to handle alone. It would be better to have Mondragone deal with the American. He picked up the phone and called.

"It's Bartolomeo," the old man said. "I have a sapphire necklace for the boss. Renato gave it to me. But now an American is here asking for it."

NAPLES TRAIN STATION

Sinclair and Luca sat in the large, modern train station, attempting to blend in with the throngs of travelers. Sinclair looked over at the kid. What kind of logic had passed through the boy's brain to run off like that? Was he that unhappy at home?

"So, Luca," he asked gently. "Why'd you go with Karl?"

Luca looked up guiltily. "He said it would just be for a day or so."

"It was a very dangerous thing to do."

"I can handle myself," Luca argued. "I'm not a baby anymore."

Sinclair sighed.

"Remember that industrialist whose son was kidnapped a few years ago? Kidnapping is a profitable business in Naples."

"Is that why the guy had a gun?"

"Yes, Luca. He probably recognized Karl. Especially after he turned up with priceless jewels."

"Well, stealing the necklace wasn't my idea. Karl did it."

"It doesn't matter; you were involved in a criminal act."

"I'm sorry," Luca said. "I really am. Don't be mad at me."

"I'm not mad. I just worry about your safety. And I've wanted to ask you about the man on the mountain? Was he Italian?"

"Yes. His name was Renato. He followed our guide and joined our group."

Sinclair looked around at the crowded terminal.

"He was probably Camorra. Italy seems a bit dangerous right now for your family. When does school start?"

Luca brightened.

"Not for another two weeks. How about I come with you to London?"

Sinclair considered. That would solve the problem. If the Brindisi family were being targeted, Luca needed to leave as soon as possible.

"Fine. And your mother should get out of Italy also. At least for a while."

"What's happening to Karl?" Luca asked.

"He's back in Oslo with his parents. I don't think you'll be able to see him."

"I felt sorry for him being cooped up all the time."

Sinclair nodded, draining his coffee. "I know. Frankly, I think the whole royal family is sad. Victoria seems desperate to break out, too."

"Well, now she'll be tied up when that bambino comes," Luca said, pushing back his chair.

Sinclair's eyes widened.

"Bambino? What baby?"

"Didn't you know? The princess is going to have a baby."

"Who's the father?" Sinclair asked, astonished.

"Charles Bonnard."

"Who told you that?" Sinclair demanded urgently.

"Who do you think?" Luca grinned. "My mom."

VIA NAPOLI, ITALY

Sinclair and Luca entered the jewelry shop, knowing the negotiation had suddenly become more dangerous. Sinclair was fully prepared for any eventuality. Dealing in the black market had its uncertainties.

As they entered, the proprietor beamed an ingratiating smile. That was suspicious in itself. Sinclair advanced cautiously, keeping Luca well behind him and scanning the shop for another presence. The green curtain at the back was a worry. But it didn't reach the floor, and no shoes were visible beneath the folds.

"Have you found the necklace we are looking for?" Sinclair asked.

The proprietor of the shop nodded.

"Yes, I have. But you will have to go to the dockyard to collect it."

Sinclair paused. "Who gets the money?"

"Bring it with you. And be at Dock C-8 at midnight. Someone will meet you."

NAPLES, ITALY

At exactly midnight, John Sinclair walked through the chain-link gate to the dockyard and noticed that the guard booth was empty. The quay was so much larger than he would have imagined. It looked as if it were a city in itself, with streets and alleys formed by the enormous crates.

Rows of containers were stacked in a rainbow of colors and labeled—MAERSK, HANJIM, CHINA SHIPPING. Exotic scripts were scrawled on the ridged aluminum. They were spiky characters spelling out names of companies in the new industrial world.

He started toward the water, making no sound. A hollow feeling of fear gripped him momentarily, and he had to push it away. Anxiety would slow his reactions, and he needed all his faculties if he were dealing with people like this.

This dockyard was Mondragone's turf. Of course, he had dispelled the naive illusion that this was going to be a simple transaction. Recovering stolen goods was inevitably confrontational. Consequently, he'd dressed for battle: a dark T-shirt and loose cargo pants, rubber-soled sneakers—footwear that would allow him to run or fight, whichever was required.

The Naples dockyards were 24/7 operations. Loading was going on all around him. Huge cranes swung overhead, and there was the continuous boom of gigantic metal boxes as they were dropped onto the cargo dock. He expected to see workmen, but the cranes were robotically maneuvered as if by some invisible remote control.

His instructions were to walk to the very end of Dock C-8 to where the *NS da Guia*, a Portuguese registered coastal freighter, was tied up. He found it easily. The name of the vessel was visible on the hull, but no one was in sight.

He waited, alert to danger. The sticky sea mist rolled in, thick with the acrid scents of motor oil, diesel fuel, and industrial materials. Overhead LED lights emitted a harsh white glare, casting shadows under every object.

He had the sensation of being a condemned man, waiting for death. Hopefully, he was summoned here for a simple transaction only.

After a few minutes, a workman stepped out from behind the crates. He wore a hard hat and an orange florescent vest, and his face was partially obscured by work goggles. Wordlessly, he gestured for Sinclair to come.

Sinclair followed the man up the gangway of the small freighter and stepped into an interior steel staircase. They climbed up three stories. The worker abruptly left, and Sinclair stepped over a portal with a raised doorsill.

This was the pilothouse of the cargo ship. The ship's bridge was a perfect aerie for viewing the panorama of the dockyard. The small enclosed room had the feel of an air traffic control tower with only enough space for two aluminum chairs and a small metal desk. A panel of navigational instruments took up most of the rest.

For Sinclair it had a slightly claustrophobic feel, although a large open window on the side helped. That ventilation also diffused a foul smelling Cohiba cigar, which smoldered in a thick glass ashtray.

Sinclair noted these details subconsciously. His full attention was on the man standing in front of him. There was no mistaking Salvatore Mondragone. Apparently, the gangster was up to his old tricks of buying valuable objects on the black market.

Mondragone spoke first. "So, Mr. Sinclair. It seems you don't take my advice to stay out of Naples."

Sinclair remained silent. All the horror stories ran through his head. This man was a psychopathic killer. He once flayed a rival alive with a paring knife and thrust another's hand into a whirling buzz saw.

But Mondragone did not appear to be planning brutality. He was dressed beautifully in business attire. Sinclair took in the details. The wristwatch was slim, his shoes bespoke, and his suit was cut in the restrained style favored by European diplomats. The drape of the fabric suggested the hand of a master tailor.

As Cyclops sat down, he fastidiously flicked a few imaginary pieces of lint from his trousers.

"I understand you are looking for a sapphire necklace?" Mondragone said.

"That is correct."

"I'm sure we can come to terms. But first of all, who are you working with? I'm not foolish enough to think this necklace belongs to you personally."

The Camorra boss produced an envelope from his inside jacket pocket and poured the contents onto the aluminum desk. There were two articles: a small gold ring and a chunky blue necklace with diamonds. The sapphires were so large that most people would assume them to be costume jewelry.

Sinclair stared. The gems didn't just gleam—the indigo stones glittered as if lit from within.

"I am only here for a simple transaction," Sinclair said.

Mondragone smiled nastily.

"So, how's your dog?" Mondragone asked.

Sinclair felt the hair rise on his arm. Just thinking about this man being anywhere near Cordelia made his blood run cold.

"I don't understand. What were you looking for?"

"Your friend Jaccorsi tipped us off. We were following him when he came to your house in London. He's been visiting FCA authorities on a daily basis."

Sinclair realized instantly that Jaccorsi had been involved in the investigation into Mondragone's dirty business dealings. The policeman, by paying a casual visit, brought the Camorra to Sinclair's doorstep. It was a horrible coincidence. But how could he convince Mondragone of that?

"Jaccorsi is a personal friend, nothing more. I am not involved in investigating your organization."

"Are you working for FCA or FinCEN?" he asked, naming the British and American financial investigatory agencies.

Sinclair shook his head. "I'm here on a personal matter. The boy who sold the necklace is a family friend. He made a mistake in taking it, and I need you to sell it back."

"Why should I? I stand to make quite a profit."

"You still can. You bought the necklace for almost nothing. I can pay you a nice sum, no questions asked," Sinclair said.

Mondragone took a puff of his cigar, squinting through the smoke. "Where is Renato Balboni?"

"My understanding is he didn't survive the eruption on Mount Etna," Sinclair said without elaboration.

"My men don't fall into volcanoes."

"That may be, but why he was following the boys?"

Mondragone's reaction was noncommittal. He laid his cigar carefully in the ashtray and then reached into his jacket and pulled out a pistol.

Sinclair began to formulate an exit strategy. The clang of the metal cranes beat a steady rhythm that divided time like a metronome.

"I'm here for a simple sale, nothing more," Sinclair stated.

Mondragone didn't speak; he walked over to the window. It was open on the side of the ship toward the water. He pushed the glass panel out farther. Down below, waves could be heard lapping against the steel hull.

"I am going to ask you one more time. Who do you work for? The Americans or the Brits?"

Sinclair didn't listen. He was plotting. Things were about to get physical. He searched in his peripheral vision for something he could use as a weapon. All his training as a fencer would come into good stead if he could find something that would work as a saber. But on the bridge of a ship, everything was bolted down and secured.

Mondragone gestured with the gun toward the window, indicating that Sinclair should walk over. There was no choice. As he approached the aperture, a faint breeze brushed his face. It carried the briny smell of the bay.

The window was not wide, but it certainly was of sufficient breadth to allow Mondragone to push him out, or shoot him and let the body fall. Either way, it would be an inevitable plunge to his death.

On his way over to the window, Sinclair observed two things within his grasp—an aluminum chair, and a lead crystal ashtray where the cigar lay smoldering. As he passed by, Sinclair reached for the ashtray, as if to seize it.

The gesture was like a decoy in a magician's trick. Mondragone's attention was drawn to the hand, exactly as planned. As Sinclair's fingers closed over the ashtray, Mondragone's gun shifted slightly toward the movement. Sinclair grabbed the heavy glass ashtray and the cigar rolled across the table and fell onto the deck.

Meanwhile, Sinclair made sure he had a solid grip on the chair with the other hand. Then, in a single fluid arc, he swung hard, slamming the legs of the chair into Mondragone's gun arm. A shot went off in the enclosed space with a deafening noise. The pistol fell and slid away.

Without pause, Sinclair swung the aluminum chair again, thrusting it like a lion tamer, to keep Mondragone contained. That tactic failed. Mondragone proved surprisingly strong. He held the chair off with one hand and extracted a thin stiletto blade from his sleeve.

Sinclair yanked the chair sideways, throwing Mondragone off balance, but the gangster lunged. The knife came toward him in a deadly arc. But after years of fencing, it was second nature to avoid the point of a blade. As Sinclair dodged the thrust, he grasped the ashtray and smashed it into Mondragone's face. It hit him squarely in the mouth, and the knife clattered to the floor.

Reeling from the blow, the gangster weaved. His lip was bleeding. Sinclair wasted no time and began to use the four legs of the chair, prodding aggressively, forcing Mondragone to back up. It was now or never. Sinclair accelerated the speed of his thrusts. Mondragone's hands stretched out to deflect the chair.

There was very little room to fight. Within seconds, Mondragone was pressed against the sill of the open window. Sinclair jabbed again and again, until the man teetered. His arms flailed, but the leather-soled shoes had no traction on the slippery deck. The fatal misstep came from the loose cigar, which rolled under his shoe.

Mondragone slipped and reached the tipping point. His body tumbled out the window. Sinclair stood immobile as the gangster hit the water with a splash.

Cyclops was gone. Sinclair took a deep breath, his heart hammering with adrenaline. He picked up the pistol, then walked to the window and looked out. There was no ripple in the inky black water. The body was submerged. Sinclair realized he should get rid of the weapon and dropped the pistol into the harbor. It landed with a faint splash

He felt no remorse, nor would he suffer sleepless nights. He had just rid the world of a dangerous murderer. He glanced around. But where were the guards? Why weren't they coming? Surely Mondragone's henchmen had seen the fight. He'd better leave quickly, before they rushed the door.

Sinclair scooped up the necklace and the gold ring and put them back in the envelope and then in his pocket.

Suddenly, there was a shift in sound out on the dock. One of the cranes was shutting down. Then he heard other cranes go silent, one after the other in progression.

Sinclair didn't wait. He yanked the door open and fled down the metal stairs to the door of the ship. Out on deck, the gangway was still in place, and he sprinted to the dock. LED lights still burned brightly, and it was so quiet he could hear the faint overhead hum of electricity. Where were Mondragone's guards?

Sinclair swiveled his head around cautiously. Nothing. So he quickly ran through the shipping containers, seeking refuge in the shadows until he reached the gate, then slipped away.

Salvatore Mondragone realized he was immersed in freezing water. There was nothing but blackness. His eyes were open in the stinging salt water. Above, he could see the dim glare of the dock lights wavering through the murky darkness. He kicked up toward the light, his heavy English shoes impeding his ability to swim. His lungs were throbbing with the desire to breathe. As he became more cognizant, he knew there would only be a few moments until his body would revert to automatic reflex. Then, his oxygen-starved body would try to ingest water, and he would drown.

Pulling with every ounce of strength toward the surface, he broke clear with a splash, sucking in deep-tearing breaths that felt like fire. His feet and knees were in torment from the impact of the fall. His nose and mouth were bleeding.

He treaded water, trying to work his way through the pain. Within moments, his respiration returned to normal, and his mind cleared. He floated on the surface, his eyes scanning the dark.

The bright square of the window of the ship was still visible, but nobody was watching. Mondragone paddled closer to the hull and the mild current carried him aft, toward the diesel exhaust pipe. There he clung to a rivet on the hull with his fingertips.

A quick inventory of his body revealed little damage. No bones were broken, despite the fact that he slammed into the water with such force it felt like he was hitting concrete. That sharp gasp of pain before he went under saved him.

Once again, he cheated death. And, in the Camorra world, there was only one response. John Sinclair would have to die.

Luca sat on the bed, staring at the television. He was waiting in the hotel room for Sinclair, exactly as he was told. It was now two o'clock in the morning. The instructions were not to open the door under any circumstances. Sinclair booked them into a hotel in Naples, to keep a low profile until they could get the necklace back.

Italian entertainment programs were simply awful. This was some kind of police drama, and three men were shooting at each other in the dark. Incredibly, the show was boring and scary at the same time.

Luca yawned and looked at his watch again. Just then, he heard the ping of the elevator outside in the hall. There was a scratching of the key card, and Sinclair opened the door and stepped in quickly.

"Get your things," he said, his lips white with stress. "We're getting out of here."

Luca jumped up and grabbed his jacket.

"Did you get it?" he asked.

Sinclair nodded, dialing his phone.

"Yes, I did."

MAYFAIR, LONDON

At 2:00 a.m., in an upstairs guest room of Cordelia Stapleton's townhouse, Charles Bonnard was sound asleep. He drifted off into a fretful doze, worrying about intruders. Now he woke to the buzz of his cell phone vibrating on the nightstand. He answered it, and Sinclair's voice cut through his fuzzy brain.

"Charles?"

"Yes, I'm here."

"I got the necklace," Sinclair said.

Charles sat up, forcing himself awake.

"That was quick. Did you have any trouble?"

"A bit. Mondragone had it," Sinclair told him. "But it worked out."

"Glad to hear it," Charles said, relieved.

"So what do we do now?" Sinclair asked. "How do we get it to Victoria?"

"She's in England, at the Cliffmere estate with my sister."

"That's no good. I'm in Italy. I can't bring the necklace."

"Why not?"

"I'm probably on some kind of watch list. My luggage will be searched coming back into the UK."

"Well, what about Brindy?"

"What about her?"

"Why don't you ask Brindy to do it? Mondragone murdered her grandmother. If there's a vendetta on her family, she should leave Italy for a while anyway."

"How would she get it through customs?"

"She has her own plane, right? They're a lot less vigilant about checking luggage that comes in on private jets," Sinclair added.

"I'll ask her."

"She can bring it to Victoria; I can arrange for her to stay at Cliffmere for a while. "

"Good idea. I'll try to convince her." Sinclair agreed. "But you know how she is. Nobody tells her what to do."

Charles laughed. "I know. Good luck."

VILLA BRINDISI, CAPRI

It was 5:00 a.m. and Sinclair sat unshaven, grubby, and exhausted on the pristine white couch in Brindy's house on Capri. He and Luca had taken the first ferry they could to get out of Naples. Luca was now asleep in bed—safe for the first time in more than a week.

Sinclair pulled the necklace out of his pocket and put it on the glass coffee table in front of Brindy. The sapphires gleamed with a deep cobalt shimmer.

"It's *incredible*," she said. "I'm astonished you got it back so quickly."

Sinclair let the comment slide. There was no use telling her all the gory details.

"I need to smuggle this back to England," he said.

Brindy's eyes shifted to his face.

"Why not just give it back to the Norwegians?"

"Victoria doesn't want her parents to know that Karl stole it. He's in enough trouble for running away."

"But I could simply say I found it here at the house after Victoria left."

"Yes, but the police have already questioned you. And you denied seeing it."

"True, but I could say it was in a dresser or something."

"No good. For one simple reason. You've been seen with me in Sicily. And your housekeeper let me in just now with Luca. The police assume I have the necklace, and you'd be tied up as an accomplice."

"So what should we do?" Brindy asked.

"Victoria has to call Scotland Yard and say it was simply misplaced, and she has found it in her bag—something like that. Since her family has asked for the investigation, the police would have to drop it."

"But how do we get the necklace to her?"

"Could you wear it?"

The contessa picked up the jewels and fastened the clasp around her neck. Sinclair looked at the gems nestled into her cleavage, and they looked exactly like a couple of the other gaudy necklaces he'd seen her wear.

"It might work," she said. "I'll rub the stones with a bar of soap. It'll look like costume jewelry when I pass through customs."

"All right. But listen, Brindy. Once you give this to Victoria, Charles and I think you should stay at Cliffmere for a while. You should keep away from the Camorra while the police investigate your grandmother's murder."

"I know," she sighed. "I should probably take Luca with me."

Just then he appeared in the doorway, eating a biscotti.

"Are we all going to England?" he asked.

Sinclair looked at Brindy, waiting for her decision.

"Yes, Luca," she said. "It will be the three of us together. Just like old times."

ITALY, TO LONDON

John Sinclair sat in the cabin of Brindy's Dassault Falcon 2000LXS staring at the orange logo of her company, Brindisi Enterprises, painted on the bulkhead. The aircraft could hold ten passengers, but there were only three of them. Luca was sitting in the back, listening to music, and Brindy sat across from him.

The airport crew removed the wooden blocks from the wheels, and the engine throttled up. It was a three-hour flight to Biggin Hill, a small private airfield outside of London. Once there, they'd go separate ways. Brindy would go to Cliffmere to return the necklace and lay low for a while. Luca wanted to come to London, so John and the boy would go there and join Cordelia. The very first thing he would do is contact Scotland Yard. The story would be simple: He'd been out at the dig in Morgantina and didn't know anything about a missing necklace.

The jet engines revved, and they began to bump along. The sky seemed to be free of ash. When he turned back from the window, Brindy was quietly observing him.

Suddenly he was struck with the unbidden thought of how beautiful she was. Brindy embodied the concept of *la bella figura*. Today she was dolled up in a blue suit, artfully mussed hair, large sunglasses, and a very low neckline. The precious sapphires were almost lost in her cleavage.

She smiled right into his eyes and leaned forward, putting her hands on her knees. The cleft in her breasts deepened, and the sapphires dangled like grapes on a vine.

"What can I offer you, John, to make you more comfortable?"

A seduction was implied.

"Don't trouble yourself," he answered levelly, "I'm perfectly happy the way things are."

Just then, a steward came over with two flutes of prosecco on a silver Christofle tray. The thought of drinking did not appeal to him, but Brindy lifted the glass.

"Cheers, John. Here's to us."

His hand stayed immobile on the armrest, refusing the glass.

"You're not drinking?"

"I see no cause for celebration."

Brindy eyed him with silent calculation.

"Why are you still so cold to me, John? Isn't it time we had a détente?"

"Tell me about the photographers in Capri, Brindy. I just can't figure what there was to gain by tipping them off."

Her smile stayed easy, but her shrewd eyes hardened.

"I don't know what you're talking about."

"Yes you do."

She picked up the glass and drained it in a single swallow. When she finished, she extended her empty glass as if to command the steward to appear. The man brought over the bottle wrapped in a white linen towel. Her dark eyes watched the pale liquid foam, and she didn't answer until the steward had left again.

"How did you figure it out?" she asked.

"Only four of us knew about Victoria in Capri—me, Charles, Cordelia, and you. I have to assume Luca and Karl were too busy with their own plans to care much about tipping off the paparazzi."

"You were always so smart, John. I'll give you that. How long have you known?"

"I won't play guessing games with you, Brindy. Just tell me why."

"I figured with your reputation in tatters, you'd have fewer options, and I might catch your interest again."

She smiled, as if waiting for him to applaud her clever scheme. He felt a surge of almost uncontrollable wrath.

"Brindy, I can't believe you would go to those lengths to have me back."

"You should be flattered," she laughed.

"And *you* should be arrested," he seethed, glancing over at Luca.

He kept his voice low. The last thing he wanted was for the boy to see them fighting.

"Oh, don't be so dramatic," Brindy hissed. "It was all done with good intentions. I was thinking of Luca."

He shook his head, furious and disgusted.

"Brindy, I swear, if those sapphires weren't around your neck, I'd strangle you."

She smiled at his idle threat. "No, you wouldn't. You could never kill anyone, John. "

"Don't be so sure," he said and looked out the window.

GROSVENOR STREET, LONDON

Cordelia Stapleton sat in the second-floor library of her townhouse in Mayfair, trying to write introductory remarks for her lecture at the Royal Geographical Society. The nib of her pen glided over the paper with a rhythmic scratching. She paused to reflect, looking up into the filtered sunlight.

Every time she worked here, she could feel the presence of her great-great-grandfather. Elliott Stapleton had planned his famous arctic travels from this very map table. The room was filled with artifacts of expeditions past: walrus tusks and Inuit art, compasses and leather journals, antique celestial and terrestrial globes by John Newton & Sons.

Somewhere in the fringe of her consciousness, she heard the door open and slam, and there were muffled voices.

Her attention sharpened. Charles? His footsteps were always rapid and light, but this was the sound of a heavy tread on the stairs. After the break-in, she was always nervous.

John appeared in the doorway, rumpled and gorgeous, blue eyes against tanned skin.

"Hello, Delia."

The Gladstone bag dropped to the floor, raising a cloud of dust. He was dressed in expedition clothes—loose khakis and a white shirt rolled to the elbow.

"You're back!" she exclaimed.

"Finally," he said with a tired smile.

His expression was enigmatic—the joy of seeing her was mixed with a shadow of sadness.

"How'd everything go?" she asked. "Did you get the necklace?"

"It was tough. But everything fell into place . . ."

The answer was terse, but that was to be expected. His stoic nature never allowed him to dwell on any difficulties.

"You aren't hurt, are you?"

"No, I'm fine . . . the necklace is on its way back to Victoria."

He looked up and realized she was waiting and held out his arms to her.

"Come here, darling. I missed you so much."

It only took her three strides to close the distance, and she stood on tiptoe, throwing her arms around his neck. His shirt smelled slightly of jet fuel and verbena aftershave.

"I missed you, too," she murmured, nuzzling his neck.

The hug lifted her off her feet. He held her against his body for a moment before putting her down and then pulled back to look her in the eye.

"Delia, I don't want to ever fight again. It absolutely destroys me."

"I know. I'm so sorry."

"No, I'm the one who should be sorry. I've been an absolute fool for not letting you know how much I love you."

He planted a kiss on top of her head, and his voice shifted to a more conversational pitch.

"So, I hope you don't mind. I brought a houseguest for a few days. This is Luca."

She turned. Luca Brindisi was hovering in the doorway, a nervous smile on his face.

"Oh! Come in, come in," she invited. "I've heard so much about you."

Sinclair drew the boy over, and the two of them stood before her grinning. She was unprepared for such physical beauty. Luca had pitch-black hair, enormous brown eyes, and the long elegant limbs of the Roman aristocracy.

"Luca wanted to spend some time here in London before school starts, and I thought it would be a lot safer than climbing volcanoes."

"Volcanoes! I think you should stick to the British Museum. I'll take you there myself."

"He promises not to be too much trouble."

"Oh, I'm sure he's no trouble at all. Besides, who would object to two handsome men in the house?"

Luca blushed and ducked his head.

"Thank you for having me," he said politely.

Sinclair ruffled Luca's hair and then walked away toward the butler's tray. It was set with Waterford crystal decanters, heavy cut-glass tumblers, and a variety of his favorite brands of Scotch. He reached for the Laphroaig.

"Tell me, how's Kyrie?" he asked, pouring a measure.

"Doing a lot better. The vet says she can come home tomorrow."

Sinclair held the glass up to the light and regarded the few inches of amber liquid, then added two ice cubes from the bucket.

"I'll go over there this afternoon to see if they can release her early."

"She's doing well. They just want to monitor her kidney functions. The police told me to be more careful about leaving lights on in the house when I go out in the evening."

"I'm sure that would help," he said, lowering himself into his favorite chair. "And now I'm here, so nobody is going to hurt you. They'll have to go through me first."

She smiled at his bravado.

Sinclair yawned. "Darling, if you don't mind, I'm going to rest for a moment. It's been a rough couple of days, and I haven't had much sleep."

"Oh. Please, John. Go ahead."

"Would you mind asking Malik to get Luca settled?"

Cordelia walked over to the boy and picked up his duffle.

"Don't be silly. I'll show him around myself. Back in a minute, John. Then we can catch up."

A spiral staircase led from the library to the floors above, and she and Luca went up to the guest suite. The fourth floor of the townhouse was like a private apartment. There was a sitting room, a few bedrooms, and a laundry—all tucked under the eaves of the gambrel roof. Furniture was upholstered with chintz slipcovers, and there were original Victorian brass beds. The view from the window dormers was a perfect vantage point over the slate rooftops of Mayfair.

Luca followed Cordelia around, as she told him about the air conditioner and how to coax hot water out of the shower. When she turned to go, he thanked her for her hospitality.

CLIFFMERE ESTATE,
OXFORDSHIRE, ENGLAND

The Contessa Georgiana Brindisi drove up from London in a red Ferarri FF. It had been leased from a dealership in South Kensington. She rented, borrowed, and purchased cars as frequently as other women changed purses. In her opinion, there was no point in motoring anywhere in a second-rate automobile.

The drive from London took about an hour, and the Ferrari purred to a stop in the front courtyard of the Cliffmere estate. Brindy stepped out of the car and looked around.

This was a beautiful spot, deep in the English countryside. The sky was darkening rapidly for a storm, and the heavy atmosphere accentuated the green foliage, turning the lawn into green velvet. A classic border garden was still in full bloom—snapdragons, alyssum, lavender, hollyhocks, lupins, phlox, foxglove, and delphiniums—so different from the arid beauty of the Mediterranean.

It was quiet as she crunched her way across the pebble drive. There was nothing except the slight chirp of crickets and the ping of the exhaust manifold shield as the engine cooled off. Just as she reached the front door, Victoria called to her from the courtyard.

"Brindy! Over here!"

Brindy turned. The princess had clearly been horseback riding. She was dressed in fawn-colored jodhpurs and high black boots. As she strode toward her, she looked marvelous, softer, and more womanly. No belly bump yet—at eight weeks, the princess was still not showing.

"Hello V, do you like my necklace?" Brindy asked, greeting her with an air kiss.

Victoria gasped. "You're *wearing* it!"

"Darling, how else do you think I could get it through the airport?"

"Didn't they spot it?" Victoria asked.

"I wore the lowest neckline I could find. Believe me, the customs officer never even *noticed* the jewelry."

"Did they give Sinclair any trouble?"

"No, they checked his passport and searched his bag, but they didn't detain him. He's under instructions to call Scotland Yard as soon as he gets home."

"I'll tell them the necklace has been found in a pocket of my suitcase."

"That should fix things," Brindy agreed.

Victoria hesitated. "Have you seen Charles?"

"I haven't," Brindy said. "I've been dying to ask. Does he know about the baby yet?"

"No. I couldn't find a suitable time to tell him."

Brindy laughed. "Oh darling, there's *never* a good time to tell a man you're pregnant. Just do it."

Victoria sighed. "I know. He's coming up for the weekend, I think. And I hear that you are going to stay with us for a few days."

"I would love to," Brindy said with a smile. "Luca is in London with Sinclair, so I'm free as a bird. "

"Good afternoon, Contessa," a voice behind her said.

Victoria and Brindy turned to see an older woman, dressed in an expensive tweed jacket and slacks, standing behind them.

"You must be Marian Skye-Russell," the contessa exclaimed. "*Delighted* to meet you."

"Please come in. Charles mentioned you would be joining us at Cliffmere for a couple of days."

"Yes, if you'll have me. I've always wanted to experience English country life."

"It would be our pleasure to have you."

Brindy swept into the front hall and stood inside, looking around at the magnificent carved oak staircase and the stained-glass windows. Tapestries hung on the walls, and a suit of medieval armor dominated the landing of the staircase.

She turned to her hostess. "What a beautiful house you have. Perhaps later you would be kind enough to give me a tour?"

An hour later, Marian led the way down the dim corridor, stepping carefully over frayed oriental rugs and turning on overhead lights. The Cliffmere estate evoked a feeling of timelessness. With its architecture ranging from Elizabethan to Palladian, almost every period was represented. The corridors were crammed with antiques. Large formal portraits gazed down with austere expressions. They passed by many closed doors, each adding to the mystery of the old house.

The day turned rainy, and the plaster walls smelled slightly of damp. At intervals, there were large windows that gave a glimpse of the inclement weather. A violent rainstorm pelted the garden. Sharp cracks of thunder and flashes of lightning produced a gothic atmosphere.

"Does it always pour like this in England?" Brindy asked.

"Usually only in winter. But we've had the most peculiar weather this summer."

"So have we," Brindy informed her. "I think it must have something to do with that volcanic eruption in Iceland."

"Hopefully, we will have a few good days while you are here," Marian said, her bright blue eyes twinkling.

"Thank you again for inviting me," Brindy replied. "It will be nice to catch up with Victoria again. I haven't seen her since Capri."

Marian took a large ring of keys out of her pocket and opened an ornate carved door.

"I've picked out a special room for you. The Tudor Bedroom. They say Queen Elizabeth I stayed here once, during her reign in 1588."

They stepped into an ornate room with crimson draperies and precious furniture. There was a mahogany four-poster bed with a richly embroidered canopy. The French doors opened out onto the terrace and offered a sweeping view of the ornamental pond and the yew hedge beyond.

"How *lovely*."

"I hope you'll be comfortable here. It is very quiet on this side of the house."

"Thank you," Brindy said. "With all this fresh air, I'm sure I'll sleep like the dead."

VENETIAN BEDROOM, CLIFFMERE

Princess Victoria lounged on her bed after waking up from her afternoon nap. She had entered a sleepy phase in her pregnancy and simply couldn't keep her eyes open after lunch. But there were no excuses for putting unpleasant things off any further.

It was time to deal with Scotland Yard.

Her parents would be greatly relieved to have the necklace back in the royal coffers. She dangled it in her hand, holding the stones to the light. What an ugly old thing, so ornate and bulky. Who would want to steal it?

The private number they had given her for Scotland Yard was answered on the second ring. The inspector sounded relieved when she told him the news.

"I assume you will drop your investigation of John Sinclair?" Victoria asked.

The inspector assured her that her "companion" would be cleared of all suspicion, and she thanked him profusely.

She put the heirloom in the suitcase at the foot of the bed and let the whole matter drift out of her mind. The necklace had been found. Sinclair was exonerated. Now everything would go back to normal.

GROSVENOR STREET, LONDON

At the Stapleton household in Mayfair, it was the cook's night off, but a torrential rainstorm had dissuaded Cordelia from venturing out for dinner. Sinclair stood at the range, fixing his standard stay-at-home meal—Turkish spiced lamb, grilled vegetables, and rice.

Cordelia nibbled Greek olives and drank a light white wine as he prepared the meal. Luca was on the floor, playing with Kyrie. The elk-hound had fully recovered from what the vet said was a "toxic event." Now her favorite squeak toy punctuated the conversation.

Cordelia picked up a cube of feta from the salad and popped it into her mouth. Her appetite was back now that Sinclair was home again. She let her eyes linger on his well-shaped form. As he lifted the cover off a dish of vegetables his shirt pulled taught at the shoulders. All that digging at archaeological sites paid off.

"What will you have for dessert, John?" Cordelia asked with just a hint of innuendo.

Sinclair glanced over at Luca, then back at her. "Well, it's my first night back. I'm looking forward to a little indulgence."

"Oh, I totally agree."

Luca popped his head up, picking up something in their tone. He looked at Sinclair with curiosity.

"What are you talking about?"

"Dessert . . . I'll make up some traditional Turkish almond pudding with grated pistachios," Sinclair deadpanned.

"That sounds good to me," Delia agreed. "Or if you want something simple, there's some of that lemon sorbet in the freezer."

Luca went back to playing with the dog, and Sinclair gave her a surreptitious wink and continued cooking.

Dinner was almost done. A drift of steam wafted toward Delia, carrying with it the spicy smells of the Mediterranean. She had a sudden memory of another evening in Capri only a few weeks before.

Cordelia watched him take a knife and slice through an onion with meticulous care. Sinclair was a much more disciplined cook than Charles. He always held the glass measuring cups up to the light to make sure the amounts were correctly poured and leveled off his teaspoons with a knife. In contrast, Charles whirled around the kitchen like a dervish, never measuring, and seasoning to taste. They had such different personalities. How funny that they should be such inseparable friends.

Suddenly the front doorbell rang, breaking into her thoughts.

"That's probably Charles," she said, putting down her wine and crossing over to the kitchen stairs.

"Check through the slot before you open the door," Sinclair cautioned. "You need to be more careful now."

Delia skipped up the narrow passage and across the black-and-white marble foyer. When she looked through the eyepiece, Charles was standing out on the step in the pouring rain. Beads of water dotted his beautifully cut jacket. He gave her a grin through the viewer.

She pulled open the door and kissed his cheek in greeting. He folded up his umbrella and stepped inside.

"*Salut, chéri.* Did you have a good day?"

"I was working on my new hydrothermal vent project in the Mariana archipelago."

"That sounds exciting," Charles said, brushing the raindrops off his jacket.

"It looks like we might be able to get organized for next year," she told him.

"I'd love to hear more about it," he said, opening his umbrella in the hallway. "I'll just leave this here to dry, if that's OK."

"Sure. By the way, John's back from Italy. I tried to call you, but there was no answer on your cell."

"I've been dealing with the lawyers."

"Oh, how'd that go?"

"I'm happy to report that Sinclair's off the hook. Victoria called and said she found the necklace."

"Oh, that is wonderful. I want to hear all about it. Come on downstairs. We're cooking."

"*Mon Dieu*, you cooking! Surely we haven't come to that."

"Oh, don't worry. Sinclair is doing most of it."

Charles vaulted down the stairs and sauntered into the kitchen.

"Ulysses has returned," he said. "So how did it go?"

"An apt analogy," Sinclair said, focusing on his chopping.

"V made the call about the necklace; you're in the clear," Charles said.

He walked over, took an olive, popped it into his mouth, then poured a glass of wine. There was still no response from Sinclair.

Charles tried again. "So seriously, how'd it go in Italy?"

"Fine."

"Fine? That's it?" Charles asked. "No complications?"

"Plenty. I'll fill you in later."

Cordelia picked up her glass and took a sip. "OK you two. Hurry up and get dinner on the table. I'm starving."

"I'm hungry, too," Luca said from the floor.

Charles looked around to see Luca on the other side of the counter tussling with the dog.

"Luca! What are you doing here? Running away again?"

"Sinclair said I could come with him to London," Luca countered defensively.

The adolescent stood up and brushed the dog hairs off his clothes. Charles looked at him with a skeptical smile.

"What does your mother think about you staying here?"

"She likes it. She wants Sinclair to be my stepfather."

Cordelia blinked with astonishment. Sinclair still didn't look up. He continued slicing the onion as if he hadn't heard.

Sinclair, Cordelia, and Charles sat around the kitchen counter finishing their lemon sorbet. Sinclair gave everyone the details about the dangerous struggle with Mondragone at the dockyard. He pulled the envelope out as he told the story and poured a small gold ring out on the counter.

"It's rare, but not priceless," Sinclair told them. "A nice Roman arti- fact, actually—probably from the ruins in Capri, if I had to guess."

"It's strange he would be carrying that around," Charles observed.

"Why would Mondragone have kept it in the same envelope as the necklace?" Cordelia asked.

Sinclair shook his head. "I really have no idea. I guess I'll just turn it in to Scotland Yard and let them deal with it."

He picked it up and put it in his pocket. Cordelia looked at Sinclair, hesitating a moment.

"What is it Delia?" he asked. "You look like you have something on your mind."

"Well . . . it's just . . . are you *sure* he's dead?"

Sinclair shrugged. "He most likely drowned."

"Shouldn't you report it to the police?" Charles asked.

"No. The Naples police are absolutely complicit."

"How do you mean?" Cordelia asked.

"They've allowed Mondragone to terrorize their city with impunity. I feel no moral obligation to speak to them."

"Funny there has been no mention of anything in the papers about Mondragone's death," Charles said.

Sinclair nodded. "I expect it will take time. You know, identifying the body and such."

"You mean, *if* the body turns up. The propellers on those container ships could chew a man up pretty quickly," Charles pointed out.

"How horrible," Cordelia said, making a face. "I can't believe we are talking about this."

Sinclair turned to her. "You know, Delia, we should be careful for a while. I don't think Mondragone's men will come after us, but we can't be too careful."

"You know, there is the possibility they won't come after you. One of the rival clans may claim responsibility for killing Mondragone," Charles said, leaning both elbows on the counter.

"One could only hope," Sinclair agreed. "You should have seen his face as he fell. He looked like a wild animal."

"Don't think about it," Charles soothed him. "We should all just try to forget about it as best we can."

Sinclair nodded and straightened up.

"You're right, Charles. Now how about that coffee?"

He turned around to get the cups, and the fragrance of fresh-brewed espresso wafted over from the stove.

"So, what else has been going on while I was away?"

"The Herodotus Foundation has a full schedule."

"Well, I'm sure you have everything in hand," Sinclair said, transferring the demitasse cups to the counter.

Charles accepted his coffee and added a spoon of sugar.

"Yes, now that you mention it, tomorrow's the gala. And you're giving away a lot of money."

LINNAEAN SOCIETY, PICCADILLY, LONDON

Burlington House was ablaze with light, and a line of limos discharged their elegant passengers into the center courtyard. Formally dressed men and women made their way up the broad staircase to the central hall where waiters circulated with trays of champagne. The noise level was rising rapidly as hundreds of people arrived. Even the British royals were expected to put in an appearance.

This was the Linnaean Society's annual gala to announce new scientific grants. Sinclair's Herodotus Foundation was hosting the event. The main ceremony would be in the hallowed room where Charles Darwin first explained his theory of evolution. Of course all this was the magic of Charles Bonnard, who put it together.

Sinclair stood at the top of the stairs, elegant in his tuxedo, welcoming the guests. And Cordelia was the belle of the ball, greeting friends from the Explorer's Club of New York and the Royal Geographical Society of London.

"Darling, you look gorgeous tonight," Sinclair murmured as he paused from shaking hands.

He surveyed her new dress. The green taffeta gown was embroidered with ferns and orchids all around the hem of the full skirt.

"I thought you would like it. I can't believe this crowd. What a turnout!"

Charles wandered up to them, Perrier in hand. "This receiving line is endless. How many people have you greeted so far?"

Sinclair turned to him. "Several hundred. I guess you would call it a success, but Charles, tell me honestly, isn't there a way to give out these grants with a little less fanfare? "

"It's my job to make you popular. You're doing fine. Keep smiling."

Charles held out his hand for Cordelia. "I'm going to take Delia away for a moment to catch her breath."

"Take me with you also," Sinclair joked.

Cordelia squeezed his arm, in sympathy. "I'll be back in a moment, John. Enjoy your adoring fans."

"I will. You and Charles go ahead; have fun."

Cordelia giggled as she walked to the other end of the room.

"Sinclair hates all this social hobnobbing. He'd so much rather be out on a dig."

Just then, there was a commotion at the door, and Charles craned his neck around. "Oh, fantastic. Prince Harry is arriving."

"John will probably take the opportunity to slip away," she observed. "He hates that kind of fuss."

"In the meantime, what should I get you?" Charles asked. "Champagne?"

"That would be wonderful. I'm parched."

"Don't move a hair; I'll be right back."

Delia watched Charles retreat to the bar and join the line for service.

A man spoke up behind her. "Well, now that you've gotten rid of your date, you can say hello to me."

She whirled. A ruggedly attractive man was standing there in elegant black tie, a glass of lager in hand. She almost didn't recognize him.

"Come on, Delia. Is that any way to greet an old friend?"

"*Jude Blackwell!*"

"De-*li*-a," Blackwell intoned, lingering over her name. His gaze held hers as he raised the glass.

"It's been a long time," he said. "You're a sight for sore eyes."

"I can't believe you're alive, Jude. I thought Iceland would surely be your last assignment."

He grinned and reached for her hand. His fingers were warm and the palm calloused.

"Does my miraculous survival earn me a lucky kiss?"

She laughed and pulled away. "You will have to accept my heartfelt congratulations instead."

"Always playing hard to get," he said, shaking his head.

He reached over and took her hand again, pulling her closer. His eyes held hers as he spoke.

"So, all kidding aside, I've been thinking. If I settled down in London, would you consider having dinner with me from time to time?"

"No, Jude, I am seeing someone . . . John Sinclair," she demurred.

"John *Sinclair*!" he blurted. "I thought you—"

Another voice interrupted, "Blackwell, nice to see you. I didn't expect to run into you again so soon."

Cordelia turned to see Sinclair reaching over to shake Jude's hand. She flushed with confusion. Did they know each other?

Jude gave her a rueful smile and explained. "Small world. I just met Sinclair in Sicily."

Sinclair filled Cordelia in on the story. "Jude was kind enough to help Luca and Karl get off of Mount Etna. In the middle of an eruption, I might add."

Cordelia stared, astonished.

"I had no idea you saved Luca. Thank you so much,"

"No thanks necessary. I did what I had to. Luckily, it worked out."

Sinclair spoke again. "The King and Queen of Norway have also asked me to convey their warmest regards. I hear they are sending you some kind of medal."

"Oh, no kidding? Well, that will be something to brag about," Jude laughed. "And what's become of the errant prince?"

"Karl is now under strict supervision. As might be expected."

"Not a bad kid," Blackwell said. "He has a real head on his shoulders. He was telling me all his dreams about becoming a scientist."

"Well it's not likely he'll be allowed to, considering his social rank," Sinclair said ruefully. "His future is rather limited."

"A pity, he has potential."

"Yes. Well, Karl and Luca are alive because of you," Sinclair said, returning to the original subject. "So thanks, once again."

"Hey, don't mention it," Jude said, edging away to join another group. "Anyway, nice seeing you again, Sinclair . . . take care, Delia."

Sinclair's eyes followed him, then he turned back to Cordelia. "You two seemed friendly."

"Yes, we met years ago."

Despite her best efforts she felt a blush creep up her neck. Sinclair noticed, and his eyes narrowed.

"I hope you weren't encouraging him."

"Why would you think that?"

"Maybe because he was holding your hand."

She lifted her chin and looked him in the eye.

"You're not the only one with a past, you know."

"Delia," he said warningly. "Let's not get into all that again."

"You started it, John."

"What do you want me to do, watch you flirt with Blackwell right under my nose?"

"Well, you'll have to get used to the fact that I know plenty of attractive men. The double standard is over."

At that moment, Charles ambled over. Cordelia accepted the champagne flute and took a long sip, regarding Sinclair over the rim of the glass.

Charles swiveled from one to the other, sensing a sudden change in mood.

"Why do I get the feeling I missed something?"

The electronic squeal of a microphone cut through the noise.

"Is this thing on?" someone said into a microphone.

As everyone turned, the director of the Royal Geographical Society was bending forward trying to get the attention of the crowd. The program wasn't due to begin for another half hour.

"Ladies and gentlemen, fellow scientists, a brief announcement if you please."

The crowd hushed.

"The volcano advisory office in London has just informed us that Iceland has entered a second phase of eruption. There are now two volcanoes. Katla and Eyjafjallajökul are both now classified at a level seven."

A silence fell over the room. Then people broke into groups, murmuring.

"I don't understand," Charles said. "What does that mean, Delia?"

She explained. "We really should ask Jude. He knows so much more about Iceland than I do. But the VAAC office in London monitors Iceland. And I know Katla has been a worry of theirs for years."

She turned and beckoned Jude over. He took another swig of his lager and rejoined their group.

"How bad is this?" Sinclair asked.

Jude took a deep breath and exhaled, his face somber. "It's bad.

Katla is one of the biggest in Iceland. And historically, it tends to show increased activity whenever Eyjafjallajökul erupts."

"What does 'level seven' mean?" Charles asked.

Jude rubbed his chin in a weary way.

"Let me put it this way: the Volcano Explosivity Index (VEI) refers to the amount of debris that is ejected from a volcano. There hasn't been a 'seven' in about two hundred years. The last time was Mount Tambora in 1815."

"So what happened then?"

"The ash blocked the solar rays, and it set off a volcanic winter on a global scale."

"Could that happen this time?" Sinclair asked, appalled.

"Actually, I'm thinking this eruption might be as big as the Laki disaster in 1783."

"What happened then?" Cordelia asked.

"Millions died all through Iceland, the British Isles, Scandinavia, and Europe. I believe the final death toll was six million. It was mostly respiratory failure from the volcanic ash, and when the crops failed there was widespread starvation."

"So you think this eruption will be a global disaster?" Sinclair asked.

All Jude's humor was gone, his expression grim. "Well, I'd venture to say it's going to be a major problem."

Salvatore Mondragone edged closer to Sinclair. The room was so crowded he could easily blend into the mob of people. This was an exclusive event, but Mondragone was not impressed. As far as he was concerned, the mission of the Linnean Society—to promote the natural sciences—was for crazy rich people who wanted to go off into the jungle with a butterfly net and an aluminum canteen.

He was all about business. And now that Sinclair had been linked to inquiries into his financial dealings, he wanted to know more. Did the American archaeologist work for MI6? Archaeology would be a perfect cover. He could go to any country and travel wherever he wanted with no questions asked.

But, if not the Special Intelligence Service, then who? Perhaps Sinclair was a free agent, hired by the British Government to gather information about the Camorra? Had he been tasked to kill the top bosses?

Even the sapphire necklace seemed suspicious. It could have been sold on the black market for the purpose of entrapment.

There was only one thing to do. Sinclair would have to be eliminated. But London was not Naples, and assassinations had to be planned carefully.

Mondragone flagged the waiter for another glass of Pellegrino and squeezed the lime wedge into the glass. He was not drinking alcohol; it wouldn't do to mix hard liquor with painkillers.

His body was still suffering contusions from that fall at the dockyard. His feet smashed onto the water first, and luckily his shoes bore the brunt of the force. But now, several days later, his ankles were as bruised as if he had landed on concrete.

Mondragone circled around and watched Sinclair and his girlfriend laugh together as if they hadn't a care in the world. And only one emotion consumed him—a burning desire to kill the man.

Sinclair walked to the podium to make a few remarks as the round of clapping died down. After a quick scan of the crowd, he located Cordelia standing by herself toward the back. Charles and Jude were conversing nearby.

Facing the spotlight, he couldn't see much; the backlight haloed everyone's head, and their faces were indistinct. But suddenly a silhouette seemed familiar, and his heart skipped a beat.

It couldn't be Mondragone, could it?

The man turned toward Cordelia and made a remark. She nodded and smiled at the pleasantry. Sinclair abandoned the microphone and pushed through the bystanders with near-frantic urgency. When he reached Cordelia, the man had disappeared. People were murmuring in confusion.

"Aren't you supposed to do your speech now?" Cordelia asked.

He brushed past her. "I need to ask Charles something."

Sinclair pulled Charles aside and spoke quietly.

"We have to get her out of here!"

"What's the matter with you?" Charles hissed. "You're supposed to announce the grant."

Sinclair leaned forward and whispered.

"I can't . . . he's here."

Charles widened his eyes.

"Mondragone?"

"Yes. He's come to finish it."

Charles reacted swiftly.

"I'll take care of Delia. You go make the announcement as if nothing were wrong."

"How can I do that, Charles?" Sinclair demanded. "We are all in danger."

"Don't worry. Security is tight. Prince Harry is here. Mondragone won't risk it."

"But what about Delia? He was just talking to her."

"I'll get her outside. You can join us as soon as you do the awards."

Sinclair noticed Jude Blackwell lingering and grasped his arm. "We have an emergency."

"What's up?" he asked, as he put his glass on a waiter's tray.

"We need help to get Cordelia to the car," Charles said.

"I don't understand."

"There's no time to explain," Charles whispered. "Sinclair, *go*! We have it under control. Don't keep everyone's attention on us."

Sinclair gave a curt nod and walked to the podium. Up at the front of the room, he raised the microphone higher and spoke.

"Ladies and gentlemen, forgive the interruption. First, let me begin by thanking you for attending our annual event."

Charles pulled Jude aside for another hurried conference.

"We need to get Cordelia to the car. First, I'm going to go check the door. You follow with Delia. Keep a sharp eye out for trouble."

"Sure thing. But how are we going to get Cordelia out of the room without her raising a fuss? She'll never leave without Sinclair."

"Use your charm," Charles said and winked.

Jude sidled up to Cordelia and spoke quietly.

"I have to talk to you."

She turned, confused.

"Not now. John is just starting his speech."

"Exactly. It's a perfect time to talk alone." Jude took her arm. "I have something I need to tell you. It's urgent."

Cordelia rolled her eyes.

"We'll just step outside. This way," he said and walked her quickly through the crowd and down the central stairs to the exterior of the building.

Jude assessed the situation. The courtyard of Burlington House was dark and shadowy. There were a hundred places for a gunman to hide. Any person emerging from the party would be outlined in the light—a perfect setup for an assassination. They had to find shelter quickly.

Jude didn't tarry on the steps. Instead, he walked with Cordelia toward a dozen black limousines. The drivers were standing around in clusters, smoking and exchanging stories.

"We can sit inside your car," he said.

"Why?" she demanded.

"Delia, please," he begged, "*Where* is your car?"

She pointed out a limo parked at the curb, and Jude opened the back door.

The driver noticed them and cast his cigarette to the pavement, grinding it out.

"You're back early, aren't you?" the man asked, checking his watch.

Cordelia gave him a wave. "We're not leaving. We're just going to sit for a moment."

She entered the car, and Jude climbed in after her and slammed the door. Inside it was dark, and the windows were tinted. Jude exhaled. They were safe.

"So what's this all about?" she demanded, arranging her gown.

"I wanted to ask you about something."

"I hope this isn't some misguided attempt to make a pass at me."

"Don't be ridiculous, Delia. I may be rough around the edges, but I have more class than that."

The door opened, and Charles climbed in on her other side.

"Charles! What's going on?" Cordelia gasped.

"Mondragone is here," he said, slightly breathless.

"The gangster?" Cordelia struggled for the door handle. "I can't believe you two just hustled me out and left Sinclair on his own."

"Sinclair *asked* us to get you out," Jude countered.

"Well, that's just ridiculous. I'm going back in."

Jude reached over and grabbed her wrist.

"Not so fast, Delia."

"Jude, let go of me, or you'll regret it," she threatened, struggling in his grip.

Charles spoke up, his tone exasperated. "Jude, let her go. Delia, cut it out. Sinclair is coming out in two minutes. We *all* have to get out of here."

Five minutes later, Sinclair stepped out onto the sidewalk and looked around, face haggard in the streetlight. Charles lowered the limo window and flagged him.

Sinclair sprinted to the vehicle and slid in, taking the reverse banquette opposite Charles, Jude, and Cordelia.

"Let's go," he said, loosening his tie and pushing the intercom to tell the driver to head home.

"You still need me?" Jude asked.

Sinclair looked over, realizing Jude was still there.

"Oh, sorry. We can drop you off. Where are you staying?"

"The Goring. But look, why don't I stick around? You might need another pair of hands if you're in a tight spot."

"Actually, we could use all the help we can get. We have a situation with Salvatore Mondragone."

Jude's expression became serious. "Charles told me. If you need help, I'm in."

"Let's all go back to the house and figure out our next move," Sinclair suggested. "Jude, you should stay over. We can send for your bag from the hotel."

"Your call," Jude agreed.

Sinclair noticed Cordelia's studied indifference in the conversation. Was she interested in Jude? He had no time for that right now. They needed extra manpower. And Jude was more than capable of holding his own, if push came to shove with the Camorra.

"Keep a sharp lookout for anyone following us," Sinclair said to Charles as he signaled the driver to go.

Charles looked nervously out the back window. "Listen, I think I should take Cordelia up to Cliffmere as soon as possible. She can stay with my sister and Victoria."

"Good idea," Sinclair nodded.

"The nerve of you two!" Cordelia gasped. "Don't *I* get a say?"

"I was just thinking out loud," Charles protested.

"Don't be difficult, Delia," Sinclair told her firmly. "Everyone is concerned for your safety."

She sat back, fuming. "Why can't I stay in London with you?"

"I'm Mondragone's target," Sinclair explained. "And I don't want you anywhere near me while this is going on."

"And *I* don't want you wandering around by yourself with a crazy gangster trying to kill you," she shot back.

Sinclair sighed. "We're going to have to compromise, Delia. You go to Cliffmere with Charles and Jude. I'm going to report all this to Scotland Yard, and I promise I will drive straight up there afterward."

"No. Absolutely not. I'm staying."

Sinclair leaned forward and took both her hands in his.

"Let's not fight about it. I need you to help me. Please. Go with Charles and Jude. I'll join you as quickly as I can."

Cordelia sat back in the limo seat, resigned.

"Fine."

"So you'll go?" Charles asked, astonished at her capitulation.

"Yes, I'll go. But don't underestimate me, gentlemen. If I find out you have double-crossed me and have exiled me with the 'women' at Cliffmere, you won't have to worry about Salvatore Mondragone. *I will kill all three of you!*"

There was a moment of shocked silence, and then Jude spoke up.

"I don't know about you guys . . . but personally, I'm terrified."

GROSVENOR STREET, LONDON

At 8:00 a.m. the next morning, the townhouse dining room was empty. Jude entered in search of breakfast and looked around the beautifully appointed room with its long mahogany table and dozens of carved Hepplewhite chairs. He seemed to be the first person up.

The discussion about Mondragone went late into the night. Sinclair, Cordelia, and Charles were still sleeping. Uncertain what to do, he stood staring out the window, watching the traffic pick up outside in the street. Eventually, the housekeeper came in, bearing a salver of toast covered with a linen napkin.

"Breakfast is ready, sir, " she said, pointing to sideboard dishes. "Please eat hearty. I don't like to see men go out of my house in the morning without a proper fry-up."

She handed him an empty china plate and lumbered out. No other invitation was necessary. Luscious scents were coming from the chafing dishes, so Jude went to investigate, lifting each silver dome.

From the look of things, breakfast was lavish in the Stapleton household: There were scrambled eggs, Scottish salmon, kippers, bangers and rashers, as well as fruit and pastry. He filled his plate liberally and sat down to eat. The scrambled eggs were rich, fluffy, and perfectly seasoned.

"Hello. You're up early," Sinclair remarked as he came into the room.

Jude turned. "I woke up at six. A late-night conversation about the Camorra tends to cut into REM sleep."

Charles arrived right behind him, perfectly turned out, as if he were going to be photographed for a men's magazine.

"Hey, how're you Charles," Jude said, surveying the clothes. "Going somewhere fancy?"

"Don't mind Charles. His sister is a fashion designer," Sinclair explained with a laugh. "He doubles as one of her mannequins."

Charles ignored the jibe. "As a matter of fact, Victoria will be at Cliffmere, and I wanted to look nice."

Jude nodded. "Oh, yeah. I guess when you're dating a princess, you have to wear snappy clothes all the time."

"Something like that," Charles said and picked up a plate.

Sinclair patted Jude on the shoulder as he walked by on the way to the sideboard.

"I can't thank you enough for all your help."

"No problem," Jude said, continuing to eat.

"Everything OK with the food?"

"Your cook is fantastic," he said, swallowing.

Sinclair sat down with his plate and opened the *Financial Times*. One article had a feature photo of the eruption of Mount Katla.

"Mind if I take a look?" Jude asked, trying to see it upside down.

"Of course," Sinclair said, handing him the paper.

The front page gave all the latest details: After decades of being dormant, the Katla volcano was now erupting in a spectacular manner.

"Is it bad?" Sinclair asked.

"Very. I'll show you something," Jude said, reaching for his pen. He found a clear margin on the newspaper and began to draw.

"What's that circle?" Charles asked, looking over at his scribble.

"It's the caldera. See, it's like a gigantic bowl, six miles across. The word Katla means 'kettle' in Icelandic."

"Mmm . . . hmm," Sinclair said moving his chair to see it more clearly.

Jude kept sketching. "The Katla crater is about two thousand feet deep and filled with ice. It's part of the Myrdalsjökull glacier."

Jude drew wavy lines down the slopes.

"So when Katla erupts, the ice melts and a huge amount of water pours down the mountainside."

He looked up at both of them. "In 1755, the flood discharge was nine million cubic feet a second, equivalent to the flow of the Amazon River."

"That's incredible! So what's happening now?" Charles asked.

Jude began drawing broad strokes through the center of the crater.

"Helicopter pilots have sighted cracks like this in the ice. That tells us subglacial activity has begun along the southeastern rim. And just yesterday there was a basaltic eruption recorded in the fissure swarm to the northeast."

"Hold on," Sinclair interjected. "Too much jargon. What are you talking about?"

"Sorry," Jude apologized. "Simply put—the eruption melts the glacier into water vapor. That changes into sulfur dioxide gas and creates a toxic cloud filled with ash."

"Where is it drifting?" Sinclair asked.

"Good question. Toward Bergen, Norway, then across the continent to Germany and France."

"Will it reach here?" Sinclair asked.

"Absolutely," Jude nodded, recapping his pen.

"But why now? We've had other eruptions in Iceland that didn't do as much damage."

"Well, here's where it gets technical. There are two kinds of volcanic eruptions: effusive and explosive. Etna was explosive, which as you know, usually shoots up into the stratosphere and then disperses."

"And this one?"

"Katla is an effusive eruption, a slow leak. So it's worse for the environment."

"So the debris will just keep coming."

"Exactly. Most of the gas and ash will stay in the lower troposphere. So with the high-pressure system over Europe, the output of the volcano will scatter all over the continent."

"For how long?" Sinclair asked.

"Months. Maybe a year."

"A *year*!" Charles said.

"That's not inconceivable. In 1783, the Laki fissure continuously erupted for four months—from July through October."

"I guess we won't be flying anywhere soon," Sinclair observed, pouring himself another cup of coffee.

They all sat ruminating on the turn of events.

Charles spoke up first. "I hate to change the subject, but we have bigger problems than the weather."

"I agree," Sinclair said, putting his cup down and wiping his lips with a monogramed linen napkin. "After sleeping on it last night, I've made some decisions."

"What are you thinking?" Charles asked him.

"I have decided to tell Scotland Yard everything about Mondragone. The entire story."

"How can you do that?" Charles objected. "You're already accused of stealing the necklace."

"And you tried to kill him," Jude added.

Sinclair took a sip of coffee. "It was self-defense. And since Mondragone survived, no crimes were committed. He's hardly going to press charges on assault."

Charles shook his head doubtfully.

"I want you to run it by our lawyer first."

"Fine, I'll call Jim and brief him before going to Scotland Yard."

"And then meet us at Cliffmere?" Charles asked. "I don't want to be responsible to Delia if you don't show up."

"Don't worry, I'll come. In the meantime, keep her busy."

"Happy to do that," Charles nodded. "She can feed the chickens with Princess Victoria and my sister."

Sinclair laughed. "Somehow I can't picture that. And speaking of, what are you going to do about Victoria?"

"What do you mean?" Charles asked, flushing bright red.

Sinclair persisted. "I know it's not really my business, but it seems my fate is closely tied to hers these days. Are you going to continue to see her?"

Charles reached into the pocket of his blazer and took out a small ring box. He put it on the table in front of Sinclair.

"Take a look," he said. "I bought it yesterday at Van Cleef."

Sinclair opened the lid and removed a ruby ring.

"Very nice, Charles. So this is it?"

"I'm going to propose," Charles said modestly. "I hope she accepts."

Jude nodded. "She'll accept. That ring is a beauty! You didn't spare the budget, that's for sure."

Charles took the ring from Sinclair and held it up to the light. The crimson stone sparkled like liquid flame.

"It's called a 'Pigeon Blood Ruby.' It reminded me of the element of fire."

"It's great," Sinclair approved. "I'm glad. Marriage is a wonderful institution. And it's better for the baby, of course."

Charles looked at him with a shy smile.

"We're just getting engaged. I don't anticipate children for a while. Victoria is pretty young for all that."

He lowered the ring and placed it carefully in the box. There was a deep silence. Sinclair stared at him.

"Are you saying that you don't know about the baby?"

Charles looked at Sinclair in confusion.

"*Wait . . . is Victoria . . . ?*"

Sinclair nodded.

"Oh, shit," Jude mumbled as he pushed back his chair and walked quickly over to the coffee urn.

Sinclair leaned forward and put a hand on Charles's arm.

"I'm so sorry. I thought you knew."

"How did you find out?" Charles asked.

His expression was complete shock.

"Luca let it slip. Brindy told him. I . . . I thought you . . ."

Charles threw up a hand for silence and then sat staring at the wall with sightless eyes. Embarrassed, Sinclair picked up the paper and pretended to read. Over on the other side of the room, Jude made a big production out of putting sugar in his coffee.

The silence lengthened until Charles finally managed to recover his composure.

"I'm sorry . . . you see I had no idea. It changes things a lot."

Sinclair smiled sadly. "How so?"

"Well for one thing, I know she'll have to accept my proposal."

Jude turned back from the sideboard. "Well, there you go. Look on the bright side."

Charles nodded. "Thanks, Jude. In fact, I would appreciate it if you would drive this morning. I'm a little shaky at the moment."

"Sure. No problem."

"Well, at least take my car," Sinclair suggested.

"Take your car where?" a voice asked.

They both turned, and Cordelia stood in the doorway, dressed in elegant black slacks and a sweater. Her long hair cascaded over her shoulders, and her face looked fresh and rested.

"Cliffmere," Sinclair told her. "Jude and Charles are driving you up there this morning."

"Where will you be?" she asked.

"We went though this already. I have to deal with Scotland Yard. I'll come up later this afternoon."

"Can I go, too?" Luca said entering the dining room.

Sinclair clapped his hand to his forehead.

"Luca! I totally forgot. Of course you should go. Your mother is there already."

Cordelia turned to the boy. "You could go horseback riding. They have wonderful bridle paths all over the estate."

"I'd love that," Luca grinned, glancing over at Jude. "Is Jude coming too? Wow, this is really going to be fun!"

Cordelia glanced over at Charles.

"What's wrong? You're so quiet."

He looked up, suddenly aware of her presence.

"No, I'm perfectly fine."

SOUTH KENSINGTON, LONDON

Salvatore Mondragone sat in the dining room at the Ritz Hotel in central London with his accountant. They were enjoying their normal three-course breakfast. Their topic was extraordinarily important. Mondragone wanted to know how many of his operations could withstand regulatory scrutiny.

The problem was most of his financial dealings were tainted by drug money and loan sharking. He was planning to cash out of everything and reestablish business in another country, somewhere with less financial regulation.

As the discussion concluded, the check arrived. Breakfast was astronomically expensive, as usual, and Mondragone flipped his black American Express card onto the small silver tray.

Within moments, the waiter came back and spoke discreetly.

"Declined, sir."

Mondragone laughed, embarrassed. "Vinnie, take care of this will you?"

His accountant snickered.

Mondragone tossed the platinum MasterCard onto the tray. "Put it on that one."

The waiter returned after several minutes.

"I'm afraid not, sir."

Mondragone flushed bright red.

"Vinnie, you need to come home with me to look into this," he snarled, digging for his wallet.

He tossed bills onto the tray with irritation, overpaying by fifty pounds.

"Keep the change," he snarled.

It was mid-morning and Salvatore Mondragone scrolled through his online financial records. The accountant had left, pale and sweating. All of his bank accounts appeared to be shut down and confiscated. One after another, the balance was tagged with the official warning: "Under investigation. Please contact your primary banking institution."

There had been hints that the financial regulators were after him, but he hadn't expected such draconian action.

Sure, pressure had been rising: A couple of his credit lines had been inexplicably withdrawn, and his interest rates had been ratcheted through the roof. But with his stream of cash from the dockyards, he didn't need very much credit.

The never-ending wealth had raised suspicion. Late yesterday afternoon, he received a hand-delivered summons from the British FCA requesting him to appear before a hearing to justify his income statements in the UK. American regulators from FinCEN would also be attending.

By his reckoning, arrest must be imminent. Mondragone ran a hand through his hair in desperation.

He'd have to flee the country and bring enough cash to travel and set up elsewhere. Returning to Italy would be impossible. The Roman police had named him as a suspect in the murder of the old Contessa Brindisi. He'd have to go outside the Eurozone. And that would take big money.

There was only about a hundred grand in the safe. Fabiola had some jewelry, but most of it was stolen and hard to sell. As he sat there at his Louis XV desk, he opened the top drawer. There was a checkbook. He could always kite a check to one of his friends. But most people who did business with him would wonder why he needed to write a check for cash. Suspicion would be high. Nobody would help.

He hadn't been this broke since he was a kid living on the streets in Naples.

Mondragone stood up and swung aside the Van Gogh to reveal the safe. Within minutes he had packed all the euro bundles into a hard-sided briefcase.

Suddenly, outside in the hallway, a door opened and closed. He hastily returned to his desk just as Fabiola came into the room.

"Good morning, *caro*," she said, coming over to kiss him on the lips.

"Happy Birthday," he replied. "Today's your big day, isn't it?"

"I know. I can't wait for the party tonight," she smiled.

For the briefest moment, her beauty distracted him. She was wearing a white peignoir trimmed with marabou, and the underskirt was sheer enough for him to see the outline of her body.

"What are your plans today, my love?" he asked, trying to keep things normal.

"Oh, nothing special. I'm going out this morning to find something to wear for tonight."

There were three hundred people coming tonight to her birthday bash. He had paid for the whole thing already, thank goodness. But her shopping excursion would be a disaster. Her credit card would be declined just as his was; their accounts were linked.

"Why don't you wear that pink outfit? I like it so much."

She smiled. "If you insist."

"Oh, I do. It's magnificent on you."

"What time would you like to go to Grosvenor House?" she asked, sitting on the edge of his desk.

"I guess we should go over there around seven," he told her.

Of course he couldn't go to the party. The police were probably on their way here to arrest him. And he had no intention of being home. His survival depended on a speedy exit from the country. Fabiola would stay here, of course. She'd make too much of a fuss if she knew all the money was gone. Women were always trouble like that.

He turned his mind back to the problem at hand. What were his immediate resources? There was enough cash in the briefcase for airline tickets. But too bad there wasn't something more portable he could take with him. He would need some capital to get started again. Wasn't there something small and salable, such as a gold box, a painting, or a ring? Unfortunately most of his trinkets were back in Italy.

"What's the matter, *caro*?" she asked.

"I have a headache," he complained.

She walked behind him and began rubbing his shoulders. The feel of her fingers kneading him agitated him even further.

"That's better, thanks," he said, shrugging her off.

She walked over and sat on the couch.

"Is something troubling you?" she asked.

"Nah. Just I have some business to take care of with Tito this morning."

He realized he wasn't sad about leaving her. His emotions had always been ephemeral, and now he looked over at her without remorse. He was simply trying to remember if she had anything valuable he could take. His eyes fell on her wedding and engagement rings.

"Do you want me to get your rings cleaned for the party?"

She looked down at her hand in surprise.

"Um . . . no, thank you. I just had the settings checked last week— the jeweler cleaned them then."

His eyes stayed riveted on the stones, trying to figure out how he could get them. Then he remembered.

The sapphire necklace!

It was worth millions. Enough to get him started all over again in a new place. In fact, there was no single object that was more transportable, or more valuable. The stones could be sold anywhere in the world. His mind went back to John Sinclair. It had only been a few days. The man probably still had the jewels. It was time to pay a little visit to his townhouse.

Mondragone stood up and walked casually toward the door, picking up his briefcase of cash.

"OK, I have a meeting with Tito. I'll be back later."

He stopped long enough to kiss her full on the lips. "Happy Birthday, *tesoro*. Have a good day."

CLIFFMERE ESTATE, OXFORDSHIRE

The ash cloud from the Katla volcano in Iceland was drifting to Northern Europe and the UK. The weather forecasters were calling it a "dry fog," predicting whiteout conditions by early afternoon. The acidic content of the debris would be extremely dangerous for anyone with asthma or other respiratory problems. Road traffic would come to a standstill and vegetation would wither. Her Majesty's Government was declaring a state of emergency, cautioning everyone to stay indoors.

At seven o'clock in the morning, Cliffmere farmhands were out working to salvage what they could of the crops. Day laborers were not driving to the farm today, and the production operations were very shorthanded. Marian and Princess Victoria were helping with the chores, collecting the eggs—something that was not usually done by the owner of the estate and her royal guest.

As the two women cut across the pasture, the princess was unrecognizable in a Barbour jacket and Wellington boots. She didn't mind being up so early. The sky was still clear; the natural fragrance of vegetation mingled with the earthy muskiness of the farm.

For the first time in her life, she was happy. Somehow everything was turning out fine. Her baby was growing, and she found the weight in her abdomen to be a comforting presence. She was calm and happy. Charles would be the father of her child. And that made the world an entirely new and wonderful place.

She and Marian approached the first chicken coop. The arrival of the two pairs of Wellingtons scattered the flock. Victoria burst out laughing at the antics of the hens.

"You hold the basket. I'll collect," Marian instructed.

The hen house was like a gypsy caravan—painted blue, green, and yellow, with large wooden wheels. Inside were small compartments, like individual cabinets, and Marian reached in and extracted a perfectly formed pale blue egg.

"What a beautiful color!" Victoria exclaimed, reaching for it.

"The blue shell is produced by Araucana chickens."

"I've never seen that before."

"We've adopted it as sort of a trademark."

Victoria wiped the straw and debris off the shell and put it in the carrier.

"Are they organic?"

"They're pastured. The chickens can roam and eat what they like, larvae and bugs mostly. Free ranging the chickens improves the quality of the eggs."

"I think they are lovely," Victoria said, turning one of them around in her hand, surprised it was warm to the touch. "Why does it feel waxy?"

"All fresh eggs are coated with secretions from the chicken. They have to be washed before they go on sale."

"I never knew that."

Victoria aligned the eggs gingerly in the wire carrier.

"I love being a farmer," the princess confessed. "I don't want to go home."

"You're welcome to stay as long as you like," Marian told her.

"Don't tempt me. I hate my life at the palace."

Marian nodded. "Well, that is understandable. I am sure it is very confining. But you may find that when you become a mother, things will improve."

"I'll have to get married first. Hopefully, Charles will come back soon."

"I'm sure he will. But if he is coming today, he'd better hurry, before they close the roads."

"I'll call him and let him know."

"Why don't we get these eggs into the barn first. I have Clothilde helping with the washing."

"Isn't she fantastic, working from her wheelchair like that?" Victoria remarked.

"She does very well."

"I'm sorry about dragging Contessa Brindisi out here to Cliffmere, but I owed her a favor for bringing the necklace back. I'm afraid she's pretty useless when it comes to farm life."

"I assumed that the moment I set eyes on her," Marian replied with humor. "With that wardrobe, I really didn't expect her to turn up at dawn to milk the cows."

Inside Long Barn, the egg washing machine was running. Clothilde was seated in her wheelchair removing two eggs at a time from the conveyer belt and placing them in cartons.

"Hel-*lo*, I see you have more eggs for me," Clothilde sang out.

Her skin was flushed, and her eyes sparkled. Victoria noticed that the old farmhand who was standing there broke into a huge grin at Clothilde's enthusiasm.

"We can finish this up after we eat breakfast," Marian laughed. "You are so efficient, we're well ahead of schedule."

"Have you heard from Charles yet?" Victoria asked.

"He just called, everyone is coming—Cordelia, Luca, and somebody named Jude Blackwell."

"What about Sinclair?" asked Marian.

"He has an appointment and will drive over later."

Victoria started collecting her hair up into a ponytail.

"Oh my gosh! If Charles is coming, I'll have to do something with my hair. And find something to wear. I'm a total mess!"

"No, you look gorgeous. Just slip on a dress," Clothilde advised.

Marian ignored them both. "Five people . . . I'll need to see about lunch."

"Don't worry about all this," Clothilde said, indicating the egg washing operation. "I'll finish up after breakfast."

"Sure," the farmhand said. "We can get these packed up in no time."

GROSVENOR STREET, LONDON

The engine of the Land Rover Defender rumbled to life, and Jude adjusted the mirrors to his height. Charles and Jude were in the front, Luca and Cordelia in the back.

"Everything OK?" Charles asked.

"Fine. Just worried about visibility," Jude told him.

"Is it that bad?" Charles asked.

"Yes, the radio says they are shutting down the major highways."

Jude pressed the button to open the garage door and eased the car out into a misty day. The ashfall was coming down like snow flurries, coating the streets with a fine powder. Jude turned on the windshield wipers. They circumnavigated Grosvenor Square. At the motorway entrance there was an orange flashing sign: "HAZARD—DUAL CARRIAGEWAY CLOSED."

Jude sighed. "Now what?"

Charles pointed left. "There's a shortcut through the back roads. Turn here, and I'll direct you."

"I'm glad you know where you're going," Jude said, cranking the wheel. "I'd be lost."

He checked in the mirror and made a left.

Thirty seconds later, a "beluga black" Maybach 57S also made the turn. It was driven by a chauffeur in a peaked cap. In the backseat were Salvatore Mondragone and Tito.

NEW SCOTLAND YARD

John Sinclair sat with three senior officers, telling his saga about Salvatore Mondragone. Their eyes narrowed with disbelief, as they took copious notes.

"So you think Mondragone is trying to cause some mischief with you, sir?"

Sinclair huffed impatiently. "Let me make myself perfectly clear. I don't *think* Mondragone is going to try to kill me. I know he is."

The three detectives stared at him. The senior officer finally spoke.

"We advise you to keep yourself aware at all times."

"What do you mean by that?"

"Unfortunately, Mr. Mondragone appears to have fled his home in London. We don't know where he is at this moment."

Sinclair sat back, astonished. "Didn't you say he was under police observation?"

"He was. But all our men had to deal with the ash, and Mondragone slipped away."

"Can you give me some police protection until you locate him?"

"I'm afraid not, sir. You see, there has been no direct threat to your life."

"But there *was* a threat; I already told you."

"That attack occurred in Italy. Something needs to happen in the UK before we can assign an officer."

Sinclair pushed back from the table.

"Well I'm going to go somewhere quiet until Mondragone is apprehended."

"Where can we reach you, sir, if there is a need?"

Sinclair stood up and collected his jacket.

"Cliffmere Estate, Oxfordshire."

Charles fiddled with the satellite radio while Jude drove. The beautiful strains of the Albioni Adagio in G minor flowed through the car. Everyone was silent, absorbed in their own thoughts.

Jude peered forward, concentrating on driving. Luca was in the backseat, rock and roll music flowing through his earbuds. Cordelia sat next to him, her head against the window, dozing.

Charles reflected on the news of Victoria's pregnancy. In retrospect, he could see that she had been trying to tell him about the baby all along. But the crisis with Karl had curtailed the discussion.

He took a deep breath and let it out slowly to steady himself. Jude glanced over with a sympathetic smile.

"You'll be fine, mate. She's a beauty. And rich, too. You can't beat that."

Charles gave him a nod and decided to change the subject to the weather.

"This is just like very dense smog," he observed.

"Terrible stuff," Jude replied. "Full of acid. You don't want to breathe it, or even eat anything that gets coated with it."

"Cliffmere must be in a frenzy," Charles observed. "Maybe we can make ourselves useful with the animals and crops."

"Not in that outfit," Jude joked. "No use getting mud on yourself before you propose."

"Right," Charles agreed, smiling.

They lapsed into silence. The haunting music inside the car was conducive to deep reflection, and he returned to thinking about the baby. He looked down at his hands and noticed that Victoria's ponytail fastener still encircled his wrist. He had picked it up weeks ago, off the terrace in Capri. The need for that small talisman was telling—he had been in love from the very start.

Victoria was a perfect match. His friends assumed she was a capricious flirt, but he had seen another side of her. V was a serious young woman who was clinging to the last vestige of freedom before she took the weight of a country on her shoulders. Her position as queen would be a lifetime obligation. And he would be at her side.

Charles looked up and noticed the ash had cut visibility to less than twenty feet. How different from the sun-drenched week in Capri. His thoughts went back to a few vivid memories: Victoria in the pool and then lounging on the chaise in the brilliant sunshine. Suddenly a vision came to him, totally unsolicited.

He imagined his infant son taking his first halting steps across a sunlit terrace at Villa San Angelo. His future was not an unknown. His son would change everything.

Charles looked over at Jude and smiled.

"I'm feeling better."

"That's the spirit."

"I think I should speak to Victoria as soon as we get there."

"Good idea, strike while the iron is hot," Jude agreed. "But if this ashfall gets any worse, I don't know if Sinclair is going to make it."

Charles laughed.

"What's so funny?" Jude asked.

"Oh don't worry about Sinclair; he'll get to Cliffmere all right."

"Why do you say that?"

"He's not about to leave you alone with his girl for the weekend."

Jude smiled. "Is it that obvious?"

Charles nodded. "Absolutely."

CLIFFMERE ESTATE, OXFORDSHIRE

The Land Rover turned into the gates at Cliffmere, and the chauffeur-driven car with Salvatore Mondragone and Tito were right behind.

"A lot of people in that car," Tito remarked.

"One of them has to be Sinclair," Mondragone replied.

The glowing red taillights of the first vehicle receded down the long line of elms in the direction of the house.

"Pull in," Mondragone told his driver. "Put it there."

They drove over the grass, tires bumping. If they parked between the trees, no one could see the vehicle from the house. Mondragone stepped out, noticing that a dusting of soot was beginning to cover the grass. It was like fine gray flour on his leather shoes.

The natural disaster was working in his favor. With the volcanic debris shutting down roads, authorities would not be out looking for him. In the next forty-eight hours there would be a window of opportunity to flee the country. Police would be occupied with other emergencies.

He slammed the car door shut and walked under the canopy of leaves. Tito climbed out, limping over to join his boss.

Mondragone watched the man struggle across the uneven lawn. His ghoulish appearance and white hair were even more noticeable out here in the country.

"You need to stay with the driver," he instructed.

"Why?" Tito demanded.

"I need you to keep an eye on the front gate and watch the car."

"OK, boss."

"Stay out of sight. Sit in the front seat like you're having a smoke."

"You got it," Tito said, smiling, through crooked yellow teeth. "I'll be there."

Mondragone set out on foot for the enormous mansion.

All this seemed a lot of trouble. A real long shot. But if he could get his hands on the sapphires, it would be well worth the effort and provide enough money to set himself up for life in Brazil, Colombia, or Argentina.

Finding the gems would be tricky. He'd have to locate the bedrooms. And in this huge house, it might be difficult. He might have to force someone to tell him where the sapphires were. He fingered the gun under his left arm. No problem. He came prepared.

GROSVENOR STREET, LONDON

John Sinclair walked into his garage in the lower level of the London townhouse and unlocked the Aston Martin DBS. It was a shame to take it out in this weather; the volcanic ash might damage the paint. But the Triumph Speed Triple motorcycle certainly wouldn't work; in conditions like this, he would need an enclosed vehicle.

Just before he started the ignition, he slid his hand into his jacket pocket to feel for his wallet. His fingertips met with another small object—smooth and round. It was the ancient Roman ring he had taken from Mondragone. He had picked it up this morning to return to Scotland Yard, but the discussion had turned serious, and it had entirely slipped his mind.

He put it back into his coat pocket, reminding himself to turn it in at another time. And Scotland Yard had something of his also: There was the matter of the diamond engagement ring the police had taken from his drawer. After this weekend, he'd take care of all the unfinished business. Right now, the police needed to focus on finding Mondragone.

The Aston Martin eased out of the garage into a foggy mist. Visibility was worse than he imagined, and there were very few cars out on the street. He'd take the shortcut and be there in less than an hour.

They all needed a nice calm weekend: Cordelia, Charles, Princess Victoria, and Luca. So much had happened. Jude especially deserved a respite; he had a terrible time on Mount Etna. And they could never thank him enough for saving Luca.

Of course, Jude was trying to endear himself to Cordelia. Sinclair smiled to himself. He'd overlook that little flirtation. Go ahead Blackwell, just try to win her over. With his Kiwi accent and ruffian manners, he was the classic "bad boy." These types were great for women's fantasies and terrible as husbands. Cordelia was too smart to fall for that kind of thing.

He was determined to make this a happy, relaxing weekend. After what he had been through in the past few days, a weekend in the English countryside would be welcome, no matter how bad the weather.

People always talked about London fog. This was the worst air quality he had ever encountered. He could barley see the road. Once out of the city, the back roads were treacherous. It wasn't so bad with the hedges on either side of the road; he could keep his eye on the wall of shrubbery. But when the road was flanked by open fields, the odds of ending up in a ditch were much worse.

He tried rolling down his window to see out the side, but the air was not breathable, stinking of sulfur and full of ash. He sealed up the car and cranked the air conditioner. The system would be ruined, but at least he'd survive the trip.

After an hour of tense driving, Sinclair pulled into the lane at Cliffmere. He'd made good time on the back roads. As he drove down the avenue of elms, he noticed a new Maybach coupe between the trees. That was a curious place to park. He'd ask Marian which of her acquaintances was foolish enough to leave their car outside during this kind of acidic ashfall.

Marian walked across the pasture to see how the men were getting on. The visibility was declining rapidly, as the ash rained down in small, almost invisible particles.

As she walked up to the fence, two farmworkers in neoprene pollution masks struggled to corral the sheep. There was a wooden ramp that led into the back of the truck with one man on each side. A black-and-white border collie worked as a header, in the lead, keeping the animals in a group and occasionally circling back to stop any movement away from the ramp.

The ashfall coated the wooly animals, leaving them muddy gray. Their eyes and snouts were pink and running, already irritated by the chemicals in the air and on the ground.

"Good morning, ma'am," one of the men greeted her.

"Good morning. I hope this is not too difficult for you?" she asked.

"It's fine ma'am. But we have the Dishley Longhorns in the west pasture that we still have to tend to."

"I'd rather you just pressed on," she said, looking at the sky. "I think it's going to get worse."

One of them agreed. "It's so cloudy now, I can stare straight at the sun."

Marian shook her head sadly. "It will be a miracle if any of these animals live. I've never seen pollution like this in my whole life."

"I hope it rains. Maybe all this will just go away," one man offered.

"There's no chance of that. It's dead calm," the second farmhand said.

"Well, we can only do what we can," she encouraged. "Thanks ever so much."

Marian strode back across the pasture; her hunter green wellies looked like they were coated with plaster. The men got in the cab of the truck with the border collie and started the engine. As they drove off, the dog began to whine.

LIBRARY, EAST WING,
CLIFFMERE ESTATE

Sinclair felt his tension fall away when he entered the elegant manor house. Cliffmere always felt like home. He and Cordelia had known the Skye-Russells for years. He'd spent plenty of time on the estate while he was courting Cordelia. And every time he came back, the magic was still there.

When you got right down to it, Cliffmere was the perfect spot to propose. He should have thought of that before. Cordelia's family had roots here. Her great-great-grandfather, Elliott Stapleton, and the owner of Cliffmere, Sir Mark Skye-Russell, had been friends. They had gone on many polar expeditions together in the early 1900s.

Maybe he and Delia would have a moment alone this weekend, so he could ask her to marry him. He'd better do it soon, especially with Jude Blackwell lurking around trying to catch her eye.

As he entered the library, he looked around, savoring the memories. This section of the house was a throwback to the Victorian era: The light levels were dim the double-height glass-enclosed cases were filled with tales of adventure and exploration.

Sinclair walked over to greet Marian. The woman was diminutive and jolly, the quintessential English gentlewoman—dressed in a soft, heather wool, tweed blazer, her white hair piled up in a prim bun on top of her head.

"So nice to see you, Marian," he said, bending down to kiss her on the cheek. "By the way, there's a car parked out at your gate."

"Oh, sometimes tourists stop to photograph the entrance," she said, dismissing his concern.

"I can't imagine any tourists today. I could barely see the road."

"I know. We're all terribly worried about this ash," Marian fretted. "The animals might make it, but the crops will be ruined. There's nothing we can do about the fruit and vegetable gardens."

She turned to Cordelia. "But enough about the weather. Delia and I were just catching up. Why don't you pull up a chair and join us?"

"I wouldn't want to interrupt," Sinclair declined politely.

Marian and Cordelia settled themselves in the large crimson wing-chairs by the bay window. Marian and Delia were the closest of confidants.

As the women talked, Sinclair wandered around, scanning the shelves. Gibbon's *The Decline and Fall of the Roman Empire* was still where he left it on the last visit.

"Hello, down there," a voice called from above.

Sinclair looked up and saw Jude on the second-level balcony, perusing the shelves.

"You just can't resist climbing things, can you," Sinclair laughed.

"There are some great books on volcanoes up here," Jude called down.

"Enjoy," Sinclair said, and ambled over to the heavily draped window to check the weather.

Sediment coated the lawn like frost. There would be no romantic walk in the garden with Cordelia today. He'd have to propose here in the library. Suddenly, he remembered another proposal that was supposed to take place today—Charles and Victoria. What a fun coincidence. Tonight they could have a double engagement party.

"Delia, where's Charles?" he called over.

"He went out to the barn to find V."

Marian chuckled. "Victoria ran upstairs to change when she heard he was coming."

"Why change?" Sinclair asked.

"Clothilde had a notion that Victoria should wear a simple country frock, to look like a milkmaid or something."

They all laughed.

"I guess having a fashion designer in the house makes life complicated," Cordelia said.

"To say nothing of a princess," Marian sighed. "We're all under terrible pressure to be chic. I've stowed all my ratty cardigans until Victoria and Clothilde leave."

"I wonder if I packed something fancy enough for dinner," Cordelia mused.

"It should be a great evening," Marian declared. "I'll have to remember to put some more champagne on ice."

"Who else is staying for the weekend?"

Marian counted off on her fingers.

"Charles and Victoria, Mr. Blackwell, Luca, and the Contessa Brindisi."

"Where *is* Luca by the way?" Sinclair asked. "Not getting into trouble, I hope."

"No," Cordelia smiled. "We sent him to the stables to find a horse."

"I don't think he should stay out long," Sinclair observed. "The air quality is terrible."

Jude spoke up. "The pollution is bad for the horse as well. The fluorine gas can turn into hydrofluoric acid and cause terrible sores on animal hides."

Marian nodded. "If he doesn't come back in a few minutes, I'll send someone out to look for him."

She turned to Jude, who held a slim volume in his hands.

"I see you found a book that interests you, Mr. Blackwell. That was given to my great-grandfather by the author himself."

He smiled.

"Yes, I can't believe you actually have a signed first edition of Frank Perret's work on Vesuvius!" he said.

"Who's Frank Perret?" Cordelia asked, glancing up.

"He is the father of modern volcanology. He ascended Mount Vesuvius during an eruption in 1906 and took photographs."

Jude sat with the volume in his hands as if he had found the Holy Grail.

"I expect that book has been on the shelf ever since Sir Mark put it there," Marian said, clearly charmed by Jude.

She walked over and sat next to him on the bench, watching as he thumbed through the photographs.

"Jude is one of the best volcano photographers in the world," Cordelia told her. "He just climbed Mount Etna while it was erupting."

Marian turned to him appalled. "Young man, I don't think that was a very prudent thing to do."

They all laughed.

Marian continued. "Why don't you take this book with you and return it the next time you visit."

"I couldn't possibly . . ." Jude demurred.

"But I insist," Marian replied. "And if you are interested in volcanoes, I have some other interesting things to show you in the portrait gallery. Why don't we all go?"

They all followed her into the next room, which was a long gallery of portraits and landscapes. There were at least a hundred paintings hung on the walls in a dense pattern, all the way up to the rafters.

"Have you ever heard of the 'Volcano School'?" she asked, walking along the row of gilt-framed canvases. "Sir Mark was enthralled with that genre of painting."

"Yes!" Jude turned toward the others. "That was a group of artists who all painted in Hawaii during the 1880s and 1890s. They did some of the first real pictures of Kilauea and other volcanoes in the Pacific."

Marian led the way, stopping before a framed watercolor of an erupting volcano.

"Well, here is a perfect example. The owner of Cliffmere was friendly with Constance Gordon-Cumming, one of the first women to paint Hawaii."

Jude stared at it, absorbing the details.

"Absolutely beautiful."

"But there is another one I wanted to show you, Mr. Blackwell."

Marian paused before a life-sized oil painting of a woman in a lace-trimmed dress and broad-brimmed hat. The lady clearly was an aristocrat, in buttoned-up gloves, holding a lace handkerchief. The sky behind her glowed red, and there was a volcano, its summit crowned with a fiery blaze.

"This portrait was done in 1784, after the historic eruption in Iceland."

Cordelia leaned in to examine it. "How gorgeous! Who is it?"

Marian continued. "It is a portrait of Abigail Broomfield Rodgers by John Singleton Copley. See—there is the volcano in the background."

Jude reacted visibly, flushing with excitement. "We were just talking about that eruption at breakfast this morning. It reminds me of what is happening now."

"Exactly," Marian nodded. "And here is another painting that is considered quite a masterpiece."

She pointed to another large canvas at least five feet wide.

"*Oh my God!*" Jude whispered.

It was a spectacular work of art. A classic stratovolcano dominated a stark landscape, and the surrounding countryside was illuminated with an unearthly glow. It was a masterful interplay of light and darkness.

"Joseph Wright of Derby," Marian explained. "He painted Vesuvius in 1775."

Jude was staring at the painting. Sinclair noticed a bead of sweat had formed on his temple.

"Jude?" he said quietly, touching his arm. "Are you OK?"

"I'm . . . not feeling . . ." Jude said and turned abruptly away from the painting. "It seems . . ."

"Sit here," Sinclair suggested, offering a bench.

Jude wobbled over and sat heavily on the seat.

"I'm so sorry . . . I don't know what just happened."

Cordelia sat down beside him and took hold of his hand.

"Your fingers are cold . . ."

"Oh my goodness . . . he needs some port," Marian exclaimed as she hurried off to get it.

"Take deep breaths," Cordelia suggested.

Marian reentered the gallery, carefully holding a glass of fortified wine.

"Have some of this, Mr. Blackwell. It's very restorative."

Jude took it, embarrassed. "I don't know what happened just now."

Marian patted his arm. "Young man, it seems to me you need a good rest. Now drink up."

He tossed the port down as if it were a shot of tequila. His eyes widened as he swallowed. "Wow, that's *good*. I feel much better. "

"Nonsense. You need a nice lie-down before lunch."

"I'd love that," he admitted. "I guess I didn't sleep well last night."

"Come along, I'll show you to your room," Marian offered.

After Jude and Marian left the room, Sinclair turned to Cordelia. "Maybe we shouldn't have brought him into this business with Mondragone. He's been through a lot lately."

"You're probably right. He looks exhausted," Cordelia agreed.

"Well he's in the right place," Sinclair said, laughing. "Marian has found someone to cosset for the weekend."

Cordelia nodded. "He's going to be her new pet, that's for sure."

"I can see it now," Sinclair joked. "We'll come back years from now, and he'll still be here, sipping port and looking at the picture gallery."

They both laughed.

Sinclair looked around. "So, shall we sit in the library for a moment?"

She looked at him and smiled. "Yes, John. That would be nice. I could use a little peace and quiet."

CHINOISERIE BEDROOM, WEST WING, CLIFFMERE

Jude entered the Chinoiserie bedroom and placed his overnight case on the luggage rack. Ever since that near miss in Iceland, he had been exhausted. A couple of days at Cliffmere should set him right.

He glanced around, assessing the place—much swankier than he was used to. Marian had given him a little museum speech when they came in, telling him the room had been decorated in a Chinese motif, dating back to the British Orientalist School of the mid-1700s. Black-lacquered furniture was overlaid with gold designs, and the walls were papered with a toile of exotic birds, pagodas, and picturesque Mandarins in flowing robes. He didn't understand half of it, but she had carried on to make him feel at home.

Suddenly terribly weary, he undid his laces, kicked off his shoes, and draped his jacket carefully on the valet stand. Then he vaulted up onto the mattress in a single bound. He stretched out and allowed his mind to drift off to sleep, hoping that if he had a dream, a volcano would not be part of it.

CLIFFMERE LIBRARY

Sinclair followed Cordelia into the empty library and turned and shut the thick oak door behind them. Alone at last. Finally, there was a moment when he could say what he wanted to her, without interruption.

She had no idea what was on his mind and walked over to the large map table to leaf through a book. He looked around the room, summoning his muses to help him. The wisdom of the ages filled the shelves: Plato and Aristotle, Socrates and Aquinas, Hume and Locke, Thoreau—all champions of humanity, all great thinkers of the past. But this moment was about the future—his future.

Sinclair walked over and took her hand, kneeling down on the carpet in front of her, his left knee creaking. The floor was surprisingly hard, something he hadn't anticipated. One part of his brain was amused at himself, subconsciously noting all the details of the moment.

He looked up into her startled eyes. She seemed so vulnerable, and he pressed her hand between both of his.

"John, what are you doing?" she asked, but the query seemed half-hearted. She knew full well. Her eyes were round and expectant.

"Delia, I can't go another day without knowing . . . this uncertainty between us has gone on entirely too long, and I blame myself for being so hesitant."

"Yes, John?" her irises were huge.

"You see . . . I was so afraid you would refuse. And that would absolutely kill me. I just don't know what I would do . . . but I'm hoping that, even with all my flaws, you might find something in me that you could love forever. So what I am asking is if you will marry me . . . if that would be acceptable . . . ?"

He faltered to a stop. The delivery wasn't great, but she didn't seem to notice.

"Of course I will marry you," she said with tears in her eyes.

He exhaled and stood up. Thank goodness it went as well as it did. Proposing was a highly overrated event—at least for the man.

Yet, there was something else he had to do. *Of course! The ring!*

"I'm afraid Scotland Yard has confiscated the diamond I had for you," he told her.

"Oh, don't worry about it. I'm sure it's beautiful."

"All I have is that ancient Roman ring. We could use that, at least for now. It *is* a betrothal ring."

"Oh, I don't mind," she said rather magnanimously.

He felt around in his pocket and found the small gold Roman band from Capri. The ancient artifact gleamed in the dim light.

Part of him didn't want to use such a tainted object. After all, it had been in the possession of Salvatore Mondragone. But then he thought back to the original owner. Some man had given this to his bride during the Roman Imperium. Certainly two millenia of history would outweigh the recent transgressions of a petty crook.

She extended her hand, so he could place it on her finger. He turned it sideways, anxious not to drop it in his clumsiness. It slid on, big and bulky but sufficient for now. Then he lifted her fingers and kissed the back of her hand.

"Delia, you have made me so happy," he said and meant it.

She stood on tiptoe and wrapped her arms around his neck. Her cheek felt cool when it pressed against his. He turned her face and sought her mouth. And this time, when he kissed her, it was different—much more tender—like they truly belonged to each other. The perfunctory engagement kiss lengthened. He had a vague impression that time ebbed and flowed as they stayed in each other's arms.

After a while, he let go and walked over to the corner where Sir Mark Skye-Russell had placed his old gramophone. It was an original American Sonora. Sinclair opened the wooden case and cranked the handle with deliberate care. Cordelia watched, absolutely charmed.

"That phonograph was a gift to Sir Mark from my great-great-grandfather."

"I know," he said. "I wanted to celebrate our engagement with the family, even if they are in absentia."

A wax record was already on the turntable, and he placed the needle gently on the exterior edge as it started to rotate. The same recording was always there—a favorite of Sir Mark's—one of the most popular songs of 1918, the year he died. It was Henry Burr's "I'm Sorry I Made You Cry."

Sinclair held out his arms, and she walked slowly over to him, tears of joy shining in her eyes.

WEST TERRACE, CLIFFMERE

Charles knew his way around the estate from past visits, so he cut across the drive, cap-toed oxfords making a loud crunch on the pebbles. Victoria was supposedly in the barn. It would be fun to catch her doing something rustic. A barn might be a very nice place to propose; the simplicity of it appealed to him.

Despite the bucolic setting, he had dressed carefully. Clothilde had made him promise to wear a certain outfit when he asked Victoria to marry him. She said that women cared about that kind of thing. Personally he found his sister's fashion dictates amusing, but he had worn the Chesterfield jacket anyway.

It was a light herringbone wool with a black velvet collar. Clothilde told him that the style—wearing a small strip of black velvet—originated in France, when aristocratic noblemen wore it to mourn the execution of King Louis XVI. She wanted his French heritage to be evident when he proposed.

In the distance, Charles could see the barn. A truck was backed up to the loading dock. Nervous, he paused in the middle of the border garden and checked his pocket for the box with the ruby ring. He'd rehearsed his speech a dozen times, but it might be good to walk around the garden to get his courage up.

He turned around and strode past a huge bed of blue delphiniums, thinking of what he was going to say. Once or twice he tried kneeling down, just to get it right. Should he have the ring in his hand, or leave it in the box? Which was the proper way to do it? There was so much to consider.

Luca Brindisi turned his beautiful chestnut mare onto a cinder track that wound through the fields and into the woods. The air was full of mist, and the horse pranced with skittish energy. The groom at the stables told him his mount was a classic British breed—"warm blood"—a mixture of hot-blooded thoroughbred and cold-blooded draft horse, a perfect temperament for a novice rider.

Luca cantered through the meadow. He squeezed his heels into the flanks and gathered the reins. The animal immediately stepped up into a gallop. Luca gave a little whoop, and they were flying along the path through the mist.

LONG BARN, CLIFFMERE

The old farmworker toted a metal carrier basket of forty-eight eggs into the sorting shed, balancing them carefully. They rattled as he put down the aluminum frame, but none of the shells were broken.

It was clouding up something awful out there. The radio said it wasn't a normal situation—and that much he knew. He'd seen volcanic ashfall before, when he was young.

Marian didn't seem to realize how bad it could get. If this kept up, they'd probably lose the harvest and half the animals. The dry fog sometimes killed the animals, destroyed the crops, and withered the grass. The effect was immediate. Entire forests could lose their leaves in a single day.

At least the eggs were all right. He adjusted the metal basket on the conveyer belt. The shells would travel through the automatic washer, and a needle jet spray would rinse them just like a household dishwasher.

Washing eggs was his least favorite job on the farm. His large clumsy hands were not suited for such delicate work. Some of the eggs would inevitably shatter as he tried to unload. By the end of the morning, he usually had yolks dripping down his clothes.

The visitor, Clothilde, was a genius at it—she could pack hundreds of eggs in just minutes. When he asked her how she managed it, she told him she was a fashion designer and had developed a light touch from years of sewing.

A lovely girl, and so was her friend, the princess from Norway. Victoria was just like her pictures in the *Sun*. But when you got right down to it, Clothilde was prettier than the princess. He'd tell anyone that, if they asked him. But of course, nobody would.

The farmworker broke off his train of thought. The first batch of eggs made it through the washer and was ready for the cartons. Focused intently on his job, he didn't see the man walk up behind him.

"Hold it there," Mondragone said.

The farmworker started in surprise, and the eggs broke.

"Blast," he cursed.

The yellow ooze seeped through his fingers. He turned, still holding the shells.

"Who are you?"

Mondragone pointed a gun at the bib of his overalls.

"I need your clothes."

The farmworker looked down at his stained coveralls in disbelief.

"Are you daft? These aren't worth half a pound."

The muzzle floated up to the level of his eyes and the soft thud of a 9mm bullet passed through his brain. The blood speckled the eggs with crimson.

The man stayed on his feet for a second, mouth open, staring into space, then his knees collapsed, and he fell heavily to the floor.

Mondragone put his gun back in the holster. The farmworker lay on the floor with eggshells still in his gnarled work-worn hands. The green Cliffmere overalls were large enough to fit over what he was wearing. Mondragone bent down and began stripping the overalls off the warm corpse.

Clothilde propelled herself across the stable yard toward the barn. The rubber wheels of her chair moved smoothly over the wooden planks. She had no trouble with mobility ever since the farmworker laid a platform of lumber across the gravel. Now she could get to the barn by herself.

She stopped a moment to rest and glanced up at the sky. The day was getting cloudy, foggy. There wasn't much they could do about the lettuce and other vegetables, but at least the eggs would be salvaged. As she approached the open doorway of the barn, something wasn't quite right. The egg washing machine was not on. Usually at this distance she could hear it doing the rinse.

"*Hello?*" she called, maneuvering her wheelchair over the doorsill.

There was silence. Perhaps the farmhand was delayed, or he might be out with the cattle.

Clothilde wheeled herself forward. There was a funny smell—sharp and familiar, like firecrackers on Bastille Day, or that time they went hunting for grouse up in Brittany. Her brain identified it—*gunpowder!*

Even before she saw anything, she knew a pistol had been fired. She stopped rolling her chair, unwilling to go farther. Then she saw the pale naked leg sticking out from the other side of the counter. All she could see was a bare foot and shin. It was a man's leg.

Some instinct of self-preservation made her look away. She froze, her hands poised over the wheels of her chair. Breathing was impossible, and the air would not fill her lungs. It felt like her heart would burst into her throat.

"*Are you OK?*" she called over to the farmhand.

She had no idea why she spoke to the man. There was no logic to it. Maybe she had the irrational hope she could bring him back. But it was useless. She knew he was dead.

From the courtyard, Mondragone watched the girl propel her chair into the barn. He stood undecided, fingering the pistol in his pocket, then walked into the barn and let his eyes adjust to the dim interior. Before him was a silent tableau. The girl was sitting in her chair, staring at the dead man's leg. Her hands were suspended over the wheels, motionless.

Mondragone came up behind her stealthily. She had all the outward appearance of shock—her eyes glazed, her breathing rapid and distressed. The rhythms of a murder scene were predictable. The scream would come at any second now.

Mondragone sprang and clamped his hand down over her nose and mouth, cutting off her ability to make a sound. She started violently like an animal that had been captured, thrashing with her upper body.

He tightened his grip, pressing his fingers against the warm flesh of her face. A quick twist would be all it would take to snap her neck.

He was prepared for a struggle, but she stopped after a moment. Her beautiful pale gray eyes looked up at him with terror and then fluttered shut. She fainted right under his hands.

Surprised, he let her go and stepped back, wiping the moisture from her mouth onto his overalls. Her head lolled back, eyelashes brushing her cheek.

Mondragone aimed the pistol at her forehead. The girl's eyebrows were light blond and beautifully arched. He aimed right in between and readied himself to pull the trigger.

Charles crossed the courtyard and walked toward the open barn door.

"Halloooo," he called, his voice echoing.

Some chickens fussed in the courtyard, but nobody else answered. Suddenly, an unusual feeling of danger flooded over him, a ripple of goose bumps on his arm. It was a familiar sensation, and he always trusted it. There was danger here.

He approached the open doorway cautiously.

Mondragone paused and listened carefully. A man's voice called out in the yard. Footsteps approached. He looked down at the girl, still unconscious. He'd better not attract attention by shooting her. Instead he ducked out of sight behind the large aluminum egg washing machine and waited. Within seconds, an outline of a man was visible in the barn doorway. It was a perfect backlit silhouette, the man's features obscured.

Mondragone aimed the pistol at the head—a certain kill. Taking this shot was as easy as a shooting range. Suddenly the silhouette was moving. The man raced toward the inert girl.

"Clothilde!"

Mondragone tracked him with professional skill, the pistol reestablishing aim. The man flew over to the girl who was slumped unconscious in the wheelchair. As he reached her, something impeded him;

he tripped and stumbled over the dead man's leg and fell, sprawling, just as Mondragone fired the gun.

Mondragone hurried out the side door of the barn, wearing the dead man's coveralls. This was turning into a debacle. He'd better grab what he could and leave. Tito was waiting for him, along with the chauffeur, at the estate entrance. But first he needed to go inside the house to find the necklace. The French doors on the west terrace were open. He slipped inside.

CHINOISERIE BEDROOM, CLIFFMERE

The volcano was shooting off projectiles—and he had to save the boys! Jude opened his eyes, and the gold silk underside of a bed canopy came into focus. He was at Cliffmere, not Mount Etna.

But there was something about that audible pop in his dream that was real. It was a pistol shot. Was someone shooting pheasants or grouse or whatever they did on these big estates? But they wouldn't be doing that so close to the house.

"Never a dull moment," he mumbled and put on his shoes.

It was time to investigate. The French windows to his room opened out to the terrace. The glass-paneled door swung open with a rusty squeal. Jude walked across the lawn and down the garden steps, crunching his way across the gravel in the courtyard.

The wide barn door was open. Inside, his eyes had to adjust to the dim interior. But something struck him as wrong, although he could not put his finger on exactly what. It was the silence, or a faint smell, that registered in his subconscious.

He started forward, and then he saw her—a beautiful blond angel, slumped in a wheelchair, eyes closed. She was the most ethereal girl he had ever seen, slim and pale, with white-gold hair that curled around her face in perfect soft waves. Jude ran over and picked up her limp hand. She was alive, her skin warm.

TUDOR BEDROOM,
WEST WING, CLIFFMERE

In the brief moment between sleep and waking, the Contessa Brindisi thought of Capri: the sun, the beautiful breeze, and the shimmering sea.

She opened her eyes and knew it was not real; the room was dark, and there was a cool dampness in the air. The heavy, red brocade curtains and the scent of greenery from the open window reminded her that she was in England.

Brindy stretched and looked over on the bedside table for a clock, but there was nothing but a vase of white roses. The drapes were closed over full-length windows, but she could see a sliver of light between the two panels. It was time to rise.

Brindy pushed off the covers. Sinclair was supposed to come to Cliffmere today, along with Luca. It would be a perfect day.

Now, where was her robe? She scanned around for it.

A faint glimmer caught her attention.

Someone was standing in the corner of the room.

Brindy sat bolt upright. She blinked a few times to make sure it wasn't a trick of the light.

The curtain billowed, and a narrow shaft from the window fell on the intruder's face. *It was a man!* He was large with a bulky build. The green Cliffmere overalls identified him as one of the farmworkers.

Brindy gasped in outrage at the intrusion.

"How *dare* you."

"Don't move," the man said.

The hands seemed to be reaching out for her, but then she saw he was bracing a pistol, aiming right at her head.

He had a thick accent. A wave of fear stopped her heart. He was Italian, Neapolitan? Suddenly, she recognized him.

"Cyclops," she said, and the word came out as an accusation.

The meaning was clear. He had come to kill her! Brindy found herself surprisingly unafraid. She had only one reaction. Mondragone must not find her son.

"You killed my grandmother," she said. "Why?"

He said nothing, dark eyes glimmering in the half-light.

For some reason, she felt perfectly calm. This man was a street thug and nothing more. He stood before her, gross and vulgar.

"Do you have any cash?" he asked.

She looked at him with disgust.

"*Cash?* I didn't bring cash with me. This isn't a hotel."

"Where is the sapphire necklace?"

"I don't have it anymore."

"You didn't fulfill the agreement."

"It's not my fault if your men are incompetent. I had it in Capri, right there in the bedroom, where I told you it would be."

"So give it to me now."

"No. All deals are off. You killed my grandmother. And now you can go to hell."

"Tell me where the necklace is," he growled, advancing with the pistol.

She belted her robe and stood before him, unflinching.

"It belongs to Princess Victoria, not you," she said. "I gave it to her last night."

"*Grazie, mille,*" he said, "Now I know it is here."

Her temper flared. "Get out of here, before I call the police."

"You will not call anyone."

He advanced closer, and she could see his coveralls were spattered and stained.

"Crawl back to your cesspool." She spat at him.

"How dare you insult me," he said. "I could kill you right now."

"You already killed a Brindisi. Isn't that enough? How does it feel to murder a harmless old woman for a few trinkets? No amount of money will ever give you class, Mondragone. You're nothing but a dirty peasant."

She took a menacing step toward him, and incredibly, Mondragone backed up, recoiling. Satisfied that she had cowed him, she started to turn away and saw their reflections in the large mirror on the wall.

It was a dramatic picture, the crime boss backing off from a woman attired in a red robe, her dark hair streaming over her shoulders. Her face was strong, angry, imperious.

The tableau in the mirror gave her great satisfaction. Mirrors don't lie, and every inch of her ancient Roman heritage was apparent. It was she who was in command. And Mondragone was a lowly thief in his spattered work coveralls, thick hands like pieces of meat grasping a pistol.

In the mirror, she saw him raise the weapon to shoot. She turned back, intending to command him to stop, but Mondragone pulled the trigger.

In the split second it took for her to realize what was happening, she called out. The word began with an S, . . . but the rest was lost in death.

The contessa fell straight back onto the bed, eyes staring at the ceiling, the pillow behind her splattered with crimson.

FRONT LAWN, CLIFFMERE

Tito walked around the lawn, smoking a cigarette. Mondragone had told him to stay put. But this was taking forever. There was no problem with him checking things out on his own. He told the driver to stay with the car and started off down the driveway.

The volcanic ash had gotten much worse; now it was so thick he could barely see ten feet in front of him. The line of elms extended toward the house, and he slunk from trunk to trunk. Soon, he could see the façade of the manor house.

His boss might need backup. He walked toward the garden, holding on to his Taser.

LONG BARN, CLIFFMERE

In the barn, Jude leaned over and brushed Clothilde's hair back from her face.

"Wake up, sweetie," he said, patting her hand gently.

She moaned, and her eyes flew open.

"*Who are you?*" she gasped.

He knelt down next to her chair.

"Don't be afraid. I'm a friend. What happened?"

Clothilde looked around and saw the body on the floor again.

"I came in and found him. He's dead," she said.

Jude turned to look. There were two bodies. The older man was face up, stone dead. The other body was face down, a younger man, nicely dressed.

"Who is the other guy?" he asked,

"*Oh my God . . . that's my brother, Charles!*"

Jude recognized the coat and rushed over to the body. He turned him over and found that Charles was conscious.

"Take it easy, there," Jude said.

He lifted the flap of the elegant coat and saw the shirt was soaked with crimson. There was a small hole where a bullet had torn through his shoulder.

Charles groaned and shut his eyes.

"Lie still," Jude ordered, "You've been shot."

"It's not so it bad, is it?" Charles asked, looking at him.

Jude peeked again. "Listen, I'm no doctor, but it seems to have missed all the important stuff."

Charles became more alert.

"Where's Clothilde?"

"She's right here," Jude said, moving so he could see.

Charles made an enormous effort to struggle to his feet. Jude steadied him as he staggered over to his sister.

"I'm here, *chéri*," he said, leaning heavily on her chair.

Tears poured down her face.

"Oh Charles, I thought you were . . ."

"I'm fine."

"No, you're hurt. There's blood."

"It's nothing. What happened?"

"I was so frightened," she explained.

Charles looked where she was pointing.

He recoiled in horror at the corpse.

"Who is that?"

"I have no idea," Jude said as he gestured to the man. "But look at that bullet hole in the forehead."

"Mondragone's signature kill," Charles told him.

"He must be around. We should leave immediately," Jude said. "Are you strong enough to walk?"

"I could push Clothilde in her chair. You run and warn the others."

"No. You're in no condition to push anyone. I'll carry your sister. And you get back to the house as best you can."

Jude turned to the girl in the chair.

"I think your wheelchair is too slow. I can carry you much faster."

"Whatever you think is best."

He bent down and gathered her up. She was so light he could have carried her with one arm.

"Charles, go as fast as you can. Keep a sharp eye out. Mondragone may not have gone far."

WEST WING, CLIFFMERE

As the clock struck noon, Marian walked down the darkened corridor to the west wing of the house. Nobody had seen the contessa this morning. Even if she were sleeping, certainly a discreet tap on her door would be appropriate. Lunch would be served in half an hour.

She knocked on the thick oak door. Nothing. Marian pressed her ear to the wood, but there was no sound inside. The knob didn't turn. She inserted the housekeeper's master key and pushed the door open.

"Contessa?"

There was silence. The breeze blew the drapes open. The heavy curtains wafted and fell, causing dim sunlight to flicker across the surfaces of the furniture. Marian got a glimpse of the upholstered chair, marble mantle, and carved wood bedposts. The covers were in disarray, pillows piled high.

"*Contessa?*"

Then Marian saw the pale arm draped over the duvet. It was unnaturally white, chalky in color, the deep red nail polish garish against the opalescent skin.

Marian approached the bed from the other side then halted, transfixed. A body was lying among the blood-soaked pillows. The Contessa Brindisi was not ill; she was dead.

VENETIAN BEDROOM, CLIFFMERE

Mondragone entered a beautiful bedroom with a large four-poster bed, needlepoint carpet, and huge ormolu mirrors. Everything was as neat as a pin; nothing out of place. Princess Victoria's personal luggage was on the rack at the end of the bed. He flipped open the top of the suitcase and began a quick search of the contents.

It took thirty seconds. The jewel case was right at the bottom—a blue leather zippered roll with six compartments. He walked to the dressing table and began shaking out the contents—gold chains, pearls, bracelets, rings.

There it was—the necklace—deeper blue than he had remembered, and somewhat dull in finish. It didn't look quite the same, but this had to be it. Mondragone put it in his pocket and walked out the door.

MAIN HOUSE, CLIFFMERE

Jude hurried through the house, carrying Clothilde, looking for someone to help. In the library, he found Sinclair and Cordelia sitting together in the bay window. They both looked up in surprise.

"Jude! What's going on!" Sinclair asked, leaping to his feet.

"We need to call the police," Jude gasped and strode over to the leather couch, carefully laying Clothilde down.

"Clothilde, are you all right?" Cordelia asked.

"Yes. But there's a dead man in the barn! A farmworker was murdered."

"Do you think it's—" Sinclair started.

"Yes, it's Mondragone," Jude affirmed, "The bullet hole was through his forehead."

Sinclair put his hand to his mouth, completely distraught. "How the *hell* did he find us?"

Jude stood up. "We also found Charles. He's been shot."

Sinclair grabbed his arm. "*Charles? Where is he?*"

"He's coming. It's not that bad. He could walk on his own."

Just then the door crashed open and they all whirled to see Charles stagger over to a chair and collapse.

"Call the police," Charles said, his voice altered by pain. "Mondragone's here."

Cordelia flew to him, but he waved her off. "I'm fine. Look after Clothilde."

"What happened, Charles?" Sinclair demanded, taking a cell phone out of his jacket pocket.

"I walked into the barn and somebody shot me."

"Clothilde what did you see?" Sinclair asked.

"There was a man with a gun."

"What did he look like?" he pressed, dialing the emergency number.

Clothilde pulled herself upright on the couch, and Jude hastened to assist her.

"He was a big man. He put his hand over my mouth. But I don't remember his face."

"Hello?" Sinclair said into the phone, interrupting her. "May I have the police . . ."

He covered the receiver momentarily.

" . . . Delia, take a look at Charles, will you?"

"I'm fine," Charles insisted.

"Sit up and let me look," Cordelia told him firmly.

He opened his coat, and his shirt and pants were sopping with blood.

"John, this is bad!" she said. "Charles needs a doctor immediately!"

Sinclair held up a hand for her to wait as he spoke clearly and calmly.

"Yes . . . this is Cliffmere Estate. We have a gunman on the property, one person dead, another seriously wounded, and will need immediate medical attention."

Sinclair listened.

"Yes, that's right. Just after A-4, past Maidenhead. Send the police. Right away."

He cradled the phone next to his ear and pulled out his wallet, searching through it for a business card.

"Also please call Chief Inspector Fenton at Scotland Yard. Yes, tell him the man he's looking for is here—Salvatore Mondragone. And please hurry."

He hung up and turned to them to explain.

"They say the police may not be coming right away. The highways are closed, and there are quite a few serious car accidents because of the ash."

"What about an ambulance?" Cordelia asked, looking up from Charles's bloody shirt.

"EMS teams are all tied up. I put in the word with Scotland Yard, but that won't be quick either."

They all stared at him in silence.

"You mean we're here on our own with Mondragone in the house?" Jude asked.

"Yes, but hopefully he's not in the house proper, only on the grounds."

"John, somebody has to check on the others," Cordelia said urgently. "Marian and Luca. And what about Brindy and Victoria?"

"We need to organize," Sinclair said, turning to the group. "The library will be our base of operations."

"What should we do?" Clothilde asked.

"Lock the doors and windows, pull the drapes. Clothilde, you stay here. And Charles you need to lie down and take it easy."

Charles nodded, and Sinclair continued.

"Delia, go get a towel for Charles and a couple of blankets to keep him warm."

"OK."

"Jude, you protect the library. We need to gather everyone into the same spot."

"No problem."

Sinclair stood in the middle of the room, a commanding presence. His directives were calm and deliberate, without emotion.

"Everyone will stay here and lock the door. This will be our strong-hold until the police come."

"What are you going to do?" Cordelia asked.

"I'll go out and find whoever is missing and bring them back."

Charles interrupted, his voice weak. "Does anybody know where Victoria went?"

Cordelia jumped up. "I'll go find her."

Sinclair looked at her undecided.

"You need help," she argued. "You can't do it all by yourself."

He gave her a curt nod. "OK. We'll both go. Check the house first. She may be in her room getting dressed. But don't take any chances. Look around and report back to Jude, no matter what."

KITCHEN GARDEN

Victoria cut through the vegetable garden. The sprinklers had just finished their automatic cycle. A row of wet lettuce leaves sparkled with water in the weak sunlight. Her printed cotton skirt billowed against her legs in the fresh cool air, and the mist made everything very romantic and dreamy.

The ashfall was dense now. Even at this short distance, it was hard to see the barn. The air had a strong smell of sulfur, and she could discern a slight metallic taste in the back of her throat. They'd all have to stay indoors. But first she had to find Charles.

When she entered the barn, everything was silent. Even the egg washing machine had been turned off. The packing operation must be over.

"*Clothilde?*" she called as she walked over to the conveyer belt.

The ceramic tile floor was stained with something—a bright red puddle. Beet juice perhaps? Victoria stopped, appalled.

Clothilde's wheelchair stood abandoned, and a man in his underwear was stretched out in a pool of blood, eyes sightlessly staring up at the ceiling.

She gave a gasp of shock. It was the farmhand who had worked with Clothilde! The eyes were glassy, the mouth slightly open, as if he might speak. But this man would never move again.

Victoria turned and ran back to the house.

CLIFFMERE KITCHEN

Marian was telephoning the police.

"Yes, please send them as soon as possible," she said.

She rang off when she saw Victoria standing in the doorway.

"Marian, someone has been killed."

"I know. We need to find the others," Marian said.

"I just found the body," Victoria said in a shaky voice.

"Who could have wanted the contessa dead?" Marian asked, bewildered. "I just don't understand."

"The *contessa?*"

"Yes, she's been murdered in her room. I've just called the police, but they knew already."

"Are they coming?" Victoria asked, stunned.

"No. They told me there were a lot of accidents out on the motorway, and all the patrol cars have been dispatched."

"Marian, it's not *just* the contessa. A man has been shot in the barn, and Clothilde's wheelchair is empty . . . she's missing."

At that, Marian's knees wobbled, and she plopped down on a chair. Victoria came over and put a hand on her shoulder.

"Where are all the men? The farmworkers?" Victoria asked.

"Most didn't come in today, because the roads are closed. All the people who could make it here went out to the west pasture. They're moving livestock."

"We need to protect ourselves until the police get here," Victoria said. "Do you have any guns?"

Marian looked up in surprise. "Do you know how to shoot?"

Suddenly, Victoria realized there was something she could do to help. The biathlon training would be useful in this situation.

"I am very good with a rifle. That might help."

"Yes, it would," Marian said, fumbling in her skirt pocket for an enormous bundle of keys. "Just down the corridor to the left is the gun room."

Victoria took the key ring. "Which one?"

Marian sorted through with trembling fingers. "This one opens the door; the cases are unlocked."

"Good," Victoria said. "Now go find everyone else and tell them what has happened."

The gun room was filled with firearms for shooting birds and game. There were antique shotguns with sterling silver stocks and modern hunting rifles. All were arrayed in glass cases.

When Victoria walked in, the sight of the weapons steadied her. This was a world she knew. Any of these rifles would do. She could easily handle them all. The latch on the cabinet turned, and the glass door swung open.

If a murderer were still on the estate, she'd try to protect the others. Her hand closed over the stock of a hunting rifle, and she checked the breach. It was empty.

The ammo cabinet had dozens of small drawers. After a quick search, she found the correct shells. With utter familiarity, she slid five into the chamber and slipped the rest into the pocket of her skirt. Then she lifted the butt to her shoulder. Gripping the forestock, she sighted along the barrel. The rifle had good heft and balanced well. This would stop him.

SOUTH LAWN

Cordelia walked out across the terrace looking for Victoria. With all the ashfall, visibility was only a few feet. As she descended into the garden, the grass was spongy and wet.

Suddenly her ankle bent, and she stumbled on the uneven stone steps. Gasping in pain, she waited until the throbbing subsided. No harm done. It was not sprained, and she continued her search.

The garden was filled with a ghostly mist. The prospect of Mondragone being out here in this fog was terrifying. There were only indistinct shapes. Every shrub seemed to be shaped like a person. Cordelia closed her eyes and tried to picture the architectural plan of the garden. It was a long sloping lawn that led down to the parkland.

Coming out here was a mistake. Why would Victoria be out on the grounds in conditions like this? She'd better return to the house. But where was it?

A thick swirl of mist made her eyes sting. Jude said the fog was comprised of acidic droplets, and she could certainly feel it. As she inched her way across the lawn, suddenly she felt a fine mist from the fountain. That would put her halfway out, in the middle of the lawn. She kept walking on a straight course, looking for the structure. From there, she could orient herself to get back to the house.

The stone fountain suddenly loomed out of the fog. The granite tower was magnificent. It was a gigantic monument, the kind of centerpiece that could be found in many town squares in Europe.

It stood about thirty feet high with a round basin that was as large as a swimming pool. Three carved sea naiads cavorted in the middle, spouting water jets. She took a moment to bend down and dip her handkerchief into the basin to wipe her irritated eyes.

Just as she stood up, a man came toward her out of the mist. He was startling in appearance, slightly deformed with white hair that stood up on end.

This was the man who had broken into her townhouse in London!

She had identified him from police photos after the incident. He was a Camorra gangster and worked closely with Salvatore Mondragone. He lifted a gun and pointed it at her! It was like a nightmare. Was he going to shoot her?

Her eyes were drawn to the weapon. It didn't look like a real pistol, more like a ray gun in a sci-fi movie. Was it a stun gun, like a Taser? She had no idea.

Her eyes shifted back to the man's face. His crooked yellow teeth were bared in a slight smile. This was almost too nightmarish to comprehend.

"What do you want?" she asked.

"Step back toward the fountain."

She understood immediately. He clearly had plans to shoot her or kill her and push her in.

"But I don't even know you," Cordelia said reasonably. "Why would you want to hurt me?"

He looked at her with flat, dead eyes.

"You identified me to the police."

She had no reply. As they stood looking at one another, her mind leapt to a variety of escape plans. If that were a real gun, he'd certainly be able to shoot her.

"Go over to the fountain," he commanded again, holding out the stubby weapon.

She backed up to the rim of the basin, her knees shaking. A plan was formed, but she'd have to act quickly. There was no time to debate.

She sat down slowly and took a deep breath of air, steeling herself for the effort. She shut her eyes and fell backward into the water with a splash. It was something she had done a thousand times, the same way she would push off a boat on a scuba entry. The splash was huge as she tumbled backward.

She was in! The temperature was freezing!

Her hair flowed across her face like seaweed, and she pushed it back, kicking deeper to the bottom. Hugging the basin wall, she felt around with her hands on the slimy bottom, looking for something to hold on to. She needed to keep herself weighted down. Feeling around, she came into contact with some large rocks and she clung to one with her fingers.

After orienting herself, she set off again, swimming rapidly, keeping one hand in contact with the marble wall to guide her around the bottom of the basin to the other side.

In her years of diving she had spent plenty of time in low-visibility conditions. The water was murky, and she could see nothing. But guiding herself by feel, she followed the long underwater curve of the fountain, flutter-kicking her way with great speed as she remained submerged.

She kept up a slow, steady exhale to reduce her buoyancy, as she often did during a scuba dive. Surprisingly, there was no fear. Her life had been spent in the water diving, and she felt more in her element here than anywhere else. She could function without panic. Survival came down to simple skill.

At about 180 degrees from the start of her dive, she let herself slowly rise up until she just broke the surface of the water. Then she took in air cautiously and poked her head out, above the waterline. As her eyes cleared, she could see there was white fog all around, and the splash of fountain jets had covered any sound she had made as she came up. The sea nymph statues in the middle concealed the gunman. She inched her way around, until she could just see the Camorra gangster on the other side.

Straining through the mist, she saw the faint outline of the figure, now a good twenty feet away. He was staring down into the water at the same point where she went in, trying to locate her.

It would be simple to climb out and run away. Yet that would leave a dangerous killer on the loose at Cliffmere. He had to be stopped.

Near her feet at the bottom of the pool she could feel loose stones. Some were square and others round. She took a breath and went under again. There was a sizeable rock at the bottom that she was able to heft with both hands. Curling her fingers underneath, she found it was very heavy, so she pulled hard, lifting it up.

Her hands were strong from hoisting fifty-five-pound scuba tanks, and this rock was comparatively light. She surfaced, hair streaming into her eyes. With a heave, she tossed the stone into the grass outside the rim of the fountain. It landed with a soft thud, and she climbed out after it.

Now crouching on the ground, low behind the basin, she took the rock in both hands. For a moment, she wondered if this was the right choice of action. She could end up in a deadly confrontation. But there were the others to consider: Charles and Victoria, Clothilde, Marian, and Luca would not be able to defend themselves against these killers. The consequences of inaction seemed worse.

Crouching low, she cradled the rock as she circled back behind the gunman. He was partially obscured by mist, but she could just see him peering over the edge of the fountain, leaning on the basin rim, totally absorbed with trying to locate her in the water.

Cordelia quietly approached from behind, lifting the small boulder with both hands. He must have sensed her presence, because at the exact moment she raised the rock above her head, he turned. The gun was pointing at her, painting her chest with a laser.

She flung the boulder toward him with all her might. It was heavier than she calculated, and she didn't get quite the loft she had wanted. She had aimed for his head, but the stone struck him squarely in the chest.

He let out a loud "umph" as the heavy projectile connected. He toppled backward over the rim of the fountain into the water. There was a huge splash and a flash of blue, like lightning. Then silence.

Cautiously, Cordelia approached to see if he would resurface. The dark water was still, a few bubbles rising.

Then the lifeless body bobbed up, floating face down. He was either dead or unconscious. The face was still submerged, but the man floated around, his shirt nearly transparent, white hair flowing like seaweed, hand still gripping his weapon. From above, a sea naiad merrily sprayed his back with a jet of water.

Cordelia knocked on the library door.

"Who is it?" a voice asked, muffled by the thick oak.

"It's Delia."

The door opened, and Jude's face appeared, gaunt with worry.

"I'm back," she announced through chattering teeth.

She walked into the library, her clothes sodden, shoes squelching.

"What happened?" Jude asked, aghast.

"I killed him," she said, her lips stiff with cold.

"Mondragone?" Charles asked from the couch where he lay.

"No," she answered, looking over at him. "His partner, I think. The guy who broke into the townhouse in London. He was trying to shoot me, so I threw a rock at him, and he fell into the fountain with his stun gun. I think he was electrocuted."

"Holy smokes," Jude said, impressed.

Charles smiled weakly. "Remind me not to ever cross you."

His face was ghastly white, eyes enormous.

"Charles you look terrible," Cordelia said.

His physical condition was deteriorating rapidly.

"I beg your pardon?" he joked, summoning his old humor. "*I* look terrible? Have you taken a look at yourself lately?"

She managed a weak chuckle, then scanned around the library.

"Where's Marian?"

Jude came back with a wool tartan blanket and wrapped it around her.

"We can't find Marian or Victoria. Brindy has not turned up either. And Luca is still missing as well."

Cordelia froze.

"Where's Sinclair?"

"He's still outside, looking for everyone."

FRONT DRIVE, CLIFFMERE

Victoria slipped out the front door of the house and ran lightly across the drive, carrying the rifle. She flew across the courtyard, her rapid footsteps audible on the gravel. One of the hunting dogs spotted her and ran to greet her, wagging its tail. It sniffed her skirt, recognizing her as a friend.

She told it to sit. Superbly trained, the dog obeyed.

"Come," she said. "Heel."

The setter trotted obediently behind her as she headed to the alley of trees. Thick elms were planted at regular intervals along the drive for at least a mile, and a row of trunks stood like soldiers all the way out to the main road.

Victoria lowered herself into a prone position next to one of the trees. She was right next to the trunk, well hidden from the house. The grass was damp and filled with ash. She settled in and flattened out, well out of sight.

The police would have to come this way when they entered the estate. Here would be the perfect vantage point to intercept them and explain the situation. And if the killer tried to leave, she'd be in the ideal position for stopping him dead with a single shot.

The Gordon Setter lay down next to her, staying close. She kept a hand on his neck to keep him quiet. The fur was silky and warm under her fingers. The dog understood what she was doing; they were hunting. He crouched low, ready to fetch a game bird as it fell from the sky.

Mondragone came out of the front courtyard and scanned the lawn. He felt for the necklace in his pocket, grasping it tightly: It was a multimillion-dollar ticket to a new life. Now he stopped to examine the stones, which seemed duller, as if they were coated with something. Yet the heft of it was the same. He spit on his thumb and rubbed one of the gems, and a substance came off. The necklace was real.

Mondragone put it back in his pocket and looked around. The best way would be to leave via the main drive where Tito and the chauffeur were still waiting. The mist was dense now, and he could taste the faint chemical residue in the back of his throat. Visibility was poor. Nothing was discernable beyond the trees.

Suddenly, off to the right, he heard a dog growl. The sound was muffled, the direction indeterminate, but it was nearby. For some reason that perfectly ordinary sound alerted him to danger. His survival skills went into high alert. Someone was out there waiting for him.

Victoria saw the man emerge from the mist. He was a worker wearing green Cliffmere overalls. Finally some of the farmhands had returned from the fields!

She started to stand up and call to him, but the dog growled and the low warning made her hesitate. Why would a dog growl at a worker who came here every day?

This was strange. The dog had greeted her without hesitation just now. And she had been here only a few days. This person must be a stranger. It would be prudent to wait and see who he was.

She settled back down, closing her hand over the dog's muzzle. The dog understood immediately. This was their target.

The man walked by, looking around to see whether anyone was observing him. He was large and powerfully built and would be a frightening adversary.

Victoria stayed perfectly still. With her pale skirt and hair, she was well camouflaged. Ash was falling steadily now, and it was covering her up, like fine-grained sand.

She could see the man's tracks on the road. His footsteps were as clear as if he had trod across a beach. He stopped, not more than three feet away. Victoria tried to quell her breathing.

There was something odd about him. His overalls were stained and spattered, like those of a fieldworker, but his shoes were laced-up dress brogues, the kind English bankers wore. Her instincts were right. Clearly this was no farmhand.

The man glanced around and then took something out of his pocket and held it up, examining it carefully. The dog growled.

It was her necklace!

A sick feeling came over her. This man had come to steal her sapphires. Brindy had told her all about Sinclair's confrontation with Salvatore Mondragone at the dockyard in Naples. Clearly the gangster had not been killed. He had returned to get revenge on Sinclair and steal the jewels.

So this was the notorious Cyclops. Her mouth went dry. She was no match for such a trained killer, yet her duty was clear.

She had to kill him.

The thought made her dizzy, but there was no time to lose. Victoria was aware that her hands were moist on the stock of the rifle. She closed her eyes, slowed her breathing, and readied herself to take a shot.

In all those years of biathlon practice, she had never aimed at a human. It was harder than it looked. And for a moment, she didn't think she could do it. Her pulse soared, and her hand trembled.

Victoria reached up and found the gold Vesuvius charm around her neck, clasping it for luck. Then she sharpened her mind, put her hand back on the trigger, and slowly exhaled to steady her aim.

Just then, another man approached out of the mist. He was dressed in a dark suit with a peaked cap, like a chauffeur.

"Why didn't you stay at the car?" Mondragone asked him.

"I can't find Tito. He wandered off. I think he got lost."

"Where did he go?"

"I don't know. He went to the house. I'm gonna go look for him."

Mondragone glanced over his shoulder at the house.

"To hell with him, let's go," he snarled.

The man stood his ground. "You can't just leave him here. The guy's crippled. They'll catch him right away, and then he'll talk."

"Fine, give me the keys, so I can get in the car. I'm waiting ten minutes, and if you two are not back, I'm leaving."

"OK, boss."

The chauffeur tossed Mondragone the key ring. They were going to split up and go in different directions.

Victoria aimed the crosshairs of the rifle on Mondragone's temple, but then shifted to the other man. She had to decide which one of them she should target.

The chauffeur now seemed a biggest menace to the others, because he was headed toward the house. But if she shot him, she'd have to follow up quickly with another shot at Mondragone. That would be two successive kills, with no margin for error.

She shut her eyes for a long second and opened them again. There was no time to wait. It would have to be now, before they both disappeared in the mist.

Again, she cleared her mind of all extraneous information and sighted the crosshairs carefully on the chauffeur. Steeling herself, she exhaled slowly and pulled the trigger.

The man fell, face down, his skull split open by her bullet. The impact blasted a spray of red into the air. The chauffeur's cap flew off onto the driveway and landed a few yards away.

He fell, clearly dead. His feet were twisted, pigeon-toed. His body was splayed in the driveway, completely inert. Mondragone whirled, reaching for his pistol, and looked in her direction.

John Sinclair emerged from the house, his footsteps crunching across the gravel of the courtyard. Victoria was still missing. He had searched every room in the house, even her bedroom, where the suitcase had been ransacked. Mondragone had been there and must have taken the necklace.

His thoughts were frantic, trying to calculate where to look next. He'd checked the greenhouse, and the barn with its dead farmworker and pool of blood. The West Garden and the maze were unlikely spots, but he tried anyway, stumbling his way through the grounds in the fog. He'd even walked all the way down to the neoclassical folly. Victoria seemed to be gone.

As he searched, his mind went back to the Maybach car parked by the gate. It must belong to Mondragone. Who else would have such an expensive vehicle? Perhaps he had kidnapped the princess. It was worth checking to see if it was still there. At the very least, he could disable the car by puncturing the tires, eliminating an escape route for the mobster.

Sinclair started down the long line of elms, using the tree trunks to guide him. Suddenly, there was a single rifle shot. He stopped. In this fog it was impossible to tell how near it was. It seemed to come from in front of him, so he started to run along the drive in the direction of the sound.

Victoria lay still with her hands shaking and her heart pounding. She'd killed the chauffeur. At least one of the Camorra gangsters was dead, sprawled in the driveway not ten feet away. Now she had to target Mondragone.

She tried to aim the rifle again, but her hands were shaking. As Mondragone approached, the dog whimpered at her side, crouching in a defensive position. A low growl came from its throat. Mondragone was standing not three feet away, pointing a pistol at her head.

Luca Brindisi rode the horse through the mist. Somehow he had gotten off course. The animal knew the route back to the barn, and he was letting it find the way. For a while, his mount seemed confused by the muffled sounds and the swirling fog, but suddenly they were cantering down a double line of trees flanking the main drive.

Lifting its head, the horse broke into a gallop, tearing toward the main house. Luca relaxed the reins and gave the horse its head. They would be at the stables soon.

A loud explosion seemed to come from behind one of the trees. It spooked the horse violently. The animal bucked, stumbled, and nearly fell, neighing with a high-pitched scream.

Luca gripped with his legs and grabbed fistfuls of dark mane. A dog barked somewhere nearby. The horse got even more agitated. It worked itself into a frenzy of panic, prancing and neighing. Luca held on with all his strength, trying to bring the horse back under control.

Suddenly, there was a man in front of him. The horse bucked and reared, pawing the air, rising up. Luca fell to the ground with a thud, smashing his shoulder painfully. Now the horse was standing over him. He looked up at the underbelly of the thousand-pound animal as the hoofs danced close to his head.

As Luca lay on the ground, Mondragone cowered from the rearing horse, his hands up as if to keep it away. He had no experience with animals, having been raised in the streets of Naples. This charging beast looked enormous and wild.

The horse was in distress, bucking and rearing in the bewildering fog. The rider lost his grip and slid off to the ground, lying there for a moment, in great danger of being crushed under the hoofs. But then the horse reared up and galloped away down the lane.

Mondragone turned back to the elm trees. In that short moment, while he had been avoiding the horse, the girl with the rifle had fled. The spot where she had lain was outlined by ash.

Mondragone shouted in frustration. He couldn't allow any witnesses. Now he had to go back to the house and find her. And there was also the boy on the ground. He would have to be eliminated, too. It was a teenage boy—dark hair, eyes enormous, cursing in fluent Italian.

Luca saw the man approach wearing green Cliffmere overalls and signaled for him to help.

"I lost the horse," he said. "Something scared it."

"It was the mist," Mondragone said, fingering the pistol in his pocket. "Are you OK? Let me walk you back to the house."

"Who are you?" Luca asked.

"Oh, I work here," Mondragone said. "I'm Sal."

"I'm Luca Brindisi," Luca smiled at him. "Thanks for the help."

"Luca *Brindisi*?" Mondragone asked, smiling pleasantly. "Isn't your mother here on the estate also?"

"Yeah," Luca said. "But please don't tell her what happened with the horse. If she finds out, she'll absolutely kill me."

Victoria ran back to the house, sobbing. She had killed the man, and now she had to warn everyone. Running across the drive, her knees trembled. She almost slipped on the gravel.

The baby! She had to be careful. Slowing her pace, she climbed the steps to the front door. There was no bell, and the latch was locked. She banged on the solid oak with the flat of her hand.

"*Let me in. Please!*"

CLIFFMERE LIBRARY

Jude tucked another blanket around Charles. He was getting weaker by the moment. Cordelia sat by his side, holding his hand, talking softly, but his responses were faint.

Marian had arrived and was making every effort to reassure Clothilde that her brother would live. The girl was frantic, sobbing uncontrollably. Cordelia was also fighting tears, grasping Charles's hand and begging him to hold on a bit longer.

Jude paced, tortured by the women's grief. There was no sound of activity outside the house. It was clear the police were not coming. With nothing to occupy his time, he made another very insistent call to the local precinct and another to Scotland Yard. No promises were made. Apparently, Chief Inspector Fenton was not able to travel from London. The highways were clogged with traffic accidents.

This was going from bad to worse. Charles was bleeding to death. Victoria was still missing, Sinclair had not returned from his search, and Luca was still out on his horse. Too many people were still at risk.

Suddenly, he heard a thumping at the front hall. He sprinted out of the library to investigate. At the front door a female voice was yelling, muffled by the thick wood. Jude unbolted the latch and yanked it open.

Victoria was standing on the doorsill, covered in ash. She was holding a rifle, her face streaked with tears.

Charles felt his life draining away. Cordelia was talking to him, squeezing his hand, telling him all about Capri and Victoria, tears flowing down her face. He knew what she was doing. Trying to keep him conscious and alive.

He desperately wanted to live. There was Victoria and the baby. His mother and Clothilde. Cordelia and Sinclair. So many people to love.

He wanted to try. It was just that he was so cold. He'd read somewhere just how much blood you could lose before you died. It was quite a lot, but the blanket around him was soaked now, and time was running out.

He heard a noise and saw Jude walking into the library with his arm around Victoria. She was a real mess: her clothes caked in mud, her hair coated by ash. But she looked alive and well. Unconsciously he glanced at her waist. It was impossible to tell yet.

She was talking to Jude, but when she entered the room, she called out to Charles and raced to his side. He was too weak to speak, but he smiled as best he could. Cordelia stood up to make room for Victoria on the couch and gently relinquished his limp hand.

"I shot him," she said woodenly.

"Him?"

"One of the Camorra."

"You *did*?" he whispered, astonished.

"Yes, his body is lying in the driveway." Victoria started to cry, her forehead wrinkling, mouth trembling. Big tears rolled down her cheeks, making tracks through the dust.

"Oh my God! I killed him," she sobbed.

Cordelia knelt down to speak to her. "Was it Mondragone?"

She shook her head, trying to speak.

"No . . . an accomplice . . . Mondragone got away. I feel just awful. He was lying there . . . his head . . ."

She started to weep again, bending over in anguish. Cordelia patted her back.

"Don't cry, Victoria. You did what was necessary to protect everyone. It was very brave."

She sobbed even harder, wiping her eyes, her face blotchy from crying.

"I can't believe I *killed* him."

"V, don't," Charles soothed. "It's over now."

"But Charles it was *horrible*. I shot him in the head. You have no idea."

Cordelia looked at her soberly.

"I know exactly what you are going through, Victoria. I just killed someone in the fountain out back."

Victoria looked up, eyelashes wet.

"You *did*?"

"I had to. He was going to drown me."

Jude stood over them, bewildered.

"How many of them *are* there!" he exclaimed. "Cordelia, lock this door when I leave! I have to go out and find Sinclair and Luca."

Sinclair heard the galloping hooves coming at him from out of the mist. A rider-less horse was charging, its nostrils flared, eyes rolled white in terror. There was only a second to react and fling himself out of the way.

This was the horse that Luca had been riding. The saddle was still on, stirrups dangling. Luca must have been thrown. Sinclair started down the lane again. The line of tree trunks stood like sentries, and everything was quiet. The ashfall had created whiteout conditions, and he could only see a few feet ahead. Through the gloom he saw two figures, a man and a tall slim boy.

His heart stopped in terror.

Luca Brindisi was walking along, chatting merrily to Salvatore Mondragone.

Sinclair stepped behind a tree, almost certain no one had seen him. Mondragone strolled along with the boy, listening to his prattle, nodding from time to time. Suddenly the mobster bent down as if to tie his shoe. Luca continued a few steps ahead, then waited for the man. Sinclair could see Mondragone's hand reach slowly for his pocket.

Sinclair didn't wait. He lurched out of the trees and tackled Mondragone, sending him sprawling. His pistol clattered to the dirt, as Sinclair put his hands around the massive neck and squeezed. Enormously strong, Mondragone hurled him off easily and stood up. They were very unevenly matched when it came to physical strength.

Sinclair lurched at him again, catching him in the chest with his shoulder, bringing him down. They locked together in a wrestling match on the ground, muscle against muscle.

Sinclair had never engaged in any close combat before; all his battles had been in the fencing lane, governed by rules. This was a primitive fight: elbows and knees, fingers gouging, teeth grinding, each trying to get an advantage.

In some kind of buried memory, Sinclair recalled the marble carvings of gladiators straining against one another in the coliseum. Taking that image as a cue, he locked his arms around Mondragone to imprison him, and then went by instinct. They rolled and grappled, sweating and groaning.

Sinclair realized he was outmatched. The man was an animal, his face contorted by rage. This thug had spent his childhood fighting in the streets of Naples. Cyclops had survived all these years by brute force. He was not going to lose now. Not when his life was at stake.

Jude ran down the line of elms looking frantically for the others. The familiar scent of sulfur caught him in the back of his throat, but he ignored it. For him, conditions like this were normal, and the stench of volcanic ash didn't bother him.

Up ahead in the mist, he saw two men grappling on the ground.

Before he could react, he was caught around the waist. Someone was clinging to him, crying out in terror.

"Mr. Blackwell, help!"

Jude peeled Luca's arms away from his waist and took him by the shoulders.

"Luca! Run back to the house. *Now!* Go to the library and stay there!"

As the boy set off, Jude approached the combatants. Sinclair was pinned into the earth, struggling for his life. Mondragone was on him like a wild beast, his thumb reaching out to gouge an eye.

Jude grabbed the man by the shoulders and tore him off. Mondragone fell, skidding along the ground. Sinclair leapt up, recognized Jude, and together they advanced toward Cyclops.

Mondragone was on his feet again, feet planted wide, waiting to take them on. His face was mottled with exertion, and the large powerful arms were spread wide, ready to swing. Sinclair saw the glint of a stiletto knife in his hand.

"I'll go low," Jude said.

"I'll get the knife," Sinclair murmured.

Sinclair flung himself forward and grabbed for Mondragone's right arm. Jude tackled the knees. The blade sliced at Jude, grazing him on the forearm, and Jude rolled away. Sinclair seized Mondragone's wrist, twisting it savagely, but the gangster held on to the knife, flailing and thrashing to shake him off. Mondragone's foot lashed out, and he kicked Jude in the head, knocking him down in the dirt.

Sinclair kept hold of the knife, forcing it up above their heads. He was taller than Mondragone by about four inches, and that gave him some advantage. But the other man was much stronger. They stood locked together, scuffling, every sinew straining. Mondragone's sweaty face was inches from his, grunting with effort.

"*Va al diavolo!*" the gangster cursed, wishing Sinclair to hell, and began to forcefully pull the blade lower. Sinclair resisted fiercely, calling up every ounce of strength. But slowly the knife moved toward his face. The sharp tip came closer and closer. A thrust to the eye would be all it would take.

Sinclair strained as he pulled on Mondragone's arm, but it was as unmovable as steel. He was nearly out of strength. This man was a brute.

He desperately needed help. Jude was near, but Sinclair couldn't take his concentration off the knife. Suddenly, he felt Mondragone buckle and fall sideways. Sinclair turned. Jude was kicking straight into Mondragone's leg, with the precise jab of a martial arts expert. There was an audible crunch as the ankle splintered. Mondragone collapsed and went down, loosening his grip.

Sinclair wrestled the blade out of Mondragone's hand and pounced on him. Mondragone was now flat on his back, Sinclair straddling his body. For a split second Sinclair hesitated, the knife poised. This monster deserved to die. But how could he do something so savage?

Sinclair gritted his teeth and then drove the knife sharply into Mondragone's neck with one clean thrust all the way up to the hilt. He forced it down and rooted the blade around in the thick neck until he was sure he had pierced the jugular. Mondragone let out the roar of a wounded lion. His eyes went wild with anger. His rage was savage, primitive. He bucked like a wild horse, trying to throw Sinclair off of him. But the damage was done.

Sinclair pulled the blade out, then stood up and tossed it away. Mondragone was on the ground, mortally wounded. Blood flowed slowly and then spurted out of his neck like a drinking fountain, the crimson stream pumping high with each heartbeat. Horrified and revolted, Sinclair stood there, his chest heaving.

Mondragone struggled to get up, but then fell back weakly, propping himself up on one elbow, still not willing to concede that he had suffered a deathblow. Now blood was pouring out of the gash in his neck in a steady rush, forming a lake on the ground. He opened his mouth to curse, but his throat was filled with blood. He gargled, choked, and spat, but the blood kept coming.

Jude came over to stand with Sinclair.

"Are you OK?" Sinclair asked.

"Yeah, fine," Jude said, nursing the cut on his forearm.

They waited silently, side-by-side, watching the beast die. Mondragone stared at them with dark hatred. Finally his eyes dimmed and his body went limp. He fell back on the ground. All life had left him.

In death, his face was vulgar and lumpy, the eyes half open, the mouth still parted as if to hurl a final curse. All veneer of sophistication was gone. This was a dead animal.

Sinclair spoke, his voice raspy from inhaling the tainted air.

"I know there was no real choice. But it's still hard to kill a man."

"With evil like that, the only option is to try to stop it," Jude agreed. "We did what we had to do."

Sinclair turned to him. "Thank you. I needed to hear that."

Through the fog, a red-and-blue strobe light moved steadily closer. An emergency vehicle had entered the long drive and was coming toward them—finally taking shape. It was an ambulance. Sinclair and Jude watched it approach.

The tires of the vehicle pulled right up alongside the corpse on the roadway. A window rolled down, but before the paramedic could speak, Sinclair pointed toward the house.

"Keep going. Your patient is in the library. This one is gone."

AUGUST, ONE YEAR LATER
RUE DE VAUGIRARD, PARIS

Rock music blared in the fourth-floor photo studio, and a young Russian model swirled with the grace of a ballerina. The drapery of a red chiffon dress wafted in the breeze created by a floor fan.

"That looks great," Clothilde observed from the back of the studio.

"I think we can do better," Jude said.

Leaving his camera, he walked toward the girl and adjusted the angle of the fan, turning her thirty degrees away from the blast. The pure silk chiffon rippled in the breeze.

"This dress, it reminds me of the color of molten lava," Clothilde told him.

"It's beautiful," Jude agreed.

"I think it would look great on Victoria. She needs a new wardrobe again."

Jude surveyed the model, finally satisfied.

"That should be better," he mumbled.

Clothilde laughed. "You are so picky about every little thing. And to think you used to photograph volcanoes blowing up."

Jude walked back to the camera and bent down to refocus the shot.

He spoke to Clothilde without taking his eye away from the viewfinder.

"Volcanoes don't blow up, my love. They erupt."

VILLA SAN ANGELO, ANACAPRI

The housekeeper, Mrs. Jaccorsi, came out on the terrace at the Villa San Angelo carrying four glasses of iced tea with fresh mint. She walked slowly and set the tray down on the patio table in between the two lounge chairs.

It was lovely working for Mr. Bonnard. She was here in Capri during the summer as she had always been. But now she could spend the winter in Naples, living with her son. Detective Jaccorsi had been promoted and now had a safe desk job with the Guardia di Finanza, relieved to no longer be a target for the Camorra.

She looked around the terrace to see if the guests needed something more.

Charles and Princess Victoria were in the pool holding Princess Sophie, dipping the baby's toes in the water to make her laugh. They were such a lovely couple—so happy and beautiful.

This was a house of great blessings and always had been. And that child was a gift from heaven; the Villa San Angelo had finally found its little angel.

There was a solid knock on the outside door. Mrs. Jaccorsi turned and went to answer. When she opened it, Sinclair and Cordelia stood in the sunlight, with Luca Brindisi behind them. The boy shoved past Cordelia and hugged Mrs. Jaccorsi, letting loose a stream of endearments in Italian.

She stepped back, eyes shining with tears. He had grown so much during the past year in London and had put on some weight. His mother should see him now; he was so healthy and strong and turning out just like her—a beautiful Brindisi. She crossed herself and kissed his hair, calling on all her saints to protect him.

LATE AFTERNOON
VILLA SAN ANGELO

Cordelia and Victoria were stretched out on the terrace in lounge chairs. Princess Sophie was in her bassinet taking a nap. The conversation between the two women was intimate and friendly.

Victoria was going on about her new foundation to promote sustainable farming techniques. She was hoping to develop organic farms in extreme climates in northern Norway.

Cordelia had her mind on more immediate matters. She and Sinclair would be married at the Cliffmere estate next month.

Sinclair and Charles were not listening to the conversation. They stood at the balustrade of the terrace, looking out at the Bay of Naples. The water was bright cerulean blue. It was a pleasantly cool afternoon. Everyone agreed that the ashfall from last year had lowered median temperatures by at least a couple of degrees.

Sinclair took a small gold ring out of his pocket and looked at it.

"What's that?" Charles asked.

"It's the ancient Roman ring. The one I got from Mondragone," Sinclair said, turning it over in his hand.

Charles examined it. "Oh yes, I remember. All that seems like it was years ago. Doesn't it?"

Sinclair read the inscription on the inside.

"Funny thing. It says '*Te Amo Parum.*'"

"*Te Amo Parum?*" Charles repeated. "Latin?"

"Yes. It means, 'I love you too little' or 'I don't love you as much as you deserve.'"

"Strange," Charles said, staring at the artifact. "What are you going to do with it?"

In response, Sinclair stepped back, wound up his arm, and flung it far over the cliff. The gold ring arced high into the air, glinting like a spark in the sunlight. They watched it tumble to the earth, carried by the wind, until it disappeared into the ancient ruins below.

THE END

KITTY PILGRIM has traveled the world, first as a correspondent for CNN for 24 years, and now as an author of international romantic thrillers. Her novels are filled with high lifestyle and luxury.

Many of Pilgrim's novels include themes of science and exploration and cover such exotic locations as the high Arctic or the calderas of active volcanoes.

As a writer and journalist, Pilgrim feels she has a mission to inform as well as to entertain. Her novels include real information, discovered through research and interviews. She also visits the places she writes about and meets with top experts in the field.

Readers are often confused about what is real in a novel. To answer that question, Pilgrim shoots and produces videos, to allow the reader to accompany her on the adventure of researching her book.

These short videos, available on her website, kittypilgrim.com, provide interesting background for those who would like to learn more about the scientific themes or the locations of her novels.

Pilgrim lives the life she writes about. She is a certified diver, a member of the historic Explorer's Club of New York, and a fellow in the Royal Geographical Society of London. When she is not traveling, she lives and works in Manhattan and spends time with her two sons William (age 27) and Beau, (age 25).

CPSIA information can be obtained at www.ICGtesting.com
Printed in the USA
BVOW07s1653270515

402100BV00001B/38/P

9 781632 990259